THE SNOW

THE SNOW

ADAM ROBERTS

The right of Adam Roberts to be identified as the author of this
work has been asserted by him in accordance with the
Copyright, Designs and Patents Act 1988.

First published in Great Britain in 2004 by
Gollancz
An imprint of the Orion Publishing Group
Orion House, 5 Upper St Martin's Lane, London WC2H 9EA

5 7 9 10 8 6 4

This edition published in Great Britain in 2005 by Gollancz

A CIP catalogue record for this book is available
from the British Library

ISBN-13 978-0-575-07651-8
ISBN-10 0-575-07651-8

Typeset at The Spartan Press Ltd,
Lymington, Hants

Printed in Great Britain by
Clays Ltd, St Ives plc

The Orion Publishing Group's policy is to use papers that
are natural, renewable and recyclable products and
made from wood grown in sustainable forests. The logging
and manufacturing processes are expected to conform to
the environmental regulations of the country of origin.

He had prepared himself for every possibility. Reality must therefore be something that bears no relationship to possibilities, any more than the stab of a knife in one's body bears to the gradual movement of the clouds overhead.

Proust, *Du côté de chez Swann*

Snow

One

The snow started falling on September 6th, soft noiseless flakes filling the sky like a swarm of white moths, or like static interference on your TV screen – whichever metaphor, nature or technology, you find more evocative. Snow everywhere, all through the air, with that distinctive sense of hurrying that a vigorous snowfall brings with it. Everything in a rush, busy-busy snowflakes. And, simultaneously, paradoxically, everything was hushed, calmed, as quiet as cancer, as white as death.

And at the beginning people were happy. They balled the snow and threw it at one another, overarm, underarm, laughing and dancing, kicking up blurry clouds with their feet. Picture that. Railway travel was not disrupted. There was no wind, and accordingly no drifts accumulated. Just the snow falling in slow motion, straight down.

After forty-eight hours of uninterrupted fall there were railway delays, but no cancellations. Traffic reports urged drivers to use caution, but cars still hurtled along the roads, swerved and interwove, poured on and gathered in metal drifts at traffic lights. Snowtrucks kerb-crawled, but the temperature was never worse than minus-seven at night, and during the day was barely below zero. There was little ice on the road, and little call for grit or salt. After three days and nights of constant snowfall, banks of snow began to stack up. Britain, which had some experience of lighter snowfalls and some more experience of frosts and slush, was poorly provided with proper snowploughs, although it had gritters and salters galore. In the United States, I understand, the A-prowed trucks cut through the snow banks, keeping the roads passable for several more days; but in England most of the gritting-trucks themselves became trapped in the snow. Those few snowploughs at the authorities' disposal were commandeered for Glasgow, Manchester, Birmingham and London, and for certain military establishments. By September 12th the snow in those places where it had not been cleared away was thirty inches deep. Trains, buses and cars were infrequent. Few people in London frolicked in the white landscape now. Nobody threw snowballs or built globy snowmen with fagends for eyes and an old pen for a nose. Instead they grumbled. The snow kept falling. People whinged about the weather: they blamed ill-luck, government, global warming, God's wrath. What had been charming, an early presage of Christmas, like the glitter in a toy snowglobe, became tiresome, and then oppressive, and then became something worse, became calamitous.

I'll tell you about London, because it is London I know about.

Everything was white. We had written on the page, London was our writing, and then nature had scattered the myriad fibres of soft paper over it so that the page became white again. A city as big as London depended absolutely on the avenues of supply, food, fuel, everything. For the first month snowploughs kept the bigger roads open, continually scouring the M4, the A2, the A3. Lesser roads quickly clogged with snow. People made their way to the centre to buy potatoes and meat at highly inflated prices, carrying them home again, using makeshift snowshoes of tea-trays or tennis bats, or else moving forward by throwing boards down in front and picking them up from behind to throw down again in front.

Any attempt to lay paths over the snow proved futile. New snowfall buried them in hours. By the month's end, paradoxically, passage about the city became easier because the snow had reached the level of the roofs of two-storey buildings and it was possible to make one's way along guttering, roof-paths and the like, at least for some of the way. But by then the government had long since given up deliveries of food.

Many people had left the city. Some, old and young, had stayed in their rooms until the chill settled on them forever. A few struggled on. There had been talk – whilst the radios still worked – of a mass evacuation by air, but this had never materialised. After forty days and nights of solid snowfall the sense that there was even a government in charge faded from the mind of those people left in the city. Its authority was lost in the blizzard.

I was one such person. I thought of going, of leaving London: I had a daughter in Southampton (although I was still only a young woman myself), and I had a mother closer at hand, just west of the city in Slough. Naturally I thought about making my way to be with them. But in the end I stayed in London. Transport had stopped working alto-gether, so I could only have got out by walking, and I told myself that I wouldn't have been able to find my way, maps having been rendered irrelevant by the snow. Or so I told myself. Maybe I just didn't want to go. Why go? The news reports were unambiguous: snow was general, as they put it, all over Europe, all over the western world. What possibili-ties did the countryside hold for me?

Like many I was waiting for the snow to stop, for life to return to normal, and whilst I was waiting I tried to roll along the usual grooves of my life. I was working at that time in a building society on Balham High Road, and for the first week I fought my way through the snow flurries and drifts to do my job. On the ninth day of snow the management closed the doors, telling us that they would reopen when the weather improved. A small group of us bickered with the local manager over whether or not we would continue to be paid – it seems bizarre and irrelevant now, but we were worried he was going to gyp us out of our wages. We had little enough money.

By the second week of snow the local stores were exhausted of necessary provisions, and the radio told us that our nearest food-aid distribution point was Clapham Northside, two miles away. For several days I undertook the wearying trudge to this temporary depot to collect food. I had got hold of proper winter clothes: a massively padded and hooded ski-jacket, snow-trousers, walking boots and overshoes, mittens. But the drifts were so high now that although this gear kept me warm it did not make it much easier to travel through the new white landscape, the whipped-cream of it, the feathery piles, snow in the air all around me all the time as I struggled on. I gave up making this journey.

For a while after that I stayed in my home, my flat on the fourth floor of my ex-council block. I ate what stores I had, I watched the scratchy TV pictures, I stood at my window. TV transmissions ended, although the electricity supply continued for a surprisingly long time. The water pipes froze, but it was easy enough (for a while) to scoop snow with cooking pans like giant spoons, and heat it on the cooker. From the window I watched the undulating surface of the snow rise day-by-day to the first floor of my block, then to the second, and only then did it occur to me that perhaps the snowfall wasn't going to stop any time soon. Or any time at all.

The phone lines were still working. I called my sister in Scotland and we talked. She said she had been unable to reach our mother. She was worried. I agreed with her that it was worrying. Neither of us could bring ourselves to say openly what it was that worried us. I tried phoning my mother but she didn't answer.

Shortly after that the phone lines stopped working.

The flat across the hall from me was occupied by a retired fellow, a gent in his eighties called Mr Martland. I had been in the habit of visiting him from time to time. One day I knocked, let myself in (he had given me a spare key in case

4

of emergency) and found him dead in his easy chair, sitting facing the blue light of the window. It moved me hardly at all. I left him there and found a surprisingly large cache of tinned food in his cupboards which I took for myself. This I ate, cooked first and then, when the electricity finally ceased, uncooked. The snow rose to the third floor, and then rose further to the bottom of my window.

I had existed, up to that time, in a kind of blank state, a sort of nerveless stasis. Snow fell constantly in my brain. Drifts of it heaped up to my eyeballs. But, finally, it occurred to me now that if I stayed where I was I might as well sit in my chair and fall asleep and not wake up, like Mr Martland opposite. This was not a prospect that alarmed me especially. My overwhelming sense (I might even describe it as the chief tenor of my life) was of the slow accretion of inaction, an erosion of the *heat* of being, the fluttery disruption of the view of the future, of where I was going.

The vista from my window was of luxuriances of snow on every surface, in every direction. Isn't it curious how snowfall looks so cosy, so *warm*, though we know that it is so very cold? It is a visual pun on quilts, white duvets, blankets, I suppose. I stood at my window for hours. The street had been wholly filled in. My eye settled on that portion of the block opposite that still protruded from the snow, its slant roof, covered over by a nightcap of snow, slugs of white on every ledge and windowsill. Behind it the roofs of Balham High Road, all similarly capped with white, could just be seen. The view was being continually scrabbled over with the interference pattern of snow falling.

Two

I decided I should leave, get out, get away. I think, in fact, that I had some romantic notion of trekking out in the snow-desert to die, like the heroic British polar explorers, the sort of men my father had always revered as types of self-sacrificing duty and strength ('I know it is unfashionable,' he would say, 'I know the *young generations* laugh at it, but these are qualities worth celebrating'). So I ripped up a stretch of my carpet and laid it on the treacherous surface of the snow outside my window. It sank six inches. I gathered another piece and clambered out to lie on the first piece, which sagged and U-ed around my kneeling form. When it had settled I threw the second piece forward and made my way onto that. It sank further, V-ed rather than U-ed around me. I began to be frightened. I was convinced that I would drown in the drift unless I could stay on the top of it. By tossing my fragments of carpet I made a precarious passage to the roof of the building opposite, leaving a channel in the surface of the snow behind me. I had to haul myself onto the guttering.

I headed north, along the roofs, still passable, that lined the road. It took me all day to travel perhaps two miles, with various painstaking manoeuvres and elaborate shifts. Where buildings were joined in a terrace the going was easier. Where they were interrupted, or were less than four storeys high, it was harder going. Towards the top of Balham High Road I met a woman coming south, heading, she said, for Balham Tube. She was the first person I had seen. 'I thought,' she told me, her breath steaming around us both, 'that I'd dig down into the Tube. Y'know? It's got to be clear down there . . . don't you think? I figured I'd wait down there 'til all this washes away.'

'I don't know about that,' I said. I lived round the corner from the tube, and it hadn't occurred to me to seek shelter there. 'It's pretty snowed over. How do you know how you'd get down to it?'

She shrugged.

'Besides,' I said, pulling my hand free from my mitten to scratch my face inside my hood. 'What makes you think the tunnels are going to be safe? They may be full of water, for all we know. Maybe all iced up. And there won't be any food down there.'

'No food up here,' she said.

'I guess not.'

'I figured I could go anywhere in the Underground,' she said. 'Anywhere in London. It's hellish travelling above ground, but I could wander the tunnels under the city and go where I liked. Is it far from here?'

'Balham Tube? Not far,' I said. 'Clapham South is about *as* far, up in that direction.' I think I was hoping she would agree to travel with me, thinking that the two of us together would make better progress than I could by myself.

She looked over her shoulder. 'No thanks,' she said. 'I'll press on.'

I left her and carried on north. By the evening I had reached the general vicinity of Clapham South. I think (I can't be sure) that I was perched on the roof of the derelict building opposite the Tube entrance – you know the one? The snow was still falling steadily, softly. To my left was a huge sheet of white, sloping slowly away from me, and pitted with tiny dots. Not a roof, steeple or pole broke the expanse: Clapham Common.

There was no wildlife of any kind, not a dog, not a bird. All dead, I supposed. Nor had I met any more human beings since the woman bound for Balham Tube. The sense of loneliness was growing around me.

I spent the last of the light that day getting across the road junction: forty feet of blank snow with nothing underneath it all the way down to the tarmac. I won't labour the narrative: I used boards ripped from that portion of the building still above the snow. I did think of spending the night inside the derelict place, but pulling the boards free of the old window holes revealed an eerie coldness and blackness inside, and I hurried on. It took three boards, and me wriggling more or less on my belly, but I reached the top floor and trapezoid roof of the terrace over the way. I cleared the snow where it had gathered in a five-foot peak all along the central portion of this roof and found a skylight. It wouldn't open, but the glass was so chilled it broke easily beneath my foot. The glass, with a wire-grid running through it like graph paper, came out of the frame in one bent piece.

Below, inside, was a storeroom; through the door and down the stairs a bar. The place had been wrecked previously, and almost all the drink taken, but I found a crate of peanuts and some unbroken bottles of vodka and whisky. It had been a week since I last drank, and I drank too much and fell into a stupor – stupid of me, for I was helpless had anybody chanced across me. But I woke, unmolested, in the morning with a miserable hangover. I was sick on the floor where I lay, and it took me half a day to gather myself.

I decided then to wait another day in that place, with its dismal half-light, the great slabs of its bars, the upturned chairs and tables. I crouched in the corner and finished the peanuts. In one unbroken glass I mixed snow from through the letter box, drizzling it with vodka.

The next morning, or what I thought was morning, I made my way back upstairs. The snow had fallen through the broken skylight, and had gathered around the rim of the hole I had made. I was able, just, to clamber back out, but wasted nearly an hour trying to find my boards – foolishly I had left them on the roof instead of taking them into the building with me, and they were snowed under. Eventually I dug them out, and dragged them on.

I made my way up the Common's south side, heading north towards Clapham High Street. A tall terrace of Victorian residential housing ran almost the whole length of it, and I picked my way rather quickly. Sometimes I was striding hip-high through the snow (I am not a tall woman); sometimes I was able to walk along gutters or roof-spines. I was, I suppose, quite the daredevil, strolling at some speed along a gutter: had I fallen from it, or had the gutter given way, I would have tumbled into the snow. There was no doubt in my mind that I would then drown in the drift. Using the boards I crossed where roads left spaces, and by nightfall I was near the top of Clapham High Street. Or thereabouts. Or so I supposed.

To my right, looming through the snow, were the distant obelisks of tower blocks. I thought about making my way over to them, assuming that people would be crowded into

8

the upper floors: but on reflection I decided against it. What manner of society I would have found, had I done so, I can only guess at. Food was very scarce everywhere now.

That night I went instead down the snow-clogged metal stairs of a fire escape and into a building. Inside, checking room to room in the almost-darkness, I found half a packet of biscuits, old and stale, under the sink in a small kitchenette. I ate them immediately. I slept in a room at the back. The windows were still half clear, the view out over the fire escape, so I could see whether it was day or night.

I awoke to darkness. The snow had covered the windows completely. I had no idea how long I had slept. I stood by the icy glass and contemplated heaving it open and clawing my way up through the snow to the surface – the fire escape must still have been there, after all. But I felt a weary sense of horror at the prospect of voluntarily entombing myself in the snow. I learnt later that, deeper down, the snow was firmed by compression such that it could be hollowed out into tunnels or cells; but the topmost layers of the snowfall, the layers that I had had dealings with, were soft like granular water: snow-quicksand.

Instead I went through the building, room by room, until I found an internal stairwell that went from top to bottom. I climbed to the very top, where I found a 'Push Latch For Exit – Emergency Only' door. This took several shoves to open, clearing away the snow from the ledge beyond it, but soon I was in the open air, panting great ectoplasmic breaths into the chill air with the exertion. The door led onto a narrow roof-pathway that was stacked with snow to my left and right; but in front of me the slant of the roof had prevented too massy a build-up.

I had a splendid view of south London, covered with snow, and I stood just staring at it for a long time. I don't know how long a time. Hours, probably. It came to me then, belatedly I acknowledge, standing in that doorway, that the world had ended, and ended blankly. Ended blankly after all. It is curious, looking back, how blithely I accepted this fact. Are we pre-programmed to accept world apocalypse? The shadow cast by our own life against the wall of the world? We each know we'll die, individually; it is the easiest thing to extrapolate that fate out onto the cosmos as a whole.

What did I do then? Well, I reasoned I was on Clapham High Street, although there were no markers I recognised. I spent the day and the night there, exploring the buildings for what I could find, clambering over snow-clogged roofs and working my way when I could through interconnecting doors. My stomach ached like a sprain, the continual pain of hunger. It was all shops and offices inside, with a few abandoned bedsits in the upper floors. I found a good knife, and some scraps of food frozen by the chill. Much had already been looted. There was nobody around, just the corpse of an old dog, curled in the corner of one brown room.

That evening, as the light faded, I stood on the roof with my head back, just looking up. I was fascinated, for some reason, with the underbelly of the cloud-cover above me. It was bubbled and pronged like floating coral, corrugated, I thought, like a colossal brain. I found myself thinking silly things. I wondered, for instance, whether the cloud might be sentient – a cloud-brain, stretched over the whole globe. Perhaps it had come to consciousness spontaneously, or (my mind wandering with the cold, the hunger and fatigue) – or been brought to life by cosmic rays, or something B-movie like that. And, looking down godlike upon the corruption beneath, it had decided to bombard us. Not with one cataclysmic A-Bomb (or Ω-Bomb) but with the atomised essence of bombardment, the bomb broken into a continuous rain of atom-sized particles, forever, forever.

Fanciful thoughts. They say no two snowflakes are alike, but I believe I saw many alike that day.

Three

The next day I saw, or thought I saw, an orange light away to the north. The trek after this gleam, which glowed brighter, faded and vanished, glowed orange again depending on the strength of the intervening snow-flurry – the trek after this faery gleam took the rest of the day and much of the night. I ran out of roofs, and it seemed as if there was an impossible stretch to cross with only my boards. But I had become fascinated with the colour, and so I found a way. I cut swathes of pigeon-netting away from the steeple of a church, and laying it out before me with my boards was able to make a painstaking path across naked snow directly towards the light. I was trembly with hunger.

Closer I could see it was a fire, and closer still I made out the half a dozen figures standing about it. I reached that place long after sunset, but the figures were still there and the fire was still burning. I was utterly exhausted.

The six figures stood about the fire, their torsos exaggerated by the bulkiness of their coats, their hands giganticised by their mittens, their heads elongated by their hats, giants standing together. There was something alarming about them, an inhuman aspect. The firelight bounced off the creases and contours of their bodies and muffled faces to Gothic effect in the darkness. It occurred to me that it had been, perhaps, rash to come so blithely amongst these people. What if they intended me harm?

'Hello,' I panted.

They said nothing, but neither did they prevent me from sitting amongst the slush on the roof by the fire.

The building on which we were now warming ourselves was topped with a cupola, wooden slats in a metal frame, and with a metal weathervane at the highest point. These people had built their fire inside this structure, feeding it (as I soon discovered) with all the burnable material they could salvage from the building itself and from the buildings around it. For long minutes the sensation of heat was so delicious, the shocking gaudiness of the orange light so refreshing after weeks of grey and white, that I did nothing but sit. The broad stone ledge on which we all were gleamed damp in the firelight.

11

'We've no food for you,' called one of the figures to me, singsong. He, or she, came and stood over me.

'OK,' I said. 'That's OK.' It wasn't OK, but what else could I say?

'Just so as you should know,' said the figure. It was a masculine voice.

Pause. I stood up, feeling at a disadvantage.

'You lot,' I said, addressing this figure. 'Are you a group? A band?'

'Just together by chance,' was the reply. The voice sounded slightly less surly.

'Right,' I said.

'Jeffreys,' he said. 'My name.'

'Tira,' I replied, unsure whether he had said 'Jeffreys' – a surname – or 'Jeffrey', a first, and not wanting to strain the mood by asking.

He ducked down to squat, and I sat down again. We were both facing the fire. A seventh figure had emerged from somewhere, and threw a whole chair and numerous sticks onto the blaze. I watched the blaze swell, and only belatedly noticed that Jeffreys was looking at me.

'Pretty,' he said.

'What?'

'Pretty – pretty eyes.'

'Thank you,' I said.

'Tie-ra,' he said. 'Kind of name is that?'

'Indian.'

'Ah.' He nodded. Looking closer I could see that his face was that of an oldish man, creased and lined like fractured ice, pressure cracks spinning out from the corners of his eyes, from the wingtips of his mouth. I later learned that he was fifty-nine years old. He smoked with the focused avidity of a man habituated to four packs a day who was now forced to husband each cigarette, not sure where the next pack was coming from. He smoked each fag right down to the filter.

Later, others of the group gathered round. I told them

how I had traversed the open snow with the pigeon-netting and planks. They were impressed. As the night wore on I slept, but woke again before dawn. Then I joined a foraging party, following two people down into the building to scavenge fuel for the fire. We went all the way down the stairs to the ground, the way lit with a hand torch. On the ground floor I saw they had dug tunnels through the now compacted snow to buildings over the road. 'How did you do all this?' I asked, amazed.

'Jeffreys,' they said.

We fetched furniture, paper, cardboard, anything. It was hard work keeping the fire going. Snow spiralled constantly into the blaze, fizzing and spitting. Metal spars running round the frame, and the metal sheet at the top, still supporting its hen-shaped vane, helped keep some of the snowfall out, but the outer portions of the fire dampened and kept fizzling out.

Despite Jeffreys' insistence that there was no food to spare, the eight of us ate together in the morning, wrapping a large ham in foil and cooking it in the body of the fire. We dug the scorching meat from the bone with our bare fingers; I can't think anything ever tasted so good to me before. Or since.

'Where's all this snow coming from anyway?' I said, after this breakfast. We were all of us sitting around, some of us looking into the flake-filled sky. 'Why is it snowing so completely?'

One of my companions grunted. 'Wrath of God,' said another.

'You really think so?' It seemed a rather fatuous explanation to me, but perhaps it was as good as any.

'Sure.' It was a man called Peter. 'Sure. You know about the rainbow sign?'

I said: 'Greenpeace, is it?'

'Na-aa-ah – in the Bible, yeah? God saw the world in its wickedness, in the Old Testament time. Right?'

'Noah,' I said.

'*Right* – Noah. So, God sent the flood, and everybody drowned 'cept Noah. Then when the waters drained away, God sent the rainbow sign, you know, like, yeah an actual rainbow in the sky, which was his promise that he ain't sending another flood. But the wickedness didn't end, did it? Humanity.' Peter drew the word out like a sort of obscenity. 'This,' he added, holding his arms up, 'this don't break the promise, you see? It's God's wrath, alright, but it don't break the promise.'

'Frozen Noah,' said somebody else, and laughed briefly.

'My old Nan,' Peter mused, 'she used to sing: *God send Noah the rainbow sign, no more water, the fire next time*. But this is one weird fucking fire.'

'Ice,' said Jeffreys. 'Burns. Sort of.'

'You agree with that?' I asked him. 'This all God's wrath?'

'Me, no, not me,' Jeffreys said. 'I'm an atheist, thank God.' He stopped, turned his head, and added, 'You get the joke there?'

They had built the fire on the roof because none of the buildings round about had fireplaces, and what Jeffreys called 'a proper fire' wasn't practicable in an unventilated room. But it was hard keeping it going, and another day and night saw the snow finally dampen it down. The party broke up.

Four

I went with Jeffreys. He seemed to have taken a bit of a shine to me, and I had nobody else to go with. Besides, he was likeable in an ornery sort of way. And more importantly he could tunnel.

'Is that true?' I pressed. 'Can you tunnel?'

'I'm one human mole, sure,' he said. 'One human ice-mole.'

We went down to ground-level in the building, and Jeffreys opened a cupboard and brought out a potholer's helmet, with the miner's lamp over its peak. Then we set off. We hurried down the ice-tunnel I had been in before, with several of the others following behind. Into the buried shops opposite, and through to the back, where two tunnels led away through the snow. We took the right-hand one and hurried on. It felt very much *hi-ho, hi-ho*. Light slid over the ruffled white of the tunnel walls in slippery parabolas.

I am a small woman, but even I had to bend forward; that's how low the tunnels were. Jeffreys was bent nearly double. But he moved quickly, and I had to hurry to keep up with his light. It cast a spectral blue-white halo off the white walls. 'How do you make these?' I called.

'Heat,' he said. 'Come on,' he added. 'I got a hideaway.'

'You got several, I'm sure,' I called back.

He didn't answer.

We cut in and out of buildings, through short tunnels and lengthy ones. The strange tunnelly environment started to become almost familiar. At one stage we came out into a huge roofed space, dark and echoing, in which Jeffreys' helmet-light was swallowed after a few yards. 'New Covent Garden Market,' he said, panting. He stopped, leaning against a rail, to light up another cigarette.

'Covent Garden?' I said, amazed that we were so far north.

'The market, no, the market. *New* Covent Garden. Not Covent Garden, not the tourist place. You know? The real market, meat and flowers. South of the river.'

'Oh,' I said, looking around me, although nothing could be seen in the dark except the shine of Jeffreys' helmet and the bullet-point of orange at the end of his cigarette. 'Any meat here now?'

'Nope.'

'Or flowers.'

He coughed, coughed again, paused, and took a longer drag on his cigarette. The end glowed brighter.

'You got one of those for me?' I asked.

'You've got to be kidding,' he said, deadpan.

We went further north.

Five

Jeffreys had used to work for the Underground, on track and tunnel maintenance. There was a machine, he told me, that was used to heat the ground if digging was required in icy weather. 'In winter that ground will be hard as steel,' he said. 'Hard as nickel. This device, it's a sort of trolley with an electric coil at its front, which we used to soften the soil for digging. But, come this snow, I used it to push right through the snow. It cuts through pretty easily, the snow melting and running away as water. About a fortnight after the first snowfall I revved it up and digged some tunnels. Dug,' he added, fumbling for another cigarette.

There were parts of his story I never learnt, and he didn't respond well to my interrogating him. After a while I gave up trying to get the information from him.

'Why not just use the Underground tunnels themselves?' I said. 'Why dig your own?'

'Rats,' he said, in a dark voice. 'Millions of rats. They get cold, get hungry, you don't want to be in the brick tunnels with them.' When he said that I thought of the woman I had met on her way to Balham Tube, and wondered what had become of her. 'Better,' he went on, 'to dig your own tunnels. There's nothing alive above ground now but a few hardy people, like me.'

Later he said, 'I was based up on the Charing Cross Road.' But he can't have meant that he lived there – it's not a place an Underground worker could afford to live. Perhaps he meant he was based at Charing Cross Tube for his work. 'I dug south,' he told me, as the two of us crossed the emptiness of New Covent Garden Market together. 'I had the notion to go to Buck House, I'm not sure why. Never went before the snow came. Too touristy. I think I figured, the Queen, she'll have supplies and such. So I dug in that direction, but it seemed futile. Halfway there I thought of walls and gates and locked doors and swung about, dug to Parliament Square. Thought I'd check out the Houses of Parliament. God knows what I thought I'd find there.'

'How did you power the heater?' I asked.

'Batteries,' he said, laconically, and said no more. We reached the far side and ducked down into the tunnel again. 'They're not going to last long,' he said, as we scurried on. 'You can be sure of that.'

'Really?'

''S true. The heater melts a path, and leaves the tunnel with a sort of sheath of ice on the inside, and that holds it up to a point. But once the snow's built up a bit further it'll collapse these little rabbit-holes. Wouldn't want to be in them when that happens.'

I hurried my step. 'You think that's going to happen?'

'What?' he grunted.

'You think the snow is just going to keep on falling, building up, falling?'

'Don't you?'

'It can't fall forever, surely.' I said. 'Can it?'

He sniffed. 'Fall a while yet, I reckon.'

We came out of the snow into a brick railway tunnel, fifty yards long, with snow packed at either end and piled a long way in. Jeffreys sat on one of the rails running along the ground and pulled off his mittens. It was an extended BR arch, probably on the run-in to Waterloo, but I wasn't happy being there; I hadn't been able to get what Jeffreys had said about rats out of my head. I sat beside him.

'Where are we going?' I asked. 'Any way?'

'Like I said, I got a hideaway.'

'Inside a house.'

'Nah,' he said. 'Once the snow really builds up one storey, two storeys, that won't prevent the pressure from above squashing it down. Tall buildings are the best. What you want is a really tall building. The weight of a thousand feet of snow is greater than the weight of a thousand feet of building – building is largely open air, you see, where the people were supposed to go. Snow is water, that's heavy. So,' he said, chafeing his hands, making an egg of them and blowing into it, as if his thumbs were the mouthpiece of some strange musical instrument. 'So, a skyscraper, acts like a sort of funnel up the snow. A one-storey building, now if that gets a thousand metres of snow on top of it – that roof'll probably cave in. But the lower stories of a skyscraper . . .'

He trailed off, and pulled out another cigarette. I pushed myself closer to him to breathe up as much secondary smoke as I could. It had been a long time since I had had a cigarette.

We hurried on, and into another dug-out ice tunnel. 'Anyway,' he said. 'I came south. Found the north side of Vauxhall Bridge, tunnelled over it. Came further south still, found those guys making the fire. Thought I'd hang out with them.'

'Where's the tunnelling machine now?'

'Stockwell,' he said. 'Batteries ran out.'

'Couldn't you get some more?' I was thinking of the sort of batteries that go in the back of a cassette-player.

'I could fetch some from the depot,' said Jeffreys. 'I suppose. But they're heavy buggers, heavy. Anyway, I'm not sure I'd want to be in these tunnels too much longer, they're not properly propped. Like I said. Snow's falling all the time. Pressure's building up over our heads all the time.'

We walked for hours, bent over, a pain growing in the small of my back all the time. The tunnel swung to the right, and started creeping up at a gentle angle. It swung down into a dip and up again. The bottom of this slight indent was covered with ice. Finally it seemed to end in a tiny hollowed out ice-chamber, like inside an igloo. On one side of this cell the walls were smooth, but the other side seemed to have been loosely packed with snow. There was a single exit.

'Nearly there,' said Jeffreys. 'This bit I dug out with a shovel.' He pointed to a sharply upward-sloping pipe, not

18

much wider than a human torso. 'Up we go.' He put his head up this snow-orifice, wriggled and disappeared, taking the light with him.

There was nothing for me to do but follow. I bent down before the white, gleaming circle, the only light in my now darkened environment, and squeezed myself inside. It wasn't too hard going, actually; I could dig my fists into the snow and haul myself up. After a while it levelled out. I crawled horizontally along behind Jeffreys. I could see ahead that this mini-tunnel terminated in concrete, but Jeffreys had squirrelled down and to the left. I followed him down into a pocket where he had previously cleared out a space outside a window and smashed his way in. I followed him. He had picked the snags and triangles of glass neatly out of the frame, placing all the shards in a concise heap against the wall. Evidence of a tidy mind.

Inside was an open-plan office space: desks still piled with paper, dead computer terminals stickered on their sides with images of film stars. It was grey and murky until Jeffreys lit a camping-gaz light. The hissing bulb grew bright slowly: it gave the impression of light filling the space as if with effort, inch by inch, pushing out against the dark. Through an open door a side-room was visible, filled with crates and loose cans and various paraphernalia. What sort of office had this been before the snow came? It was difficult to say.

There were dozens and dozens of pot plants, from little bushy things in bowls to large Swiss cheese plants in big tubs. I later discovered that most of these had been in place when Jeffreys found the place, that indeed he'd chosen this office amongst all the thousands in London because its former occupants had filled it with so many plants. He was thinking ahead, you see: plants soaking up the carbon dioxide and breathing out the oxygen that we needed. Living off the light of our artificial lamps.

Jeffreys sat on a desk. Sheaves of paper were stacked beside its blank monitor. One mug, packed solid with pens and pencils, bristled like a fox's brush. Another mug beside it was one-third filled with black coffee, as dead and cold as diesel oil. A gonk, a blue ball of artificial fur with yellow felt seagull-feet and outsize cardboard eyes, perched on top of the printer. I stood on the carpet and looked around. At every window save the one that served as entrance the snow pressed up close like the densest mist. 'It's a wonder the windows haven't broken,' I said.

'A wonder,' Jeffreys murmured. 'Upstairs two flights they have broke, most of 'em. Snows all piled in, filled half the space. On the other floors, on this floor, I don't know. Double-glazed I know, for I had the devil's trouble breaking in. But the floor where the windows broke, that was double-glazed too, so I don't know. Maybe the street's narrowness prevented too great a pressure – that side is Charing Cross Road, and it isn't too broad. And *that* side,' he said, swivelling to look at the far wall, 'is a narrow yard and another tall block beyond, Leicester Square. I'm glad for the snow at the windows, though. It insulates marvellous well. I can light a fire in here and almost none of the heat escapes. The warmth stays.' He looked at me. 'A small fire. We don't want to use up the air.'

'The air?'

'We could be down here some time. I got a scrubber,' he said and gestured at a grille-faced box on one side of the room. 'And,' he said, 'and there are the pot plants, but they'll probably die. Or some of them will, but hopefully not all. Still, we need to be careful. Don't want to asphyxiate.'

He thought, I suppose, that we'd be down there a few weeks. We were down there a lot longer than that.

Six

We slept that night together, cuddled up, but Jeffreys didn't make any advances. It wouldn't have been too easy anyway, with the pair of us swaddled up in so many layers of clothing. We ate beans, heated in their tin over a tiny gas fire, and afterwards Jeffreys made two cups of tea with a tea bag. 'No milk,' he apologised. 'Nor lemon neither.' But I was only glad it was hot. Then we snuggled up together on the carpet under a desk and he fell almost instantly asleep.

I lay awake for a long time in the silent darkness. The lack of traffic noise was a distraction. I kept thinking about something Jeffreys had said on the journey through the ice-tunnels about the snow just falling and falling and never stopping. I thought: it can't go on forever. But that night, lying under that desk with my arm for a pillow, I wondered. I imagined the whole world covered with snow, every square yard of it. What would happen if it kept snowing? Would it accumulate and accumulate, heaping up and up? The world swollen to twice its size, a massive globe of white, snow reaching up towards the moon. I fell asleep to dream of creeping through tunnels, and the snow falling silently over my head.

But this is how life is. It doesn't land on you all at once, like the house in the Wizard of Oz that flattened the witch – or perhaps for some people it does, but not for most. For *some*, maybe, I guess, I can see that some instant catastrophe, their own illness or some disaster, knocks them down, concertinas them into a hat and feet. But for most, for the many, it doesn't come all at once. It drifts down, tiny torn-up pieces of your heart, of your job, your body, your weariness, responsibility, pressure, expectations, of little day-to-day specifics, of ordinary setbacks and difficulties. It settles and settles and then, one day, you look out of your window and you see that all of the stuff has covered the ground all around you, has built up without your noticing. And then, another day, you look to your windows and realise you can't even see through them, that the snow has cataracted the glass, and your only surprise is that the panes can withstand the pressure of all that snow pushing in from outside. It is not that you really care, either. Some mini-ature, mandrake-shaped core of you cares, perhaps: but the

21

peripheries – the face and the limbs, the heart and the brain – are too numb, and cold, and weary to care.

To give you a for-instance.

You're a foreigner, an Indian girl. You spent your childhood as a lawyer's daughter in an East African country, part of a small Indian community in a mostly black land. It's a privileged existence, really, but since you've never known anything different you don't realise that it is. You read a lot. You love books, and when they call you a *bookish girl* you think they are being complimentary. Everything in your childhood is hot, the landscape glowing orange and yellow with the heat, the sky low and dropping continual daytime pressure of hot light. The night sky is glorious: enormous, gleaming with stars like snowflakes scattered thinly over the widest, deepest, purplest depths of sky. And when the sun rises each day the buff plains warm and seem to breathe out joy, and the sunlight glows almost neon off the white hair of the horizon mountains. Today is not a school day, so you play in the garden with your sister, although she is too small to be much of a playmate. The dust and dirt is warm. The leaves of grass tower and sway around you. Here you creep through the grass. Here is a bug, sluggish in the midmorning heat, as big as an electrical plug, and as strangely pronged. You lift it from the blade and let it creep over and over your turning hands. You discover more of these bugs, a little colony of them, and lie on your front watching them for hours as they make their bumptiously tiny way about their inscrutable business.

But then your father's house is set alight by one group of malcontents or another (for there is a great deal of political unrest in this country in which you live). The arsonists evade police detection, which makes your father more bitter than he was. You don't like the stale, damp-burnt smell of the kitchen and lounge after the firemen have quelled the blaze. Everything is blackened, ruined. And in this country, where goods are sometimes hard to come by, it takes many months for the new kitchen to be installed, for new carpets to go down. Over months the house comes together again, and you settle back to normality. But a year later the house is set alight again. This time your father's hand is tautened to a claw by the burns he suffers trying to rescue some of his belongings. You are twelve. 'We're going to London,' you hear. But you know nothing about London except what you've gleaned from Dickens and Sherlock Holmes and James Bond movies.

You're still twelve when you step from the plane at one of the London airports, but there is something wrong with the sky. It seems to be clogged with cold white fluff falling, and it takes you a moment to realise that this is snow, because you've never seen snow before. You've read about it, seen it on TV, but somehow you thought it would be more crystal-line, more defined, than this puffy nebulous matter. And then you stand there, amazed, with your mouth open for these drifting insects of ice, but too soft to be ice, to drift in, to meander lazily through the cold air and into your mouth, touching your tongue like a cold fingertip.

And London, you discover, is not like Dickens or Sherlock Holmes or James Bond. London is filled with cars and dirt, and grim people shouldering you out of the way on the pavement, and for every day of luminous, stilling snowfall there are fifty days of relentless rain and three hundred of dull cloud-covered grey. Grey is London's colour. Buildings and roads are grey. The pigeons are grey; even their shit is grey.

Your family – your two parents, your sister, you – live in a three-room flat in Hounslow that is so poky and run-down you literally cannot believe it when you first come through the door. The African house was three storeys tall and had fifty acres of garden. 'This could fit in our *shed* in Africa,' you complain, tears in your eyes. 'I hate it, I'll *never* get used to it.' But you do get used to it. You get used to sharing your bedroom with your sister, and eating your food off your knees in front of the TV, and used to brushing your teeth in the bathroom whilst your father is sitting on the lip of the bath changing the dressing to his burnt arm, inches away from you. You get used to the constant serenade of traffic sounds, and the incoherent noises of yelling and sobbing from the flat above. You do get used to these things, but at the same time they rub away that part of you that was carefree and child-like and lying in the sun watching the insects in the grass. This flat has no garden, and there is no grass.

In Africa your school had been an elegant timber building with a well-watered lawn and acre upon acre of open ground running away to the purple-shouldered hills. In London your school is a concrete building with a twenty-foot-square walled yard. In Africa you had made friends with the Indian and Pakistani children and with white children, and even with those few black children whose parents did the same sort of well-paid work your parents did. But in London your schoolfriends are Indian because you are Indian, just as white kids all have white friends – although white boys, you discover after a few years, are less picky than white girls in their associations, provided you grant them their intimacies and their touchings-up. Worse, in this school you find yourself mocked for your love of books, for your studiousness, and so you learn to mimic interest in the cares and passions of your peers. You yield to the urgent necessity of *fitting in*, which is the most important thing in the life of a child. You start dressing to attract boys. With your girlfriends you talk about boys, and relationships, and love, and sex. Everything you talk about comes down to this – not books, or study, or future career, or ambition, but love and sex. Playground discussions about celebrities and pop-stars are, in essence, about the love-lives of the stars. Discussions about boys are about who is dating whom, about whom you'd be prepared to date yourself.

Boys are really not interested in you though, no matter how much make-up you wear or how low you unbutton your shirt. And then, mysteriously, boys *are* interested in you – you don't know why – although their interest is wholly physical, and fades off as rapidly as it comes. Your father shouts at you that you are too young to wear such make-up or such clothes, but you shout back that you are fifteen now and you'll wear what you want. You have sex with various boys standing up in tucked-away places, in cloakrooms and toilets, lying awkwardly in cars, and this brings with it a sort of acceptance, but mostly you hug to yourself the melancholy satisfaction that if your father knew he'd be horrified – that he doesn't *know* you, that you don't *need* him, that it's all his fault and that, in some obscure inarticulable way, you're paying him back.

Then you're sixteen and you have a steady boyfriend. When he has sex with you he says he loves you, and he coos and caresses your skin. Because he loves you he omits to wear a condom and you fall pregnant, and although he says he will stand by you, marry you, he doesn't – he's only sixteen, after all. So you give birth to a baby girl, and spend two years making the cramped flat even more cramped, with an infant crying in the middle of the night and all the paraphernalia of child rearing. You love the baby some-times, when she smiles, when she sleeps; but more fre-quently she is noisy with colic, or vomiting, or growling with a miserable look on her face, and then she just grinds you down. You sleep on the settee in the TV room with Minnie, your daughter, in a cot; and you wake with a jolt at 3 a.m. because her whimpers have caught, like a petrol engine coughing into life, and flourished into actual cries. So you get up, the weariness registering in your inmost bones, but you get up because you must, and you pick her up and cuddle her, bounce her in your arms, pace the tiny room until she calms. When you try to replace her in the cot she begins crying again, so you hold her and feed her and jiggle her and soothe her for an hour or more. You stand by the window and outside, below you, is an orange-stained lamp-lit road, troubled by occasional cars. The traffic lights, to the right, go through their pavane-like changes of colour, apparently equally indifferent to the traffic or the absence of traffic. Then the night starts snowing, the scene fuzzing, grey flakes swirling up against the glass like an infinity of moths.

Life goes on, and death also, but mostly life. Your father dies of an asthmatic attack when Minnie is fourteen months old. His last words, gasped in between attacks – although they are not literally his last words, but rather the words you remember most clearly afterwards – are: 'you could have done great things, great things, my daughter,' and 'I love you.' But this latter phrase only focuses the oblique rebuke of the former, because you don't go to university, or get a good job, or meet a good high-caste husband, or do any of these things. Instead you move into a tiny council flat in Streatham and you raise your child. Just the two of you, the twosomeness, queerly, more lonely than actual solitude. Your friends are other single mothers, none of whom read books. You smoke. You drink. You take turns looking after one another's children on a Saturday night so that the rest of you can go as a group to a Salsa dancing club. Boyfriends come and go. Years pile on years. Your mother moves to Slough to stay with very distant relatives, and your sister marries a dentist and moves to Dundee, and you see neither of them as much as you ought.

Sometimes in your life the skies clear, the sun emerges, the light reaches you. One relationship, with an older man called Sam, lasts several years. You live with this kindly, tubby bloke in a house – a real house – in Collier's Wood, behind the superstore. With him you go on holidays to Portugal two years running. It's almost exactly as if you are a proper family. Minnie seems happier in school. You take an access course and plan to go to university as a mature student, to study literature – rebelling against your world as always, although this time it is a secret rebellion against your circle of friends. To wallow in books, to read and read! But the relationship with Sam ends. Nothing catastrophic happens between you, just the build-up of rows, of nagging and sniping and bickering, of day-to-day petty unhappinesses. Sam helps you move out to a flat in Balham. It's only up the road but it is a different educational authority, so Minnie must change school. You find work in a shop, then in a bank, then in a shop again whilst Minnie goes to secondary school and does her equivalent of what you did when you were her age. She pierces her face, she wears make-up and short skirts. You want to communicate with her, not to warn her off exactly, not to nag her, not to be a tyrant-parent, of course not; just to explain to her what your experience was like, to let her know that she doesn't have to follow the same path that you took. But you don't have access to those forms of communication. Those train-lines were long since snowed under. The only language you have as a mother is to nag, is to be to her what your parents were to you. Love takes that form too, sometimes, or so you tell yourself. But your daughter can surprise you; despite her Hindu heritage (although you never raised her as a Hindu) she decides to convert to Islam. That, ultimately, is the form her rebellion takes. It's hard to name a more serious form of rebellion a Hindu girl could undertake – more shocking than having sex with boys, even with white boys, more shocking than drinking, or smoking. You tell yourself that she's chosen the one thing still capable of shocking you, that by comparison all those other things would have been positively welcome to you. But there's nothing you can do. She covers her head and goes to a mosque and has earnest discussions with you about how vital it is to live a life that embodies the will of Allah. It distresses you, for some obscure reason you cannot articulate to yourself, but you do not berate her: you don't tell her that this is just a phase, that she will grow out of it. You keep your disapproval hidden, and with the see-saw nature of the dynamic that exists between the two of you this lack of disapproval on your part conjures forth a violent form of disapproval on hers. She criticises you in vehement terms for your boy-friends, for the mode of your dress, for the cigarettes and alcohol. You try to take this in your stride but it grinds you down; the weight of her teenage scorn, and the added

27

weight of the whole world of Islam on top of that, it presses down upon you. But she is sixteen now, and you are thirty-three, and in a moment she has gone – married to a good Muslim man and living in Southampton with a baby on the way.

That's just a for-instance. There are a million similar stories.

Seven

I soon lost track of how much time we spent in that discarded old office. A month passed, perhaps, or so I thought, but when I taxed Jeffreys he insisted it had been a week, no more. I explored every room in the block, from the glass-doored entrance lobby on the ground through to the office at the top, a copy of the one we occupied on the second floor, complete with windows whited out by snow-fall. Six storeys of tall building long since buried. Walking through it with nothing but a torch, blowing a delicate bubble of light into the sheer weight of darkness. Going from room to room I felt like a drowned sailor haunting the cabins of a five-fathom-sunk liner; and then, with an unpleasant twist in my intestines, it occurred to me that this was close to the truth, that there were millions of gallons of water over my head.

But, in general, it was comfortable enough, being buried. For a while at least. We got used to the dark all around; hours and hours of pure dark, with a few hours of gazlight a day, throwing our vast and fuzzy shadows on the walls. There was food, some of which we heated on the camping-gaz stove, although Jeffreys husbanded the blue tins of fuel with something approaching ferocity. There was alcoholic drink, for a few weeks at any rate, until we drained it all; after that we made do with meltwater. Each floor had its own toilets, with three cubicles and urinals against the wall like cowls of ice. We used each toilet bowl in turn until they filled, and then moved on; when we had filled them all we took to shitting in the fifth-floor office. It was cold though, despite Jeffreys' boast about the insulation. The chill all around us chilled us too, and we could venture only a little heat with our precious supply of gaz.

To begin with, Jeffreys ventured out through his ice-tunnel on several occasions to try and gather more supplies; mostly, I assumed, to find more cigarettes, for we had many months of food in tins and frozen tidbits. But he could find no more cigarettes.

Each smoke was now a little ritual for him; the most significant moments in his day. He would take out the tiny white tube, like a hyphen made of snow, and simply look at it for a long minute. Then he would run a finger along its length, and press it against his upper lip to sniff the tobacco smell. Finally he would snap the lighter flame into being and caress the cigarette-end with it, like tickling a small brown button with a ghostly orange finger: running the foxtail flame past and past the end of the cigarette before finally clamping his lips on the filter and sucking the fire in to ignite the tobacco in the tube. When he did this, his eyes would roll white in their sockets and the creases and lines of his face would visibly relax. He drew each breath in as if it were more precious to him than air – which, of course, it was. And he exhaled with a drawn-out shuddering reluctance. The smoke came out of his lungs and throat fine and white as talcum.

I watched him do this many times. It was virtually a sexual ritual for Jeffreys.

In fact, if I am honest, there was more ritual and a more sensual pleasure for him in this than in actual sex. We had sex a few times, but after the first few occasions it became more and more rare between us. Partly this was simply a function of the cold. We might start cuddling and hugging one another, working up a degree of heat inside our many layers of clothing, but as soon as either of us pulled any part of our skin out into the air it would chill at once. Even

29

kissing was difficult, the fat rims of our hoods getting in the way unless we bared our heads, and if we did that our scalps felt the chill in moments. Such sex as we did have was more or less fully clothed, and didn't take long. Jeffreys seemed unengaged. I didn't feel strongly one way or the other. 'Difficult to get turned on in this cold,' I said, one morning.

'I like the heat,' he replied. 'Heat's more erotic.'

He told me almost nothing about his personal life, about his situation before the coming of the snow. 'You married?' I asked once, in as offhand a way as I could. 'Separated? Divorced? Widower?'

'No,' he said, and that was all.

I told him various things from my own life and whilst he demonstrated no great interest in these revelations he did not quite discourage me either. I told him about my daughter, and mentioned that she had a girl of her own. 'You a granny?' he said at this, and grunted his half-surprise. 'You don't look old enough.' The following day he followed this up with, 'What happened to the father?'

'Father?'

'Of your daughter?'

'Him,' I said. 'I lost touch with him.'

'Were you married?'

'No,' I said. 'We weren't married.'

He was lying on his back on the carpet, looking straight up. He said: 'I used to go to Thailand.'

'Really?'

'Hot, there. Very nice. Steamy. An annual thing, me and a couple of mates.' He got up and went through to open another tin. It only occurred to me an hour or so after that this apparent non-sequitur had been Jeffreys talking about his sex life before the Snow. I remember feeling quite startled by the thought of it, and even, for a while, worried: to think of all the sexually-vectored diseases he could have picked up. But when I reflected on the situation it seemed daft to fret. The world had ended, after all. Why worry about anything more personal?

Jeffreys' occasional trips out of the building came to an end when, with a sort of shuffling noise, the ice-tunnel outside fell in. The little collapse pushed a few cubic metres of granulated snow in through the broken window to pile up like a miniature model of a ski-run. The noise woke Jeffreys, who had been napping under a desk. I had been rereading one of the books we had found (all the books were about the cinema industry; presumably the office had housed a film company, or something similar). He got up and went to examine the window. After standing in front of it for a while he grunted and turned away.

The glass doors in the entrance lobby downstairs opened inwards, and the two of us spent one day trying to undo them. 'I could just dig through to the block next door,' he said. 'There might be more supplies we could find.'

'Didn't you already check it out? This block next door?'

'Sure. There's a newsagent's, some offices.'

'And you cleared them out?'

He didn't answer this. I understood that it was less a need for supplies and more a simple matter of boredom that inspired him with the desire to break into a new building. But we didn't open the door; the two of us heaving on the handle shifted it slightly and the whole mass of snow beyond creaked and shuddered, showering dusty white powder through the miniature crack at the top. We hurried back, and up the stairs, hearts pounding.

Eight

Week succeeded week. Jeffreys kept the light on in the main office for hours each day to give the plants light. 'We need their oxygen,' he said. I wondered whether gazlight was enough to keep the plants alive. It felt very different to sunlight; a bluer, Hadean quality. But the plants seemed to be lasting; going a little yellower maybe, but still alive.

31

Jeffreys would scoop snow from the broken window and lay it carefully around their stems.

I became convinced that the snow had stopped falling, far above us. I'm not sure where this conviction came from, but I badgered and badgered Jeffreys that we should dig up to the surface and find out. 'I'll wait 'til the thaw,' he said. 'Til the flood washes up and down Charing Cross Road and the world emerges clean and new. Besides,' he added, carefully bending back the cut rim of a tin-can with pliers all around its circumference, so he could run his finger around the inside and sop up the last of the food inside without cutting himself, 'besides, even if it has stopped it'll be thousands of feet above us. Thousands and thousands. The snow looks as compacted at these windows as it does at the topmost set of windows. Mark my words.'

But I was getting more and more restless. I paced up and down the room, wandered pointlessly up and down the stairway, wasting the torch batteries.

'When's it going to stop then?' I asked, one day.

'Dunno.'

'You said before that this building could stand a mile of snow on top of it – is that how much snow you think is going to fall? A mile?'

'*I* dunno.'

'So why did you say a mile, then?'

'Leave it. Alright, Tira? Just leave it.'

'What if it's more than a mile.'

'What if it is?'

'How *much* more? Ten? Fifty?'

'Leave it, I said, just leave it.'

But I couldn't leave it. I was the Rat In The Cage. I went round and round. How deep will the snow get? How long will it keep snowing? Where has all this snow come from? 'You're like a kid, you know?' Jeffreys yelled at me one day. 'On and on and on. Give it a fucking *rest*, will you?'

But we were too far gone to conciliate one another. '*You* give it a fucking rest,' I shrilled. 'Don't take that tone with me – I'm only trying to think of the future, of how we get out of this mess.'

'Maybe we don't,' he barked back. His face had gone red. 'You think of that? Maybe we're going to die. You're certainly going the right way about killing *me*, and no mistake. So we're both going to die and I'm glad.'

We shouted and yelled at one another for quarter of an hour, although no blows were struck. After the fight we both curled up under different desks and went to sleep, worn out with our bickering. For a day or two after such fights we would be wary of one another, and then we would fall back into easier habits. Then another fight would brew, and the words would come flurrying out in their petty tempests.

'Even if it lay five miles thick,' I said one day, 'there would still be mountains and high grounds poking above the snow. Wouldn't there?'

'Doubt it,' said Jeffreys. He didn't say anything else. This was one of his traits I was finding increasingly annoying, the way he would speak gnomically and then not explain. So I pressed him.

'Why? Why d'you doubt it?'

'The terrain is up and down, I agree,' he said. 'But if the snow is falling everywhere, then it'll just lie unevenly over the world. Your mountain might be ten miles high, but it'd still have several miles of snow over it. Your lowlands would have the same amount.' He was playing with a cigarette, drawing out the foreplay with the tiny tube.

'But the oceans would be clear,' I pressed, unsure why I was so eager to prove this point.

'Unless they froze. Think of the polar ocean, the what's-it-called Arctic Ocean. That was frozen over. Maybe all the world's oceans are like that now, frozen with bergs and smothered with snow.'

'You have to be *so* down, don't you?' I cried out, the anger buzzing out from god knows where. 'It would *kill* you to be even a little optimistic.'

'Don't start,' he retorted.

'You're like death, you're the figure of death himself,' I said. 'You're dragging us both down. Bastard, bastard.'

'Don't blame me – I fucking saved you.'

'Wish you hadn't.'

'*A-men* to that.'

'And *so selfish*,' I went on. My voice was rising into uncontrollable levels. 'You must have smoked a hundred fags since we got here and you've offered me none at all.'

He looked startled at this, as well as angry. 'I,' he said, hiding his cigarette inside his fist as if ashamed of it. 'I *gave* you one, you cow,' he said. 'Last week, or before. You begged and begged and I gave you one then.'

'One,' I said, furious. 'One! And you only gave me that because I had sex with you.'

'It wasn't worth it,' he yelled.

'Well I shan't bother you again,' I called, stung into a feeble sarcasm.

I slept that night in the office above, but it was less comfortable because all the light, the minuscule heat and the food was downstairs. The next day I came down, and we spent a day of surly silence. After that we started exchanging pleasantries again, and soon enough we were back to normal. Except that the normality was constantly simmering, ready to break out into another fight.

Dark, dark, dark.

Let's say I was there for a year. It might have been less; it was probably longer. I don't know. After a while you become bored with being bored, the monotony achieves its own tenor of variety. Jeffreys ran out of cigarettes and spent a long time in a torpid state, unresponsive and depressed. When he came out of this, it was with startling bursts of energy. He concocted a plan to dig a roofed tunnel, making use of the objects in the office. 'We could use the chairs and the desks,' he said. 'They might not hold out for ever, but they'd be good for a while.'

'You're bored,' I observed.

'I thought you wanted out of here.'

In fact I wanted that escape so desperately that I did not dare name it to myself. Instead of facing that fact I sulked in the corner, rereading one of the cinema books again and again by gazlight, whilst Jeffreys pranced about the office like a goat. All the books in the office were about cinema, or about education. I don't know why.

Jeffreys wasn't a reader. 'Time to turn out the light,' he said. 'We're going through the tins at a fearful rate.'

'But the plants,' I said. 'They could do with more light.' And, indeed, they were starting to die, going sepia and brown and losing their leaves. I didn't care about the plants. I wanted the light for myself. I was a plant myself.

Jeffreys gave the plants another ten minutes.

Let's say we were there for a year. The plants died, all of them. 'I don't understand it,' said Jeffreys, muttering in the dark. 'We ought to be asphyxiating.'

'Maybe we are,' I replied.

'No,' he said. 'No, we ought to be dead. We ought to have breathed all the oxygen in here. Where's the oxygen coming from?'

I didn't know where the oxygen was coming from. I didn't know if it was coming from anywhere.

'We can't wait around here to be suffocated,' Jeffreys said. 'I'm going to start digging. Maybe we can break out and up, get to the surface. At the very least we'll need to dig to a new building – there'll be air in other buildings. Maybe we can go from building to building, breathing the air, like bottled air.'

'The plants have been dead for months,' I said. 'We must have already asphyxiated. We must already be dead.'

'It doesn't make sense,' he fretted. 'It can't be months – that must be an illusion. We'd die. Where's the oxygen coming from?'

I still can't answer his question.

Jeffreys became agitated about his tunnel. He had to start the tunnel now, he said. I didn't see the urgency. We'd been

35

there, in the dark, for so long. There were only a few canisters of gaz left, and the batteries had long since expired. We tried to bring power back to the batteries by warming them in our armpits and tucked into our groins. This brought us a few extra minutes of power, but it wasn't a trick we could repeat too many times. Eventually they refused to be resuscitated. Jeffreys insisted that we ration the remaining gaz canisters. He took a lamp upstairs to illuminate his digging of the escape tunnel.

Dark.

He didn't start digging at the window he had originally broken through – superstition, perhaps. Instead he went up to the top office and broke a window with a chair. He had a little shovel, originally a gardening implement I think, with which he cleared away the packed snow outside, and started hollowing out a space large enough to fit a chair in.

I went up from time to time to watch him do this, but I was going through a depressed phase myself (I think), and mostly I lurked on the second floor in the dark. A week passed. 'You should help,' he told me. 'Those tins won't last forever.' And indeed the supply of tins was starting to come to an end; another canister of gaz was sputtering to a halt. But I didn't care. I had no energy in my system at all. I went downstairs and slept. I woke thirsty. When we needed a drink, we usually scooped snow from the broken window into a metal mug and heated it, but lately we had decided we couldn't afford the heat, so I munched miserably at gum-chilling ice for a minute or so. I sat in one of the wheeled office chairs and stared at the pattern of wall-tiles until the lines started creeping and twitching in my weary eyes, and the light finally went out. I toyed with a tin of beans for half an hour, wondering whether to open it.

Eventually I began to think it odd that Jeffreys had not come down. Making my way up the stairs involved a conscious effort at each step, boredom, not exhaustion, making the climb interminable. It occurred to me that I hadn't seen the colour *green* in a very long time. The office walls were white, the carpeting a deep blue that looked black in the half-light in which we lived. There were orange and red and purple objects, plastic devices and pictures here and there, but I could not remember seeing anything green. But that was absurd: there must have been something green in one of the many illustrated books I had read so many times. There *must*. Mustn't there? A photo of grass, or trees, something? Was it (I was physically straining my mind, trying to remember) that the inks in the colour process made the green look more aquamarine? Dark green, conifer green, bottle-green. But what about the bright green of sunlit lawns? The uncomplicated green? The way my mind was then, I could almost have believed that this colour had been banished from the world forever.

In the topmost office I found Jeffreys lying on his front. His breath was coming in steam-like little hisses, and when I bent over him I could hear that he was swearing on every whispery indrawn breath: *fuck, fuck, fuck, fuck*.

'What happened?'

'Stupid fucking thing,' he gasped. 'Fell off the chair.' I looked behind him, and saw that he had placed one chair on a desk, the better, I supposed, to be able to fiddle around with something on the ceiling.

'Jesus,' I said. 'Let me help you up.'

But when I tried to lift him he howled like a beast in pain. I was so startled that I dropped him and flinched back. 'What is it? What is it?'

'Leg,' he gasped. 'Hip. Leg. Dunno.'

'Oh Jesus,' I said. 'Is it broken?'

'Fucking stupid,' he panted. 'So fucking stupid. The chair slipped. The desk, slippy, or. Something. Fuck. Fell off, like. Stupid.'

'Let me try and roll you over,' I said.

He howled again and again as I shifted him, but as he screamed he flopped over onto his back. I couldn't see anything wrong with his leg, but that was because it was so bulked up with the layers of winter clothing.

'D'you know,' he hissed, 'first aid?'

'Nope,' I said. 'I was working in the Abbey National when the Snow came. First aid was no big requirement for my job.' I was thinking that he couldn't have fallen that far, that he couldn't have done that much damage. He had put a chair on top of a desk, and stood on top of that. But how far was that to fall? Six feet?

'Got to do,' he gasped. 'Something.'

'Do we have any painkillers?' I asked. But I knew the answer to this question already. Jeffreys had not salvaged any when gathering his supplies together; we had found a half-used first aid box in one of the offices, but the only paracetemols inside had been gobbled months ago to counter an intermittent bout of Jeffreys' toothache. And what good would paracetemol be, anyway, for a broken limb?

'We should splint it. Can you get downstairs, do you think?'

'Fuck off.'

'Let me have a look at it.' I took off his shoes, fumbling with the chilly, wormy laces, and drew down the snow-trousers that were the outer layer of his legwear. Each shift in the material made Jeffreys wince, or shout out in agony. I tried pulling down the second layer, the canvas trousers he was wearing underneath, but the massed-up bulk of the snow-trousers got in the way. In the end I had totally to remove the outer trousers to get the canvas pants down, and then take those off to get the inner jogging-pants down. Finally, Jeffreys was lying on the carpet, cursing, more naked than I had ever seen him; his legs were white, with twig-shaped blue veins running up and down. At the top of his left thigh, just below his underpants, was a bruise, the size of a fist. The area was swollen, and a comma-shaped protuber-ance was visible at its centre, poking up underneath the skin like a thorn. I didn't want to think that this was a splinter of leg bone propping up the skin from within. The very thought of that made me feel queasy, dizzy. I told myself that it couldn't be, that he hadn't fallen far enough. That his hip would have been cushioned by his clothes. But the evidence was there, unmistakeable. The bone had broken to put up a little spike that lifted bruised skin like a tentpole.

I felt my shrunken stomach spasm. It was horrible.

'What could I use as a splint?' I said, in a forced, breezy tone of voice to distract myself. 'Chair leg?' But the chairs were all metal and plastic.

'Jesus,' Jeffreys was saying. 'Jesus, fuck.'

'What do you think?' I pressed. But I was losing him. Maybe, I thought, distantly, he was in some sort of shock. The pain must have been terrible. I stood up and paced around the office in an unfocused way. I thought of pulling down one of the neon-lights from the ceiling, half-thinking that I could break splints from the square plastic casings. Then I thought of breaking up a desk drawer, of using the wooden sides to one of the drawers. I went down the stairs to the second floor, because the two of us had started breaking up the furniture the week before in anticipation of our using up the last of the gaz-fuel. I'd had the vague idea of preparing a supply of burnable material to make an actual fire, although Jeffreys had forbidden it, scolded me, told me that without a chimney we'd asphyxiate ourselves. I think I didn't really care. 'We should have asphyxiated anyway,' I said.

But I didn't make the fire.

I selected two or three pieces, and ran back up the stairs. But I had no idea how to splint even the simplest break; let alone a complicated fracture up near the hip, or possibly of the hip itself. I dropped the fragments of wood beside Jeffreys and went down again to retrieve the first-aid box we had found. It still contained some bandages and plasters, which I supposed would be useful. I ran back up again. Then it occurred to me that I ought to fetch up the camping gaz. It was our last tin, and only had an hour or so of use left in it, but it occurred to me that I ought to make Jeffreys some tea. 'Hot sweet tea,' I said to myself as I went down the stairs again, a mantra. 'Hot sweet tea.' It was stupid, really, because we had neither tea nor sugar; but I scooped out some snow and gathered up the little cooker. I was halfway up the steps when I thought to bring some beans as well, that he should have some food, so I left my stuff on a step and went down again for a tin.

When I finally emerged at the top again Jeffreys had stopped breathing. I dropped all the material I was carrying with a clatter and rushed to bend over him, but his naked legs were cold as any stone, and his face had settled into a sort of icy grimace. I tried pumping his chest, not sure what I was doing, but it made no difference.

Eventually I gave up, and sat in one of the office chairs looking down at his body. I tried to work out whether he had died of the break, the pain, the cold, but there was no way to know. I think, maybe, that the pain had over-stimulated his heart. I have talked to doctors, subsequently, and they said it could have been that. The pain would have produced a lot of adrenalin in his blood-system and the adrenalin would stimulate his heart, and this might kill him, because his heart wasn't really very strong. He had smoked all his life, after all. Sometimes, though, I think that it was my stripping his legs bare that did him, because it was so very cold in that place. I'd prefer not to think that, because I would prefer not to think I was so directly responsible for killing him. But who can tell?

Nine

I went through a phase of wanting, with an animal despera-tion, to be out of that place, to be away from Jeffreys' dead body. I couldn't bear it. He was a much more potent presence in the building dead than he had been alive. I don't know why this should be. For a day I lurked on the second floor, carrying the cooker and the beans back down with me. I used up more precious heat to boil some water, I ate the beans I had been going to take up to him, but all the time I was aware of him – up there – pressing down on the floor as if it were my skull. I imagined him magically swollen in size, his corpse so huge it stretched from one side of the building to the other, his hands as big as desks, the veins on his legs big as hoses. Like that scene in *Alice in Wonderland*. Or is it *Looking Glass*? – where she zooms up in size inside the room and her foot goes up the chimney? You know the bit I mean. I fantasised that Jeffreys' body had grown like that. I'm not sure why. It created this sense of morbid wonder in my head. I lay under a desk, but the thought of the dead body was palpable. I imagined it bruising all over with the slow violence of decay, imagined its skin going black and olive and cyan, filling like an air bag with corruption from within, but infinitely slowly. I tried to sleep, but the more I thought about it the larger the body became in my imagination, until it was packed impossibly into every corner and crevice of the top floor, grown like a sea cucumber of prodigious dimensions. Lowering over me like a black cloud, threatening what unspeakable storm I could not say.

Eventually, after maybe twelve hours of fretting and scaring, I crept back upstairs. I turned on the lamp with trembling fingers. Jeffreys was still there, still normal size, his skin white as paper, his face stuck in a slightly uncomfortable expression. It was almost an anticlimax.

I tried leaving the body there, but it continued to prey on my imagination. Eventually, summoning my courage, I moved it to the top-floor toilet, dragging it through and leaving it lying on the floor by the window. That reduced its presence in my thoughts to a certain degree, although I still woke from clammy gelatinous dreams.

One morning I snapped. I couldn't bear it any more. I went to the broken window on the second floor and started scrabbling at the snow with Jeffreys' little shovel. I didn't have anything planned clearly in my head. I probably thought of digging clear through to the surface – impossible, of course – just to see the sunlight once again, just to feel the

41

sun on my skin before I died. The thought of simply giving up and lying in that mausoleum with Jeffreys was obnoxious to me. To lie there in the cold for ever and ever?

No.

But the snow had packed so hard that I could barely dent it. On some level I think I realised that this meant the weight of total snow must have been very great, and that accordingly the snow must have fallen to a very great height above me. But I was crying, with the frustration, and with the effort of cracking the shovel at the bulging wall of white like an axe. A small quantity of tiny fragments flew off the ice with every blow, like sparks, but after an hour of digging I had made so little progress that I gave up in self-disgust.

When I was a little calmer, the following day, I tried to cultivate a philosophical frame of mind. I told myself that a thaw might still come; that one day I would hear the ice cracking, and see it run away as water down the glass in fat rivulets, and see the sun shining brightly through. This, I said, was surely going to come. There had been a million snowfalls in the history of the planet, I said to myself, and a million thaws. How could this *one* snowfall, the million-and-first snowfall that I had experienced, be the single exception to this universal, planetary rule? It was impossible that this would be the case. All I had to do was wait until the thaw, and then I could go back to my ordinary life. I did not dwell too completely on how this ordinary life might be changed – how many people had died – how much had gone forever. Instead I told myself stories about the strange escapes that my various friends had made from the catastrophe. Improbable though it all was, I needed the fiction. I fantasised about meeting up with them again after the thaw, about sitting in a pub with a glass of wine and a cigarette and laughing at the absurdity of it all.

Then, some mornings, I would weep at the futility. I would cry those sorts of tears that squeeze out between reluctant eyelids, whilst the side of the hand is pressed between the lips to stifle the sobs. There was never going to be a thaw, and everything was finished, and that was that. I vacillated between the two states. The most likely fate I ignored, mostly: even with the food wholly to myself, even without Jeffreys eating half the store, my supply of food was running low. Soon I would be without light or food or heat, and soon after that I would fall asleep with starvation and cold in the dark and not wake up. But I didn't think about that.

I slept more than I had before. I put the one remaining lamp on its lowest setting to reread all the printed matter in the office, with a bizarre avidity: everything I could find, from books about cinema to accounts documents and inventories, going through the lists of things as if my life depended on checking each thing and memorising every number. The food ran out. I had been on starvation rations for a while, so the cessation of eating did not strike me with any too pronounced pangs, although it was uncomfortable. And still the hoped-for thaw did not come. And two days after I wiped clean the food from the last tin, just two days later (as if on cue), the building shivered.

First a noise, a sort of soft groaning. Then silence. Then the noise again, and I noticed that a sheen of ice particles on one of the desks was trembling slightly. At first I thought it was an earthquake. Then, my heart thudding, I thought perhaps the weight of snow had built up to the level where the entire building was going to be collapsed. I leapt up, uncertain how to meet my fate. Being squashed out of existence in one push downwards. I wanted it *not* to happen, it horrified me; and in exactly the same motion I wanted it to happen, I wanted to rush to embrace it.

There was a crack and a crash from upstairs, and I could barely control my trembling legs as I rushed up the stairway with the lamp turned up bright. The third and fourth floors were empty, but in the fifth floor Jeffreys was standing, swaddled in strange gear. I called out 'You're dead,' or something, I don't really remember what. Then I noticed that the figure was not Jeffreys at all. He pulled back a visor from his head-hugging helmet and I saw it was a young man with bright blue eyes.

It was a shock. I had forgotten how other people looked, it had been such a long time. The shock was so profound that I started laughing.

Ten

This was the captain. He didn't tell me his Christian name, he said 'call me the captain'. The first thing he said was, 'Jesus my Saviour, there's somebody alive in here.'

From behind him came whoops of disbelief. He had emerged from a tunnel cut in the ice, taller and broader than any tunnel Jeffreys had ever cut. It took a few moments for me to piece together all the visual detail my eyes were being presented with after so long in solitary isolation. This figure was carrying a device that looked like a leaf-blower. Over his shoulder another helmeted head emerged.

'Alive?' said this second figure.

'Who are you?' I said.

'Jesus my Saviour,' said the first man. 'It's a woman. You a woman?'

I blinked. 'I am a woman,' I said. I pulled the hood from my head. I saw his eyes widen. 'And a damn pretty one,' he called back, over his shoulder. 'Pretty woman. What's your name, honey?'

'Tira,' I said.

The second figure emerged fully from the tunnel, stepping down from the window sill. A third head was visible in the shadows. 'Never mind that now,' said the second. 'Lady, tell me one thing.'

'Who are you?' I said again.

'Tell me *one* thing, lady. This the bank?'

'Bank?'

'Bank of London,' said the second. 'Bank of England, whatever.'

'No,' I said.

'Found a sign, a subway sign,' said Charing. 'Charing's one step away from the Bankment, according to our maps.'

'The Embankment,' I said, slowly. My head was chilly, so I pulled my hood up again. 'That's not far, but there's no bank there.'

'So why is it called what it's called?' The second figure seemed very cross.

'I don't know.'

'Stupid fucking city.'

'Is this a bank of *any* kind?' said the first figure.

'It's an office.'

'Jesus. How long you been here?'

'I lost count.'

'Alone here?'

'Yes.'

'I'll have a look through,' said the second figure. 'You want to take her with us? Better than nothing.' He bustled past me, and started checking the desks. As I was being helped up the window and into the ice-tunnel beyond I heard him say, 'I guess we can use some of these computers.'

'How long you been down here, ma'am?' asked the third figure.

'I don't know,' I said.

Still dazed I was led along the tunnel and through a hatch into a low-ceilinged metal chamber. It was all so new, and my mind was so poor at taking it all in, that I barely remember any of the many details, for all that I stared and stared at them. I have a hazy sense of a positively Christ-massy profusion of lights, of a sharp stink like a fox's hole, of a further door through which I was bundled. The first figure introduced himself to me, as the captain, and asked me to sit down on the floor. I sat down. I don't know how long I was sitting there.

Eventually the second figure came through, and deposited an armful of stuff from the office. He went out and came back several times, bringing computers, chairs, pens and pencils, paper, ornaments, all sorts of things. He said nothing to me at all, and I watched in a sort of blissful non-comprehension, just sitting in their odd craft.

Later still the three men in the strange craft started yelling at one another – in anger, I thought at first, until I realised they were simply preparing the craft for cast-off. 'Doors locked!' one shouted. 'Doors locked!' echoed another, further away. 'Heating!' 'Heat*ing*!' 'Central fan – check it, Harry.' 'Checked!' And so on. There was a change in pitch of the engines, and a huge shuddering that grew and grew, like a washing-machine on spin-cycle. Then we tilted, tilted back, shifted, and started to creep away.

I was in some sort of daze. It occurred to me that these people might be the angel of death, might be some new incarnation of the angel of death, and that they had collected me to carry me away to the afterlife. I thought: perhaps the angel of death came with a scythe in the older days of hand-harvesting, and now He comes as a technical crew and a large machine. That's how muddled up my brain was.

'Where are we going?' I asked the captain, when he came through to see how I did.

'Up top,' he said. 'You really been down there since the snow started?'

'Yes.'

'So – what? Did you work in that office, or something?'

I thought about explaining the true state of affairs, but I couldn't – really – be bothered. It seemed unnecessarily messy. 'Yes,' I said.

'Man. That's some survival. How you last that long? What did you do for food? For *air*?'

'We stockpiled some tins,' I said, vaguely. 'Air, I don't know. I don't know how we managed.'

'We?'

'There was this other guy.'

The captain seemed hugely interested and energetic to my tired perceptions. 'Other guy,' he said. 'Really? Work colleague? Husband?'

46

'Friend.'

'Dead?'

'Yeah.'

'We did find this, like, body in the rest-room,' said the captain. 'That him?'

I nodded. For a while we were silent. The conversation had taken place at an exaggerated volume, because the engines of this strange sub-ice craft were so noisy. After a while, I said. 'We're going up top?'

'That's right. We're going to the Free World. I guess it'll all be new to you.'

'The free world,' I said. 'It's still snowing?'

He laughed at this, and went out through the little door. I stared at the door after him; it was a hatch, not a door. The shuddering and trembling of the walls and floor struck me paradoxically as symptoms of the big chill – I say paradoxically because it was very hot in that little, cluttered space, so much so that I had to take off my coat. The first time I had taken off my coat for the longest time.

After an hour, or five hours, or perhaps a few minutes, the whole craft gave a lurch and tipped through fifty degrees. I fell along the floor. There was a sort of rubber matting down to provide grip, but the tilt caught me off guard. Then everything stopped. The engine noise shrank to a sort of purr.

I got to my feet and manoeuvred my way through the hatchway, leaning against whatever might provide purchase. In the cockpit (I assumed it was the cockpit) the three men were huddled around a tiny screen. There were no windows, and the sense of clutter, the oppressive hot fug was even stronger in here. 'What's happened?' I said. 'What's going on?'

'We're at the surface,' said the captain without looking at me. 'More or less. We're waiting for our hovercraft to come collect us. Shouldn't be long now.'

'Did you go to the bank?' I asked, slightly febrile with the unusual heat and all the excitement.

'Bank?'

'Bank of London, *she* means,' said the second figure, the guy who had pushed past me in the office.

'No, we didn't. We didn't have the energy to manoeuvre through the streets all the way along. I mean,' he added, enunciating carefully as if it mattered very much to him that I understand, 'we found it, we got our map-book and we found where it was, so we can go back another day. But we don't have unlimited energy to go crawling through the icebound streets. You know?'

I didn't know. 'OK,' I said, uncertainly.

'We'll try and book another dive, dig out some new tunnels closer to the site.'

'You want money?' I said.

'Money, food,' said the captain. 'But, whatever, we didn't manage it. We got some other stuff.'

'Junk,' grunted the second figure.

'Whatever. Plus we got you.'

'How you mean?'

'He means,' said the second figure, 'we went looking for valuables and all we found was you.' He laughed, obscurely, and then was silent.

'Valuables?'

'Young women,' said the captain, beaming. 'They're valuable in their own right, women, you know.'

'Valuable how?' I said, a nervous sensation crunching in my stomach. 'What am I, some sort of slave? Some sort of . . .' But in my nervousness I couldn't think of a synonym. 'Slave?'

'Jesus my Saviour,' said the captain, loudly. 'No, no. No slaves in New America. What you think we are?'

'Sorry,' I mumbled.

'But women are welcome, of *course* they are. Young women. We got to look to the future. But go getting yourself a husband, maybe a wealthy husband, that don't make you a slave.'

'Sorry,' I said again.

'Here we go,' said the third figure. 'Mama.'

The captain heaved open the hatch, and clambered out. I understood later that he was going to attach the crane-hook to the grapple-point so that the whole craft could be winched out of the snow and loaded onto an enormous hovercraft. I understood that later, and understood too why there was such a deal of clanking and banging. But at the time I knew none of that, because I was hypnotised, utterly hypnotised by the sudden, glorious sight of clear sky. Clear blue sky, through the rectangle of the hatchway.

'Out you go,' prompted one of the other men, heaving me on my rear to help me up and out. And, wide-eyed as a child, I climbed through into endlessness, into the white and the blue and the sharp, clear, ozone tang of fresh air. I stepped onto the fringe of the hovercraft without even realising that it was there, so astonished was I by the breadth and depth of the colour, of the blue.

Around me, bright as a searchlight, was the sunlit snowfield, white to all horizons. And above it stretched a cloudless sky of such purity, of such distilled essence of blue, that it made my heart yammer. It made my heart flip and buck about in my chest like an epileptic having a fit. I stood for long moments with my head back just looking up at it. It was the colour of a gas flame turned low, bright and shining from horizon to horizon. Blue. Blue. 'Jesus,' grunted a man behind me, wanting me to hurry up, wanting me to go inside the hovercraft. But I was hypnotised, I was the snake looking into the infinite blue eye of the snake charmer. And, as softly as a lover's caress, falling from a clear blue sky, occasional flakes of snow brushed against my face.

So You Want To Be A Food-Miner?

[You've read Tira's narrative.][1] Its account of the world before the Snow either reminds you of what you have lost, or perhaps awakens you to a knowledge of what has passed away (depending on how old you are!). But do you want to know the truth? The world has *not* passed away completely! The world described in this tale is *still there* – still perfect, preserved by the cold. For many, the snow is the roof of their tomb, and may they Rest in Peace: never forget that their sacrifice helped us forge a new world here in the broad sunlit snowlands. But there is a great deal else down below, pristine, waiting for enterprising and brave citizens to dig it out and bring it up to us. Even a small list of the sort of wealth locked underneath the snow would be too long for us to list here: all sorts of money, all manner of technology, raw materials – metals, plastics and wood – precious things, beautiful things, fine art, self-defense equipment. Above all, *food*.

Understand this: our Democracy needs this wealth! Our enemies grow stronger, and threaten our very existence, our very way of life. Make no mistake the challenges are severe and testing. But God and the People will prevail, and this great mass of raw material will be properly exploited. Heroic companies like Novadic, Novemi, NovaMicron and New Affiliated Miners undertake the constant struggle to wrest

[1] This sentence changes according to which personal account or memoir the *So You Want To Be A Food-Miner?* appendix is added. *IP Order*: all accounts or histories of the Coming of the Snow should also include statements tending towards the recruitment of workers for the public good and the increase of public wealth.

profit and glory from the dangers of the deep snow; heroic Food-Miners like Sam Appleseed, Bernard le Farrar and the great Andy d'Intino make lucrative careers for themselves and bring glory and wealth to the People. Perhaps *you* have what it takes to follow in their great steps?

Contact your nearest certificated Ladder agent, and take the first step up to a lucrative and publicly important career – start to train as a *Food-Miner*! Contact: 756–778–8570. 3-yr min medical insurance a requirement.

Interview with
Gerard Louis Seidensticker

{{<<G S Seidensticker is one of the most eminent scientists to have survived the Snow. A household name for his dedication to Freedom as well as the brilliance of his technical and scientific work, he talks here to *Science for Freedom* about the question on everybody's lips – *the origins of the Snow.*>>}}

SCIENCE FOR FREEDOM The question, of course, is: where on earth did all this snow come from? It's a question we all hear constantly, of course.

G S SEIDENSTICKER It sure is – and I've heard as many theories as there are flakes of snow in a blizzard! It's in the nature of science to play with theories. That's a natural and healthy thing.

SFF But, perhaps, a little distracting for the general population?

G S SEIDENSTICKER Indeed. But the mystery, if I can call it that, is not such a big one.

SFF You say that, but most people don't know the real cause of the Snow. Do you think the government is justified in restricting knowledge on such an area of – we might say – pressing public interest?

G S SEIDENSTICKER I don't think you can say that the government is actively restricting knowledge. The government has a very difficult job to do, a difficult balancing act. Society has changed so much, and preserving the things that are important to us – free enterprise, freedom, quality of life – means making some tough choices. I think they've got it about right at the moment; actively disseminating the truth might be destabilising to our fragile new order – that, after all, is how people in government tend to think. But neither have they actually *banned* the information . . . not yet anyway!

SFF You say the truth of the situation might be destabilising, yet you're talking to us here today?

G S SEIDENSTICKER Science is about the truth, first and foremost. I believe, deep down, that the truth cannot harm us. I believe in freedom, of course, but I also believe the old adage, that the truth will *set* us free. So I'm happy to talk about things if anybody asks me – and you guys asked me!

SFF When you describe knowledge of the true source of the Snow as 'destabilising', what do you mean?

G S SEIDENSTICKER I mean it might turn people against science and scientists. This would be destabilising because so much of our future depends upon the proper development and articulation of science. We have so many new challenges in this new world, and new enemies as well: we need scientific and technological innovation to address these problems.

SFF In what way would the 'truth' about the coming of the Snow cause resentment against scientists?

G S SEIDENSTICKER It's very difficult. Rationally we know that all the most significant technical advances in human society were produced at risk, with some often unpleasant side-effects along the 'research 'n' development' way. Marie Curie died of X-ray poisoning, yet X-rays are a crucial component of our modern society's fight against disease. We know this sort of thing, know it *in our heads* if you see what I mean; but *in our hearts* there is sometimes an instinctive revulsion against the price that science asks of us. It's that kind of knee-jerk that I'm talking about.

SFF So the Snow was an unfortunate by-product of scientific research?

G S SEIDENSTICKER I was part of a team that had been working for six years, or nearer seven, on a number of topics in magnetoanisotropy. In particular we were developing and testing the concept of the *electron sheath*. Now, we know about electrons from TV, from scanning microscopes and the like, but the genius of our team was in finding more and more stable ways to arrange electrons.

SFF Who funded your research?

G S SEIDENSTICKER Defence Industries Corporated; the old Novadic.

SFF So it was military research?

G S SEIDENSTICKER Actually, no. The shooting-off point for the research *had* been military. The Navy was interested in the compacted focusing of electron beams as a possible weapon. But it became pretty evident pretty soon that the military applications were negligible. Credit to Novadic, DIC as was, that they didn't pull the plug when they realised that.

SFF Why didn't they?

G S SEIDENSTICKER They saw the commercial possibilities, I think. The market in patent trades and – especially – patent futures was very large back then, and my understanding is that they were speculating on the futures market for what they thought would be a very lucrative commercial patent. Assuming we could get the electron sheath properly working, that is!

SFF Tell us more about this electron sheath.

G S SEIDENSTICKER Electrons occupy certain positions around nuclei, certain energy levels, called their shells. For a while it was thought that electrons circled their nuclei in set orbits, like little planets around a star. Then, with quantum physics, we began to think of electrons as occupying certain bands, like the skins of an onion. But it's more proper to think in terms of what the physicists call *orbitals*;

the electron is not so much a well-defined point as a quantum-uncertain wave that moves in the orbital. If you're doing basic calculations about the charge of an atom and the like then you can think of the orbital as an area around the nucleus in which the electron is, like, smeared out – and not necessarily evenly smeared either. Scientists have spent a lot of effort now mapping out the shape of these orbitals, and perhaps surprisingly, we discover that they're not necessarily circular, or even elliptical, in cross-section, although obviously they *can* be. Indeed, there are some very peculiar shaped orbitals out there in nature.

The idea behind the electron sheath began with us manipulating some of the weirder shaped electron orbitals. We began to think that we could fit some of these things together into a circle, like a carbon-ring only without the nuclei – a stable form of electron existence. Link these together, stripping electrons from the outer orbitals of heavier elements and realigning them in an interlocked series of these rings, and you have the sheath. Early experiments took place in very attenuated vacuums, which were very expensive to maintain, because we found that the electronegativity of ordinary matter was too great for the coherence of the sheath. But after a year or so of tinkering, we discovered a form of the orbitals jigsaw that was much, much more stable. We called it the lattice. Since then, we've discovered seven variants on the same lattice, and we've also very much speeded up the way in which these sheaths can be spooled out of the originary matter. Our best time, I think, is under an hour to spool out a nineteen-thousand-kilometer electron sheath – pretty good going!

SFF You said that these electron sheaths had no military application. What sorts of commercial applications were you thinking of?

G S SEIDENSTICKER Well, it's not really a researcher's job to think of practical applications for his or her work, but as we worked through the project the sorts of possible uses for the technology were just so obvious to us. Imagine a tube running, let's say, for the sake of argument, from a fresh-water lake in northern Europe all the way down to the Sahara[2]; a tube in which the electrical potential of the thing itself meant that it acted like a siphon. You could irrigate millions of hectares of barren ground. You could put out forest fires with the flick of a switch; you could revolutionize the trade in a thousand products – fresh goat's milk from India could be piped to consumers in Canada as cheaply as it could be hauled down the road to the next village in pails. A million uses. A million and one.

SFF I've heard the electron sheaths described as 'worm-holes'.

G S SEIDENSTICKER They are most definitely *not* worm-holes. Wormholes are a science-fiction invention, some sort of instantaneous tunnel through the fabric of spacetime. I hate science fiction. Electron sheaths do *not* 'tunnel through spacetime', they are *part* of the spacetime fabric. Travel down an electron sheath is most certainly *not* instantaneous – no faster-than-light travel here. Think of it as water coming down a hose. Although, having said that, travel along the sheath *is* very efficient, because the electrical potential insulates the product from friction. And, if I remember my *Star Trek*, wormholes are supposed to just 'open' like doors, aren't they? Well, electron sheaths have to be spun out using some very high-tech equipment. So, no, they're real, not sci-fi.

SFF How stable are the sheaths?

G S SEIDENSTICKER Perfectly stable.

---

[2] Before the snow much of northern Africa was hot, dry and barren. The Sahara was a waterless place.

SFF What were the downsides of the technology?

G S SEIDENSTICKER Once we got the proper matrix developed – the lattice – there were very few downsides. The major drawback is the volume capacity. We hoped to be able to manufacture electron sheaths of industrial diameters – let's say a metre across, or ten. But the Planck Constant won't let us do so. We can squeeze one lattice out to a sizeable fraction of a millimeter, but that's the best we can do. We got around that by binding a hundred or so sheaths together, twining them about one another and upping the capacity. It was a very workable technology for fluids, provided only they were not too viscous. With time I think we'd have been able to handle any sort of fluid, and maybe solids too.

SFF You ran out of time?

G S SEIDENSTICKER The Snow overtook us.

SFF How is the coming of the Snow connected to your research?

G S SEIDENSTICKER We had done a number of larger-scale experiments. By larger scale, I mean spooling out longer and longer electron sheaths to see how far material could be practicably transported. Theoretically, we couldn't see any reason why an electron sheath tethered on one of Jupiter's satellites, Europa say, couldn't transport water all the way to – I don't know, Earth's moon. There's no *theoretical* limit to the length of these things, although I suppose physical shearing forces would compromise the integrity over really larger distances. But, anyway, we were trying out different lengths.

The trouble happened with a sheath of a little under nine thousand kilometers. It was braided, which is to say it was made up of over a hundred individual sheaths coiled together into one rope. So, we hoped to generate it between our American laboratory and an affiliated institution in the Nederlands. It was the sort of experiment we had done before.

SFF You had done this exact experiment before?

G S SEIDENSTICKER Not that exact one, but very similar ones. We'd run a very lengthy sheath down from the USA into South America without any problem at all.

SFF So why was there a problem with this one, do you think?

G S SEIDENSTICKER With hindsight I'd say that it was the lateral lay of it. It spooled out and up into the atmosphere before coming down in Europe, which meant that it crossed the global lines of magnetic force at a right angle. The sheath we'd sent down to Latin America had lain neatly within those lines of force, and they hadn't disrupted it. But this US-Europe sheath got tangled up in the lines of force.

SFF You didn't anticipate that?

G S SEIDENSTICKER No, we didn't. Easy to be wise after the event, but it didn't occur to us before. Think of the Earth as a huge bar magnet, with lines of magnetic force running from north pole to south. That was the problem, right there. We set up the sheath – we hoped to send some coffee from a cup in our lab to our colleagues in Holland.

SFF Cold coffee!

G S SEIDENSTICKER Oddly enough, it *was* cold coffee; it took us so long to set the thing up, the coffee went cold! The stuff would have been heated a little by the environment of the sheath as it passed through, but no more than a few degrees – so it would have come out cold at the other end. Still, some people *like* cold coffee, I've heard; some people actually *prefer* it!

SFF Give me my joe steaming and hot!

G S SEIDENSTICKER Me too. Anyway, we set up the sheath: nine thousand kilometers of it running latitudinally across the globe. Now we're still not entirely sure how or why, but the lines of magnetic force disrupted the thing. Didn't interfere with the coherence of the sheath itself, but did wrench it out of position. Ripped it clean from its tethers! In a way, the very fact that the sheath didn't then disintegrate is a testament to the integrity of our original design.

SFF Shouldn't it have disintegrated?

G S SEIDENSTICKER What probably happened is this: some of the outer sheaths – remember there were over a hundred, all braided in together – probably did degrade. But the bulk was preserved by the highly energetic environment of the magnetosphere, through which it was whipping like a string in a hurricane. And afterwards, when it settled down, the likelihood is that the passage of so much water produced a sort of electron rub against the insides of the sheaths that kept them coherent. Water is very reactive. Or maybe the thing is maintained purely by the electrical potential of the magnetosphere – there are several theories.

SFF Did the sheath go straight to the north pole?

G S SEIDENSTICKER Probably not; it probably slid up and down along the lines of force for a while, empty, high in the atmosphere. But given the electrical potential, it was inevitable that it would be attracted to the north pole, and our best guess is that it slid northwards in a matter of days.

SFF And then?

G S SEIDENSTICKER Well, the results are well known! The mouths of the sheaths lodged in the ice pack at magnetic north, and the tails broke free from one another, unbraided we would say, and thrashed through the atmosphere nine thousand kilometers south, buoyed up by the lines of terrestrial magnetism. About sixty of the sheaths retained their integrity, and the tails of these began spitting out ice water drawn from the polar cap. The sheaths were – are – in constant motion with the variations in the magnetic field and the pressure from above and along the lines of force of solar radiation, so the tails thrash about a bit, varying their height from few hundred meters to thirty thousand meters depending.

SFF This produced the Snow?

G S SEIDENSTICKER Almost certainly. This would explain how the snowstorm has maintained itself. There is only *one* way for a snowstorm to maintain itself, and that is by being fed constantly with new water as the old water freezes out and falls as snow. In the old days the Atlantic, the Mediterranean and the Norwegian Seas were the main suppliers of moisture for all those snowfalls from our childhoods, those snowfalls that used to be characteristic of northern European and North American winters. But the way the older weather systems worked meant that eventually the falling snow would chill the air, and without warm air to rise from the ocean surface carrying moisture with it the snowstorm eventually peters out.

SFF But the sheaths changed that.

G S SEIDENSTICKER Exactly. They deposited a constant supply of moisture into the atmosphere. It was drawn directly from the Arctic ice, warmed only very marginally by the passage through the sheath, so these very cold layers of moisture were being constantly laid out into warmer air – that's how you get the precipitation needed for snowfall. The rubbing together of warm air and cold chafes water out as snow.

SFF One question I've heard very often is how can *so much* snow have been drawn from any one place?

G S SEIDENSTICKER The polar ice cap used to represent about 2% of the world's water; maybe 20,000 cubic kilometers of water. Now, that would be enough to cover an area of 20,000 square kilometers in a kilometer of snow – Europe is about a thousand times as big as that, and North America is twenty-five million square kilometers, so you're right, the ice cap alone doesn't explain it. Clearly what happened is that the sheaths started draining the polar seas, and then shrinking the world's ocean layers. There seems to have been some kind of malign chain reaction. By the time the ice pack was (shall we say) *redistributed* via the sheaths, so much snow had fallen that the whole northern hemisphere had altered. Ice had formed all across the northern seas, and snow had settled on top of it, the ice packs freezing out the water from saline. And it was this that the sheaths were sucking into the air, so the snow kept falling from the sky and the ocean got saltier and the levels got lower and lower.

SFF Isn't it the case that snow occupies a greater volume than the same quantity of water?

G S SEIDENSTICKER That's right; the snow packs down under its own weight of course, but even at ground level, miles beneath us now, it's slightly less dense than water. At the higher levels it's mostly air. So if the water from the oceans was redistributed around the globe as snow it would occupy a great deal more space – it could fill up the oceanic basins and then cover the land to a height of many kilometers. I guess that's the most likely explanation for what has happened.

SFF The million-dollar question: how long will the sheaths hold out? How long will the snow keep falling?

G S SEIDENSTICKER We're all amazed at the longevity of the sheaths – it's quite exciting, actually, from a scientific point of view. But no reputable scientist believes that they'll last forever. There's already been one major change in the weather pattern – in the early days of the Snow, the sheaths were depositing cold water and ice directly into warm air, and so we saw those great billowing cloud fronts, cloud-ceilings, those spectacular nimbostratus formations. We don't see those any more, of course: the snow still comes down, but from high cirrostratus, or sometimes from what seems to be open blue sky.

SFF Your prediction?

G S SEIDENSTICKER Another five years of snow at the most. That's as much, I think, as the sheaths will bear. Perhaps much less than that – two years, one maybe.

SFF And after?

G S SEIDENSTICKER No more snow from the sky. After that, all bets are off: weather, climate and landscape are the classic instances of chaotic systems; it's nigh on impossible to predict them. Big thaw? A thousand years of chill? Something else? Who can say?

SFF Professor Seidensticker, thank you very much.

G S SEIDENSTICKER You're *very* much welcome.

Know Your Snow!

DENDRITES The pretty six-sided flakes – no two are alike! Each flake has six sides because of the way the *molecules of water* fit together to make ice crystals. Each water molecule is a bit like the letter V, with two oxygen *atoms*, one at each of the topmost prongs, and a hydrogen *atom* at the bottom. It just so happens that this shape makes up into ice crystals with six sides. *Dendrites form when it's not too cold!*

NEEDLES When the air is a little bit colder, the water can grow into tiny needles – between about four and seven degrees below zero you'll find these forms, but they're so small it's hard to see them with the naked eye!

HOLLOW PRISMS Colder still, down to minus nine, and the needles form as fatter tubes, layered one inside the other.

SECTOR PLATES Plates are what their name says! – six-sided flat plate-like crystals. Sectors are tiny budded versions of the same. Plates and sectors form when the air is colder than minus nine. If the air carries enough water in it (what is called *water supersaturation relative to ice percentage*) then the two forms combine to form fat flakes called sector plates.

Doc 08–999 [Clouds]

[Warning: this is an Illegal Document under the Texts
(Restricted) Act of 15. The minimum punishment for reading, possessing or disseminating this document in part or
whole is a 2nd degree fine and up to five years in con-
finement. Do NOT proceed beyond this legal notice; notify
your nearest certificated police officer or certificated military officer AT ONCE, quoting your provenance for the
document and your period of access.]

[Tampering with the official seal on this document is an
offense under the Government of the People (Emergency
Powers) Act of 2, punishable by fines in the 6th or 7th
degree and up to two weeks in confinement]

One

Question: where did all this snow come from? I'll try to
answer that question. My name is Tira Bojani Sahai. I
published an account of my time with the Snow years ago
– it was issued in an unexpurgated version first of all, and
then in an expurgated version when the government
brought in its restrictions on printed text. It was never
banned altogether, although I suppose that this current
letter, this document you are now reading, will be banned.
Times have changed. I cleared the writing of this text in
advance, as the law required me to, but I don't believe it will
do me any good. I can see the censor now, sitting in his hut,
wearing woollen gloves from which two fingers have been

cut off so he – or she – can hold the red pen properly; see him reading this opening paragraph and giving his head a melancholy shake. And his pen cuts through the tissue of the writing like a knife leaving a red mark. Slicing through sentences that lie there like arteries. Separating word-cell from word-cell. These eight sentences I have just written, for instance; I'm sure they aren't a promising start to a narrative, as far as the official line of the government of New America is concerned. I'm not even supposed to use that term, 'New America', although (and the phrases people would use here are: come *on*, get *real*, let's be *honest*) most people call it that. I should say 'the Free World Coalition', of which NUSA is only one delegate. But in reality the Free World is NUSA, we all know. How could it be otherwise? NUSA companies are the ones that control the mining, and so control the food supply; and it is NUSA companies that promise us new developments in food supply to take over when the food-mines are all mined out. Crow called it 'New US', sometimes pronouncing the acronym as 'noose', which I thought had a certain mordant applicability. Of course, jokes like that were rather lost on Crow. But fish are swimming, so I suppose we needn't worry.

When I arrived I was billeted in the immigration compound. I was the first person to arrive at Liberty for several months, and the first to be pulled out of the snow for over a year, 'something,' the officer told me, 'of a celebrity. People are more or less giving up on the under-snow now as far as survivors are concerned. Miners keep going down and keep finding corpses and corpses and nothing else.'

'So where do the immigrants come from?'

'Oh,' the officer replied, his mouth a moue. 'From the other cities, sometimes, the over-America cities, though to be honest people *tend* to move the other way – who'd want to come to over-London from the over-States? People want to go back, you know. They want to go back. Where else?' He mused for a moment before adding, as if wanting to be scrupulously accurate, 'Sometimes we might get a for-eigner.'

The officer, whose name was [Blank], had been a miner until he had trapped his foot in a factory machine, under the snow, one time. 'Buried for over a year and the thing was *still* primed to go off. Can you believe that? God knows where the power came from,' he told me. We talked many times during my ten days in the compound. 'Must have been some sort of battery, some sort of cell. Amazing it didn't just run down during that year, but, you know. Especially in that cold. Whatever.'

'What happened?' I asked him.

'I was standing on something to reach some boxes, wondering what was in them. This was in Liverpool-under-snow. So I jigged something, and the machine coughed into life and the next thing my foot was being eaten.' That phrase seemed to me childlike in its horrible vigour and simplicity: *my foot was being eaten.* That past-continuous sense. I winced, and he grinned, wanting to force the point home. '*Chewed* it up,' he added, 'the bone all *munched*,' and laughed.

After his accident, the authorities gave him a managerial post running the immigrant compound.

'What were you looking for?' I asked him. 'What were you mining?'

'Eh?'

'When you had your accident. What was it you were looking for?'

'Food,' he said, laconically. 'Where else you think the food comes from? There're no animals and there're no plants left alive up here, that's for sure.'

The scientists were asking: where will the oxygen come from? The biomass had been entirely smothered, and not a green thing was left alive. 'Where's the oxygen going to come from?' [Blank] asked, rhetorically, waving his right hand generally in the air over his shoulder to indicate oxygen. 'That's what they keep asking. Me, I'm not worried.

The way I see it is, God'll keep us alive. He's kept us alive this far.' In this manner I learned that [Blank] believed in the 'divine wrath' theory of the Snow's origin. But then he went on, 'Besides which, there's some green stuff left south.'

'In the south?' I pressed. 'You mean, the snow hasn't covered the whole world?'

He shrugged. 'So they say. They say some bits of the southern hemisphere are clear. How should I know? We're not supposed to talk about it.'

'Not supposed to talk about it? What you mean?'

'*They* said,' said [Blank], winking mysteriously. 'The guys, you know. Anyway, it doesn't really matter. *You* know.'

'I don't,' I said, genuinely baffled.

'It don't matter – do – *not* – matter overmuch. Some say that there are places in the south clear of snow. Or likely only snowed under to a few feet. Some say not so, that the whole world is sunk as deep in snow everywhere as it is here.' He shrugged again. 'Difficult to know who's right.'

'But it is *really important* to know,' I said, slowly, the whole notion of clean land, open under the sky, blossoming gloriously in my head. 'Isn't it?'

'The government says that the whole world is snowed. So it's not a good idea to gainsay them. When is it ever a good idea to go against the government?'

But that night I fantasised about leaving the compound, leaving the Free World that I hadn't even seen yet, and travelling across the globe to – I didn't know where – Australia, maybe, to sit on an orange beach thrummed by the surf, looking out over a purple sea, drinking beer in the heat. To think, only, of heat!

It was the heat I missed most. I would go for weeks without ever feeling warm. Really, it's almost incredible to recall, but it's true. I'd be cold when I woke in the morning, and colder when I washed and dressed, and then chilly in my clothes during the day, and in the evening I would slip beneath cold cotton and leaden blankets and shiver myself to sleep. Matters weren't too bad in the compound apart from this, as it happened, apart from the ubiquitous cold. I had space and privacy. The original stream of immigrants had died away to a trickle, and then to nothing. I was [Blank]'s only charge, the solitary occupant of the dorm, his only companion at mealtimes. 'When they set the place up,' he told me, 'there was a hundred or more coming every month. Nobody for ages since.'

'A hundred a month?' I said. 'What – pulled out of the snow?'

'Rarely that,' he said. 'Rarely pulled from the snow. Usually they trekked here. One group came on the snow from Denmark, wearing these great snowshoes like winnowing-nets – walked the whole way, believe that? Another couple groups came by air, gliders, planes, whatever. Some by hovercraft. But that supply of population, it's mostly dried up now. Mostly. On the other hand, there's always you!'

'There's always me,' I said.

'I think there won't be many, after you,' he opined. 'I consider that we're to be thrown on our own resources now. The seven cities'll have to look after themselves now.'

'Unless there are people in the south?' I said. 'They may find their way up here. It's still snowing,' I observed. 'Maybe they'll be driven up here.'

He shrugged. 'We're not supposed to talk about the south,' he said.

It still snowed sometimes, though without the intensity I remembered from my last time above ground. Instead of packing the sky with cold down, the flakes were sparse and often fell from a clear blue sky. Instead of the horizon-to-horizon cloud cover that I remembered from before, the clouds were now high and streaky, barely staining the blue. Or else there would be a parade of little cottony clouds, each one curled into a ball, six of them, seven, eight, nine. I could watch these clouds forever. [Blank] told me not to loiter outside. 'The air may be cold,' he said, 'but the sun'll burn you sharp.' So I sat at the window in the dorm and simply stared as the pattern shifted, slowly, in the sky above me. It was a sort of procession. Victory parade, maybe.

A government official came and interviewed me. 'A formality, really,' he said. 'I think I can say, pretty much without fear of contradiction, that a young woman such as yourself will find a sponsor in the Free World easily enough.'

I didn't know what to say to this.

This new official, [Blank], asked me a series of questions. I wasn't sure where the line of questioning was going, but I answered faithfully. 'Do you suffer from any contagious diseases that you are aware of?'

'No.'

'Are you or have you ever been a member of a terrorist or governmentally-proscribed organisation?'

'No.'

'Do you have any criminal convictions?'

'No.'

'Would religious or other dietary considerations prevent you from eating food deemed fit for consumption by the government? Before you answer,' he added, with an unconvincing smile, 'I could prompt you. Food is not a thing to get high and mighty about, as I'm *sure* you realise. Until Novadic gets some home-grown veg into market, we have to eat pretty much what we get given, so it's not worth your while to make a *fuss* about – I don't know – being exclusively vegetarian, eating pork or whatever. You're not Jewish are you?'

'No,' I said, surprised at the question. 'Would that matter?'

He widened his eyes. '*That's* not one of the questions. I mean, are you Jewish isn't one of the immigration questions.' He was speaking hurriedly. 'There's nothing to stop a Jew from immigrating to the Free World, of course not. The law is clear. I was only saying . . . don't misunderstand me.

70

I'm asking about diet. Any Jew could apply to immigrate, just as anybody else. I'm asking about *diet*.'

'I'll eat anything.'

'That's good.'

'Should you have a list?' I asked. 'Or something? Should you be ticking these things off a list?'

'Paper's too precious for that sort of thing,' he said. 'I'll remember it, don't worry.' He poked his forehead with his thumb, in dumbshow emphasis of the point. 'There's a couple of other things,' he said, 'but we can pretty much skip them. I think we should be able to move you out of the compound soon – tonight if you like.'

'OK,' I said.

'Now, I'm assuming you don't have any money.'

'I don't.'

'That's OK. We'd have to confiscate it if you did anyway. The government's got to keep control of the money supply, or inflation would get going. So the supply's got to be limited and official.'

'What's the currency here?' I asked.

He looked at me as if I was stupid. 'Dollars,' he said.

'Real dollars?'

'What other kind?' he said, with a geeky sort of snorting laugh. 'We try to keep things normal in the Free World. The government has dug up a proper balance of currency, and if you – say – had a million dollars in your underwear, like, stuffed in your *bra* or something,' and he snickered snortingly again, 'then I'm afraid I'd have to confiscate it. But you don't?'

'No,' I said.

'OK,' he said, 'That's OK. I have no doubt you'll find a sponsor. In fact, given that you're the first immigrant in a while and a woman to boot, an, if you'll excuse it, attractive woman, you know, you know what I mean, there's been a certain amount of interest. Can I make a suggestion?'

'Go ahead.'

'It's only a suggestion, though.'

'That's fine.'

'Right,' said [Blank]. 'Well, I could organise a little get-together this evening, a basically mealtime get-together. Let's say half a dozen gentlemen, you, me as broker. You'd get some nice food, and maybe something to drink – you never know. And you'd get to meet half a dozen nice guys.'

'Wait a minute,' I said. 'Why would I be meeting these guys?'

This question stumped him. I might as well have asked him *why is the sky blue*? A line appeared across his forehead, and then another, and then his forehead was weighted down under a drift of worry lines. 'I,' he said, eventually. 'Isn't it obvious? I mean . . .' He trailed off.

'Put it this way,' I said. 'What's my alternative?'

'Alternative?'

'I'm new here. Say, for whatever crazy reason, I'm not in the mood to meet these guys. What do I do?'

'Do?' This possibility was clearly an absolute remoteness as far as he was concerned.

'Can I stay here? In the compound?'

'Of course not.'

'So where else can I go?'

He shook his head, like a wet dog shuddering itself dry. 'Look,' he said, smiling. 'I think there's a misunderstanding. You can go where you like – it's a free world, after all. But you got to ask yourself, how you going to pay for things? How you going to pay for your food, for where you live? Where you going to get the money?'

'I'll get a job,' I said.

'Exactly,' he said, as if to a child. 'But how? You don't know anybody, to get a job. There's no governmental employment exchange as such, not up here. So here's a chance for you to meet some people, to get to know people, to get yourself a job.'

'I kind of got the impression, from what you were saying,' I said, 'that the point of the meeting wasn't strictly employment-related.'

72

He was grinning now. 'It's just a meet,' he said. 'No obligation! But these guys are all *real* interested in getting to know you.'

I discovered later that this guy, this immigration official, took a finder's fee from all the interested men, and took an additional fee from the one who managed to grab me. It was one of the little ways of the Free World. Even if I didn't want to marry any of these men, he still took his finder's fees. The government didn't pay him anything at all. The only people to draw 'government' salaries were the higher government officers and the military (and almost all the higher officers were military anyway). But there were no taxes as such, because the government controlled the money supply as a raw material, rather than, as in the old days, something they printed up. Accordingly they took what they needed directly from the supply, limiting themselves to a non-inflationary amount, or so I suppose. That was the theory. Miners bringing up dollars from below had to surrender them to officials; they were stamped with a braille-like starburst of dots and released back into circulation in various ways – official salaries, government purchase and contract, welfare, that kind of thing. That was the official explanation, at any rate.

Two

I went to the meet. I met.

I met [Blank], who worked as a [Blank] – a famous guy in the NUSA, as I later discovered. He already had a wife, but was hoping for a second. 'No harm in trying my luck,' he told me, disarmingly. 'I know the odds are against me.'

'Odds?' I said. I was drinking: a sort of fruit vodka. I did not then realise how rare a thing alcohol was in the Free World. If I had known I would have appreciated it more.

'Seven men to one woman, ratio,' he said. 'But I say to myself, you know, this isn't communism, none of that equal-shares baloney. Hey! This is the Free World. I'm wealthy . . . hey, that's no secret.' He was grinning, his teeth wholly filling the space between his lips like white mosaic tiles. 'I can afford more than one wife. You want a cushy job, maybe we should get to know one another better. You know? I could help you with that. A cushy job.'

'Cushiony?' I repeated, not quite hearing him properly.

'Something warm; something inside, where the hours aren't too bad. What do you say? Why don't you,' he said, lowering his voice and sliding over to me, 'why don't you come have dinner with me and my wife? You might find you like her.'

'Is that legal?' I said. The drink was making me less diplomatic than I, perhaps, should have been. 'That's not bigamy, is it?'

The smile shrank a little. 'Hell,' he said. 'You want a nice desk job in Novadic? Or not?'

'I think I'd like to be a miner,' I said. I can't remember why I said this. I don't think I had been pondering possible careers before the Meet, and I'm certain it had not crossed my mind to be a miner. But the phrase popped into my head from somewhere, and I said it.

[Blank]'s smile irised away to a tiny 'o'. He looked at me for a moment. 'Not my area. You need at least three years medical,' he said. 'They say three years when you apply, but you'll probably need more than three to have a realistic chance of a job.'

I didn't know what this meant. 'OK,' I said.

[Blank] turned and left me. I felt a little giddy with the understanding that I had alienated a man evidently powerful in this little community, but the vodka new in my blood meant I didn't really care. Another man approached me, chatted for five minutes about this and that. The only thing I remember about that conversation is that at one stage he said 'Miss London?' and I replied, 'Sure, a little. Still there though, isn't it, underneath everything?' and he looked puzzled. Afterwards I realised that he had been addressing me: *Miss London*, like a beauty queen title, because my name had been entered on the official form as Tira London. That didn't seem to bother me much either. Maybe, a little tipsy, I even quite liked the idea; a new land, a new identity, like that guy, whatever-he-was-called, becoming Godfather Corleone in the movie, because he came from a town called Corleone although his name was something different. I can't remember what his name was, originally. You know the movie? You'd need to be my age to remember it.

My age or older.

A man called [Blank] was the most persistent – not, it turned out, on his own behalf, but rather as subaltern to a high-ranking military man called General [Blank]. This intermediary – Pander I called him. You know the way you think up secret names for the people around you, names that never leave your own head? Only sometimes you slip, and your tongue betrays you. Well, that was my secret name for [Blank], Pander; and I never let it slip. He's Secretary [Blank] in the government these days, a powerful and senior man. Anyway. This Pander talked to me seriously for half an hour, pressing my elbow between his thumb and fingers like a lobster gripping its prey. The general is a senior man, a great man, a man with greatness in him. He walks with God. He will be Interim President some day, be sure of it. And he has fallen in love with you, Miss London. He has fallen in love with you.

I was a little scared, actually, of Pander's intensity, and so I reacted with lumpish humour, trying to scour out my weakness. 'Is he married already?' I asked.

'No,' said Pander, looking shocked.

'Has he got a wooden leg? Is he *ugly*? Dewlaps hanging from his face like folds of cloth?'

Pander stared, as if in dismay that his general had fallen in love with a madwoman. 'Miss London,' he said. 'Believe me, he is pre-eminently serious about you.'

It occurred to me that [Blank] did not know exactly what the word *pre-eminent* meant, but used it anyway because he liked the sound of it, a sort of rhetorical malapropism. It was something he did a great deal in his speaking. 'How can he be in love with me?' I asked, more serious. 'He doesn't know me. He's never met me. [*expletive deleted*], he's probably never seen me.'

'Miss London,' said Pander, as serious-faced as a six-year-old; 'please don't swear. I implore you. And the general has indeed seen you. He came to the immigration compound to observe you.'

'Observe me?'

'From one of the towers.'

'Watching me, without my knowing it? Like a stalker?'

'Please, Miss London,' said Pander, his voice quiet. 'Believe me; the general is unimpeachably interested in you. His feelings are genuine. You'll not get a better offer.'

I felt the seriousness bear down upon me, like the weight of snow on my head. 'Well, why don't we meet?' I said. 'He and I?'

'What sort of career were you hoping for, Miss London?' Pander asked. 'What were you hoping to do with your new life?'

'Miner,' I said. The notion had become a sort of fixed idea over the course of that evening, although, as I say, I don't know where it came from.

Pander's eyes widened, a *you don't say?* expression. His mouth curled into a smile like a slice of bread going stale on a plate. 'Well, Miss London, you've cottoned on quick enough, I'll say that. OK, I think the general can help you with that. Not mining itself, of course, not *snow face*, of course, but work in the mining industry. OK, as I say, I think the general can help you with that.'

'Excellent,' I said, although I didn't really know that it was.

'Lunch tomorrow,' said Pander, briskly.

'Why couldn't the general come here, anyway,' I said, the vodka now manifesting itself in my manner as a sort of petulant crotchetiness. 'Why did he send you?'

Pander was standing as if to attention. 'He's a very busy man, a very great man,' he said. 'We'll call by the compound tomorrow noon, sharp.'

This was how I met Crow – Crow was my nickname for him, you see, because he was angular and had a beaky nose and for some other reasons that elude me now. I called him Crow at that first meeting, to his face, and he liked it: he was not used to people speaking back to him. He was used to automatic deference. That's how it works in the army, after all. I think he found my spiciness enticing.

You know what? He thought I was Irish. He thought Tira was, like, a version of Tara; and he thought my black hair and pale skin had an Irish look about them. His own roots were Irish, he told me, on his mother's side. I said, wow, excellent, or whatever, and didn't understand the relevance of the remark until much later.

He liked me, though. We were married within a fortnight. That's a hurry, I know, but times and manners change after a thing like the Snow. I went to live with him in his apartment in the Liberty Barracks, near the heart, surrounded by military men all day. Things were OK for a little while. What can I tell you?

Three

Everybody went to church, but I didn't want to go. I'd never gone, I didn't believe, I didn't see why I should. Crow thought it was because I was Catholic, where the church was Baptist – he told me this long afterwards, and I laughed about it. He was too awkward to tell me about it at the time. But for two Sundays I managed to stay out of church. Come my third Sunday as a married woman the pressure came to be applied. 'It looks odd,' Crow said to me; 'you need to be in church beside me. Come today.'

'OK,' I said. But at the last minute I ducked out, and Crow had to go without me again. I wandered the barrack-compound, and then slipped past the church-house and wandered the streets. It was a feeble sort of rebellion, though I say so myself. As I look back on myself from the vantage point of so many years, I can see not a principled woman, but a petulant one. I see her standing by the perimeter fence, a sort of rail, looking out at the snow-desert beyond the city limits. I can see her real clearly – *Hey there! Stay out of the sun, don't get a tan, it'll ruin your life!* My words don't reach her, of course not, course not, course not. The past has a different language from the one you and I speak today, and there's no linguist can translate between them. I want to tell her, *you'll tan and it'll destroy your life*, but she flat can't hear me.

Standing at the rail looking out. The snow banked up, rising away from the perimeter into a low hill-ridge all round the city that was caused by the weight of Liberty itself, bedding down into the snow despite its under-balloons and spread-supports. These hills shortened the perspective, giving the horizon a weird stage set-like closeness, like a special effect.

I was struck by the thought that the whole city – all of the cities of NUSA – were based on a kind of insubstantiality, on nothing but floss, on nothing but cloud stuff. It is the clouds that are frozen solid beneath us. It's not snow at all. It's a whiteness that signifies emptiness. The night-sky emptiness should be white: if there were no smuts in the interstellar sky, if there was no dust or planets or dark matter, then the nothingness itself would blaze white with the light of seventy trillion trillion stars. What might this mean? Only that it is the dirt and the dark that save our eyes from burnout. Up! *Hey! Don't tan!*

She's still not listening.

I looked at the sky all the time. I couldn't get enough of looking at the sky.

People talk about 'the blues', as if *blue* were somehow a colour intrinsically associated with depression. What a crazy notion. For me, blue will always be the colour of transcendence, the flag the sky waves in promise of depth, in promise of something *more*. White is the colour of depression. How could it be otherwise? Because white is what is left when the colour is bleached away and when life is smothered, horizon to horizon, under the pressure of unhappiness. There are things underneath, true, but they can only be excavated, they cannot be alive. On the other hand, white is all colours, isn't it? It is the magic paintbox in which red, blue and yellow are stirred up together and make not mud-brown but purest, dazzlingest, opaquest white. The colour wheel spins, blurs, whites out. This world-drift is white according to this logic, since all the world has been whipped up in its creamy concupiscence.

And colours are colours because of different wavelengths – isn't that right? Short wavelength, blue; long wavelength, red. It's a function of an overly literal mind, I know, but I could never read the word *wavelength* without thinking of actual waves, at the beach at Brighton, say, where Minnie sat dour and self-contained even as an eight-year-old, picking up pebbles and turning them over and over in front of her face, and putting them down neater than nature had contrived. Before the Snow, of course. And me, my chin on my knees and my cigarette flaring brighter in the sea breeze, looking out at the waves. The sky, clouds with sunlight shifting through their greyness, a sharkskin colour. A forceful breeze coming right into our faces, and the collars buttoned up on our wool coats. Long ridges of waves lifting slowly in the swell, coming towards us, then curling down on themselves as they approached the shore, like the closing of sleepy eyelids. Twelve feet, maybe, between each wave. The water in between stretched like lycra, swelling up and down, foam webbing on the indigo water – like the shreddy pattern you see on the skin of some black grapes, you know the thing I'm talking about? A fungus, is it? (The pattern you *used to see* on grapes, I should say, since nobody has seen a grape in many years, of course.) But those waves, those long wavelengths – difficult to think of them as red-shifted. They were *so* purple, so dark.

And waves break against the shore. Their splendour is in their ending. Do light waves *break*, in a spume of shattered photons, when they reach the eye?

I suppose not.

The English Channel was usually grey, or brown. But sometimes it was a beautiful deep shade of blue-purple.

When I was a kid I had an argument with my sister. She had a silver-coloured plastic dagger, a toy, plastic curlicues on the hilt and a fat seam running in an unbroken line around the edge of handle and blade. She called it her gold dagger. I told her it wasn't gold, it was silver. *Gold*, she insisted. And the bickering went back and forth like ping-pong, *Silver! Gold! Silver! Gold!* I tried to convince her with more complex, considered arguments: *only an idiot*, I suggested, *would call that gold*. But she did not take the force of my reasoning. *It is gold, it is, it is. Ask Ma, she'll tell you. If that's gold*, I said, snatching a 10p piece from the windowsill where somebody had left it (next to an orange train ticket and an empty key ring and an unwrapped sweet) – *if that's gold, what's this? That's gold*, she insisted. *It's not gold, it's a silver ten-pee. No-it's-not-it's-gold.* And so on.

I got very worked up. I cried, even. Why did this stupid spat upset me so much? It was not my sister's intransigence, exactly: it was rather (although I didn't think of it in these terms then, of course) – it was the abyss of relativism that her insistence opened up. I knew what colour was meant by the word 'silver', and what by 'gold', but they're only names after all. If everybody agreed that the red light meant go and the green one stop, traffic lights would still work perfectly well (*if* everybody agreed). I look at an object and see it as silver, and I say the word 'silver'; but what if somebody looks at the same thing and sees gold? Maybe their brains are wired up wrong in their colour-recognition centres. Or maybe it is *my* mind that is wired up wrong. Maybe everybody else who reads the word 'silver' sees, mentally, what I would call *gold*. How can I convince you of the colour as I see it, without just using other colour-words? They're just as slippery. Grey, yellow, blue, white, white – what do they mean to you? Your whole spectrum may be different from mine. It's unsettling. There's no higher authority to settle the dispute. That's what upset me, I think, when I was a kid bickering with my kid sister. It was the sense that what I had assumed was solid ground under my feet was in fact a thin crust, and could drop me through into an abyss at any time, into I don't know what.

Talking of colour, here's a conversation on that topic I had with Crow. We had been married a month.

'So,' he said. He was brushing his uniform with a dry toothbrush. A clothes-brush couldn't be had for love nor money; not even for somebody as senior as Crow. The tooth-brush took longer, but did the job just as well. And actually I think Crow liked the work, liked the sense of preening himself, liked to dilate upon that task and thereby dwell on his status. General [Blank] of the New US Army! As he brushed, he said 'So, Tira, I was thinking. There's a Jack London.'

'A who?' I was in bed, reading.

'A writer, you know. Last century, I think.'

'Oh,' I said, not much interested.

'Didn't he write *Call of the Wild*?'

'Yeah,' I said, vaguely.

'Or was it *Claw of the Wild*? Jack London's *Claw of the Wild*?'

'That,' I said. 'Or the other title. It sounds familiar.'

The little scratching noise of bristles rubbing over military cloth.

[Blank] cleared his throat. 'Is he, like, a relation? A family member – ancestor?'

I laughed at this. 'Why on earth would you think so?'

He looked a little hurt. 'You know – your surname.'

'London's not my surname,' I said. 'London's where I come from.'

A twenty-second pause.

'Like,' he said, working carefully over an epaulette, 'the immigrant thing.'

'Immigrant,' I said. 'That's me.'

His voice acquired a cautious, downward inflection. 'So – what's your actual surname?'

'Bojani Sahai,' I said. I didn't give it a second thought.

Crow scoffed. 'What sort of name sounds like that?'

'An Indian name,' I said.

'Chief Sitting Cow,' he said, and laughed in little noises like hiccoughs. 'Don't joke, though. What's your surname – really?'

'Not American Indian. Indian Indian.'

Another twenty seconds. The toothbrush scrub had stopped. 'I don't understand,' he said. 'We're *married* now. I don't understand.'

'What's not to understand?'

'You're, like, Indian?'

'Sure.'

Crow was looking intently at me. 'But you're *white*.'

'I've been out of the sun a long time,' I said. 'Give me a month of good sunshine and I'll brown up nice and tasty.'

'You're *black*?' he said, his voice still non-comprehending.

'Brown,' I said, cross. 'Or black if you like.'

'I can't believe it,' he said.

'Look—' I started to say, my temper rising.

'I don't get it,' he said. 'You can't be black – brown, whatever. Brown skin just doesn't, you know, change to white. Black guys don't go white in winter.'

'I do,' I said. 'I tan, like you. Only maybe a little deeper, that's all.'

'I can't get past this,' said Crow. 'You're *black*?'

'I'm,' I said, fiercely, '*brown*, and what's the problem with that? Is that not allowed in the NUSA or something?' I said, my voice hardening.

'Jesus,' he said, his most extreme expletive. He stood up.

He looked rather angry. 'You're joking – you – right? A joke, yeah? Look at [Blank]' (one of Crow's lieutenants), 'he's black as beetroot, and he hasn't been sunbathing any more than you have.'

'Black as beetroot?' I said, unable to keep the mocking tone away from my words.

Crow's face darkened with an angry blush. 'As eggplant, I meant to say. As eggplant. Don't avoid the god-heck-it question.'

I got out of bed, and faced up to Crow. 'What is this?' I screeched. 'You're interrogating me, now? What sort of racist [*expletive deleted*] *is* this?'

'You married me under false pretences,' he blustered.

'*You* married *me*,' I said. I had lost my cool by this time. 'I was the [*expletive deleted*] goods and you *purchased* me. What, you want to change your mind now? Is that it?'

'You never told me you were – uh, a woman of colour.'

'I never knew you were the sort of racist [*expletive deleted*] for whom it mattered. Anyway,' I said, throwing my arms up and stalking round the bed, 'anyway, what kind of a [*expletive deleted*] is that to say? *I never told you I was black?* – look at me! You looked at me, and you liked what you saw. And how has that changed now? Because my surname's *Sahai* not [*expletive deleted*] *London*? Because you pronounce my surname differently you suddenly don't want me any more?' I was dressing now, clumsily, determined to march out, to walk out on him for ever, although I had no idea where I was going.

'Now,' Crow was saying. 'Settle down, settle down. It's just a shock, you know, finding out like this. You know? You'd be shocked if I told you *I* was black, all of a sudden, wouldn't you?'

'You're the whitest man in the world,' I told him, vehemently.

'Just settle down,' said Crow, coming over to me and putting a hand on my shoulder. 'Just get back into bed and settle down and let's talk about this.'

That was our conversation on the subject of colour.

I fumed and huffed around, calling him some more names, but there was no point in me storming out dramatically. Where would I have gone? Crow put his uniform away, went through to the bathroom and didn't come out for a long time. When he re-emerged he looked no different, except for a sort of flush over his neck and up to his ears. We went out together and had supper together in the mess, and he was his forced-jolly self. But everything had changed.

We had by then been married a month, and every single night of that month, without a single exception, we had had (as he might put it) marital congress. There had been a quaintly military flavour to it: we'd go to bed, and the light would be turned out, and we'd both lie on our backs not touching, not speaking. But I could feel his muscles tense, the miniature vibrations transmitted through the material of the mattress, as he prepared with painful obviousness to ambush me. The unspoken notion that he was taking me by surprise was so transparent, and therefore so preposterous, that it was almost endearing. So he would lie still, lie still, and then suddenly flex his body and twitch himself round and get on top of me. Then it would all be happening at once: he'd be kissing my mouth and chin and neck (he was shorter than I was) with a rapid padding motion, urgent and yet oddly restrained, as if he were holding back – think of an overly lipsticked woman kissing tissue paper to remove the excess. At the same time his right hand would be thrust between my legs, his fingers working me, the muscles of that arm palpably tensing and pulsing, pressing into my belly and across my chest, his finger [*text deleted*]. He would not say so much as a single word, but he would inevitably go through a series of set-piece physical movements. At precisely the halfway point he would grip my hips firmly with his hands and turn me over. A few minutes from the end he would repeat this procedure, put me again on my back, start kissing my face and chin and neck again, and pull my knees up. [*text deleted*]. His pushing motions would become abruptly more rapid. Then it would be all finished, and he would pull away to lie on his back again, breathing a little more deeply. There was never, in our time together, any discussion of sex – neither preliminary discussion to establish preferences, nor after-sex anatomisings of what we'd just been doing. Certainly there was no indication that he wanted me to play a more active role. I don't believe he did. And as for me, I didn't mind. Perhaps that sounds like a rather crushing judgement for a woman to make of a man, *I didn't mind*. That's not what a man wants to hear, I suppose: he wants to hear I moaned, I loved it, the earth moved. But *I didn't mind* was how I felt. It was by no means the best, but equally certainly not the worst sex I had ever known. I didn't mind. Some nights I was even quite into it, not because of the sex itself, maybe, but just because of the luxurious laziness of absolute passivity – of not being expected to initiate, to twist and throw my body around, and most particularly the complete lack of pressure to simulate any enjoyment, all that operatic panting and gasping. And in that not uncomfortable void of expectation, that play-acting of submission, I sometimes even discovered some sparkles of pleasure myself. I've no especial yen towards submission, I've never had fantasies of being dominated, never gone for that S&M scene. It wasn't that, that was not where the liberation lay. Rather it was that Crow, instinctively or otherwise, took away all the constraints that make sex a *performance*. In this one arena he did not ask me to pretend in any way.

But after we had our conversation about colour the sex stopped. That night I lay on my back, waiting, and [Blank] lay next to me, tensed up and motionless. But the pounce did not come, and after a little while I turned and shuffled myself into a sleeping posture on my side. And sleep settled on me like snow falling until I was buried in it and far away.

The next morning he strode around the apartment like a spring-heeled man, clearing his throat mightily, bouncing up and down and stretching his arms out in front of him with his palms out and his fingers interlaced. 'Gotta get on, today,' he told me, with a brightness so forced it was nearly metallic. 'Things to do, things to do.' And he positively marched out of the flat.

The next salient, as it were, was when he announced between mouthfuls of supper that he wanted us to sleep in separate beds. But although my memory wants to flip forward to that moment, I would be glossing over a whole long stretch of time. Was it as long as two whole months? Part of me thinks it can't be, can't be so long, but I rather think it was. Sixty days. Sixty nights, more to the point, of lying next to me in bed in the darkness with every muscle in his body tensed up, as if he were a stage strongman and was holding himself prepared to receive a punch in the stomach from a member of the audience. Was it sixty nights? How could he have persevered so heroically in his physical withdrawal and unease? I can't put myself, imaginatively, into his place. I just can't do it. Wouldn't *you* relax, despite yourself, after a few nights? Wouldn't the seepage of ordinary life erode your principled stand? Let's say – and I can't even go so far as to suggest that this was truly the process going on inside Crow's mind, but let's, for argument's sake, say – that he felt aggrieved, tricked, that what he had assumed to be pure revealed itself tainted, that a marrow-deep physical revulsion was blended with a sense of wounded honour. His white wife had been stolen away and replaced by a black wife he found repellent. Even if that was how he felt, how long could he cling on to such wilfulness? Set on one side the purely mental idea, the symbolic signifier of whiteness, or of blackness; set on the other all the myriad actual touches, a caress, a hug, of conversations and differences of opinion, the myriad joys and comforts of companionship, of a smile on the face of the person you are talking to, of irises and pupils (that mean so much in human communication and which are the same range of colours the whole world over – in fact, pupils are the same *actual* colour the whole world over, and that colour is black), not to mention the sexual release, which was obviously something important to him. Doesn't one side so wholly outweigh the other?

It seems so to me.

But nevertheless we lived that life, that freezing up of personal relations, and I think it did indeed last two full months before the first crack shot across the frozen surface with the pattern of lightning striking. He acted colder and colder, though he expressed this coldness through a frosty brightness like sun on snow. 'Good morning good *morning*,' he would say as we took breakfast together. Always the double greeting, as if the second utterance cancelled out the first, sine mixing with cosine to leave no actual greeting at all at the start of the day. 'Busy day today, yes indeed,' he would say, briskly, bolting his morning pasta in his hurry to be out the door and away from me. 'Back late, back late.'

And gone.

And then one evening we were enjoying a meal of meat – rare pleasure. It was tinned meatballs, half a dozen each, like eyeballs that had shrunk as they rotted brown and slimy. We had bread too, and that was a luxury item, though I think it's more common nowadays. It was pasta-bread rather than real bread, which is to say dried pasta ground down to use as flour and then baked up with water and yeast. But I can no longer remember what real bread tastes like. The city had a supply of four hundred thousand tonnes of dried pasta, mined out of a supply somewhere far below us, so pasta was the meal that month.

He slid the prongs of his fork very carefully into one meatball, and lifted it to the level of his eyes, moving it very slowly as if it were an enormous weight. This, I could see, was his externalisation of 'thinking', a sort of dumbshow to me that he was revolving ideas in his head. He examined the meatball for a little while, placed it in his mouth, chewed and swallowed.

'You know,' he said, and I knew with those words that something serious was about to be said, because they were uttered in a level tone of voice, and without the pressured brightness of his usual conversational manner.

I looked at him.

'You know, I think we should maybe have separate beds. In fact,' he added with a hurried emphasis, as if urgently cutting off my shocked protests, although I had not made a sound, 'in fact, in fact, I've decided it. I've decided it. It'd be better for you, nee-ah-aw' (a sort of mewling noise), 'would, it would, really. You'd sleep better, I'd—' and he laughed briefly '—I'd sleep better. It's the whole sleeping better thing, you know.'

He stopped, and looked at me.

'OK,' I said.

He blinked both eyes in unison once, twice. 'We can,' he said, 'still sleep in the same room.' It was, I think, a concession that he had been prepared to grant me after prolonged argument, and which was startled out of him by the immediacy of my capitulation.

'OK,' I said again.

His face darkened a little as if growing angry, but his tone of voice remained plain. 'Or not, if you'd prefer. Whatever you'd prefer. Separate rooms, maybe.' He ate another meat-ball with studied slowness. Then another. I was waiting for him to say something else, but he was silent for the rest of the meal. I think I would have preferred it if he had said something. Maybe: 'it's nothing to do with me finding out you're black.' I don't believe I would have challenged this, had he said it. I don't believe I would even have contradicted him ('oh let's be honest with one another, of course it is' and so on). But at least it would have meant that an actual, active point of view would have been established, planted like a flagpole. Even had he said something brutal, like 'I can't [*expletive deleted*] you now I think you're Indian', I think I would have been happier. But with nothing said, the dynamic between us was nebulous, sticky and unformed as melted ice cream, and I was nagged by the sense that I had missed something important, that there was some crucial fact that I was stupidly overlooking. Maybe it had nothing to do with my race. Maybe it was something else driving him from me that I just could not see. As I thought about it I didn't truly believe this, but I couldn't quite rid myself of that suspicion. It nagged, as the cliché says suspicions do: but it really nagged, it chided away in the back of my mind.

That night Crow rolled himself in a blanket and slept in the dining room under the table. The following day a couple of his subalterns, or whatever they're called in the NUSA marines, brought in some sticks and some short planks and assembled a bed. We no longer used the room as a dining room then, and took to eating in the kitchen – still together, mostly, but often without saying anything. On the other hand, sometimes we *would* say things to one another. And on occasion our conversations would be quite animated and even cosy. Once, much later, he kissed me: a touch on the cheek that turned into a drawing together of our four lips, into a single circle. It was nice. It was wonderful, actually. And he didn't yank himself away, or hurry off muttering, or anything like that. But the kiss stopped, and we talked some more, and he went through and lay on his bed and rolled himself tightly in a blanket and went to sleep. It was strange.

No, I must be exact. Our life together became a less traumatic but more sterile sort of thing than perhaps I am implying. There was no great tension, no drama, no fuming suppressed racial hatred. It was more a sort of antiseptic going-through-motions. It was frustrating. From time to time my temper would leave me, and I'd yell at him that he was racist, that he was gay, that he was stupid and idiotic, all the random noise that comes flying from a person's forge when their temperature is up and the hammer of anger is clattering down. But it is hard to argue, properly to argue, with somebody who is not engaging with you. He could wear down my explosions by applying a constant drip of 'calm down's, or 'hey's, and perhaps hug me until I stopped. He could be very tender.

He wasn't sleeping well, I could tell, but there was no communication between us of that sort, no 'Tira, I have nightmares' or anything like that. I could tell he was having nightmares, nevertheless. Every morning there were bags slung under his eyes, like tiny smiles. He stumbled into the furniture, backing off with a sucked-in breath and a frozen grin. In the night I sometimes heard him gasping in his sleep, or heard his truckle bed creak and creak as he writhed on it. Still, what could I do? It wasn't my call. Did he go to the officer's mess and drink a tiny shot glass of wine (for alcohol was very hard to come by, even for the most senior people) with his fellow officers, and blub about it? I don't know. *She broke my heart, I loved her, she tricked me, she whited herself up somehow, but she's a nigger underneath, I'm not racist, you know I'm not racist, but I just can't do it with an Indian woman, I just can't, it's not something I can help.* And the brother officers would place precise, sharp, manly slaps on his shoulder, and murmur their support. I can picture the scene, but that doesn't mean it actually happened. Maybe he said nothing to anybody. That was more his way. It's even possible, though I find this harder to comprehend, but it's possible that he didn't even say anything *to himself.* We don't know what it looks like, do we, the inside of another person's head. We try to read faces, but faces are not windows. They're more like clouds of unknowing, the features forming temporarily in the transient flesh like cloud-shapes and then passing away, and inside holding rainstorms or maybe nothing at all. Perhaps his mind was an utterly alien thing. Wouldn't that be ironic, in the light of what later happened?

I started work, which was entirely his doing. He had arranged the job before our disaffection, although I didn't actually start working until after we were sleeping in separate beds. For the week immediately following the wedding I did nothing, and Crow and I were sort of on honeymoon, although he still called by the mess, and did little bits and pieces. Then for two weeks after that I hung about, attending a couple of classes on food-mining with some other prospective miners, and reading a bound printout of the technology. This last pamphlet was so well thumbed the pages were greasy and frayed. Then there were several more weeks of nothing at all, of me sitting bored in the apartment, or wandering about Liberty with my hood up. But then Crow came home one afternoon and sat me down. 'You start work tomorrow,' he said, his high-pressure smile and high-pressure body language pumping jolliness into the situation. 'You've been kept hanging around for way too long, and I spoke to [Blank] today. Block four, Science Street, eight-thirty.' Suddenly I was employed.

'Great,' I said.

I'll talk about my job in a minute, but first I want to say something about my husband, about [Blank]. I really don't think I've caught, precisely, the way he was. I worry that I'm giving the impression that he was a one-dimensional man, when he really wasn't. I've been suggesting he was – if you'll pardon the punning – a black-and-white-man. He wasn't merely a black-and-white-man. So, for example, although my anger (which was frequent) made me think of him as nothing more than a racist pig, and although I used this term and many like it to his face, I now look back on that time and I'm not so sure he was. Clearly there was some racist component in his make-up, but racism – or homophobia, or hatred of women (again, all of which accusations I threw at Crow from time to time) – cannot make up a whole person. There's not enough material in such attitudes to make up a whole human: a grotesque, a cartoon villain; real people aren't like that. I'd believe that not even the Chief of the Ku Klux Klan could have been a racist *all the time*, through *every* fibre of his body. However distorted their mind were, there must have been gardens and comfortable rooms in there as well as burning deserts of hatred. Mustn't there? And Crow was no KKK villain. He never said 'I'm not a racist' (and he never said 'I'm a racist', either). Though his actions were sometimes bad they were sometimes good. There were, for instance, the many little courtesies and kindnesses of cohabiting life. In addition to which, of course, he got me the job. When I started working, and saw how many people were on the committee only because of their skill in [*expletive deleted*] their husbands, I was impressed that [Blank] would still go to the trouble of finding me work when he and I were sleeping in separate beds.

One day I said to him, 'It'd be no bother if we got a divorce.' The phrase sounded callous to me as soon as I uttered it, and it wasn't one I had premeditated, but that was the offhand phrasing that my mind chose at that moment of utterance. *It'd be no bother.*

[Blank] looked at me as if a piece of ice had slipped down inside the back of his collar. 'I beg your pardon?'

'I could just move out.' I was sitting on the sofa, and [Blank] was sitting at his desk with some paperwork.

'Move out?' he said, turning his whole body on his chair to look at me properly. His wide-open eyes annoyed me, for some reason.

'I'm trying to make it easier on you, you racist queer-[*expletive deleted*],' I said. The spot anger cooled immediately, and the words tasted ashy in my mouth. 'Look,' I said, 'look, just look. This isn't easy, right? Not easy for you. Not for me. Shall I just move out?'

'Where would you live?'

'There must be somewhere in this [*expletive deleted*] city,' I said. Every time I swore a little wincing shudder of the lines in his forehead, a twitch of his eyebrows, made it clear that my words were causing him pain. Naturally, I swore often, to try and magnify this migranic flutter.

'Tira . . .' he said.

'I've walked about the city,' I pressed. 'There's plenty of places to stay. I've got a job now. Surely my salary could cover rent and food. Wouldn't you prefer it? You could start over. You could divorce me, and get a white wife, a lily-white wife, all blonde and pink and smelling of [*expletive deleted*]. Wouldn't you like that? Wouldn't you?'

'Tira, I don't understand you,' he said. I was crying.

I don't know why I was crying by this stage. It had started as a genuine attempt on my part to break the logjam of our relationship. And I didn't cry often. Hardly ever. I had turned away from Crow now, and was trying to breath in deep and calm my sudden sobs, as if breathing in would blow me up like a balloon and smooth the teary crumples from my face.

When I said *I hardly ever cried* back there, I may have been exaggerating. I'll be honest with you on that point. Actually I cried from time to time. Or I cried a lot.

In a minute I had got myself under control. I wiped my face against the back of the sofa like a dog, and turned back. [Blank] had been quiet the whole time.

'Are you OK?' he said, in a softly consolate voice.

'I'm fine,' I said. 'I'm happy, perfectly OK, no I'm not. I'm *not* happy that we never *talk* about this stuff.' I clamped my jaw. I presented a strong face to him.

'We can talk,' he said, looking genuinely concerned. 'I don't want a divorce.'

'You could marry again.'

He said: 'There's nobody.' Then, perhaps thinking that sounded too much like *I'll just have to make do with you, scrapings-of-the-barrel*, he added, 'There's nobody else I'd want to marry.'

I looked at him. 'OK,' I said, getting to my feet. 'We'll carry on as we are then.' Then, I added, the thought spurting up in my head from nowhere, 'Is this a keeping-up-appearances sort of thing? Is this a running-for-office thing? [Blank] told me you were thinking of running for IP.'

'It's nothing to do with that.'

'Are you thinking of running for IP?'

'That's politics,' he said. 'That's not real life.'

'It's real power, though,' I said. 'Is it *I need a wife and*

93

respectable-looking life if I want to run for IP? Is that what it is?'

'Tira,' he said, looking weary, running the tip of his forefinger along the tiredness lines under his eyes, first his left eye, then his right. 'Tira.'

'It's OK,' I said, high-pitched. 'You don't need a row right now. OK.' And I left him there, at his desk, and fumed through the kitchen. I put on coat and mittens and boots and stomped around outside in the talcumy snow. Then I came in again, and put my head through the door of the room, and there he was, bent over his desk doing some paperwork or other.

The notion that I was a sort of window-dressing companion became one of those fixed ideas, those obsessive little notions that grow like crystals in our minds. When I was more rational I could dismiss it. It wasn't very likely. The sexual politics of NUSA are different from the more conservative old USA. Of course they are. That guy at the meet, [Blank], who suggested I become his second wife – he wasn't a Mormon. He was simply registering the seven-men-to-one-woman inequality of the new world, the scarcity and therefore collectibility of women. If Crow had divorced me, other men would have bid for me, not because I was necessarily wonderful or beautiful but just because I was a woman under a certain age. People would not regard Crow as immoral, or unelectable, for divorcing me; they might, at worst, regard him as a touch foolish to let an eligible woman go, but that's all. I don't believe that would have stood in the way of him becoming elected Interim President. Or, at least, it would have figured as a very small thing compared to the fact of his military rank, his reputation, his ability to say 'go' and they go, 'come' and they come. Maybe it would even have worked the other way around: people would have admired his marital profligacy, as if he were saying *look, I'm so powerful I don't even need to cling on to the one woman I've been lucky to snag, like the rest of you – see! I discard her!* I don't know.

Of course, that leaves open the question of why Crow didn't simply divorce me. Maybe my furious fixation on the notion that he wanted me to stand beside him as he stood for political office was actually, and simply, a way of distracting me from that more fundamental question. Why didn't he just leave me, kick me out? There isn't a straightforward answer I think.

Four

Let me tell you about my job. I was a mining administrator, committee-level. This meant that I sat on a committee and discussed questions relating to mining; nothing more. Eight-twenty the following day I was standing in the metal hallway of the metal building at four, Science Street. A corporal showed me through. I went up a metal-grid stair-case into a larger first-floor room. The door was of a different colour and design from the walls; it had the word STROSSEN printed in sharp black capitals, over the handle. That stuck in my mind for some reason, although I did not know what the word meant.

Inside was a formica table and some scuffed plastic chairs. The walls were bare, thickly corrugated like metal corduroy. A single large window was icily, painfully bright with morning light. Half a dozen people were in the room, crowded at one end. When I went over I could see that they had gathered around a small waste-burner, and were trying to absorb the heat.

'Eight-thirty,' said the corporal. He was not a young man. 'Time for the heater to go.'

Without complaint, the little group zipped and buckled themselves into their various fat coats and took their seats around the table. The corporal swung a lid onto the heater, picked it up by two handles, and hoiked it out of the door.

'No heater?' I said, to nobody in particular.

I was answered by the Chair, a man I was to later to know

very well indeed. At the time I thought him just a crumpled face, swaddled and padded about with bulky coat and hood; but I don't want to play the tease-you writerly game of, you know, gradually revealing more and more about him, of keeping you hanging on whilst I slowly reveal his significance in my story, all that nonsense, so I'll tell you all about him right away. He said: 'Seven of us in this room, our body heat will warm it eventually.' Later that day I discovered his name, [Blank], and his courtesy rank, although he had not been a serving military officer from before the Snow. He was old-US, his family originally from Eastern Europe, from Poland I think. They'd been called [Blank] which they had Englished to [Blank] when they emigrated. It was a little while later that I discovered the more personal details about him, his habits, his little fetishes, his dead wife, divorced then killed by the Snow, his previous career as a writer. And later still, after we had been [*expletive deleted*] for a month, that he told me his secret life: his hopes, his suspicions about the NUSA administration, the whole Che-Guevara side of him. I didn't realise he was a terrorist until I had known him for a long time. Should I say terrorist, or freedom fighter, or should I say *agent of change*, or some euphemism like that? He certainly talked about change, and he talked about freedom, and sometimes he talked about 'terror'.

Perhaps it sounds strange, but when I started working I had no idea what I was supposed to be doing in this committee, other than the fact that it was something to do with mining. So I sat at the table, and listened attentively to try to winnow the clues from the discussion.

[Blank], chairing, began by introducing me to the group. 'People,' he said. 'This is Tara, recently married to [Blank].' I didn't bother correcting him about my name. 'We all know [Blank], he's a friend to this committee. And I'm sure we all want to congratulate Tara on her marriage to such an important person.'

A murmur went round the table. People seemed genuinely appreciative, as if marrying Crow had been some sort of actual achievement on my part.

I smiled, nodded at people.

'OK,' said [Blank]. 'Let's get on with it today. Let's get this show on the road.'

Now, as I write this, and as I recall that day, the memory is overlaid with later memories, like drawings on transparencies laid over a painted backsheet in the making of an animated movie. [Blank] was, that day, pompous and exact. He kept holding things up to pronounce on breaches of the necessary protocols. My first impression, I am sure, was of a tight-arse, a government man. His constant little catch-phrases infuriated me: 'let's get this show on the road', 'we can drive that past them (the military) in an open-top Mercedes and see if they salute', 'well, there are fifty ways to leave this city' (or 'fifty ways to skin this cat', or 'fifty ways to get yourself killed'). But now, as I write this, I can picture a different [Blank]. I see him lying in my arms, his chest hair prickling against my bare skin. I picture him talking about the Seidensticker memo, or sometimes about the Seidensticker interview, although (he would say) the two things were probably the same secret document. I picture him saying 'the government is lying to us, just as it always did. Things are worse now, because they control communication much more efficiently. Only somebody halfway inside, like me, gets even a whiff of the truth. This Snow was not a natural disaster; it wasn't caused by Russian environmental abuse, it wasn't reactors in Siberia that kick-started it, all that stuff is *just a lie*.' And he would tremble in my arms with the suppressed fury of saying those last three words, actually tremble with this sweet, loveable, innocent hippy-outrage. 'The government is lying. If we can find that Seidensticker document we'll know the truth.' The long conversations we had in the pale afternoon light, with him telling me everything he knew about this man Seidensticker – a scientist who had been working for the government at the time the Snow started falling, who had written something that proved that it was the *government* that was responsible for the disaster that had ruined mankind. This was a completely different [Blank] from the pompous man who chaired that committee when I first met him.

But maybe I'm getting ahead of myself.

Our meetings, I slowly learned, involved one particular large construction project. There was a much smaller quantity of snow falling out of the air every year. The massive falls that had blanketed the world were, according to the best guesses of army scientists, a thing of the past. 'We can start to think of our basing ourselves at this height of snow,' said [Blank]. 'That seems assured now.'

'Totally?' asked a woman I was later to come to know very well as [Blank].

'I can confirm,' said a man in a major's uniform, [Blank], 'that the snowfall is now less than four inches a year. There is reason to believe,' he said, looking at the Chair, 'that it will reduce even further.'

The plan, then, was to *base* the city. Previously it had been built up as the snow built up, supported on old Air Force barrage balloons filled with helium in the early days of the emergency. This had worked well enough (I discovered) because encasing the balloons in snow had effectively cut leakage from the balloons. As the snow levels rose the balloons had been dug out and moved to the side, a couple of hundred yards or so, one at a time; a new platform had been laid down on top of them and the prefab buildings moved one by one onto the new base. I discovered this recent history of the city in the first week of meetings, I think, and I can remember my astonishment at the amount of work it must have involved; all that physical labour, like squaddies building the pyramids. 'Oh,' said the major, when I expressed my amazement, 'that's nothing. Liberty is a recent build. By the time it was sited, the snowfall was starting to slacken off anyway, and the place has been moved only a couple times. You should have seen how the original survivor cities were constructed, over-Stateside.' He told me epic stories of military installations growing into small cities with the influx of essential personnel; of platforms built on stilts, like oil rigs, with their legs being extended month by month as the snow rose, until it became clear that the world was looking not at hundreds of yards of snowfall-depth but at *miles*. Each of the six over-US cities worked on their solutions, some placing inflated balloons at the base of their stilts, some working networks of gridwork into the snow at angles, most having to abandon everything and simply rebuild whilst their populations struggled in the whiteout frozen chaos.

The most striking thing, he said, was how utterly *ordinary* this whole apocalyptic labour became. How used people became to it, such that it was just another day's work, digging the city out of the accumulating snow and hauling it physically upwards, upwards. Amazing, really.

I sometimes think that the human being is a machine designed to take the extraordinary and make it ordinary, habitual, banal. What would you call a machine designed for that purpose?

Now that the snowfall was finally dying down, plans were being drawn up for more permanent habitation. Our committee was addressing one aspect of that normalisation. Specifically, we were discussing the best way to construct a mineshaft down to the food-mines beneath. Up to now, all the food, all provisions and supplies, were mined out of under-snow sites by adapted military craft. These burrowed down through the snow, most of them on battery power. Their crews excavated supplies, filled their holds, and burrowed back up to the surface. There was much talk about the design of these machines, of the ways in which former submarines had been adapted, how former trucks had been welded together with former airplanes, how hovercrafts were salvaged from every military location, and hovercraft blowers and skirts added to the most unlikely machines to enable them to skim over the snow's surface. Some of these mining craft were little tubs, lowered from the side of the larger hovercraft, such as the one that had dug me out of the snow. Some were larger machines that could hover to their dig-site and then burrow in.

But it was a troublesome and dangerous technology. The machines required complex and continual maintenance, with an extremely limited supply of spare parts. Sometimes they went down and did not come up again. Worse than this, their capacity was very limited. Their hold-spaces were small. They couldn't surface if they were carrying too much weight, so not enough heavy metal, machine spare parts and other weighty things were coming up from below. It was all, I realised, terribly unsatisfactory. I didn't take in too much about the specifics about diggers, skimmers, ice-subs, the blueprints and wiring charts and all that boys-toys stuff, because I really wasn't that interested. But the picture it painted in my head, the webwork of human interaction, the struggle and labour, the social organism contracting like a muscle and pulling together, sent trickles of electricity up my back and neck and made my hair stand up a little.

Our committee was one of several discussing the construction of permanent tunnels, reaching down through the snow to the resources buried beneath. That was what we were about; that was our big project, part of the bigger project of *siting* Liberty. We were not the only government committee engaged on this talking-shop work. Given the fact that, of the seven of us, four were wives of senior military officers I'm prepared to wager that we weren't even the most important. But we did our job. We read documents, and pored over plans, and discussed and discussed.

The advantages of a permanent tunnel were obvious: we could roll trucks down the ramp, fill up with goodies, and roll them back up again. We could dig them with manpower, mine stuff with manpower, avoid all the breakable electrics and fuel-hungry machinery we were using up to that point. We could up productivity enormously. Of course, it was the problems with our project that were more pressing. We were not talking about digging through a firm substance, such as earth; even when compacted at depth snow is a friable medium, highly sensitive to heat, and at higher levels sensitive to vibration, to sideslip, to many other problems. Do you dig it straight down? Say a thirty-degree angle, straight down, you're thinking of a tunnel fifteen or twenty miles long. Do you bend it, concertina it down to the ground? Do you curl the tunnel in a helix, to arrive at the place directly beneath you? Liberty had been built by NUSA directly over the site of buried London, but had, it seems, slipped a little out towards the buried Thames estuary. This slippage was common to all the Seven Cities, I was told: some of the ones built in mountainous areas that slipped several kilometres. Snow is not rock, and deforms and moves and slides around underneath you.

How do you keep the tunnels intact? Do you sheathe them, internally, floor-walls-ceiling, all the way down? What do you use? Wire mesh? Where would you get so much material from? What about tunnel supports for the deeper areas of the mine, where the pressure of so much weight overhead was hundreds of pee ess eye? How do you actually excavate the snow? Dig it out, deposit it on the surface, like old-fashioned mining? Or heat it and pump the water away? How do your miners breathe? Maybe thirty degrees was too steep an incline for fully-laden trucks to make their way up; how about fifteen? Double the length of your tunnel, and of your problems. How about five degrees? How many hours' drive away would the excavation-face actually be? You'd be surprised how much discussion these questions can provoke in a group of seven where only three of the seven have any actual, technological know-how, but the other four are determined not to seem like wastes of space.

I've mentioned [Blank], the Chair, the man with whom I was soon to begin an affair. A dangerous man. There is one other person on that committee, a woman, I should mention, for she is also important in the story I'm going to tell you. She was called [Blank], and was married to Chief of Staff [Blank], who was a four-star general then, I think, and now is a five-star. Or maybe he was already a five-star? I ought to know. The number of stars that defined her husband, like a recommendation in a guidebook, was a matter of great importance to [Blank]. She used to talk of it often, so it is rather ironic that I can't remember the details.

My first day of working on the mine-shaft committee came to an end with this woman catching my eye. 'Tara,' she said. Most people called me Tara. I no longer cared. 'Tara,' she said. 'How's [Blank]? I hear he's a changed man since you married him – lucky girl, he's a fine fellow, a good man. A good catch. How is he? How is he? We haven't seen him since his wedding. Is he well?'

'He's fine,' I said.

'I've a little coffee,' she said. 'Would you like some?'

Of course I said yes. She might have been the devil herself offering me coffee and I would have said yes.

So we walked through the compound and back to her apartment. She walked with a self-consciously stately walk, the way a beautiful person walks when they really know that they are beautiful. And [Blank] was certainly very beautiful. She looked the way models looked: tall and pale and slender, with an amazing display of ink-black hair.

Her husband was an inch (or whatever is the proper mode of measurement) above Crow in the military hierarchy that ran Liberty, and their apartment was accordingly a little plusher than ours, although only in petty ways. A slightly nicer sofa, salvaged from who-knows-which under-snow city. The window in the front room was not plain, but was rather a piece of criss-cross leaded glass. It looked out of place in the white-painted, metal-walled room, like fishnet stocking on a man. The apartment was essentially the same prefab block of metal rooms as my own apartment, the same layout.

102

I sat on the sofa. [Blank] brought a small metal pot of coffee from the little kitchen, and poured warm and black-sandy coffee into two cups. It was fantastic to me. I drank, I'm rather ashamed to say, greedily. There was no sugar, but that didn't matter. The coffeeness of the coffee was like a spike going into my mind. I had to restrain myself from gulping the whole cup in one go. [Blank] sat herself in a chair, slightly higher than my low-slung position, and looked down upon me with a faint smile, almost condescending. But it really didn't matter. I was swept away by the hit of the coffee. I took a mouthful, and held it behind my teeth for a moment, letting my tongue hang in the middle of the fluid like a blissed-out person in a sensory deprivation tank.

'The troops get coffee every day,' she was saying to me. 'That's where most of the coffee goes.'

I swallowed. 'It's enough to make you want to join the army,' I said.

She laughed politely at this, as if it had been a great witticism.

I finished my coffee.

'Don't take this the wrong way,' she said, leaning forward a little in her chair. 'But I think you're *lovely*.'

'Thanks,' I said, nonplussed.

She lifted her own cup of coffee and took a dainty sip. 'Such pretty eyes,' she said. 'I can see why [Blank] fell in love with you.'

I shifted my position. 'So tell me,' I said, awkwardly trying to reorient the conversation. 'How long you been on this committee then? This mine-shaft thing?'

She smiled again, but I could see her teeth were shut behind her lips. 'Oh,' she said, 'weeks. But let's not talk about *work*.'

And, in my head, the caffeine was starting to work its bright-lit magic on my mind. I looked up at her again as if there were some small revelation happening. Her black hair was so sheer, so completely black, so perfectly brushed to fall in an uninterrupted wave to her shoulders that it looked almost as though she was wearing a black scarf over her head.

'I love your hair,' I said, the coffee pricking a slight extraversion out of me. 'It's so black—'

'Not a grey hair,' she replied with feline smugness. 'I am glad you noticed. Not *one* grey hair. I've never had a grey hair. Imagine it!'

I smiled. I wanted to reach out and touch her hair. Its blackness was a kind of perfection. It was more than black. It was the colour of blindness, or of oblivion. I wondered if she dyed it, and then decided that she obviously dyed it, it was too perfect not to be dyed, but then I wondered where she found hair dye nowadays. Or perhaps the colour was real.

'D'you know what?' she was saying. 'I never used to believe that people just went grey. Never really believed that. I mean, it's funny, isn't it? Hair changing colour. Your *eyes* don't start brown and then go grey when you hit forty, do they! Your *fingernails*,' (she was looking at her own nails, immaculately purple: ink-dyed, almost certainly, since nail varnish is incredibly hard to come by up here) 'your *finger-nails*,' she said, 'don't start pink and go, you know – white.'

I looked obligingly at my own brown nails.

'So why?' she said. 'Why should your hair start one colour and go another? It doesn't really make sense.' She smiled at me again as if she had spoken some great profundity. 'What I mean to say,' she added, with a little spurt of energy, sitting straight up and jerking her hand forward so that it touched my knee, 'I know people *do go* grey, of course. But it is weird when you think about it. Isn't it? It's not like you ever see people with, like, half their head grey, at the top, and half, like, black. Do you? Does it mean that hair just, you know, *goes* grey, like—' and she lifted her hand from my knee and clicked her fingers. 'I don't know,' she concluded, serenely, sitting back in her chair and smiling at me again.

I smiled back. I imagined blackness draining from her head. I imagined each hair as a supple transparent quill, filled with black ink, and then I imagined each one broken off at the tip so that the ink poured slowly away, and the whiteness spread slowly from a line along the crown of her head all the long way to the fringe at her shoulders.

She had a slimline heater mounted on the wall, and she had turned this on when we entered. Another function of her husband's seniority: we had one in our apartment too, although Crow was too fastidious actually to use it. By the time we had finished our coffees it was warm enough in the room for us to unzip our jackets. She slid herself completely out of her coat, and stretched as if it had been rather constricting inside. She was an extraordinarily thin person. Two small breasts poked like elbows against the fabric of her shirt. The crossbar of her clavicle was very sharply defined against the cling of her skin. Her face was pert, a sharp little nose and a wide mouth under axehead cheekbones. There was nothing *fat* about her flesh at all; only her hair was fat, a big spread of glorious hair. Her hair, and possibly, in a smaller sense, her eyes; for her eyes were huge, porcelain curves with glistening brown pupils, dark brown sprinkled with shreds of a lighter brown. Only the sweep of her hair and the circles of her wide eyes gave her any sense of female curviness at all.

'You're so thin,' I said, I guess still a little addled by the coffee. I had not tasted coffee in weeks, and on the rare occasions when I did get some it was always a plastic instant coffee, not this grittily real brew. 'You're so slender,' I said.

'Thank you,' she said, blithely, as if that had been the last thing on her mind, although surely she had removed her coat to show off her figure (and she slipped her arms back into the sleeves of the jacket soon afterwards). 'It's a draw-back, of course.'

'Drawback?'

'In the cold. You've no *idea* how much I'd love to be a fuller-figured woman. Like you are. You know, a little insulation.' She drew the sides of her open padded jacket closer around her body. 'It never gets warm here, after all. Never warm. A little insulation would be good, a little padding like you have. But, then again, [Blank] does like me to be slimmer, rather than fatter. I wish he was more like your husband, and preferred a little more body-fat, but what can you do? A wife has a certain duty to please her husband, don't you think?'

We chatted for a while. I hated her more and more as the afternoon went on, and yet she seemed to grow fonder and fonder of me. 'I do so love making new friends,' she said. 'Yeah,' I said. 'Right – me too.' Later she said something that struck me: 'There's so much *rear-end-kissing* you got to do, you know? There're so many people you got to pretend to like, just to get on in this life. You know? If you had any idea how much *work* it was getting on this committee. It's nice to meet somebody you can just like for who they are.' And she took my hands in her hands and gave them a squeeze. Her hands were cooler than mine. I smiled, nodded, but thought to myself that I didn't understand, that I hadn't worked at all to get on this committee, I had kissed no rear-ends at all, it had just fallen into my lap. I think it was dawning on me that this committee was a platform from which ambitious people could launch them-selves. I didn't care about that, however. All I cared about at that time was the fact that this woman, this Mrs [Blank] with her extraordinary black hair, was about the most self-centred, vain, bitchily irritating human being I had ever met.

Our little session came to an end when [Blank], her husband, blundered in. He was a stout man in a blue uniform, with a bald head and a half-startled, half-sneering expression. 'Uh,' he said. 'N'see ya there. Sorry.'

'That's OK, darling,' said [Blank], affecting a southern drawl.

'Didn't know you had company.'

'Darling,' said [Blank], standing up, in her usual voice. 'This is Tara [Blank].'

'Didn't see ya there,' he said to me. 'Sitting down there. Didn't know my wife had company. Uh.'

'Tara [Blank],' repeated his wife, with emphasis.

'Uh!' he said, this time in surprise. 'You [Blank]'s new wife? That's fine, is *fine* to meet you. [Blank]'s talked of you. Said plenty about you.'

'Good things, I hope,' I said, because I was nervous, and because it's the kind of thing a person says in that sort of situation. [Blank] looked at me with a little crease of non-comprehension sitting vertically in his forehead.

'Oh he adores you,' said [Blank], coming round behind her husband and kissing his shoulder. 'You don't need to worry there; he loves you. Doesn't he?'

But [Blank] was too much the military man to be drawn into such talk. 'Got to go out on the snow,' he said, to his wife. ''Nother collision, or detonation, or whatever. I was talking to [Blank] just now, but I got to leave him. Come and speak to him whilst I'm away, keep him sweet.'

'[Blank],' she repeated, with an inflection of happy surprise.

'Yeah, yeah, uh, I know,' her husband drawled. 'It's been hell getting him to come on board with us, and it ain't done yet. You sweet-talk him, some. I got to go on the snow now, got to go inspect this thing, but you keep talking to him. Tell him about the ticket, but spin it good, yeah? Make it sound like the sort of ticket he *wants* to join. Uh,' he added, turning his face towards me as if remembering I was still there. 'Sorry to break up your tate-a-tate.'

'That's alright,' I said.

'You British?' he said.

'Yes.'

'Right. Good. Here.' He had a small piece of card in his fingers, covered with tiny print. I took it.

'He's a big fool, really,' said [Blank], apologetically. She stepped away from him and slipped her arm around my shoulder. 'That's his election card. He's only had a hundred printed, so you're lucky to get one.'

'Pass it on,' he said, gruffly, 'to somebody else, when you've done reading it.'

'Election?' I asked.

'He's running for Senator,' said [Blank].

'*Thinking* of running,' said her husband, looking cross.

'Oh he'll run,' said [Blank], knowingly. She steered me to the door.

'Is it politics season around here?' I asked unwitting. 'Is it election time? My husband is talking of maybe running for IP.'

[Blank] froze in her steps. There was silence in the room. It occurred to me that I should not have said what I said.

'He's never even been Mayor!' said [Blank].

'—Senator, darling,' his wife corrected him, with a distracted expression on her face.

'Senator, Mayor, there's not a [*expletive deleted*] difference.'

'Bad word!' shrilled [Blank], in rebuke.

Her husband shook his head. He was blushing a little. 'That don't matter. Tara here's no prude. That don't matter, that I swore. Uh, that I swore, slipped out. Uh, what *matters* is that he – I mean your husband – that *he* has never run a city. Never sat in the Interim Senate.' He smiled unconvincingly. 'Nobody'll elect him IP without that experience.'

'Nobody will elect *you* if they find out you've got a garbage mouth,' said [Blank].

'Never mind that kinda thing now.'

She bridled. 'I *will* mind it. You don't think about these things. But it's not just soldiers who have the vote, you know. Swearing may be fine and hip in the barracks, but it *will* alienate the voters. You *will* stop swearing, you hear?'

'Uh,' said the chastised husband, as he searched his mental filofax for my name. 'Uh, Tara, is he serious, though? Your husband?' He came over towards me. His was a bland face, poorly defined, composed of notes towards facial features rather than the features themselves. A blocky nose, bald head, cuphandle ears, a brow that was a vague protuberance rather than a ridge, damp-looking grey eyes. It was as though rough face-shapes had been positioned beneath a soggy white cloth. 'Uh, Tara. Is he really going for IP?'

I shook my head. 'I don't know, really. Hey, sorry, you know? I shouldn't have said anything. It's probably just a, you know, a vague idea. I don't know.'

There was a hiatus. Then [Blank] took my arm again and resumed her movement towards the door.

'Anyway, it was lovely to have this chat together. You'll promise to come for coffee again? Soon?'

I was out in the street, saying goodbye to her, saying goodbye to him over her shoulder, and then the door shut. I stood there for a while. The sky was cold and as blue as gunmetal over the top of the buildings. Pedestrians had made slush of the snow on the street. I looked down and realised that [Blank] had made a short pavement outside his front door with an old piece of wooden board that must have been salvaged from the food-mines. Despites smears of sludge, the slogan that had been painstakingly and neatly painted on was perfectly legible: *99% of People in Turnworth Say No! to GMO Trials*. I thought to myself that a bourgeois coffee-morning had suddenly gaped to reveal depths of realpolitik beneath. I told myself I really didn't care.

Five

[Blank] approached me, seeing me in the main street. 'Not chairing any meetings today?' I asked him.

'I only chair your meetings,' he told me. 'I only chair that one committee.'

'So what do you do with the rest of your time?'

'Hey,' he said, smiling broadly. 'I loiter about the streets, trying to pick up young women like you.' Then, as if fearful of overstepping some puritanical conversational code, he added, 'That's a joke.'

'I assumed so.'

We walked to the end of the street. In those days Liberty was smaller than it is today – it's not that long ago, but it has grown a lot in a short time. It was just a village then, really, a barracks-turned-village. There were hardly any of the things I remembered from old pre-Snow cities. There were cubes and cubes of accommodation, larger blocks for the communal sleeping spaces of the ordinary soldiers; prefab apartments for officers and their families; three churches built of panels with wooden roofs. There weren't any bars, because the barracks had several messes. No: there *was* one bar, a single room that sold miniscule glasses of watered alcohol, coloured soft drinks, anything that could be brought out of the food-mines for ridiculously high prices. Or did that place open later? Ackroyd's Liberty Bar, it was called. But I tell you, I can't remember if that place opened later, or if it had always been open. When I married Crow I sometimes drank in the senior officers' mess, and it's not likely I would have frequented another bar. There were several shops, a big foodstore staffed by soldiers, and several smaller places. There was a noodle bar, although it could not, obviously, restrict itself to noodles, and served whatever food it could get hold of and heat up. There was a soup place, I remember. The little array of shops on the central main-street row: most sold clothes, but the affordable things were usually inappropriate (summer-wear, bikinis, that sort of thing), and the winter-wear was extremely expensive. There was a bunch of make-do-and-mend places; seven, or eight, that I can call to mind straight away. You took everything to one of these places sooner or later. Getting new stuff was expensive.

On the far side of the city, out by the perimeter, were workshops. Mechanics worked on hovercraft and mining subs and anything the military needed. Because any money mined out of the snow, or flown out from the over-States, was government – which is to say, military – business could only make a living by attracting military custom. By the same token, it was all the grease monkeys, the mechanics who serviced the machines, who earned the most money, because these were the civilians who did most of the work for the army. They'd strut up and down main street with tremendous self-importance. They'd spend lavishly at this shop or that shop, and so the money would start its trickle down. At the same time there were a couple of doctors I knew, and they earned hardly anything. The barracks had their own medical orderlies, I guess, and civilians had better things to spend their money on than healthcare, especially when medicine and equipment was in such short supply that, often, the best a doctor could do would be to diagnose, not treat, a sickness. Doctors would stand in the chill looking through the display windows of the shops, like tramps, yearning but unable to pay for anything whilst grease monkeys swanked past in new coats with women on their arms. That was Liberty, in those days. Paper was so scarce that there was no newspaper, although there was an official sheet that was pasted up in front of the military-police block with government news on it, a sort-of-*Pravda*. There were no bookstores. There was a library, where you paid for each book, each day. I could rarely afford the lending fee, and when I did, the pleasure in reading was undercut by my sense of hurry, the feeling that I absolutely had to finish the book today so as not to incur another day's fee.

There's a bookstore now. Lots of things have changed. I've changed, myself. I've all the paper I need to write this account, although of course that's because I have chanced to be near the centre of important events, and NUSA wants a record of that. But of course, some things don't change. You hardly need me to tell you that. Then, as now, everything in Liberty depended on the military. I don't have the figures for the proportion of military to civilian inhabitants of the city when I was first living there: probably sixty-forty; maybe seventy-thirty. I don't know. Half and half former-US and former-Brit, with the smallest proportion of other types (there was [Blank] of course, from Thailand, or Vietnam or somewhere; but he was so completely the exception rather than the rule). Almost all the faces you'd see were white. It was as if the human animal had adapted so as to be better camouflaged in the snow.

The army ran everything. Wrongdoers were arrested by the military police, and served time in military lock-ups (reinforced prefabs on the edge of town). The political set-up was entirely staffed by military types. They were in charge of the economy too. But the economy was so messed up – the military handled it poorly – it was tragic. They released a predetermined amount of money into society through purchases and so on, the amount increasing each year by something like 4%, so that inflation could not exceed that amount – it [*expletive deleted*] did, though, I'm sure of it. So much for the theory. One day a loaf of bread would be $5, the next week it could be $20, the week after that $8. Supply was not regular enough to guarantee the sort of economic tweaking the government believed in and pretended to practise. But people put up with it. What else could we do? It was an Emergency, with a big, pronged, capital 'E' and ice hanging in shaggy wedges from the cross-bars. Humanity was gripping on by its fingernails. So, you have to spend your whole weekly salary on a loaf of bread and a tin of corned beef? Make the best of it. And, I should say, in the interest of being honest, that I didn't suffer the way plenty of people in the city did, because I was married to such a senior military man. But many people did. And since I'm pursuing the cause of honesty, I should add that – although we lived officially in a state of Emergency – people didn't think of it that way. Emergencies don't go on and on, month after month, year to year. They become the normal state of things; State of Normality. That's how it felt. Everything got normalised. Even the billions of dead. It was as if they had stepped out of the picture for a while, and we were making do through an unusually cold and prolonged winter.

Each city was supposed to be run by a Senator, with an administrative staff beneath him; the Senators were supposed to attend Senate back in one of the six over-States cities, I don't remember which city. Our Senator was rarely in Liberty, I know, because people used to kvetch and complain about it. His deputy was a colonel, called [Blank] I think; or maybe [Blank]. I forget the exact details. He's dead now, I know. He died in the first attack. No, the second attack – I can't remember.

Does it matter precisely which attack killed him? I don't know how precise you want me to be. It was one of the early ones, at any rate.

The Senate. When I got to know him a little better, when he became my lover and revealed his Che-Guevara side to me, [Blank] used to gush out scorn upon the Senate. 'Some Senate!' he would say. 'A seven-man star chamber more like, with the IP sitting over them like a medieval baron. Accountability – that's a joke. They're *all* military, they're *none* of them used to the idea of democracy. True democracy, I mean, not this sham.' And so on. I used to think it sweet, that he had such passion. He acted like a nineteen-year old, like a revved-up student high on Justice and Right and so on, not like the bald fifty-something he actually was.

But I'm getting ahead of myself.

Let me go back to that day. [Blank] hailed me in the street, and said, 'I loiter about the streets, trying to pick up young women like you,' and smiled at me. We walked to the end of the street, and turned up a side-row. Past the Unity Church, and to the railing at the edge of town, and stood there for a while looking out at the blankness of the landscape. We both fumbled with our sunglasses in mittened hands, and fitted them onto our faces. Squaddies with great circular snowshoes on their feet were visible on the land outside the city, laying semi-dirigible slabs out on the snow, to form a temporary runway.

'Plane coming in,' I said.

'Looks like it,' said [Blank].

I wasn't sure why we were standing there, the two of us. But at the same time it seemed natural, easy. We stood in a perfectly unawkward silence for a while. Then I turned and looked down the street. 'That chapel,' I said, without pointing.

'Unity church,' he said.

'My husband attends regularly.'

'I know,' he said. 'I see him there. But never you.'

'I don't like to go.'

'I'd heard you were Catholic,' said [Blank]. 'There's a Catholic church in New NY, where I lived before I came here. It's big, nicely made. I'm,' he added, cautiously, 'Catholic, I used to be Catholic.'

'Lapsed?' I asked.

'More complicated than that,' he said. 'It's more complicated than lapsed or not lapsed. It's a complicated thing, my relationship to Catholicism.'

'I'm not a Catholic,' I said. 'I just don't fancy it. Church, all that.'

'OK,' he said, easily. 'It doesn't really matter to me, one way or the other.'

'Matters to my husband,' I said.

'He's got a public reputation to maintain,' said [Blank]. 'That's understandable.'

'Understandable, but a pain in the arse.'

'In the . . . ?'

'Ass, you call it.'

[Blank] chuckled at this. 'Yeah, I thought that's what you said.'

I turned to face him. 'You're not,' I told him, 'such a jerk as I thought.'

'Thank you,' he laughed.

'I only mean, in your official I'm-chairing-this-meeting persona. Your *there are fifty ways to build this tunnel, let's run it up the flagpole see who salutes* persona. But, actually you're OK. Are you married?'

He laughed more loudly at this.

'What's so funny?' I wanted to know.

'Like I'm *any*where near rich enough to have a wife,' he said. 'Too old, too ugly – but, no, that ain't the problem, too *poor*, that's the rub.'

'Is that how it is?'

'It's always been that way. It was that way before the Snow for many people. It's just a more focused version of the same thing up here.'

'You were married before the Snow?'

'Married and divorced,' he said. 'You?'

'Never married,' I said. 'I had a kid,' I said. It all came out easy, as if I were chatting with a close friend, although I barely knew this man. 'Don't know where she is. Maybe she got out. I like to think so.' Saying that made the tears tremble inside my skull, like pieces of glitter nudged in a snowglobe. But the tears didn't come out.

'Yeah, it's possible,' [Blank] said, leaning on the rail and looking over the whiteness.

'What did you do?' I asked him. 'Before, I mean? Were you always in the army?'

'Jesus, no,' he said. 'No. I was a writer.' He grinned a teenagery grin as he said this. 'You believe that? Stupid profession.'

'Not at all,' I told him. 'I love to read.'

'I wasn't that kind of writer,' he said, rather mysteriously. He stared at the white landscape and said, 'You had a kid? That's great. I never had a kid. Sometimes wish I had.'

'There's still time,' I told him.

'That's not the way it works up here,' he said. 'For non-military, for poor folk.'

'I thought you *were* military, these days anyway. I thought you had a rank.'

'It's a courtesy rank. I was doing work for the military, writing speeches and press releases and stuff like that, when the Snow came. And, OK, yeah, this is a fairly big committee I'm chairing. Important, I concede it. I'm not a nobody – if I'm giving the impression I'm just a nobody, a bum, then I'm misrepresenting things. It's just that, there's a bunch of senior military staff, more senior and more rich, who come first in line before me when it comes to available women.'

'It sounds like you're angling for a charity [*expletive deleted*],' I told him.

He barked with laughter at this. 'You're not like any other officer's wife,' he said, grinning. 'You see straight through me.'

'It's this light,' I said, gazing out over the snowscape. 'This penetrating light.'

'This is some light,' he agreed.

I worked. The committee met from eight-thirty to one-thirty. The afternoons were mine, so I had plenty of time to myself.

This is what I did with my spare time: I watched clouds. I'll tell you: I became something of an expert cloud-watcher, a connoisseur. There were no birds to watch, and this was the next best thing. On the days when the sunlight was bright as a splash of cold water in your face, and the sky was blue without blot, I was less happy. But when the clouds came above me I watched them and a delight crept into my heart.

It was partly the shapes of the clouds that fascinated me. As a child I had played the game that all children play, and conjured imaginary faces, maps, and monsters from the sky. It was as absorbing a game for an adult as it had been for a child. The sort of cloud that was pregnant with apparent texture, a fish-scale silver. Or the sort that seemingly carried bruises on their chubby white limbs that threatened heavier-than-usual snowfall. Or the sort, very high up, that looked exactly as if they were painting, such that you could actually see the brushstrokes.

Why did clouds fascinate me so much? It's hard to say. It's hard for me to remember. If I were pressed to explain, I might say that there was some deep connection for me between clouds and memory. It is difficult to say why this should be. Why are clouds like memory? There's a question. *There*'s a riddle.

And, you know? – I'm tempted to produce intellectual answers to the riddle: because both memory and clouds are fluid, both fleeting, because they shift their shapes and allow you to map your imagination and desires onto them, because they are both very far away, and so on. But to say any of those things would simply be to rationalise after the fact. The sport of similes: find a connection between these apparently unconnected things. Why is memory like an onion? Why is memory like a piece of madeleine cake? Why is memory like a shark? (it must keep moving on or it dies – or, no, because it bites). Why is memory like a snowfall? It's a soft smothering of the past, a slow erosion under the newly whitened page. But that, surely, is forgetting rather than memory.

Well, this is only a sort of parlour game. Why *was* that raven like that writing desk? Because they both start with *rr*, no other reason. Why is a mantis like a twig? To catch its prey. Why is a glass of wine like a glass of blood? Because we're all vampires, or rather because Catholics are. Why is liberty like tyranny? Because life isn't structured in terms of choice. Why are women like men? Why is night like day? Why is sleep like death?

The sense I had looking at the clouds was something much more visceral, not an intellectual parallelism. Something in the gut. Clouds thrummed my nerves as memory, the thing itself.

There is some sort of connection here.

At school we studied *Hamlet* in the sixth-form English classes. Then, in the proper manner of the contemporary English schoolchild, I had pretended uninterest in the class. It was expected of me by my peers. I giggled and bickered at the back of the class whilst the teacher whined at us from the front to be quiet and pay attention. I rolled my eyes in dumb mockery as he declaimed the famous speeches at us, his copy of the play perched on his hand like a bird. But despite the external ritual behaviour I was compelled to adopt, in my heart I loved the Shakespeare. I loved the text because it stroked my heart in an ineffably tender and thrilling and disturbing way. It caressed my heart with infinitely more skill than the boys I was seeing then caressed my flesh. I kept my secret love hidden, as I'm sure you can understand, but I loved it. And I remember being especially struck by the dialogue Hamlet has with Polonius about a cloud. You remember it? It goes like this.

POLONIUS My lord the queen would speak with you presently.

HAMLET Do you see yonder cloud that's almost in the shape of a camel?

POLONIUS By th' mass, and tis like a camel indeed.

HAMLET Methinks it is like a weasel.

POLONIUS It is backed like a weasel.

HAMLET Or like a whale.

POLONIUS Very like a whale.

HAMLET Then I will come to my mother by and by. They fool me to the top of my bent.

I wanted to get a copy of Shakespeare out of the City Library, to reread and remember, but it costs a dollar for three days and I don't have a dollar.

Maybe I'm misquoting. The point here, you might say, is that Hamlet is pretending to be mad – or perhaps he actually is mad. It's the Turing-test thing; if a person *acts* mad with enough depth, even to himself, then he is indistinguishable from mad. This dialogue is the sort of disjointed thing that a mad person would say. But we read it on another level, and we see that Polonius, who is a sort of adviser to the king, is so completely in the habit of flattering the royal family that he's prepared to say ridiculous things just to be ingratiating. 'It looks like a camel,' says Hamlet. 'Yes it does!' replies the puppy-Polonius. 'It looks like a weasel!' 'Yes it does!' 'It looks like a whale!' 'Yes it does!' Our English teacher, a Mr Stalybrook, was of the opinion that no cloud could look like a camel *and* a weasel *and* a whale all at once, and that Shakespeare was obviously mocking Polonius through this speech. The rest of the class didn't care one way or the other, and I pretended not to care. But in my heart I wondered about this. Clouds can look like the funniest things, weird and amorphous. Don't you think? I *felt*, I think, for Polonius.

It was like my mother with my father, always agreeing with him to make life easier, regardless how self-contradicting his anger and frustration made his consecutive statements.

'It looks like a camel.'

'Well I suppose I can see why you might say so, my dear. Those blobs towards the end, they're sort of like legs, and that could be a long neck with a smallish head on it. In a way it is rather camel-like.'

'No – woman, must you contradict me? – It looks like a weasel.'

'A weasel? Have you changed your mind, dear? Well, looking at it again, if I squint my eyes a little, I *suppose* it's a weasel. The long neck and the small head are weasly, I suppose, and those legs do look rather tiny. That camel-hump could be the weasel bending, wriggling into a hole. Yes, I see what you mean.'

'Are you trying to provoke me? I said that it looks like a whale!'

'Oh, a whale now, is it? Well, if we imagine one of those whales with the long snout, that could be what the neck was, and that curved back you thought was camel-humpish could be the whale flexing in the water, yes, I see it.' And so on.

I remember when we lived in a flat in Hounslow, my father used to raise his voice, and my sister and I would huddle together, frightened at the noise. He used that phrase several times: *woman, must you contradict me?* But our mother was always able to placate him.

I think my heart responded to something else about this speech in *Hamlet*. It was the implied progression, not a logical progression but somehow intuitive and profound, from camel *to* weasel *to* whale, *therefore* I shall come to my mother by-and-by. As if some symbolist, irrational truth linked these three creatures and brought me back to the family, to home, to the mother. Desert beast, wetland beast, ocean beast, and home. Dry, moist, wet. A thawing of the snow; a transformation from desert to ocean. Clouds drifting before my eyes and cavorting like a carnival of animals. Home. It's all memory, you see, memory and remembrance and memorialising.

A Sunday. I wandered the empty streets, through the sunlight and the lightly falling snow. Snow from a clear blue sky. Drifts of snow everywhere, over every building like white camel-humps. The compound buildings looked draped with white sheets, as if the owners of the town had gone away for a two-month holiday and had not wanted dust to accumulate in the upholstery during that time. The sense of emptiness was absolute.

At the compound edge, looking over the wall, I stared at the wilderness outside town. The snow lay like light petrified, like white light solidified as it fell on everything. Is this what God looks like? That was an appropriate Sunday thought, wasn't it? Cold Heaven, and the sound of hymns sung coming from inside the compound church, the sound of piano and guitar chords holding wavering voices together like stitching on cloth. I walk towards the building, wander along its side-wall and turn the corner. The street is empty. New snow has blurred the outlines of the older footsteps, melting them to a cobbled vagueness, and eventually to flatness again. I am the only person in the compound not in church. I had weaselled out of attendance by claiming I was a Hindu, but I'm not, and they didn't really believe me anyway, and I didn't see how I could keep them at bay for much longer. Hymnal melodies rose through the air as the snowflakes came sparsely down.

Six

Let me tell you about [Blank] and about my affair with him. That is, after all, the main point of this document I'm writing here. That's what you want to know about, isn't it? Let me get to it: plots against the government, terrorist action, war and destruction raining down. My suntan, and the baleful effect it has had on my life.

Here, to begin with, is a little study in contrasts. One time I asked Crow, as we were eating supper together (tinned asparagus and a drift of white rice like a snowfall on the plate): 'Is it true what they say about Australia?'

'What do they say,' he replied, his eyebrows curling in suspicion, like those diacritical marks that sometimes go over the letter 'n' in Spanish, 'about Australia?' (what are those little marks called? I can't remember).

'I'd heard that parts of the southern hemisphere—' I started.

'Where did you hear that?' he interrupted me.

I was startled by his brusqueness.

'Now listen,' he said. 'That's a rumour. That's started by subversives, and terrorists.'

'OK,' I said slowly. I felt an inappropriate urge to laugh. He looked so serious, so intense suddenly. There hadn't been any razors for a week, and his old razor had gone blunt, so the beginnings of a beard were peppering his chin and upper lip. And his eyebrows were pursed, like a petulant child. What *are* they called, those funny little curvy accents that go over the 'n' in Senor and words like that, to make the 'n' into 'ny' – is it *tilde*? Or *cedilla*? Mañana, man[y]ana. That's what his eyebrows looked like.

'The government is clear, the IP made a speech specifically on this subject. Right? The snow is general, over the

121

whole globe. The depth of snow varies, of course. But the snow is general.'

'Right,' I said.

There was an awkward moment of silence.

'And,' I said, looking at my plate, 'it was started by a Russian environmental disaster, yeah?'

'That's right,' he said, quickly. 'It started in Siberia, and snowballed over the world. It was a Russian disaster. The deregulated Russian nuclear industry.'

'Snowballed,' I said, pushing my fork through my meal. 'That's funny. You're a funny guy.' He glowered, he was silent. It wasn't a comfortable moment.

That was my husband.

Now, here's a version of a conversation I had with [Blank] on the same subject.

'Have you heard,' I asked him, 'the rumours about Australia?'

He looked instantly suspicious, but in a quite different manner from Crow. He glanced about him, like a central-casting actor playing paranoid. 'What do you mean?'

'I'd heard a rumour,' I said, 'that some parts of the southern hemisphere weren't so badly snowed under. Maybe that they weren't snowed under at all.'

[Blank] looked at me. 'Listen, Tara,' he said. 'I'm going to trust you, OK? I'm going to ask you, first: did you say that because your husband set you up to say that to me?'

'No,' I said. 'What do you mean?'

'OK,' he said. 'That's OK. I'm going to trust you, alright?'

'You can trust me,' I said.

'I heard that rumour. I heard more. It's the truth.'

'You're *kidding*.'

'Large bunches of southern Africa are free of snow. Southern Peru. Pretty much the whole of Australia. And a whole lot of ocean. All snow-free. That's what I heard.'

'Jesus,' I said, my heart sparkling with hope and excitement and perhaps fear. 'And there are people down there?'

'Sure. I mean the climates have changed, so the societies

down there are bound to have changed too. It could hardly be otherwise. It'll be much colder than it was, and crops and so on will have a hard time growing. But I heard that the Australian government is still pretty much in control, that Australia is pretty much the way it was before the snow.'

'Christ,' I said.

'They're fishing – the cold-water fish are now swimming at much lower latitudes, and I heard there are big cod and other fish to be fished off the Australian coast. They've got rainfall now in their deserts, and they're growing wheat. Imagine it! Real bread, real fish!'

'Christ,' I said. 'This is fantastic news. Why are we struggling along here? Why don't we all just go down there?'

'Hush,' he said. 'You got to be quiet. The official line is that only subversives talk about Australia being snow-free.'

'I don't understand,' I said. 'What's the story? Why don't they come and get us?'

'They? Australians? They got in communication with the NUSA government, that's what I heard, and we told them to stay well away. We've got a whole lot of military hardware still, don't forget. If the Australians sent a jumbo up here, it could easily get shot down.'

'But I don't understand,' I said. 'We're barely keeping alive up here. Barely keeping alive. Why *wouldn't* we want help from Australia, or anywhere still snow-free? Why wouldn't we want to just *go* there?'

'Think about it,' said [Blank]. 'If this was widely known, then that's exactly what would happen. Everybody not under direct military orders would simply go south. The government wouldn't have anybody to govern. They'd lose all their power. They're a government – power is their reason for being. They don't want to sacrifice that. And, listen to me, Tara.' He gripped my shoulders with his hands and looked into my eyes. 'Listen to me. You may be [Blank]'s wife, but that won't necessarily protect you if you start blurting this all around town. OK? They'll lock you up,

I wouldn't put it past them to execute you. So you – be – discreet – OK?'

'OK,' I said, my head buzzing. My heart was slapping at the inside of my ribs.

Hope. It was a lot to take in. In the earlier stages [Blank]'s own certainty was contagious. Or perhaps, if I am to be more honest, it was, on my part at least, a sort of nostalgia. There was something deliciously old-world about his anti-government paranoia. It reminded me of the way things had been before the snow, of the sorts of people I would sometimes encounter in pubs or via friends. The revolutionary socialists, the conspiracy addicts, the aliens-Roswell people, the Queen's-a-lizard people. There was that addictive element of blame about it: that's an almost sensual pleasure if it is indulged at the right level, with the right degree of emotional investment. I'd like to blame my dad for getting asthma and dying. Sweet. The problem is that I can't persuade myself to think that it was actually his fault. What can you say? I'd like to blame Minnie for – no, actually, I'd rather not talk about that right now.

Let's leave that subject well alone.

This is one of the things [Blank] said: 'the government are responsible, yes? It's *their fault.* Of course they're going to cover that up – that's what governments do when they're culpable for some giant crime.' Even at the time I thought that was classic anti-government paranoia, of the sort that inadvertently grants the government super-competency, super-rationality. Faced with the situation in which they find themselves, *of course* the government has covered it up, *they'd be mad not to.* Or – to take the first statement. 'The government are responsible'; just the way that is put folds together 'it is the government's fault' and 'the government are capable'. Who, after all, would want an *irresponsible* government? Not even a conspiracy theorist – in fact, *especially* not a conspiracy theorist – would want that. By positioning the government as being in charge of a disaster you are still unwittingly presenting the government as being in charge. And *being in charge* is all that matters to a government.

But [Blank]'s enthusiasm was thrilling, in its way. I was caught up. He told me that the snow was not, no indeed, *not* the consequence of Russian nuclear incompetence, but of the US government prosecuting some secret project, some new technology that went wrong. He wasn't sure what this technology was, but he was sure it existed. He was as certain of the personal complicity of all seven members of the Senate as a geocentrist is that the sun circles the earth. 'There's a scientist called G S Seidensticker,' he told me. 'I've never heard the name,' I replied. 'No?' he said. 'He's pretty famous, for a scientist.' 'I guess I don't know my scientists,' I said. 'I guess you don't,' he said.

We were naked as we had this conversation.

[Blank] did not know precisely what this Seidensticker had done, or how it had brought about the Snow, but he was certain that it was something culpable, some military-governmental project that had horribly backfired. I would ask him, how can you be so sure? He would look at me with an almost-pitying face, and then he would hurry on with his theory. 'There are a number of secret official documents,' he said, 'that make plain Seidensticker's part in this cata-strophe.'

'Is he still alive?'

'Sure he is. Still alive and still working for the govern-ment.'

'Why not go and ask him?'

'Well,' said [Blank], 'for one thing, he lives in New LA'. He pronounced it 'newla', the way people were starting to do then. 'For another he'd deny it all, of course he would. He's the government's man.'

'I guess so,' I said, rather admiring the way [Blank]'s theories presented a smooth, impermeable roundness to inquiry. They could have been wholly true, or wholly false, but there was no place where they could be tested and checked. There was no getting through his intellectual armour. It was the same with everything he said. But, I reminded myself, this fact in itself was not enough to render his theories invalid.

However much we talked about conspiracies and government complicity and culpability and so on, I never got [Blank] pinned down on what practical good was going to come of it. Say the government were exposed, and the remaining population of the seven cities rose up and overthrew them – then what? Maybe we'd all trek down to the Australia that became, with each of [Blank]'s mentions of it, more and more like a terrestrial paradise. Maybe there was something about the technology that would mean we could reverse the Snow, if only we could find out what it was. He believed that secrecy was the evil. I don't know how much I agreed with him, but it was a more entertaining mode of living than the drudge of reality. Besides, it was undeniable that at least one impossible thing had happened – the Snow itself, I mean. Given that unnatural, or supernatural, or quintessentially natural (I'm not sure) impossible phenomenon, other impossibilities became more, not less, likely.

[Blank] and I became lovers. I mentioned that already. At least one person I've spoken to thought it an unlikely pairing, but I don't think it is. He was older, it's true, and less able to offer a woman the status or privileges some other men might have offered. But he was one of the few men unawed by my status as Crow's wife. And the energy of his beliefs, as well as the fact of those beliefs being secret, drew me to him.

He was, then, in his forties, or maybe his early fifties, with a large, well-inhabited face. Regular features, and eyes with a zing of sharp blue, but a nose more proboscoid than aquiline, and jowls that sagged like little saddlebags. His eyebrows were finger-thick over each eye, and both ended in the middle of his forehead with two little upward poking thorns of hair, like smudgy sketches of worry lines over the bridge of his nose. His ears protruded markedly. I quite liked this feature. When he stood with the sun behind him they would glow red-pink, their flattened upward-pointing ovals somehow accentuating the line of his smile, catching and mimicking the curve of the corners of his mouth. His hair, which he kept cut very close, had retreated to the sides of his head, leaving a tongue-shaped stretch of pink scalp from eyebrows to the top of his crown. This area of skin was often ruddy, or flaking slightly, with aftermath of sunburn. Sunburn was extremely common in NUSA. Suncream was dug out of the mines often enough, but people seemed not to use it. It was as if, deep down, nobody believed the sun could burn them with so much snow and cold around.

[Blank]'s was not, then, a face that could ever strike you as handsome, but it was the sort of face you felt comfortable looking at, which meant that it was the kind of face with which you could – conceivably – fall in love. You know? An expressive face, mobile and full of feeling. A pillow of a face, not like Crow's sharp, die-cast features.

I knew [Blank] for nearly half a year before anything happened between us. First he let me into his secret world, his conspiracy theories, and we would sometimes meet and talk about that. Only later did we become lovers. I remember asking him, once: 'Don't you ever wonder about the clouds?' That looks like a ridiculous question, written down, but it's the sort of thing that pillow talk dignifies with significance.

His room, that tiny room; those tinny walls, those squared-off corrugations in the metal. Moisture used to freeze in dribbles as it ran down the grooves.

'Meteorology,' he said, gruffly. 'Meteorology,' he repeated, as if by saying the word he was pinning clouds down, fixing them. 'Not my thing, not my tha-a-a-ang,' he said, pulling himself up in his skinny little bed, into which we were both crumpled. 'Clouds. They're a kind of smoke, aren't they?'

'Smoke,' I said.

'But you know,' he added. 'That doesn't settle the answer, does it? I mean, what's smoke? Particles in air. But everything, if you think about it, is particles in air. *Air* is particles in air.' He liked that, and chuckled to himself. 'You might say that that just shuffles the answer one notch along. What *is* smoke, after all?' He said this as if the question had struck him for the first time. 'What is it? Why does it sometimes rise straight up? Why, on a cool morning, does wood smoke sink into the hollows?'

'Stop it,' I said, happy-chidingly, pulling myself up beside him. 'You're giving me the yen for a cigarette.'

'Ah,' he said, 'cigarettes. Been a long time since I saw any of them around. You know? Man, I'd kill for a smoke.'

'It's surprising,' I said, 'that they don't pull more cigarettes out of the food-mines. I mean, there must be millions of packets sitting around down there. You could surely dig along any former high-street and go into any former little shop, and see racks and racks of the things.'

'Tara,' he said, smiling at my childish ignorance. 'Of course the miners come across cigarettes. They come across them all the time. But they're under secret government orders not to bring them back.'

'Secret government plots?' I said. 'Again?'

'Don't mock, it's an example of the larger pattern. On a trivial level, but it's the same thing. The government thinks it unhealthy to smoke, and its instinct is – secretly, of course – is to act out its puritanical impulse on all of us. They were always that way, with drugs for instance, only now they control the supply. It's another aspect of their fascism.' He was always at least half serious when he talked like this.

Later, returning to Crow's apartment – my and Crow's apartment, I should say – I found myself thinking about it. It seemed to me more plausible that a government would act out this sort of petty denial on its people than the grandiose world-destroying plots [Blank] was always going on about. I cooked food, and was in the middle of eating it when my husband came in. Crow, my husband.

'The other half of this,' I said, pointing to the soup in my plate, 'is in the pan, on the stove. You want?'

'Has it gone cold?' he asked, with a slightly whiny, fastidious tone of voice.

'Tepid, maybe. I heated it five minutes ago. You want I should heat it up again?'

'No,' he said, wrinkling the bridge of his nose. 'No, I'll eat it as is. It'll be fine as is.'

He sat next to me, and we ate our meal together, and carried on our strange puppet-show simulacrum of married life together, and he chatted glumly about trivia for a while. Then I said, 'Did you ever smoke?'

'Smoke?'

'Before the Snow?'

'No,' he said. 'No. That's not healthy.'

'I used to,' I said.

And there was silence. Thoughts pinged and ponged through my brain. If I had to categorise my thought processes at that time, I guess I could say I thought about proximity. How recently I had been naked and pressed up against a different man from this man, from my husband. I thought about how near [Blank] was, in his little room, a few hundred yards away, a few minutes away. I thought of all the people in the city crammed together, rooms tidied closely up against rooms, boxes against boxes, with the air in common. Cooking smells insinuating their way along ice-glinting side-alleys, and people coming and going, noise, presence, the whole of the city (zooming, in imagination, up into the air) compressing itself into a compact node of multiple humanity in the acres and acres and continents of open white nothingness.

'You alright?' Crow asked me. 'You off in your own world there, maybe?'

'Do you think,' I said, 'that it's funny how you can't buy cigarettes in any shop?'

'What's that?'

'Surely miners must come across cigarettes down below?

Don't they? Why don't they bring any up? You don't think,' I said, 'that there's a secret government interdiction against mining cigarettes?'

'Cigarettes?' said Crow. 'Well, they'd hardly be the priority of miners, would they. You can't eat cigarettes, can you?'

'They do sometimes bring up luxury items. They brought up all those pictures, recovered all those pictures from that gallery.' Many members of the senior staff had benefited from that. Crow had bought a two-yard-wide oil painting from, its tag said, the nineteenth century: Collins's *The Sale of the Pet Lamb*. It was hanging in our front room now as we ate; a rural scene of a country mother selling her weeping daughter's pet to the butcher. I don't know how much it was worth before the Snow, but I daresay it had once been traded for a deal more than the twenty dollars Crow paid for it.

'That's hardly the same,' said Crow, slurping his soup. 'Man cannot live by bread alone. That's art, food for the soul, if you see what I mean. That's hardly the same thing as tobacco. Tobacco's a drug.'

'So's wine,' I said.

He shrugged. 'I don't think there's an official embargo on tobacco,' he said. 'There are probably some shops that sell cigarettes, if you've the money for them.'

'They probably sell out as soon as they get stock in,' I said, dourly.

Crow shrugged again. 'The way I look at it,' he said. 'The snow has wiped a lot of old habits out. Cigarettes are just one of those things that will go down the dinosaur road. When we get fields of things growing, as God willing we will soon, you don't think there'll be any spare space for growing tobacco? Of course not. We'll be growing food. Better to let it go, to think about other things. We should be thankful to the snow for getting rid of cigarettes for us.'

Later that night I did a strange thing. I got out of bed in the dark, walked through the flat and out the door into the cold in my night-things. I wasn't naked, of course; I wasn't

Lady Macbeth. I slept in a long-sleeved top, long johns, night-socks; some nights I even pulled a cap on my head. So I didn't get immediate frostbite, but it was still ferociously cold. I wasn't sleepwalking. I just wanted to go outside. I couldn't sleep. I couldn't quite wake up either. And outside the night sky was immensely distant. There were some wall-lights lit in some part of the barracks to my left, staining the night-time with a milky patch of illumination, but there was nothing but blackness to my right, and in that direction the stars were clearly visible. In that direction I could see right through – black being the transparency of night, not its blockage: white being its opacity, not clarity. The chill and the darkness gave the world a deep, deep-sea feel, the black-est of blacknesses. The road outside crunched under my feet. It only took a moment for the cold to come through the material of my bedsocks. A fiery cold. I rocked side to side to shift my weight from my right foot to my left foot and back again. For a long time I was looking down at the ground all around me. I was trying to make sense of the pattern made by starlight on the glitter of the night frost, orange sparkles reflecting the artificial lighting, and a dimmer, silvery set of gleaming points that must have been from the starlight. But they were swelling before my eyes, spreading out as if flattened between two glass plates prior to being placed in a microscope, beading and blurring. By the time I realised what was happening the tears were freezing on my cheeks with little soft pinches.

I was crying because I was thinking of my daughter. If I look back on that moment now I can say to myself that, illogical as it sounds, some tiny trigger in my head had been flipped by the cigarettes conversation from earlier. It didn't occur to me at the time, but with hindsight that's what it must have been. Looking back, I might represent my own state of mind as a series of interlocking support-sticks, like a Dali painting, and with every shock or every little trauma I had propped up this or that part of my mind from collapse with one more crutch-like assumption or suppression. Let's just hold on until things get back to normal. It'll all be over soon. The whole world's gone mad, not just you. I got to the surface, other people maybe got to the surface too. Maybe *she* got to the surface. Each one of these pit-props kept the roof of my consciousness from caving in, and they all held one another up, which was both a strength and a weakness. That last thought in particular was a comfort, *other people got out, maybe she did.* I thought, sometimes, of hundreds of thousands of enterprising human beings, scrabbling their way up through the thickening environment of snow, each in their bubbles making their way to the top, moling their way upwards to the light. I did not imagine my daughter doing this, not actually picture her doing this, because if I had done that the implausibility of it would have collapsed the whole fantasy. But I thought, vaguely and non-specifically, that a lot of people made it out of the snow, and that left open the possibility of somehow, some-day, seeing her again. But it wasn't true. When I thought that way, I – very deliberately – wasn't facing the truth.

Now, the thing about cigarettes is that my daughter had always scolded me for smoking cigarettes, so there already existed in my head that connection between cigarettes and guilt, between my selfish pleasure and my daughter's dis-appointment in me. But I don't think it was only that. I think it was when Crow said that the snow had put an end to cigarettes, that we would never again see cigarettes. That was what twitched over the pit-prop, that brought all the other pit-props down, and with it the sagging collapse of every-thing. I thought to myself: *I'll never see her again.* Never. The least comfortable word in the English language. It echoed and reechoed in my head. I would never see her again. I could live to be a thousand and never see her again. I cried.

Crow came outside and fetched me in again eventually, but I don't really remember that. I only remember the things he told me the following day. 'You were out in your socks. When I got you inside and took the socks off you your feet had gone blue. You were *crying.*'

I was upset, I said. It didn't sound like me talking.

'Do you know what you were saying?' He had made up some coffee, a special treat, and although it was instant it was better than nothing, and he had brought it to me in my bed. I was sitting there as listless as a doll. 'Do you know what you were saying?'

What was I saying?

'You kept saying, over and over, "Do you think the snow is haunted?" What kind of a thing is that to think? That's just going to get you depressed. Isn't it, now? *Do you think the snow is haunted!* You shouldn't be thinking like that.'

All those people down there. All buried underneath it.

'You see? You're doing it again. Stop. Just hold up, there. Stop thinking that way, Tara.'

I sipped my coffee, and thought, but didn't say aloud, that their spirits had nowhere else to go, that their spirits must be weighed down by the weight of it, squashed and cold. I could picture a woman, a young woman, in a room; and the snow had forced its way in through every window and through the door and had squeezed up, cold and deadly, through the cracks in the floorboards, until the whole room had been filled with it, and the woman crammed close about with whiteness so close it became blackness. How could the snow be anything other than haunted? Of course it is haunted, all of it, all around us.

'You've got to think of it positively, Tara. Think of it as a new start. A blank page. Think that God has given us a new start.'

'He didn't,' I said, the sobs starting again, 'give Minnie a new start.'

'Minnie? Is this about your daughter? You can't *think* like that, Tara. You can't! You've got to look forward.'

Easy for you to say.

'And anyway,' he said, bouncing anxiously around the room in his imaginary high-sprung heels, 'anyway, you don't know she's gone. You don't know it, do you? She might have got out. A lot of people got out. Maybe she did.'

Crow repeated this line several times over the course of that day, I suppose because he could see it reviving me, almost against my will. It was even, in a sense, sweet of him; because he hated lying, or told himself he did, and yet he was saying this to me – a lie, of course – in order to try and rouse me, as if my spirits were more important than his truth-and-honour.

In the end this was the lever with which I pushed and brought some sort of normality back to my life. Over that day I tried repeating that as a mantra, and told myself that things weren't so bad, that maybe she had got out. It was possible, after all. It was not impossible, at any rate. And by the day after that I was able to go back to the committee, and go back to work. [Blank] expressed her sympathy for me, that I had had flu (for so I told them), and as we walked back from work that afternoon she became solicitous, urging me to 'take better care of myself' and other similar phrases. 'You can't be too careful in this sort of weather,' she told me. 'Make sure you're eating enough.'

Here are a couple of moments I remember from my daughter when she was young. These have nothing to do with [Blank] and his terrorism, and his threats to the state, and the detonations, and of course I know that you're only interested in [Blank] and you're not interested in my daughter. But she matters to me. I'll limit my maternal reminiscences to two. Bear with me.

One is very brief. When Minnie was tiny, less than a year, I used to put her to bed at seven. She would, often, not go to sleep: either because she had colic, or sometimes just because she was a restless soul. But I would try and keep her to the schedule, and then I would bite my nails, because at that stage I was living in a very small flat with my parents and my sister, and Minnie's cries would disrupt the evening meal, the evening TV rituals. I would sit there wishing her asleep, and quiet, and getting myself more and more stressed and upset. But you can't force a baby to sleep. She sleeps, or she doesn't. If she didn't go to sleep straight away, she would cry; but sometimes this crying would be a gradually diminishing sobbing sound that would lead eventually to sleepy silence, and sometimes it would be an increasingly frantic stabbing series of howls that would go on and on, worse and worse, as she became more and more hysteric. 'Leave her,' my dad would say. 'She'll tire herself out crying, eventually.' And then, later, '*Surely* she'll tire herself crying, won't she?' But it is so exhausting, the pressure of hearing your child cry, it's like metallic scratching inside your skull. It is very hard to bear. I remember one night she was crying in this fashion, the noise growing and growing. Finally I went through to the other room, and in the light from the hallway I could see her in the cot. She had sat up in the cot, and didn't know how to lie down again, and in her exhaustion and desperation for rest and her frustration she had cried more and more vocally. As she saw me come into the room she started flapping her arms up and down, like a chicken trying to fly, and calling out 'mama-mama-mama' with a piercing, bell-like intensity. I don't believe that I can convey to you, with sufficient force, the full, tart, marvellous, overwhelming mixture of love and hilarity that swept through me at that moment. I felt again the pungent epiphany of how much I loved my child, of how beautiful and funny and endearing she was even in the midst of her crying and her distress. I swept her up in my arms and hugged her as she sobbed, and kissed her as she settled, and walked round with her in the darkened room until she fell asleep against my shoulder. There was a brilliant-lit buoyancy in my heart. I was happy. I really don't believe that I can properly convey to you, given the complete breach that has been effected between that time and this, how happy I felt in that moment.

If I'm right (and memory plays tricks, so I may not be) my father died less than a month after that. He had always suffered from asthma, and wasn't as regular about taking his medication as he should have been. But that's another thing. Let's not talk about that.

Here is my second remembrance. Minnie was nine, or ten; a thoughtful, soulful little girl. One day she came back from school and came up to the bathroom. It was a summer afternoon, and I was having a bath. I seem to remember having a great number of baths during that time of my life. I was between jobs, I think, and so home all day, and so I took a lot of baths. I was smoking a cigarette in the bath, looking up where the sunlight oranged the pebble-patterned glass of the bathroom window. I was admiring the way steam from the hot bathwater interwove itself with smoke from my cigarette until I couldn't tell which was steam and which smoke.

Minnie hovered at the doorway. 'Hi, mum,' she said, but she was reticent about coming into the bathroom.

'Hi, love,' I said. 'How was school? OK?'

'School was OK.'

'Good. How was Miss Cicero?' A favourite teacher of Minnie's, or, at least, a teacher about whom she was often talking at that time. You know the way kids get favourites, how important their favourites are to them, at that age.

'Miss Cicero is off sick,' said Minnie. 'Miss Cicero weren't in today.'

I didn't say *wasn't in today* in a motherly-condescending tone, as I might have done – as I would have done another time. The nicotine and the warm lassitude of the bath had temporarily robbed me of the urge to correct her.

'What's she got, a cold?' I said. 'Flu?'

'Maybe she's got cancer from smoking,' said Minnie, coming a little further into the bathroom to make her disapproval plainer. 'Maybe that's why she didn't come to school today.'

'I've only had two cigarettes today,' I lied, squashing the fag to death against the metal ashtray I had balanced on the side of the bath.

'Cigarettes give you cancer and you die,' said Minnie, matter-of-factly, dragging her feet through the strands of the carpet on the hall-floor just outside the bathroom door.

'They're stupid, and smelly.' But she said this with a sort of desultory tone, as if she didn't really want to press the point. She had certainly made her position very clear on the topic of my smoking over many months.

'What did you learn today?' I asked, to forestall further anti-tobacco preaching.

'We did drawing with Miss Harth, and PE with Mr Doody, and we did God with Mr Felber.'

'God?'

Her voice faded slightly, and then grew clearer slightly, as she shuffled her way around the tiny hall outside the bathroom. 'He said that Christians call God Jesus, but I knew that anyway, 'cause we have assembly. And he said that some people call God Zen, and that some people call God La-la.'

'La-la?' I said. 'He said that?'

'Like the Teletubby,' said Minnie. 'Isn't it funny?'

'You sure you've got that right, darling?'

'That's how Arabs call God,' she said, firmly. 'And Indians. I said I was Indian and *I* didn't call God La-la. No,' she said, correcting herself without any change in her tone of voice, 'I said I was half-Indian, but he said it didn't matter where you were from, that God can see everything and that he'll help with everything we do.'

'Some people,' I said, trying to be diplomatic, 'think so.'

But she wasn't asking my opinion, she was telling me about her day, and so she continued with her narrative. 'You got to pray to God, and call him the right things like big and strong and so on, and then he'll help you with everything. So I asked God to make Picture number one in the charts, and to make you stop smoking, or stop getting cancer, and for Melissa Salzman to get fat, because everybody hates her.'

The band-name I am remembering as *Picture* may have been something else, something that sounds like that word or that has, in some other way, an association with it in my mind (was it *Pin-up*, I wonder?): the latest pop sensation, four toothsome young boys who could dance in unison and sing in a melodious, high-pitched tone. Minnie had images of them on her wall, half a dozen glossy posters. She had her favourite band-member and her favourite songs.

'That's not very nice,' I said, meaning it wasn't nice to pray to God to make Melissa Salzman fat.

Minnie was quiet for a time. 'Everybody hates her,' she said, after a while.

I got out of the bath, with the usual sound-effects of water pouring and trickling, and the unsteady steps onto the bathmat reaching for the towel. 'I don't think,' I said to Minnie as I wrapped myself by the sink, 'that you should pray for things like that. I don't think that's what praying is about. Did Mr Felber tell you to do that?'

'Oh no, Mum,' said Minnie, with disdain in her voice. 'He said that people sometimes say God is an old white man with a big white beard, but he said that God doesn't look like that at all. He's not an old white man, and he doesn't have a white beard.' Later on, as I cooked fish-fingers for our joint tea, she told me more about her theory of God. 'I think he's all wrapped about the Earth, cause he's got to protect the whole world. He's all around us, Mr Felber says. It's kind of like the air, I think, covering the whole world. But some places in the world are covered by his, you know, face and things, and that's better; and some places are covered by his toes and knees and things, and that's not so good. So some people on the Earth are happy and rich, and some are sad and poor. That's why.'

This seemed to me a very good theology, or, at least, as good as any I had heard. Years later, when Minnie converted to Islam and then married an Islamic boy only a year older than herself, I sometimes baited her with this memory. I regret that now. I regret that because it taints the memory in my head. I like to think of the yellow-bodied alien-shaped creature, the Teletubby, curling itself around the world, cushioning and protecting us all with its yellow fur. The Teletubbies were, you see, these children's-TV creatures, multicoloured baby-things living in a pure green landscape with a pure blue sky, and one of them was called La-la, possibly as an oblique religious critique, but, then again, possibly not. It's a sweet memory in my mind. But later, when Minnie became more wilful, and more single-minded, I polluted that earlier memory. I did it myself. I railed at her. 'You're abandoning yourself to this Allah,' I said. 'You used to call Him La-la, you know.' She denied that she had ever done so, and seemed genuinely to have no memory of it; but then a child's memory works differently from an adult's. And she was deeply wounded that I would accuse her of such a thing. 'La-la, La-la,' I would taunt her, in a sing-song voice. 'So let us now praise your *fantasy* creature' in a sonorous voice like a priest. 'Like a [*expletive deleted*] space alien, up there in heaven, with Father Christmas and Rudolf the [*expletive deleted*] reindeer. Oh!' I might say, as she wrapped her head up before going out, 'Are you off to the temple to worship your La-la? Your big furry yellow god?' For all the time we lived together after her conversion to Islam, which was the best part of a year, I baited her in this fashion. La-la. It upset her, genuinely, I think. Looking back on it now, I'm sorry for that. But I can't say sorry to her about it, of course. That's the difficulty, right there, that I can't say sorry. Or that once I could have said sorry, but now I can no longer say sorry, the chance has gone. I look back and I am sorry, and I'm also faintly amazed at how juvenile I was. She was fifteen, and I was thirty-one, thirty-two, and yet we quarrelled and bickered on the same teen-age level. I fought with her in the most juvenile ways. My regretting it won't change it, of course.

Seven

Eventually the snowfall stopped altogether, and, quite quickly, the nature of the snow underfoot changed. Soon it became easy to walk on naked snow. Where, before, the unsettled snow had been like quicksand, sinking you hip-deep, or in some cases dragging you wholly down, the settled snow was more compact. It also developed a kind of frozen crust, a granulated icy carpet caused, as I understand it, by the actions of warm daytime sun and cold nights softening and then refreezing that surface layer. Snowshoes became unnecessary. Hovercraft were still used, but it became possible to run wheeled trucks and cars out on the surface of the snow. It became possible to expand the city beyond the supported base that had formed the core of Liberty; buildings could be placed directly on the ice, provided they weren't too tall or heavy.

Over the period of a year various physical restrictions faded away. Other ones came to fill their place. Food was a worry.

Other things happened. [Blank]'s husband stood for the position of Senator, and lost, despite his expensive campaign – the printed cards, such as the one he had given me, the posters, the advertisements on the radio, all that. The incumbent, [Blank], won again, though with a reduced majority. Something like eleven thousand votes for him, eight thousand for [Blank], and a few thousand for [Blank], the third candidate. The IP elections approached, and Crow decided not to stand. Or his backers decided he shouldn't stand. Radio was becoming a bigger thing; at first only military receivers had been salvaged from the Snow, but with every forage more things were coming up, and soon there were hundreds of radios, and then thousands. Soon most people knew somebody who had a radio; and with that a radio station was set up. Crow went on the air to talk about politics. 'People have asked me,' he said, 'to run for IP. Good people, friends of mine, friends of Liberty, who think I can do a good job. But I've decided not to run against Interim President [Blank]. I've decided that this is not a time to rock the boat. Next election is soon enough for me.'

Another thing Crow did: he started the talk of political

parties. 'We need more of the trappings of traditional democracy,' he said, on air. 'We need parties to which people can belong, that express their differing political affiliation.' To begin with the idea was for a Democratic and a Republican party, like the old days. But there were so few Democrats. Most of the population were military, or had connections to the military, and so most of the population were Republicans. The Republican party was established, and [Blank] declared himself for it, which meant the sitting president put his weight behind the party. Then somebody decided to set up Free Republicans, a more libertarian sort of patriotic party. But the policy differences were tiny, really. Tiny.

I can't tell you how boring I found all this. It bored me then, and it bores me now to recall it. It seems like something of a crazy interlude, except that for that space of time – a year, was it? – it filled everybody's lives. Politics. Hustings, street-corner meetings, radio debates, the paraphernalia. Then the attacks started, and politics vanished like breath into the wind. Suddenly voting was the last thing on our minds. We were all in the army, in one way or another. I mean that some of us were in uniform and others not, but we were all under attack. But I don't need to tell you about the attacks. You're not interested in them, so much as you want to know about [Blank].

We all remember the attacks, of course.

It's a strange feature of the affair we had, [Blank] and I, but I could talk to him endlessly about books. After we'd made love, on our trysts, we would sometimes discuss books for ages, even though he had 'never been much of reader', as he put it. I told him it was daft, because he'd been a writer before the Snow. How could a writer not read many books? He said he'd written for the TV mostly, and hadn't read books. But he'd read some, and we could talk and talk about it.

Now, [Blank], on the other hand, was another matter: she was *terribly* literate, and *terribly* cultured. She had come

from a wealthy Hamptons or Cherry County set or something like that, or so she said. Money. She'd been skiing in
the Rockies when the snow started, and a group of them had
holed up in a tent, and each day had dug themselves out and
pulled the tent behind them and sat in it again until the
snow covered it, until eventually they emerged on the top
and found their way to an army base. That was her story.
But the point is that no matter how much she boasted her
reading, I couldn't help myself dumbing down with her. I
think she reminded me, with her long black hair and her
vanity, of some of the girls I'd known at school, and so
automatically I slid back into the ways of being to which I'd
become habituated with them. I became, as the phrase goes,
as a child again. It was almost ironic: with her I could have
talked about the books I loved, but I felt I had to hide my
passion or she would mock and degrade it; with him,
though, I talked and talked and he smiled and hugged me
even though he knew nothing at all about what I was saying.

I was taking coffee one morning with her one time – a
watery, third-rinse dregsy sort of coffee, and a poor imitation of that first cup I had taken at her apartment, it is
true, but the important thing was the social occasion itself, I
suppose. She smiled her scimitar smile, and pushed her
extraordinary hair over her shoulder with a gentle movement of her hand. 'Do you know what?' I said, my voice
registering crassly even on my own ear. 'Sometimes this life
reminds me of that movie. You know the movie? It was
about a plane that crashed in the mountains, I forget where.
And the survivors lived in the wreckage, in the snow, for
months and months, just living in this metal shell and
eventually eating the dead bodies. That's how it feels like,
living in this place.'

This was an inappropriate conversational gambit. The
food situation was getting worse week by week, with food-
miners digging out further and further to find necessary
supplies. But, still, to suggest cannibalism. This was beneath
the dignity of the occasion. Other people were there. There

was Mrs [Blank], another senior wife. She died last month, I remember hearing about it, but she was vigorous enough on that occasion. I can't remember the other person's name; perhaps it was [Blank]. But, for sure, all of them looked a chilly look at me, and [Blank] laughed awkwardly and played with her long black hair, as if saying *indulge my friend, she is not of our class.*

As the snow settled beneath us it sometimes sent tremors through the city. Window panes rattled in their frames. Snow was shaken like flour from cornices. Cups chattered to one another on table-tops. These miniature earthquakes would happen in batches. For two weeks they seemed to come every half hour, then for months they wouldn't happen at all. Intermittent. They fed my intermittent paranoia that the snow was haunted; that these miniature quakes were the unquiet souls of the crushed and dead. The radio assured us that we should expect such trembles as the snow settled, even years after the cessation of snowfall, but this didn't calm my subconscious.

There's a long pole, perhaps a communication antenna, ten metres tall, or more that I can see when I get up from my writing and walk in the yard. Its shadow is crisply laid over the snow by the morning sun. That shadow is precisely edged at the base, but grows marginally fuzzier further along its length until it becomes a vague wedge at the end. As if the shadow is greystone at the base, and raincloud at the top.

For a long time I floated along, cloud-like, through life. My husband was a tremendous help. Isn't that a funny thing? We were no longer husband and wife, yet he helped me with a persistent and rather touching tenderness. He used his position to obtain antidepressant drugs, and I took them. This started about a month after my vision of the snow as haunted, my vision of Minnie under the weight of snow. For a month, or so, I carried on, somehow. But each day was a struggle. Every single day. And – you know? – as I write that it strikes the wrong note, it really does. It implies too much effort to the process of being depressed; it gives the impression that depression is a strenuous, laborious business, fighting against the darkness, fighting to go on. But depression is not like that. The essence of that acute sort of melancholy is a lassitudinous disinclination to fight anything. It's a grey arena, and you grapple with the problems of the day without any great belief in the value of your struggle, without hating your enemy, without craving victory. Sometimes it strikes you how strange it is, in a distant sort of way, that you are undertaking that struggle at all. You get out of bed, and it feels like you've climbed Everest. The sheets are splotched with wetness. Perhaps you were crying.

Everest is below us now, of course.

This modern world—

So [Blank] fetched me some antidepressants from military-medical supplies. This was good of him, because I had been [*expletive deleted*] another man for several months. He wasn't to know this, of course. But the secretive meetings with [Blank], the illicit connection with him, the sex, these meetings represented the few occasions when I felt the glimmer of something. Sometimes [Blank] would pull out of me and drop his tiny fall of white seed onto the mattress, or the floor. Sometimes he would come inside me, and I would chide him, remind him of the dangers we ran, but I wouldn't do this very forcefully. I think I was telling myself, or not even telling myself but somehow registering down in my subconscious that I could make another baby, and that this would make some small amends for the loss of Minnie.

We met, usually in [Blank]'s tiny apartment, and usually in the afternoons. We began super-cautious, anxious not to give ourselves away. As our affair continued, and weeks became months, we probably became more careless. We had a great deal of sex. On a regular basis we experienced that sensation of making ourselves hot, of even working up a sweat, and then lying side by side panting and feeling the sweat freeze on our skin. That is a strange sensation.

You'll tell me you're not interested in our erotic grapplings, but in the terrorist plotting and scheming that [Blank] shared with me. I don't believe you. I bet you're fascinated with our love life. I just bet you are. Of course you are. But I shan't press the point. For a time I was caught up in it all, excited at the prospect, fidgety with anticipation when [Blank] and I met up. [*Text deleted*]. But after a while the sex lost its savour. After I began taking the anti-depressants my libido seemed to snag inside me somewhere, so that I couldn't become aroused beyond a certain point. I don't know why it should've happened that way. I stopped coming. Despite [Blank]'s best efforts, his increasingly red-faced struggles with me, I could not come. And then the whole sex connection seemed to recede from me, so that I felt as if I were observing the liaison third-hand, and the two semi-clad bodies wrestling like sea snakes became a kind of performance art, a disinterested athleticism, something in which I was not involved.

Soon after that [Blank] and I stopped sleeping with one another. For a year, a little more, we were not lovers. That was it. We still met up, of course, from time to time; we talked, and bumped into one another in the streets – Liberty was a small place. And he would still press upon me, in discreet confabs, his conspiracy theories. But until the eve of the attacks these talks had a slightly conventionalised, heat-less feel to them.

When we were still lovers, [Blank] would proselytise. He'd be like an old-world preacher, eager and driven. 'You see, it's a *conspiracy*,' he'd tell me. 'The government is behind the whole disaster.'

Sometimes I would pooh-pooh him. 'I don't believe that,' I would say. 'I've always believed history is cock-up, not conspiracy.'

And he would shake his head slowly, with a tenderly

patronising expression on his face. 'You think those are mutually exclusive? Of course history proceeds by foul-ups. That's why so much conspiracy is *necessary* to governments. You think the USA wanted to drown the world in snow? Of course not – it *was* a foul-up, of course it was. But now they're *hiding* their part in that foul-up from the people. They're hanging on to power. This memo, this document by the scientist called G S Seidensticker . . .'

And on he would go. Sometimes I would believe him, just to go along with him. Weird stuff had happened; why not weird theories to explain the weird stuff? What did it really matter? Later, of course, I discovered it did indeed matter, but that was later.

At the time I was less interested in this alleged government cover-up and more interested in the idea that the southern hemisphere was free of snow. It was a bolt-hole. It was the fantasy of escape. I gabbled and gabbled on and on about it. 'Let's get away,' I would say, and the fog of depression would lift for a moment as I fantasised. 'Let's steal a truck and drive over the ice – to Australia.'

'Drive around the world,' [Blank] would say, shivering and drawing his clothes around his body again. 'Sure, that's a doable idea. Drive for three months, maybe. But the fuel? And eat – what? And get across crevasses, ice-cliffs – how?'

But I didn't want to get bogged down in the practicalities of it. I wasn't interested in the practicalities of it, I just wanted the dream. Hot sun, yellow beach, the sound of the sea. [Blank] was always bringing the real world back in.

'We could steal a plane,' I would say.

'A plane to fly around the whole world? And refuel it – where?'

'Don't be a downer,' I'd plead. 'Think of it! Think of starting a life on firm ground, not on the ice. In the sunshine. Think of that!'

'You got to think practically,' he would grumble. 'The government doesn't want its citizens leaving en masse, now, does it?'

'Always the government,' I would say.

'Sure,' he'd reply. 'Make fun. Go on. But it does all come down to the government. We change the government, and it all becomes possible. We take back the government – they've been lying to us, you see? Keeping us in the dark. If we *overthrow* them . . .'

Does that get your attention? Yes, he did talk of over-throwing the government. He said that government should be by the people for the people and of the people, all that declaration-of-independence-stuff; and he really believed it. To me he sold it as a means to an end – with the govern-ment gone we could work out a concerted plan to move the whole populations south, devote all our resources to the trek, wagon trains like the Mormons, and talk like that. But I don't think that was truly his motivation. I think it became a kind of obsession for him, an end in itself. I think he felt that if he could overthrow the government he would die happy. It was the purest revolutionary fervour.

During the time of our affair he did not talk about terrorist stuff. That came later, when we were no longer lovers. A year later. I was on the antidepressants, and I was no longer getting a buzz from the illicit connection of it, the physical thrill, so I called it off.

'Now—' he used to say. 'Your husband. You should talk to him about it. He's going to be IP one day, that's the rumour.'

'You reckon?'

'That's the rumour. But if we – if you – could talk to him . . .'

'Talk?'

'You know, persuade him.'

'Isn't he the enemy, as far as you're concerned?'

'But if!' in a hurried voice. 'But if he could be *turned*. Different. And if he could be *placed*, you know? If he could be shown the memo, the Seidensticker memo, shown that we know *everything* – threatened with public exposure, maybe, then he could be manoeuvred on *our* side. If you could talk to him, if *you* could persuade him! Imagine the advantage, if the IP himself was on our side!' His eyes were wide, glistening, his breath short.

We had that conversation twice, I remember. The first time it didn't really strike me as out of the ordinary; it seemed just the sort of thing that [Blank] was given to saying. That first time I replied: 'You mean you've got this Seidensticker memo that you keep talking about?'

'Yeah,' he said, excited. 'Yeah, I've seen it. It'll blow the whole government out of the water, really.'

'What does it say?'

'You can read it,' he told me, hopping from the bed, pacing the tiny room, getting back on the bed. 'I'll bring it. But it proves that the US government was to blame for the Snow, and that the NUSA government is covering it up. Proves it!'

'Wow,' I said, drawn in almost despite myself. 'That's amazing. How are they to blame? What did they do? Was it secret nuclear testing?'

'That whole nuclear testing thing, that attempt to blame the Russians, that's way off the mark,' said [Blank] earnestly. 'I'll show you the memo.'

He didn't bring the memo the next time I saw him, and that knocked my faith rather. I believed, then, that it was all a fantasy spun out of [Blank]'s brain. 'I couldn't get the memo,' he said. 'I'm not alone in this, there are plenty of people involved. I can't just pick up the memo and walk away with it.'

'Copy it,' I suggested. 'In case it gets lost . . . you know?'

'Oh it's easier said than done, *copy it*. What, get access to an army photocopier without clearing the documents first? Besides a copy's no good to us. If we present a copy then *they*'ll say that we forged it. We need the original.'

'So what's in this original then?'

'I told you. It lays the blame for the whole disaster, for the whole Snow, fair and square at the feet of the govern-ment . . .'

'Exactly,' I said, sternly, 'how?'

'What?'

'*How* did the government bring disaster upon the world?'

'Look,' he said, grasping my shoulders with his hands, 'the details don't matter. It's the *blame* that matters. Don't you see?'

'I think you're making this whole thing up,' I said.

The next time we met he was on about my husband the whole time. 'Did you speak to him about it? Did you mention it to him? I'm thinking if we set up a time, maybe I could show him the memo . . .'

'I feel,' I said, sourly, 'like I'm living out a cheap Robert Ludlum thriller called *The Seidensticker Memo*.'

'Robert who?' he replied.

Then I lost my temper. 'You're not interested in me,' I bawled. 'You're using me as a means to get to my [*expletive deleted*] husband, aren't you? You've been using me the whole time to get to him. That's what it's all been about.'

[Blank] turned gruff at this. 'That's insane talk,' he said. 'Don't be so stupid Tira. You think I could fake this? Fake what we got together?'

'Fake this?' I said. 'Fake bad sex with an ugly man, sure, that would be hard to fake.'

'Now,' said [Blank], with a warning inflection.

'I don't ever want to see you again,' I told him. 'I'm sorry I ever set eyes on your ugly mug.'

'Mug?' he repeated, with a hurt-baffled expression on his face. 'What do you mean, mug?'

'Just [*expletive deleted*] off,' I told him, 'and leave me alone.'

'What mug?'

'[*expletive deleted*] you.'

'Will you just stop feeling so *sorry* for yourself,' he barked at me. 'Hey, you know what? – there are *more important* things to worry about than your hurt feelings.'

We got into a row. We yelled at one another. He grabbed my hair at one point, like a toddler in a tantrum, though he didn't actually hit me. Finally, though, we seemed to end up in one another's arms on his bed, with me sobbing and sobbing and saying 'Minnie' into the cold air.

But after that I called it off. It felt wrong, doing the sex thing. I wasn't enjoying it. His fanaticism had turned from being an amusing character-trait to being an alarming obsession, acted-out in the world. The next time he and I met for one of our assignations I sat him down and told him that I didn't want to have sex with him. He took it pretty calmly. He said, 'We can still meet, though, yeah? Friends, yeah?' I said yes.

I should have asked him – you want me to tell *you* – what he meant by *I'm not alone in this, there are plenty of people involved*. You want names, numbers involved, all that. But I didn't want to talk about it any more. I think I was more hurt than I let on. I think it upset me that [Blank] had been interested in my husband all along, and not in me. There's naïve, I guess.

Certainly my husband was an increasingly influential figure. I would often come home to find the front room filled with senior, famous military personnel, or even famous civilians: [Blank], for instance. [Blank], or [Blank]. You remember him? [Blank] was sometimes there. And Mayor, Senator I should say, [Blank].

I was on the outskirts of it, but I would come and go, pass into the meeting and pass through the other side, and it gave me this definite sense of things coming together. Of stuff happening. The depression had removed me from that world. And I was numb to the various little kindnesses my husband arranged for me. Getting me the medication was no small achievement, for instance. I didn't mind the medication. Tiny little blue sector-plates. They didn't make me feel happy or girly, but they made the depression shrink away. Let me put it this way: before the drugs I Didn't Care, that's the nature of depression; but in some deeper sense I *cared* that I Didn't Care, it *bothered* me that I Didn't Care. That's where the emotional pain of depression comes from. But after the medication I no longer cared that I Didn't Care. I lived easier with myself. I could focus on the meaningless tasks I was doing to fill the day.

A month would go past in which I would hardly see Crow. Then we'd spend three evenings together in sequence. One evening we ate a meal together, with nobody but [Blank] in attendance – he was a jolly sort, one of Crow's junior staff. He was the sort of man who has made a career out of being inoffensively jolly. He gossiped, too. My husband was too serious, too straitlaced, to gossip; but this new guy chatted away. Some of the people he gossiped about were unknown to me, but on one occasion his gossip really stuck home.

'And [Blank],' he said, speaking to Crow rather than me. 'Do you know her?'

'I know her,' I said. 'I used to be on a committee with her. We have coffee sometimes.'

The junior guy looked at me, looked back to Crow. 'Married to General [Blank], of course. Our would-be Senator.' He made a scoffing noise; Crow only smiled, weakly.

We were eating a sort of semolina, set in slabs and drizzled with tomato sauce. There was no wine. I remember that meal very clearly.

'What about her?' I said.

'Well,' said the junior guy, with a feline expression. 'She's been seen.'

'Seen?'

'Keeping company with, my mother used to call it,' he said. 'A man, but not her husband. An official.' He sucked in breath, disapproving. 'There you go.'

The conversation moved on to other things. But I knew, without needing further information, that the man with whom beautiful [Blank], with her beautiful long black hair and her politically ambitious little husband – that the man with whom she was now sleeping was [Blank]. He had tried

me, to get at Crow, and had failed. So now he had, somehow, seduced the beautiful [Blank], and was trying to get to
her husband.

The thought infuriated me. I suppose it should have
saddened me, or piqued my jealousy, or, perhaps, left me
indifferent, but it did not do these things. It infuriated me.
When I next saw [Blank] I yelled at him, right out there in
the open air, shouted at him across the street. He hushed me
and pulled my arm and tried to get me to be quiet. But that
evening when I first heard, with Crow and his junior, I just
fumed. I sat silently and glared at the food on my plate.

Later, after [Blank] had saluted primly and gone, and I
scraped the last crumbs of food into the re-use bag and
wiped the plate clean, Crow asked me to sit down. So we
sat down on the couch together. 'Are you feeling OK?' he
asked, like the line on the record. 'Are you feeling OK?'

'Sure,' I lied.

'Tira, I don't want to pry, you know? How is it going,
with the pills?'

'The antidepressants,' I said. 'Fine.'

'They make you feel better?'

'Feel better, sure.'

He looked at me intently for a while. He smiled. 'You
look great,' he said. 'That's a great tan you've got. You look
so much healthier.'

'You know,' I said. 'We're not stinted for sunshine up
here.'

'I'm glad the pills are helping,' he said. 'You deserve more
than being depressed you know.'

I didn't know what to say to that.

'Anyway,' he said. 'Goodnight.'

'Goodnight.'

He didn't move. 'I thought,' he said, after a little while,
'that maybe [Blank] upset you this evening. He's an old
woman, in some ways. He loves to gossip.'

'He loves to gossip,' I confirmed.

'I don't much like gossip myself,' said Crow. 'I try to

discourage it. But a commanding officer needs to cut his men a little slack sometimes. Anyway, I'm glad the pills are, you know, helping.'

Crow leant a little closer. 'Goodnight,' he said. He laid his lips against my cheek in a dry, almost ticklish kiss. But he didn't withdraw his mouth; he lay his lips against my tanned, dark cheek. I thought, what's this? But I was also thinking that *that's a great tan you've got* was probably Crow's private self-talk for *you're pretty but I mustn't forget you're really black*, and this combined with my annoyance at the gossip about [Blank]'s new lover to fuel a fierceness in my heart. I sat without a single tremor, without even breathing, my body a perfectly motionless shell wrapped around a thundering heart. Then he brought his lips across my face until they met my lips, and our two mouths became a single warm circle. My heart juddered. It was exciting, the buzz you get when you're a teenager and making out, that slightly taboo thrill. It was nice, actually. It lasted as long as it lasted.

Then Crow leant gently back, away from me, and our one joint-mouth became two mouths, four lips, and there was a pause.

'Tira,' he said. '*You* know [Blank]?'

'[Blank],' I repeated. It felt strange saying the name of my ex-lover to my husband. My head was experiencing interesting swirly effects on the inside. 'Sure.'

'He chaired the mining committee you used to sit on? Before you sat on the supply committee?'

'Mining committee,' I said.

'I don't want to – look. I've heard, things about him.'

'Heard things?' I said, starting to come out from the spell of the kiss. 'Gossip, you mean?'

He smiled at this. 'Touché,' he said, pronouncing the word without the accented final 'e', as if it were *tush*. 'Maybe it is gossip, and maybe I oughtn't pay it any heed. But he may be a dangerous type. That's all I'm saying.'

'Dangerous,' I said.

'I'm only saying that you should, maybe, steer clear, you know?'

'Right,' I said. 'I don't see him too often. Just bumping into him from time to time.' This was strictly true, but it felt to my heart like a lie, and so I couldn't help myself embroidering it. 'You know it's a small town? Sometimes we'll say hello on the street, that's all.' The truth, but sounding more and more like a lie. 'I guess we might have a coffee or something, but only really infrequently. Hardly at all.' I stopped.

'It's OK,' said Crow, after a pause. 'It's probably nothing. Like you say, I shouldn't pay attention to gossip.'

And he said goodnight, and he went through and lay on his little wooden bed and rolled himself tightly in a blanket and went to sleep. I took myself to the bigger bed and lay in it, and my heart was still keeping loud time in my chest. I thought to myself: why did that happen? The kiss? Where did that come from, after a year of living like brother and sister? I thought of *that's a great tan you've got*, and tried to imagine inside Crow's head. I believed that he was so much a creature of habit that, once the habit of celibate cohabitation had been established, it was easy for him to maintain it. But he kissed me. Had it been a momentary lapse? And then I thought of *I'm only saying that you should, maybe, steer clear*, and I wondered if maybe it was a jealousy thing, an alpha-male possession thing. I could take her to bed, but she's soiled goods, another man has had her. Could that chain of thought start up a kiss and then curtail it so abruptly? I found it hard to go to sleep.

Eight

So I'm trying to remember what's important to remember over that year, that eighteen-month period. I transferred from the mining committee; several shafts were sunk, braced with wire and concrete, down to the ground, and shafts spread across the frozen, bleached-out floor. Some videos were made. I never went down the shafts, but some videos were made – freaky things, really. They were, effectively, films of the life you remember, only yellowed and gloomy in white-walled tunnels. I understand that they cleared bodies away before shooting the videos, but the Pompeian evidences of death-interrupted lives were all around. To follow the miner, vicariously, video-linked, through these bizarre tunnels, dark all around except in the twin white ovals of illumination cast by the miner's head-light and the camera's bright bulb – to watch the TV footage of men trudging down nondescript shafts and turn a corner to see a shopfront, a house, and to realise that this strange urinous-coloured stubble underneath their feet had once been green grass, that this oddly short metal fence was actually the radiator grille of a car still almost wholly buried in the snow. It was spooky. I could hardly bear to watch the footage, although some people became obsessed with it – paid their dollars, sat in rooms with the screens on, time after time.

Reminded me of some of the scenes in *Titanic*. I don't need to tell you which scenes. You'll need to be my age to remember that film, of course. My age or older.

Food was the most pressing concern, general across the seven cities of NUSA, as it certainly was in the various unaffiliated encampments and communities scattered around the overland, over-UK and the overstates. And all across the world – a lot of East Russians had survived the snow, we heard; and odd communities scattered here and there. There were several cities of Azerbaijanis and Pakistanis, apparently, although most of the Arab and Indian nations were ill-prepared for the snow. Two Israeli cities, under military control (I am tempted to say, of course) as was NUSA. Most European nations had been able to undertake the effort to float cities up through the slowly accumulating snow, like superslow-motion bubbles, but the co-ordination and discipline required meant a military regime in most cases. Equatorial nations had survived very patchily if at all. There was little contact with Japan, although scratchy shortwave and satellite reconnaissance suggested that some cities had survived. This sort of information was not in the public domain. Either the military were covering something up, as [Blank] insisted, or else they couldn't quite shake their automatically secretive habits. I don't know. Then there was the question of Australia. Was it open land? Officially there was no comment, no comment, but the rumours grew, people focused on the chances of a normalised life in the southern hemispheres, and there was no official comment, and then – without preliminary – there was a front-page story in *Truth*. Few people could afford the paper, and it was posted on barracks walls for people to stop and read. So, out of the blue, there was an announcement: destabilising rumours, possibly of terrorist provenance, claiming that large amounts of the southern hemisphere was unaffected by snow. The IP, the Senate and the People of the Free World Coalition denounce this cruel rumour. There is no truth in it. Snow is general, over the whole globe.

Is there a quicker way to root a belief in people's hearts than for an official to deny it?

There was another front page, I remember, a week or two later, reaffirming the official explanation of the snow: Russian nuclear experimentation, unregulated, had got out of hand. We were living, the government said, in a form of nuclear winter provoked by this tragic accident. Scientists had long been theorising Snowball Earth, the occasional catastrophic ice-age events. We were caught up in one of these. This was in response, I suppose, to the general currency of rumours circulating throughout the cities. The Seidensticker memo, the same document that occupied such a large proportion of [Blank]'s paranoid fantasies, was whispered about in the food queues, in the streets, in the general rooms (they're out of fashion now, aren't they, general rooms – rooms where people simply sat, trying to share their general warmth. They used to be popular). Mostly the rumours assumed that the cause was correct, but the nation wrongly blamed – that, in other words, the Snow had been caused by some non-specific nuclear shenanigans, but that the culprit was the old USA. People grumbled about this, but I met few people – in fact *no* people – who became as worked up about it as [Blank] still did. It seemed, perhaps, a pointless thing to complain about it. Complain about the weather: as idiotic as a sailor complaining about the sea, as an old person complaining that they are old, as a young person moaning that they are young – a citizen complaining about city, government, world. Why expend the energy? You needed your energy for other things. You needed it to keep warm. Food was more expensive and wages were down, so people had less to eat. Fat people were rare. Everybody swathed and swathed themselves with as much clothing as they could. Anything warm would attract an audience – a truck idling in the street for five minutes would draw half a dozen people to its throbbing bonnet, like flies on jam. A laundrette down the road from me earned more money selling fifty-cent tickets to loiter in the room with the machines than it did in actually cleaning dirty laundry. The steam clouding out from the machines as they opened, the hot wet cloth, the warmth generated by the motors as they strained to spin the big drums; people paid to immerse themselves in this environment. A ticket bought you thirty minutes, I seem to remember, in the room with the machines and a dozen other people.

More food would have helped, but food was a great problem. The food-mines were having to stretch their tunnels further and further; a greater and greater number of mining missions was coming back empty-handed. And everybody knew that we needed a renewable source of food. Renewable. We needed crops and livestock and farms and market gardens and all this was as plain as the frost-pinched nose on my face. Plain as the nose on my face –

what a strange phrase, a strange hangover from previous times. Nothing was obvious about faces any more. You only saw an unswaddled face if it was warm, and that was only in the brief Arctic summers. Otherwise noses were never plainly there, they were muffled up. Don't misunderstand me: I had a better time than most, because my husband was a senior military man. We had heating in our apartment, we had more food than average. But over the year I remember thinking how hidden everybody was. The cold made them so. Men and woman and children all wore all-over woollen-plastic burkas, with only the letter box eyeslot revealing their humanity. And often that slot was covered with sunglasses.

Renewable food. I sat, briefly, on a renewable food committee, before moving on to a supplies committee (which was not at all the same thing). But I knew the problems. Optimists would say: we have abundant sunlight, abundant water, we must be able to grow things. Seeds had been saved from before; some other natural resources were cold-stored as well. But what could we do with them? The greenhouses that spread in great luminous patches to the north and south of Liberty were expensive to build; the soil that was packed into them had been expensively dug out of the mines (hard to dig frozen soil) and carted up; the heating pipes that ran the length of them were expensive to maintain. And a city of ten thousand people cannot wholly be fed on a score of greenhouses. The fruit that was grown was extraordinarily expensive. Ordinary people never saw it.

But what could we do? Crops will not grow in snow. Science will save us, people sometimes said. They'll genetically engineer something that grows in the snow, and we'll plant the snowfields and make them green.

But we didn't do this. Perhaps it is just beyond our scientific ability. I don't know.

Our best bet, we were told in committee, was fish. Many breeds of fish don't mind cold water, provided only it could be kept from freezing solid. An array of fish eggs had been cold-stored, and could be cultivated. Senator [Blank] put a deal of publicity, and public money, into digging a seven-acre pond to the east of the city. This was lined with black plastic – enormously expensive – and with heating elements laid in a web pattern. Then meltwater was pumped in, and the whole thing left to settle, and then scientists bred up fish fry and released it into the water. It was wonderful; exciting. Everybody talked of it. The pond had guards assigned to it day and night to prevent *poaching*, as fishing was now called.

Ice formed on the surface, but we were told that this was alright, that the fish inside didn't mind. Then the news went all through the city that all the fish were dead. Some said the whole body of water had frozen solid, because the engine that was supposed to keep the heating elements working had broken down and nobody had noticed for twelve hours. Others said that the mix of the water had been wrong – not enough plankton, or fish-food, or something. *Truth* carried the story: Fish Disaster. It was enormously depressing. NewLA has a working fish pond, *Truth* reported, and New NY was working on one, but what use was that to us?

I remember playing cards often. There was a mania for that pastime. What else was there to do? Gin rummy, and bridge, mostly; people were too canny with their money to play big-stakes, to play poker, or anything. But every house had a pack of cards, and every slack half hour was filled with a quick hand or two. What other pastimes were there?

You don't want me remembering card-games. You want to know about [Blank]. So let me tell you. Though no longer lovers we continued meeting, irregularly, throughout that time. It was towards the end of it, shortly before the first attacks, that he tried to – what would the phrase be, *recruit* me.

'Tira,' he said. 'We're reaching a crisis now.'

'Oh yeah?'

'Crisis. Now the time comes. You got to decide whether

you want to be on the side of freedom or the side of the government.'

'This again?'

'No, seriously, Tira.' He was genuinely agitated. 'Seriously. I'm not kidding. They're behind such things – I can't even tell you what things.'

'They're behind the Snow itself, you told me.'

'[*expletive deleted*],' said [Blank]. It was unusual for him to swear. He was, despite himself, too much part of the puritanically-inflected American culture of which he was also such a critic. 'Worse than that – can you believe it?'

'What do you mean, worse than that?'

'Jesus – Tira, join us and I'll tell you. Treason against mankind! Humanity cries for vengeance.' He was saying all manner of things like that, in a strangely heated, jittery way.

'You're pretty agitated,' I said, trying to step a little away from him.

'Will you join us?' he said.

'Join what?'

'Justice,' he said, in a hurried, urgent, low tone. 'Take the battle to them – what they call terrorism, but we *got* to reclaim that word. That word. Imagine a world without terror? Can you imagine such blandness? Terror is our idiom, all of us. Terror is where we live. Christ, [*expletive deleted*], we don't live in the cosy leafy suburbs any more, Tira. There's nothing *comfortable* or *cosy* about our world now. Our environment is defined now by its terrible potential. Nature is the terrorist now. This propagandist, ideological bubble that the government is trying to blow around the cities, around the people in the cities – this *lie*, this lie that we can trot along with our lives more or less the same as before, the same pettinesses, the same mundane little stuff – we can't! Look around.' And he threw out his arm horizontally in front of himself, and turned, theatrically, through three-sixty, drawing a circle with the gesture as if taking in all the city and all the white fissured landscape of snow and ice behind it. 'It's not ordinary. It's not petty. It's terror, it's terror, and we need to *wake* people up to this.'

'Terrorism,' I said, stepped back again.

But my expression, or my tone of voice, only seemed to infuriate [Blank]. 'Jesus Christ my God,' he called, his head moving up and down in little jerky nods of outrage or exasperation. 'Don't you, *you*, Tira, don't you fall for the conventional *Be Ess*. Don't you – terrorist is just another word for *I haven't been taken in by the government prop-aganda*. Don't you know that?'

'What are you planning?' I asked. He was starting to scare me, if I'm honest with you.

'Think, Tira,' he said, advancing on me with short, deter-mined steps. 'Think. We're living in an army dictatorship. You wanna deny it? The Senate, the President, they're all army, air force. It's a dictatorship.'

'Which is to ignore all the fuss,' I said, my voice less certain, 'with political parties and election, all the vogue now for democratic—'

But he cut me off. He snapped: 'Cover-up, bread-circuses for the masses, distract them from the truth – the truth – that we are slaves. Slaves.'

This, unexpectedly, almost made me giggle. It was a false step. But his eyes were intense.

'You know the logic under which we live, Tira,' he said. 'It's *Mili*tary – Equality – Fraternity. You're a woman, so you're no fraternal brother, you ain't *equal* in their eyes, you're not part of the military machine, so you're nobody. Nobody. We have to strike – we have to remind the bubble-wrapped, sleepy-eyed people of this city of terror—'

His voice was now so loud that people were stopping and looking at him. Sometimes, especially in the early days, people would go cabin-crazy under the general pressure of ice and snow and whiteness, whiteness, so it wasn't unpre-cedented for men or women to stop in the streets and start yelling. But it's always a show. It's always a diversion from the day-by-day grind. It's the same visit-to-Bedlam experience that was so popular, in one form or another, before the Snow. Lunatic asylums used to make cash by charging tourists an entrance fee to goggle over the loonies. It's a basic human impulse. Then TV served it, in the days when we had TV. Nowadays we might feel a twinge of unease as we watch somebody – a human being, memories and hopes, lovers and friends, the nexus of innumerable complexities – shatter like dry snow into particles, shouting at the sky, yelling at a passing truck. We might feel unease, but we feel a stronger impulse to spectate. It would be inhuman not to watch.

But [Blank]'s madness was not the trampish sort, vague, and windy and entertaining. It was focused and political, and he didn't want to give himself away by yelling at all the passers-by so he bore down on me, only on me. I don't know why, to be honest, he was so eager to recruit me, why it mattered so much to him. But he conquered his urge to yell at me, he put his head down, and when he raised his face again a moment later he looked sane and balanced once more.

'Anyway,' he said, eyeing me carefully. 'Maybe we can agree to disagree. Agree,' he said, managing to sound vaguely sinister, 'to disagree.'

'What you going to do?' I asked. But it was a dumb question. I knew what he was going to do without him telling me.

But, abruptly, he looked around, and stepped away from me.

'See ya,' he said, backing away. He turned and started crunching through the snow towards the covered walkway that led to sixville and the make-n-mend stores.

'You slept with [Blank],' I called after him.

He stopped, half-turned, looked at me.

'Was it to get to her husband?' I asked, my voice clear in the cold air. 'Or was it for her own sake? She's a beautiful woman.'

He turned again and hurried away.

'She's a beautiful woman,' I yelled after him, into the cold air, as if it were a rebuke.

I didn't mention [Blank]'s threats to anybody. I wasn't having, at that stage, the sort of conversations with Crow that would have admitted such expressions at any rate; *do you know I met [Blank], – and he's going to start a career as an anti-government terrorist* – this wasn't how Crow and I talked any more. Maybe I hoped nothing would come of it. Maybe I didn't care. It's a hard thing for me to think myself back into my state of memory at that time. Had [Blank] really tried to recruit me to some terrorist cell? Or had it just been an amplified version of the sort of ranting he'd indulged in when we'd been together? Or was it nothing to do with the government, was it a transferred anger at my no longer sleeping with him? Military! Equality! Fraternity! That was cute, in a sophomore sort of way. But the first explosion happened two days later.

Shall I write about the explosions, the attacks, chaos raining from heaven, fire in the snow? You know about it, you remember it. I really don't need to write about it.

I'll write about it.

I'm so sick of this city. If I could only travel to another city – but it'd be the same, more or less the same. I could go out on the ice, but that's the very definition of same. Look up monotony in the dictionary and it should have a picture of the snow. But a picture of the snow would be – what? A blank page.

I went to work in the morning, one morning. I felt weary, chilled, underfed, like everybody else in the city. I moved through the multicoloured crowd – the red, the green, the blue, the black, the yellow, the luminous orange, all the various grimy, stained, dirty shapes made by winter coats, ski-jackets, wraps and scarves. So much whiteness, and humanity had put on butterfly colours. The crowd on the street looked as if it was composed of fat people, but underneath the padding and layers everybody was thin. It looked like a rainbow nation, but underneath nearly everybody was white. Whiteness had got into our bones.

The first explosion happened mid-morning. Boom! Then, boom-*crac*.

Bewilderment. Then people crying aloud.

A great bending sock of smoke, a hundred feet tall, reaching up to the empty sky.

People running, or standing and staring at this new apparition.

Enough.

What I mean is: is that enough description for you of that first attack? It's not the first two explosions that interest me, actually: it's the later ones. But the first one is the one that shocks, of course. I don't want to blank it out. But how can I do it justice? People of my generation, we've been conditioned by TV and cinema to think we know what explosions are: great outrushes of fire, streaking out in every direction, sparkler bunches of dune-grass, orange and yellow and white, like fireworks. Yeah? Energetic splashes of painterly colour. But this is not what I saw. The first explosion I didn't see anything at all. I heard a noise, that was all. It was the sound that a paraffin lamp makes when it ignites, only magnified a hundred fold; a sort of folding, heavy, flabby noise, a *wh-umf*. Then almost immediately after this I heard a deep-throated crackling sound, like aluminium foil being crunched and rustled, again magnified by a hundred times. Mixed into this was a distant tinkling noise, like fairy-bells – glass splintering and breaking into tiny needles and prisms and sector plates and falling through the air. A deadly snow, this glass: of the five people who died in the explosion, four died from glass injuries.

The committee building in which I worked was located on the north of the city, so we were quite close to the detonation. Of course we all hurried to the window, but we were ground-floor and could see nothing except the buildings around us. The bar of sky visible at the top of the window gave nothing away. Some of the people on the committee – [Blank] amongst them – ran upstairs to get a better view. I was one of three who rushed out through the main entrance and ran through the cold streets to the edge of town. From where we were standing it wasn't possible to see things clearly, but it was evident what had happened. A column of smoke was rising from the middle of the northern greenhouses, bent by the wind a little. Sunlight glittered remorselessly on the myriad little specks of brilliance that seemed to hang in the air, as if glitter had been applied liberally to the sky. Eventually, of course, all those dendrites of glass fell back to the ground.

For the rest of that day there was no official news. Rumour invented appalling stories – a malfunction, a build-up of flammable oxygen, a weapons test that had gone awry, a terrorist attack. This last notion gripped the gossip-imagination, and variants of it circulated throughout the afternoon: a plane had crashed nine-eleven-style into the greenhouse. A rival city, a Russian city, had launched a missile at Liberty, for reasons of its own. It was (some anonymous person whispered to me, as we sat in separate cubicles in the toilet) the *Australians* – this was why the government refused to admit that the southern hemisphere was uncovered by snow, it was because the southerners now considered themselves the world superpower and were acting haughty, belligerent, as they thought befitted their situation. 'We made overtures, I heard,' said the cubicle-woman, 'but they rebuffed.'

Nine people had been working in the glasshouses when the bomb was detonated. Of these, two had escaped injury, two more had suffered only light wounds, one had suffered severe burns and had later died, and four people had been killed by airborne glass. That last phrase, *airborne glass*, stuck in my mind for some reason. Glass born in the air, and fluttering down. A glittery glass-cloud drifting overhead and downpouring a billion droplets of glass shards upon us. Great drifts of ground glass, a hundred miles high. This is the way the world ends.

After that there was a deal of scurrying. Troops quick-marched up and down the streets in formation, holding their weapons before them. Police were suddenly evident everywhere. Helicopters circled in the air over the bombsite. Soldiers cleared crowds away, sweeping them off with the length of their rifles in both hands. People stood, looking stunned.

The radio had no news all day, which, since its only broadcasting station was officially sponsored, raised levels of worry. The six o'clock news show announced that 'terrorists' had planted a bomb in greenhouse four, two blocks of glass away from the perimeter of the town. It had been a bomb of such-and-such tonnage (I forget the figures), and had caused 'injury and death'. I don't know why they weren't more specific, because that phrase resulted in wild gossip-speculation about scores and hundreds of corpses. The next day the crowds huddling to read *Truth* as it was pasted up were the largest I've ever seen. Even here the gossip followed its natural course; people waiting at the back of the crowd heard the news from people who had just read it and were now leaving, even though they were only moments away from reading it themselves. It is one powerful impulse, this urge that grips us to tell friends and strangers gossip-news.

I didn't see the first explosion, and I didn't see the second one either. In fact, of all the scores of explosions I only saw one, and that was out on the ice. But I'll recall it now, so that there's something visual to add to the otherwise mere sound-effect of my memorial here. I was in the snow, away from the city, and I heard a scratching, screechy sort of noise. The noise was coming from above. Then I saw the brown threadworm track of a projectile coming down, and I followed it with my eyes until it crashed into the snow a couple of hundred yards from me. Maybe less. The impact made a rushing, almost a splashy sound, and at the impact point I could see an oval of spreading orange-white, roiling and flickering, like a brain, expanding briefly and then opaqueing, turning to brown-white smoke and hurling off in various directions a few skittering arms of flashy smoke with shrapnel at their tips. By the time these had arced through the air and hit the snow the whole thing was over, except for a curling belly of smoke rising into the air over the impact point, and threads of dark steam coming out of the crater.

That happened out in the snow, this thing I've just described, but when I talk about the explosions in the city itself maybe you should imagine something similar, a rapidly-expanding oval of orange fire, and smoke, and skeetering smoke-trailed trajectories of shrapnel.

But, as I said, I didn't see either of the first two bombs going off. I didn't see the explosion that blew up several engineering workshops on the northwest, in fourville and sixville. The perimeter suburbs are not named logically, one after the other, with oneville in the north, twoville northeast and threeville east and so on – nothing like that, that would be too straightforward for humanity. Oneville and twoville are north and south, fourville and threeville west and east, of centreville. Sixville is north west. So fourville and sixville are actually next to one another, and the engineering shops blown up were on the border between the two districts.

I didn't see the second explosion, and because my office was in oneville east I didn't really hear it either. I sort-of-heard it. I heard a clunking sound, like a huge door being slammed shut away in the distance. This was followed, after what seemed to me a very long pause, by a series of cracks, or shots, and then – odd detail – somebody out in the street yodelling, putting out this high-pitched wavery singing noise. But we knew something was wrong. Our sensitivities had been primed by the greenhouse bomb.

And running out of the office on to the street we could see people running; a police truck hurtling along the street in low gear with the engine howling, cops in the back with their rifles up like flagless flagpoles, the thunderous wheels of the truck spraying up ice and grit behind them. People approached people, faces slack with questioning, 'what's going on? – what's going on?'

'It's another bomb,' said somebody.

Of course it was.

The radio was quicker off the mark this time. 'There has been another terrorist attack,' said [Blank], the soft-grumble-voiced radio presenter who had become a celebrity simply by reading out government news headlines in the evenings. [Blank]'s smooth and sexy avuncular tones. 'This is an emergency news announcement. There has been another terrorist attack. At eleven o'clock this morning a bomb was detonated on the edge of an army engineering shop in fourville. The explosion destroyed a mining combine. Fire spread quickly through the shop, and through two make-and-mend establishments in south sixville.' Of course there would be fire – all that petrol and oil, that's what those shops deal in. 'The fire ignited military equipment causing further damage.' Those were the additional bangs we heard, I said breathlessly to [Blank], a woman who sat next to me in committee. That was stuff exploding in the fire. What stuff I wonder? Military stuff, said [Blank]. 'There has been another terrorist attack,' the news repeated. 'The government is calling for calm – the situation is under control. Arrests are imminent. The government is calling for calm.'

And [Blank] on the radio saying over and over *There has been another terrorist attack* was indeed, oddly, calming. We all felt privy to the government's actions now, because the news was released officially on the radio at once, rather than in the papers the following day.

'There have been casualties,' said the news.

That night Crow was as close to depressed as I ever saw him. Because our marriage was merely play-acting it was difficult for me to offer consolation, to do what a normal wife would have found easy – hugs, gentle words, that sort of thing. We ate our supper (bread and four steamed carrots) in silence. Afterwards we sat in silence in the front room. We had the radio on for a while, but it was only news, and it was only the same news we'd been hearing all day, so we turned it off. Then Crow took off his shirt and did squat-thrusts in the middle of the floor, with his arms straight out in front of him and his legs folding and unfolding beneath him, like a sleepwalker bobbing up and down in one position.

'It's pretty terrible,' I said. I can't say I felt it to be terrible, in my own heart, but it seemed like the thing to say.

'It makes,' he said, bobbing down, puffing out a breath and coming up again, 'my blood,' bob, puff, up, 'boil that,' bob, puff, up, 'citizens,' bob, puff, up, 'could be,' bob, puff, up, 'so *evil*.' He stood tall, jogged on the spot on his toes for a bit. Then he put his shirt back on, and sat next to me again.

'The radio,' I said, 'was talking about arrests.' I was thinking of [Blank].

Crow sat perfectly still, looking ahead of himself. 'I mean, Tira,' he said, in a doleful voice, like a hurt child, 'I really don't understand it. I really don't understand it at all.'

And I could see that he genuinely didn't, innocent that he was. And at that moment I felt a thrum of almost-tenderness for him, this supposed trained killer, this soldier. I remembered everything that [Blank] had said about terror, and then I looked at this senior military man, my husband, and understood that he had no conception of terror at all. That he had devoted his life to being a warrior, to making war, and yet he could not comprehend terror. Everything was rules for him; rules (even!) of war. The parade ground as the type of the cosmos. You kill people according to the rules. Killing people outside the parameters of the rule book was not so much evil, though he called it so, as *incomprehensible* to him. It baffled his mind. A soldier acted a certain way because that was the way a soldier acted, and to act another way would mean that you weren't a soldier. I don't suppose he rationalised it to himself, but just such a circular pattern underlay everything about Crow. Let's say you were a woman, and you married a general: that made you a general's wife, and you acted in the ways appropriate to a general's wife. But to act inappropriately, to swear and bitch, to reveal yourself as *black* (and what white general ever had a black wife, for crying out loud?) – all this was not so much reprehensible as simply beyond comprehension altogether. It was like that episode of *Star Trek* where the humans plot to destroy the machine intelligences by showing them a picture of a logically impossible polyhedron, such that they'll take it into their brains and try to make sense of it and their minds will be corroded by their inability to rationalise it. Crow had something of that expression on his face, as if a worm were eating his consciousness.

'I mean,' he said, imploring me, 'don't we already have it hard enough? Doesn't everybody already have it hard enough? We're struggling for survival of everybody here – don't these people see that? Are they crazy, or something? I mean, I could understand a *death wish*,' he said, and I nodded although I didn't think he could, 'I could understand a death wish, but why try to take everybody down with you? Kill yourself, yeah, but kill everybody else with you? I don't get it. What good is it? What good does it do? Why blow up the food and the engineering that everybody needs? I mean I literally can't see, I *literally can't see* what they think they're going to achieve.'

He looked at me so imploringly, that I wanted to try and help him see.

'I guess,' I hesitated, and he seized on my words.

'What? What?'

'Well – it's terrible,' I said. 'It's really atrocious.'

'Atrocious,' he agreed, firmly. 'Yeah, an atrocity. Eleven men died in fourville and sixville. What good is that?'

'No good at all.'

'No good,' he said. 'No good means evil. It's an atrocity,' he said again, as if having the word helped him understand things better. 'Atrocity.'

'But I guess,' I said, trying to modulate my voice so it was coo-ish, trying not to inflame him with my contrary views. 'I guess *some* people – not me, but some people – might see the greenhouses and the engineering shops differently from the rest of the city.'

'What?' he barked. 'What? It's a crime to grow food, is it? Everybody needs food – it's not as if food is easy to come by up here.'

'Sure, everybody needs food,' I said, my voice growing a little firmer because his dogmatism was starting to rasp against my temper. 'But who gets to eat the food from the greenhouses? Rich people, only. You get a tomato, it costs forty dollars.'

'That's not true,' he said.

'Well OK, not forty dollars, but you know what I mean. It's not like the food from the greenhouses gets very far into the general population. It's food for the rich, a little delicacy to tickle the palates of the rich. It's really *really* expensive, the food from those greenhouses.'

He looked at me as if I'd said this last speech in Swahili. 'Expensive?' he said, in a *what has that got to do with anything?* tone of voice.

'And the engineers—' I said.

'No, no, wait up. Wait there. You're saying that the greenhouses are *legitimate targets* because their food costs a little more than regular food?'

'I never said they were legitimate targets.'

'That's insane. Of course it's more expensive – it's fresh food. Everybody wants to eat fresh food, and there are only so many greenhouses.'

'OK,' I said, trying to placate. 'Forget about the green-houses. You got to admit that some of the engineers . . .'

'What?' he snapped. 'What about the engineers?'

'Well, they're pretty rich, some of them.'

'Tira,' he said, slowly. 'Are you saying that this is some kind of anarchist anti-wealth thing?'

'It's not that,' I said.

171

'Like the globalisation protests used to be?'

'No,' I said. 'I'm not saying that. But you got to admit – some of those engineers, making all that money on government contracts and whatnot. They do swank themselves around.'

'They work hard,' he said. 'Essential work.'

'Sure they work hard. But most all of us work hard. We're all of us working hard. But most of us aren't rich. Doctors are starving half to death and pressing their noses up against soup-restaurant windows whilst grease monkeys are walking around buying thousand-dollar coats and boots and fresh food.'

Crow looked at me. 'For this they deserve to die?'

'I didn't say they deserved to die,' I said, getting annoyed. 'Will you just listen? I'm sorry I started this whole conversation now. I'm not saying these bombings are justified, I'm only saying.'

But Crow hopped off the sofa, in a state of obvious agitation. 'I don't get what you're saying at all, Tira,' he said, and dropped to the floor to start press-ups. He didn't take off his shirt. 'They're evil,' he said, to the floor. 'Evil, that's the only explanation. The Devil is behind it. You'll laugh, but it's the truth. He tried to destroy humanity with the Snow, and now he's working his baleful evil in the hearts of a small minority to finish the job.'

I didn't know what to say to this. I watched my husband's rigid body flatten against the floor, raise itself briskly with piston-arms acting against the hinge of its toes until it subtended an arc of twenty-degrees, drop again, raise again, like a pulse.

Crow did fifty press-ups. When he hopped back to his feet afterwards his face was choler-red with the exertion.

He was outraged. Outrage became the mood of the city. People muttered platitudes about evil. Arrests, said *Truth*, had been made: six people, including one woman. This last detail provoked particular fury in [Blank], who sat next to me on the committee: a red-haired, wrinkled female of fifty.

'A woman?' she said to me. 'How could a woman get herself caught up in this?'

'I don't know,' I said.

None of it really touched me. I don't mean to represent myself as a callous person. I'd like to think the anti-depressants were responsible. But I didn't feel the outrage, or the horror, the horror, or any of the other extreme emotional reactions of the people around me. It swam past me. I wasn't indifferent, exactly. I think the word to describe it would be intrigued. It was interesting, a diversion, it made the day-to-day grind of coping with the cold and eating next-to-nothing and struggling through tedium – it gave all that a little bit of savour, a spark.

Nine

I wondered whether [Blank] had been one of the people arrested for the bombing, but after two days I saw him in the street, talking to two other people. I didn't go over to him, partly because I was late for work, and partly because I wasn't sure I wanted to be seen in his company.

After a week the outrage seemed to recede in our heads a little. Without TV it was hard to keep the fact of the bombing fresh in our minds. There seemed to be many more aircraft in the sky, skidding through the air, hovering over the snow outside the city. A man was shot in twoville by the police, I heard from an acquaintance, although the news didn't report it. Was he a terrorist? I asked. My interlocutor looked dumbly at me, as if to say, of course, why else would he be shot? Conversation ran along a strictly limited number of lines. There was no weather to talk of, no rain, hardly any snowfall now; there was no natural world, no pets, cats, dogs, no birds. Very little happened in the human world except the same old routine. People talked about their food (what they had for supper last night, what they were going to have for supper this coming night, dwelling rather plaintively on every single detail of the meals). Sometimes they talked about their work (but there was little to say about that, for most people), or the radio (especially the radio-soap *Liberty Family*, an everyday story of everyday people) – and, after the bombs, people talked about terrorism. Each new snippet of news was chewed over and over, examined under the light of one or other of the three theories that were current. It was insiders, malcontents, evil-doers; it was the Russians; it was (whisper it) the Australians. Nobody had any hard evidence to support any of the theories, but people inclined temperamentally, as it were, either to the 'insider' or the 'outsider' theory. For example, the mysterious individual shot by the police in twoville was a lone lunatic, heading out towards the southern greenhouses with a bomb strapped to his torso. Or he was a Russian agent, parachuted into the city and trying to foster havoc. Or he was part of a secret army of terrorists inside the city, a group who had infiltrated Liberty and were now trying to destroy it from within. Or he was part of a dedicated Maoist cadre of extremists who were trying to bring down the democratically elected government. What do *you* think, Tara? What do you think?

I think it's probably insiders, I said.

Twelve days after they bombed the engineering shops, they bombed the hospital. This was located in that part of town named, unimaginatively, Barracks, because the original barracks had been located there. Most of the troops were now housed in new buildings in threeville, spreading out onto the snow, east of the city, and the old barracks building had been adapted to become a factory, a hospital, and a relatively plush residential block.

This time I heard the detonation distinctly; a faint whistling noise, like tinnitus, that couldn't be shaken from the ears. Then a swelling of sound to a moment of intensity, a sort of sonic folding-in, and a huge, complex, dry cracking sound mixed with an enormous gush of white noise. Two alarms were immediately set off – car alarms, they sounded like, except that nobody had car alarms any more – their high-pitched yaw-yawing keening distinctly in the air. I turned to my window and saw a funnel of smoke bubbling up through the air over the rooftops away to the south-east.

'Not again,' shrieked somebody in the room. [Blank], who was chairing the meeting, said in a clear voice, 'Let me just jot that last figure down,' as he scribbled something on the paper in front of him. Wasn't that an odd thing to say? As if he were in an examination, and the invigilator had called time, and he just wanted to note down one last thing before standing up and coming to the window with all of us

The hospital was the worst atrocity yet. Forty people died. In fact, I think that the number was even larger than that, forty-two, forty-three, something like that, I can't remember the exact number. A lot, anyway. Dozens were injured. The bomb – a mortar, this time – fell onto and through the roof of the main ward and exploded inside. All the windows were blown out.

I went down there later that same day and walked right round the building, and all the glass from the windows was shattered and arranged on the ground outside – neatly, almost – in fan-shaped patterns. Inlaid into the snow beside each of the now gaping windows, like some kind of artwork. There was a smell from the shell of the building, a sort of wet-cardboard smell, and it was dark and charred in there. I discovered a hand. It was sticking out of the snow, with little shards of glass embedded along the backs of all the fingers like toy stegosaurus spines. At first I thought, alarmed, that somebody was buried in the snow, so I crouched down and tried to pull them free. I grasped the hand in my mitten and hauled, and tumbled backwards, because the hand was not attached to anything. I fell on my back, and rolled over and stood up holding this severed hand.

I felt like laughing, but I didn't laugh. It was horrible. I wandered around in a circle for a few minutes, just holding the hand, and then, half-dazed, I wandered down to the main entrance where medics and MPs were milling around. 'Hey,' I called to one of the policemen. 'Hey, I found this hand.' He looked at me, looked at what I was carrying. 'Where did you get that?' he asked. 'I found it over there,' I said, holding out my hand to indicate where and inadvertently pointing, ghoulishly, with the severed hand as well. The policeman looked uncomfortable. 'It looked like somebody was buried in the snow,' I tried to explain, 'and I pulled it, but it must have been blown through the window by the blast. Here it is,' I said, offering it to him. '*I* don't want it,' he said, recoiling slightly with a pained expression on his face. I said: 'Well, what should I do with it?' 'I don't know,' he said, turning away. 'Lieutenant,' he called, and a white-coated officer came over. He looked at the hand, at me. 'It looked like somebody was buried in the snow,' I said, and held the hand out to him. 'What should she do with it?' asked the squaddie. 'You got glass on your jacket,' the lieutenant said to me. Then: 'Take it over there, where the medics are.' So I went over to where the medics were standing, and they had a sort of bin in which (I didn't look too closely) various body parts were being collected, and a medic wearing a blue balaclava and a florescent yellow jacket indicated that I should put the hand inside. It had looked, I explained to him, like somebody was buried in the snow.

So many people buried down there. I thought of Minnie's beautiful little hands, the way they had been when she was a baby. I remembered the first time I had tried to cut her nails, when she was very small indeed. Her nails had grown so sharp, and she was scratching herself in the face, marking her eyelids with little red ticks, when she rubbed her eyes. So I had taken the nail-clippers and grasped her left hand in my big adult fingers, her little baby hand with its chubby dimpled palm and its tiny golf-tee fingers. Of course she had wriggled and squirmed, and I had tried to slip the blade of the nail-clipper under the little pale fingernail of her forefinger whilst she jerked the hand and tried to wrench it free. It was hard to see what I was doing, and the blade seemed too clumsy, too thick, to go under the nail, and she wriggled some more, and finally I pressed the handles together to cut the nail and Minnie piped a little cry of pain. I had cut the delicate skin at the end of her finger. A tiny bead of blood, red like claret, swelled on the finger. She cried and cried. It was terrible. I felt a huge sense of horror swell inside me. I suppose it was only a little thing, but I felt so terrible about it. She cried, and I hugged her and hugged her and told her how sorry I was. She stopped crying eventually, of course. I did eventually learn how to cut her nails: first by biting them with my own teeth, and later by quelling my fears and acting decisively and holding her hand firmly so that it was still.

After the hospital bomb there was a palpable increase in the amount of hurrying about the military were involved in. More helicopters in the sky, flying low or buzzing away to the horizon and vanishing over it. Where did they go to? I asked Crow. Where did those 'copters fly off to, away over the horizon?

'Reconnaissance,' he said, gruffly. 'I'm not supposed to talk about it.'

What was over the horizon?

It was a foolish task to try and persuade Crow to talk if he had been ordered not to talk. But I persevered. 'Does that mean that we're under attack from outside?'

'Tira,' he said, weary. 'I'm really not supposed to talk about it.'

The new bomb, and the many casualties, stoked up the gossip again, and rekindled the outrage and Liberty-patri-otism. [Blank], the red-haired woman who sat on the service committee with me, had an almost boasting tone. 'My husband knows a guy,' she said, 'whose wife was killed in the blast. They're best buddies, and his wife was in hospital with frostbite in her feet, and she was killed.'

How terrible! I said. How terrible!

'I hurried over there as soon as I heard the blast,' said [Blank], an eager middle-aged man of small stature also on the committee. 'I ran straight down there!' He was so happy to have been one of the first on the scene. I remember this guy, I suppose, because he died in one of the subsequent attacks; a man in his forties, I'd guess, his face whittled by hunger to a desperate thinness, but with this large, aquiline, harp-shaped nose. I remember his eyebrows, complex tangles of brown and grey hairs. Why would I have such a precise memory of this dead man's eyebrows, I wonder? He wasn't a friend. I can barely remember his name. 'I ran straight down there and the fire was still burning through the windows. There was this great balloon-shaped cloud of black smoke rising over the building.'

People shook their heads, cooed 'terrible'; but their eyes were bright and alive. I was the same. I made the same social noises, shook my heads and mimicked outrage like everybody else. But I thought to myself: black clouds over the city. The first black clouds for many years. But they presaged no rain, except possibly a rain of shards of glass. I was not moved, that's the truth of it. I think, in fact, if I look back on the occasion, that – in my own head – I set great store by my not being moved. I accepted that it was probably a result of the antidepressant chemicals marinating my brain, but that wasn't important. What was important to me then, I think, was that my detachment gave me a sense of myself as a superior person, somebody immune to the disagreeable hiccoughs and bumps of everyday life. Smooth, like a plastinated body, with the quick-hurtling flakes of glass just bouncing off my skin. That's how I liked to think of myself, at any rate.

Ten

For several days after this last bomb there was a sense of hiatus in the city. I doubt that Liberty had quite digested what happened. Then troops arrived from NNY: a troop-plane arrived, with military reinforcements, twenty or so new men. *Truth* announced that troop barges had started their hovering passage from the cluster of Confederacy of Free People cities in the east over-States. I had never seen one of these devices, but had heard of them. Some people, with nostalgic turn of phrase, called them ice schooners: but this gives the wrong impression. Sled-based devices, wind-powered or otherwise, proved inefficient means of travel over the rasping, cracked surface that day and night, wind and chill had made of the snow. The barges were developed from hovercraft technology, I think: old barges with flat-tened bottoms. Two small jets mounted at the front shoul-ders, as it were, of the craft blew air hard underneath providing a tiny cushion of air, and also provided a forward momentum. Once the craft had been put in motion (shoved by trucks down an specially smoothed ice path) they plunged forward with increasing momentum, riding over smaller cracks and ripples in the surface of the snow. 'Three hundred of the best troops in the confederated cities of free peoples,' said the radio's comfortable voice, 'are on their way to help Liberty combat this terrible menace.'

'Why,' I said, almost absently, 'don't they just say NUSA? Confederated cities of free peoples. For crying out loud.'

I was at home with Crow when I said this. We were listening to the radio together in the front room, and I was making fists and pushing them slowly into my stomach to try and distract my guts from their hunger-gripes.

'I guess you're right,' said Crow. His instinct for follow-ing the rules didn't extend so far as to endorse the official mouthful-of-marbles name for our nation. 'Everybody says noose-ah,' he conceded. 'I don't see what's wrong with it.'

'I guess somebody up there thinks that New USA makes it sound like the old USA is dead and gone.' I was going to add *which of course it is*, but held myself back, because that was the sort of comment that would send Crow into a bad mood. 'When you're IP,' I said, trying to sound more chirpy, 'you can dispense with that whole confederated cities nonsense.'

Crow grunted. He didn't like talking about his possible political future.

The first new troops arrived in a conventional plane, and unloaded at the airstrip outside the city at sevenville. People huddled all along the pavements to watch them march in.

Later that same day I saw [Blank] again; so he obviously hadn't been arrested, for all his bravura talk of terrorism. It wasn't, of course, smart to associate with him, especially at that time. But I just bumped into him, I could not avoid him. 'Tira!' he called out, from the doorway alcove of a boarded-up shop. 'Tira!'

I stopped, and talked with him.

There was a fury, a controlled fury, in his manner. His arms and legs moved with an almost marionettish jerkiness. His carotid arteries stood visibly proud of the neck. His face had become a glaring mask, eyes opened a little too widely, lips parted just a sliver to show the closed teeth inside. He kept twitching his head round, to look up and down the street, constantly on the alert for pursuers. 'You look like you've been electrocuted,' I told him, which wasn't quite accurate, but which expressed something of his charged, powered aura.

'We used to have a Bill of Rights,' he said, and I realised that we weren't to begin with niceties, or even with accusations ('those bombs were your doing!' and so on), that we could take those as read. [Blank] was launching directly into the ideological discussion, the justificatory dialectic. Perhaps he had been rehearsing my lines, or the lines that would be spoken by an accuser like me, in his head, and felt that he had disposed of them. I, I'm afraid, was not so quick.

'What?' I said.

'The old USA, Bill of Rights,' he said, twitching his legs in a funny little shuffling stomp in front of me, like a condemned man pacing his cell. 'But the New United States, as we're not even supposed to call it – nothing, no *rights*, no citizens' *rights*. Do you wonder why we're supposed to talk about confederation of freedom and all that [*expletive deleted*]? Because they want to forget that there ever was an old USA, with its old constitution and its old Bill of Rights.'

'Hey,' I said, with the palm of my left hand up. 'You picked the wrong woman with whom to have a constitutional discussion.' I remember, particularly, that I used that over-precise locution; *with whom to have*. I don't know why. Odd mannerisms of speech pop out at stressed moments. [Blank] didn't notice. He wasn't paying attention to what I said.

'Freedom of speech,' he said, snarly-sarcastic. 'That used to be a right. Yeah? You going to tell me we still got that right? No you're not.'

'These are,' I said, awkward that I be seen to be defending the government, but feeling that somebody had to bring his paranoia a little back to earth, 'these are unusual times. There are – just maybe, is all I'm saying – *more* important things than freedom of speech at a time like this?'

He glowered at me. 'The *Truth*, the newspaper. That's some sick joke, that name. You know the editor?'

'I'm just saying,' I said, 'that maybe the freedom-of-speech thing would go over better if we weren't all a month away from starving to death . . .'

'[Blank],' he said, naming the editor of *Truth*. 'Same surname as [Blank], our Senator-Mayor. Yeah? Same surname, because he's his *brother*. The assistant editor is [Blank], different surname but same family, cousin. News editor? [Blank]. Sister-in-law. This is free press?'

'Look,' I said, but he cut me off.

'You know what [Blank] said? You know what he said in his Senatorial-Mayoral-[*expletive deleted*]-dictatorial capacity? He said he was in favour of a relatively controlled press. A relatively controlled press! He meant a controlled press run by his relatives.'

I'd heard this joke before. It was an old joke. For some reason it annoyed me to hear it from [Blank], it ired me up.

'This does not persuade me,' I said to him fiercely, 'that you're justified in killing people – in bombing the hospital, for Christ's sake. The hospital? I mean, I guess I can see the greenhouses, though you killed five there, ordinary people not government high-fliers, not assistant editors on *Truth*. But OK, you bomb the greenhouses, you make your point. Don't agree with you, but I can understand it. But the hospital?'

[Blank] growled, looked away. 'We didn't hit the hospitals,' he said.

I didn't think I'd heard him right. 'What?'

'I said we didn't hit the hospitals. We're not monsters, for crying out loud.'

'You bombed the *greenhouses*,' I said. 'That's not under question. You bombed the *repair yard*. You don't deny that. But the hospitals. The hospitals you didn't do.'

'No.'

'Somebody *else* did the hospitals?'

'Yes.'

'You're insane. You can't pick and choose which atrocities you want attached to your name.'

'We can,' he cried, 'if we didn't [*expletive deleted*] *do* it.'

There was a silence. I thought I could smell cordite, gunpowder, just the faintest whiff of it, and looked past [Blank] at the street, wondering if there was a bomb. But then I realised that it must be coming from [Blank] himself. That he must have picked up the odour in proximity to one of the bombs.

'You're insane,' I said, again.

He pulled off his glove and rubbed his eyes. Suddenly his whole body language underwent some subtle slump, as if the power had run out of limbs and spine. 'It don't really matter whether you believe me or not,' he said, slipping his hand back in its glove. 'It happens to be the truth, that's all. Why would I lie about it? Why would I lie about it?'

182

'You're insane,' I repeated.

'Terror is a means to an end,' he said, 'not an end in itself. Bombing the hospital puts our cause *back*, it doesn't advance it. It *hurts* us, it doesn't help us.'

'The greenhouse, the repair shop, they didn't hurt you?'

'We know what we're doing,' he said, fiercely. 'We didn't *do* the hospital. That would be *counter*productive, you understand? So somebody else did it, not us. Somebody else. Who might that be? Who might have the motive to do something that would damage our cause?'

I shook my head slowly. 'Listen,' I said.

'Who?' he pressed. He wanted me to say it. 'Who?'

'Listen, believe me, you hurt your cause with the *first* bomb. Bombs aren't the way to do it.'

'Who?' he asked again, desperately insistent. 'Who would have that motive?' And then, because I evidently wasn't going to play his game, he answered his own question. 'The *government*, that's who – that's who bombed the hospital.'

I let out what I intended to be a dismissive 'hah!' but it came out under greater pressure than I anticipated, more of a howl, or a shriek. Momentarily [Blank] looked genuinely startled.

'You really really need,' I said, insistent now myself, 'to step back from yourself, to listen to yourself. You kill all these people with bombs, and now you're saying that it was actually the government who planted the bombs?'

'Just the hospital,' he said, loudly. 'We didn't do the hospital, that's all I'm saying. Why would we bomb a hospital?'

'Why would you bomb a greenhouse?' I demanded.

He spluttered, made scoffing noises, and then was quiet. After a pause he spoke to me in a subdued voice. 'I had hoped you could understand it a little more, Tira. I had hoped that.'

'I understand,' I said, because my blood was up, 'that you're insane. That's what I understand.'

In an instant he was no longer haranguing me, and

instead was clinging to my arms like a needy child. His voice changed from ranty and insistent to whiny and tearful. 'You got to help me Tira, you got to help me, they're after me, I haven't slept in days, in days, you can help me, you got to help me.'

'Jesus,' I said, in disgust.

'They're after me,' he said. 'I don't – like to think what they'll do to me if they get me in a small room. Feelings are running high, at the moment.'

'You didn't think of that before you planned the bombs?'

His eyes were as perfectly circular as Polo Mints. 'I didn't see how much slippage there would be in the cadre,' he said. 'People can be so *untrustworthy* – [Blank] has already vanished. I think he's gone to the government, he's probably telling them everything, probably he's put the MPs on to where I live. So much for loyalty to the cause, that [*expletive deleted*] miserable traitor. So much for loyalty!'

'You sure he's gone to the police?'

'He's disappeared,' said [Blank].

'Unless,' I said sourly, 'he died in the hospital blast.'

For one pathetic, terrible moment I saw the flickers of hope pass over [Blank]'s face: hope, I suppose, that his co-conspirator, colleague and friend was dead so that he himself would not have to face police interrogation. But this morbid hope faded as soon as it came. 'Why would he go to the hospital? He wasn't sick. He was strong as an ox.'

'Well,' I said, impatient, 'maybe he went to plant a bomb?' As I said this I momently forgot that the hospital had been destroyed by a mortar rather than a bomb, despite the fact that the news reports had been very precise about that. [Blank] clearly forgot it too, because he replied with a doggy eagerness.

'And blew himself up by mistake? Yeah, that would explain why we haven't heard from him. But, no,' he added, his face falling, 'that can't be right. The hospital was hit by a mortar, that's what the news said. Oh Tira,' he pleaded again with a sobbing catch in his throat, 'you *got* to help me.'

'I don't see what I can do,' I said, striving for formality, and unfastening his mittens from my arms.

'Talk to your husband – tell him I've got names, if he'll grant me anonymity. I'll tell them everything if they get me a deal.'

'What about loyalty to the cause?'

'Come *on*, Tira, don't—'

'Don't?'

'Just *don't*, OK? Come *on*.'

'It'd do no good, talking to my husband,' I said. 'For one thing, he's only an army officer. He's got no official political standing . . .'

'Don't *give* me that!' [Blank] shrieked. 'People talk about him as a future candidate for IP, for *Christ's* sake.'

'For another thing,' I went on, keeping my voice steady, 'he's not too level-headed about the bombings. He'd shoot you himself, I reckon. For a third, I'm not in a position to sway him on this sort of thing. You should know, better than any, that we're not what you'd strictly call man-and-wife.'

[Blank] was actually crying now, little mucusy tears coming out of the corner of his eyes. 'Jesus, Tira, don't you *want* to help me? Isn't there any tenderness in your heart for me? Didn't we have something? Didn't I once mean something to you?'

I looked at him. 'Ish,' I said.

'Ish?' he replied, with a sucking noise in his throat. 'What do you mean?'

'I mean yes and no,' I said. 'Didn't you *also* mean something to [Blank]? Why don't you go whinge at her.'

'[Blank]?' he repeated, his eyes glinting and drooping down, guilty-afraid. 'What – what about her? I barely know her.'

'You're pathetic,' I said. 'You [*expletive deleted*] her. You did, didn't you?'

'Tira, listen to me, you've got the wrong end of the stick.'
I said: 'I'm going.'

I didn't move, but he turned away from me, hiding his face by shuffling up against the wall. 'Go,' he said, forlornly. 'Go on. Go.'

I stepped away, but my heel caught the icy wooden bar of the shop's step at the wrong angle and I lurched forward, hopping on my other foot and waving my arms like a loon to try and keep my balance. I didn't want to fall over. I'd heard of a person who fell on a slippery pavement and cracked her spine, and was now in a wheelchair. For all I knew (I thought of this as I hopped over the ground flapping like a dodo) she'd been in the hospital when it was bombed. I didn't want to fall. Six yards out I regained my balance, and looked over my shoulder to see if [Blank] had witnessed my behaviour. But he was still facing the wall. So I put my head down and hurried on. The way to walk on ice, you know, is to turn your toes in as you walk; so that your wide-spaced heels make it unlikely you'll fall backwards, and if you tumble forwards you have more chance of being able to regain your balance.

Eleven

For five days after the hospital attack there were no further attacks. The army was on every street, patrolling in twos with their rifles angled towards the ground before them like metal detectors; trucks rumbling back and forth; occasional roof-skimmers helicoptering through the air. The radio announced that there had been more arrests. Senator [Blank] gave a speech over the airways in which he declared that the government was on top of the situation. 'We know who the perpetrators are,' he said, boomingly. 'We are rounding up the troublemakers.' After his speech he was interviewed by salad-voiced [Blank], the city's radio presenter of choice. 'Are these troublemakers Liberty citizens,

186

or fifth-columnists who have infiltrated our city?' 'I'm not prepared to comment on that at this time,' the Senator replied.

On the sixth day there were three further explosions, one in centreville-south and two in twoville. Two further mortar attacks, destroying some shops and a housing development. There were only four casualties: the residence was empty because everybody was at work; two of the shops were empty. In the third, selling mink towels, the shop-owner and the customer were killed, but a second shop assistant escaped with only scratches. Two soldiers were caught in the blast. The fourth death was somebody hit by a falling wall two hours after the attack.

That night there were three further attacks, again in twoville, on the edge of the city. Our apartment was in Barracks, almost all the way across town, but even I was woken by the clatter these explosions made. I went to the window, but couldn't see anything. In the front room Crow was pulling on his uniform. He left that night, and although he told me he would be back in four days, I wasn't to see him for many weeks. A message was delivered to me at work the next day: *military business, an away mission*, it said. That was all. I didn't expect tenderness, or even the conventionalised sign-offs, *miss you, love you*, of course; but it was still, strangely, inexplicably, upsetting not to see them.

The day after there was nothing. But the day after that three mortars hit the snow south-east of Liberty. 'It's as if,' people said, 'the range-finder for some long-distance weapon were slowly going off target.' Bombs had traced a path right across the city, from the north-west to the south-east. The radio had nothing to say.

Then there was a bout of ice-quakes. The snow trembled near continuously for forty-eight hours, little quaking bursts every ten or fifteen minutes. On main street the snow cracked right open, little crevasses forming lengthways, grins in the fabric of the ground. It was not obvious why. The radio announced that the bombs had destabilised the snow beneath the city, but that it wasn't serious, but I couldn't see how that could be. The explosions, after all, had been on the surface of the snow, not underneath it. But people were happy to ascribe every woe in their life to 'terrorists' now.

'They arrested another dozen last night,' said [Blank] one morning. We were in the committee room together, even though the meeting had been called off – the chairman had the flu, I think. But rather than loiter outside we tried to share our body warmth inside. 'Another dozen.'

'Good,' said somebody else, with feeling.

'That's what I say too,' said [Blank].

'Too right,' said [Blank], lifting the cuffs of her mitten to blow hot air in over her hands. 'Hang them, make an exhibition of them.'

'Evil,' said somebody.

'I heard,' said [Blank], 'that they are going to hang them. I heard that they're going to hang them from helicopters and fly over and over the town, in a figure of eight, to show off the bodies.'

We all contemplated this gratifyingly savage possibility. In my head I pictured only one man dangling from the air-noose, and I pictured him wearing a placard 'lover of Tira' around his neck. I shuddered; but that was the cold more than anything.

My reality followed my fantasy. The next day I met a person in the cold street who told me, 'You know [Blank], who used to chair our committee meetings?' I said I knew him. My heart was boiling inside my cold chest. 'He's been arrested – he's a terrorist. Fancy that!' Terrist. Turrst. Really? 'Yeah, they picked him up and a dozen more people last night around midnight – I just heard it from [Blank] who was in the swat team. Picked him up, bagged his head, took him away.' Oh God, I said. 'I know, isn't it shocking? Terrorists everywhere – and he had army rank! He wasn't *actually* in the army, of course, but he had a courtesy rank!

Why would he do it? What could possibly drive him to do it?'

I said I didn't know.

That night I ate alone, and wondered about [Blank]. I knew I would never see him again. I knew he would disappear. I tried to envision the small room, the single unshaded lightbulb hanging like a dead man from a cord in the ceiling. [Blank] strapped in a chair. A herd of angry bullmen all around him, their fists hard as stone, meteors smacking into the increasingly cratered, moon-like surface of his face. A red moon rising is an ill omen. But I couldn't concentrate on those images. I knew [Blank] to be dead, already dead, like everybody else in the world. I felt him to be drifting downwards, slipping, drowning in snow and sinking down from the wreck of the Titanic on which we still grasped for existence, and tumbling through the opaque oceans of snow down and down until he came to rest on the bottom. All of us would eventually go down there eventually, all of us.

I fell asleep easily. But after midnight the door was clanging and clanging, gong-like, with the knocking, and I staggered out of bed to open it. It was the military police, and they had come to arrest me. So that was how I ended up in custody. Which is the end of my story, I think. I don't need to say more, because you'll have my interrogation on file, won't you. All the questions I was asked, and all the answers I gave. [Blank] had given them my name in the very first exchange, given it up without a blow being struck. Love, love. I've used all my paper up, close-written, both sides. I need more paper. This is the last line, and I'm having to squash my writing so that it looks compressed by the weight of words above – but if you give me more paper I can talk about the people behind the other bombings, the bombers 'external' to Liberty, those ones responsible for so much destruction – not [Blank] at all, but [*illegible*].

Confession

ADMISSION [this section is mandatory]: My signature below performs the act of my swearing that the following is wholly true. My name is *Friedrich Gimmelfarb*, and I reside ^^for a period not exceeding two years I have resided at^^ [text added] seven Dale Street, Liberty City, Over-UK. [Optional]: Previously to this I lived in New New York, and before that in Old New York. *<note: details of life pre-Snow cannot legally be required of a confessor without judicial special warrant>*

{MS notes, handwritten in margin: *of course Gimmelfarb is not the name; family changed it when he was a kid in old USA. Likely breach of law here. Jerry, any update on this? His birth cert. may say Gimmelfarb but we know different. Can we prosecute for perjury here? KK.*

The law requires he give his real name here, that's all. But what counts as 'real'? JL

I'm sure the court would surely argue that 'real' must mean 'the name by which you are generally known': and, clearly, Gimmelfarb was not the name by which he was generally known, at least not up here in the NUSA KK.}

CRIME(S) [this section is mandatory]: Conspiracy to commit treason; conspiracy to commit terrorist act or acts; commission of terrorist act or acts.

PLEA [this section is mandatory]: Guilty

CO-CONSPIRATORS [Optional]:

PERSONAL STATEMENT [Optional]: I chaired one committee in New London, on mining. I have given the army some names. I have been in custody now for a week, and I make the following statement of my free will.

It started before the Snow, which means that – which is to say, I'm happy for it to mean that – I hereby waive my rights to pre-Snow anonymity. That's nothing but a legalistic fiction anyway, let's be honest, the notion that pre-Snow activities are magically erased by some statute of limitation, by some fiat. Everybody knows it's not really like that. Everybody in the city judiciary has access to my military file; my pre-Snow life is no secret. But there are things not in my file, and I'd like to detail my pre-Snow revelation. It's not too strong a word. It was with a revelation that my disaffection with the system began, with everything as it was constituted. When I was a young man, still with most of my hair, I worked for a time in Bridgeport CT, for a company called SponsorCam. A man called Bruce Kirkland got me the job. He's dead now, dead and under the snow. They were a private TV-media company, but they were for a time very successful, and it's possible that you've heard of them. I had done other TV work for other companies, banal stuff, live-competition, dial-in, ad tie-ins. But I took the Sponsor-Cam job out of that same sense of idealism that had never

191

really abandoned me, not since I'd left college. And the irony is that I believe Jeb Prior and Andy Creaton (pronounced *Critten*), the two people who established the company, had the same ideals. It was wholly axiomatic, it was the American way. Doing good for other people and making money for yourself were two sides of the same coin. More than that – making money for yourself was actually a *way* of doing good for other people. That's what America meant. It's not that American people were not any more greedy or soulless than any other people: only that money is a powerful *lever*. You knew that already. So I could see that people were starving in the world when my neighbors were so fat that one day they broke the stair-rail in the communal hall by just leaning against it. I could see that these people in Sudan or Afghanistan were starving, and I had the urge to do something about it. That's not ignoble.

SponsorCam sounded like a good idea. You sponsored a starving person from the comfort of your couch in Des Moines or Jersey or London, you paid the TV company and they passed money along (after taking their cut naturally) to the needy community. Their cut was the least you expected, and you didn't think of that: you were actually buying something with your money, buying a unique televisual viewing experience. SponsorCam were just the facilitators, providing the reality television, but that's just the medium, the important thing is the reality itself. As if there's a difference between reality television and reality itself! I mean, maybe once-on-a-time, but now?

This was the SponsorCam idea: you the viewer buy, effectively, the right to tune in to this person's life in Sudan or Afghanistan. So SPTV set up a bunch of ten-dollar cams, and they were set running twenty-four-seven, and you bought the right to watch the feed from those cams. It was perfect: you buy entertainment – reality TV at its realest, the hottest commodity in the media. I remember thinking what a cool idea. You know? They get the money, the poorest people. They sell one of the few things they have left to sell, the TV rights to their lives, and those rights weren't doing them any good as they starved to death. Those Sudanese, those Afghans, who draw the highest number of US viewers get the most money. Ratings-based charity TV, but not really charity because the recipients are genuinely selling something for their money: access, intimacy, entertainment. And they get a whole bunch more, or so the purists tell us: buildings, bridges, all the things the money from SPTV could do for them. No – it was more than that. More important than that, it was fleshing out the cliché of the starving sub-African with the reality, with actual people, people you get to know and get to care about. People whose name you know. Globalization via humanization. TV that helps you care about real things.

But it didn't work out that way. *Could* not. And as I came to understand that, my disaffection began. It still sounds like a good idea, of course it does. But it's not, and here's why: money flows where people's desires make it flow. The money goes to those people who provide the entertainment that people want – and to be precise it's not even *want*, it's less active than that. But, look: people don't want to pay to watch a person milling corn, even if it's a person whose name they know. They don't pay to watch somebody sitting around reading a book, or praying to Mecca, or whatever. You know? This is not what we can call entertainment. You know what? People preferred the violence. There was a big violence problem in all these regions before SPTV got involved, since violence naturally goes along with poverty. But it's fair to say that SPTV didn't help. Audiences wanted to watch the more *televisual* stuff. Put it this way: where did the ratings go? The ratings followed the members of the local militias, the gangs, the gun-guys; ratings did not go with the ordinary people living the dull lives. The gun-guys had dull parts to their lives too, I guess, and a lot of the time you'd see them reading a book, praying to Mecca, whatever – but there was always the *chance* that you'd see them get into a firefight. That was what brought in the viewers.

People don't want to watch farmers farming on TV. They want action. Action is simply what people want to watch. Which is all just a very elaborate way of saying: crime makes better TV than ordinary life. Result? The *money* pushed culture that way. These guys had nothing left to sell but entertainment, and the *money* told them that carrying a gun made better entertainment. That they'd get more viewers, more sponsors, if they pistol-whipped their neighbor, if they fought with passers-by, if they shot and killed a market trader, whatever. So that's what they did.

I thought that SPTV would improve life in those regions, but it made it much worse. Gun-toters acted up for the cameras because that way more people watched them, and more people watching them brought more money along. Ordinary people took to doing dangerous, crazy, violent things to try and draw the viewers. It was quite a scandal in the US media for the five months it ran. Any number of individual people would curse and call out shame-shame, and any number of individual people would insist that it wasn't their fault the gun-crazies were getting audience, that *they* spent their evenings watching Abdulla or Ibrahim feeding pap to their children, or painting the front room, or reading a book by an unshaded electric light, or whatever. But no matter how many individuals claimed this, the *audiences* were not watching Abdulla or Ibrahim, they were watching members of the Mahdi gang shoot up a local coffee bar, with real people taking real bullets and twitching the way actors never quite get right in the movies. Violence went mad in the region, and ratings soared with it, and SponsorCam made a whole bunch of money, but we were all secretly glad when the government closed us down. I walked away with a pile of money, like everybody involved, but I did not feel clean. After a year I still did not feel clean, and that was when I was forced to consider the reasons why.

You might think that I would have a different perspective on things now that the Snow has happened, but you'd be wrong. The superstructure may have changed, got snowed under, but the base remains the same.

After SponsorCam broke down as a company, and after the Congressional hearing, it was a straightforward matter for me to find other work in the TV industry. The pay was high, as were the social rewards; the parties, the drugs. Of course, I took drugs. What exactly are the anti-drugs laws up here in NUSA? Would there be any point in having such laws, when there are no drugs for people to abuse? But of course you have them. That's your style.

I worked as a writer for several years. I wrote *The Lodging House of Love*. Remember that? No? Well, it's a transient medium, TV. I wrote *Doctor Marigold* with Jack Mahoney – that won a *TV Selector* award for 1999. I wrote two dozen episodes for a long-running soap called *Holly Tree Hotel*, set in Los Angeles in the early 1900s. I wrote the script for all ninety seconds of the Kimmeens ad, the one with the two women sitting on top of the skyscraper. I wrote that in a day, sitting in a hotel room trembling with the cocaine and the elation in my blood, and it earned me more than all the six episodes of *Wonderful End* that I wrote with Mare Obenreizer and Sandy Dean. I got married and got divorced in a year, blowing all the money I made from my writing in a blizzard of lifestyle. You know the kind of lifestyle I am talking about; the sort of lifestyle that gives America a bad name in less decadent parts of the world. I don't want to rehearse all that again.

Then I wrote the script for a TV movie about a lifeboatman who lost his religious faith, and had it restored to him after he was able to rescue a family of five from their pleasure yacht during a perfect storm, 'a miracle, I saw the lightning about the mast and it had the face of a man, a compassionate man' and so on. I wrote it with Jez Morrison. That was based on a true story. Believe that? The real lifeboatman was a drunk in Lowell, separated from his wife, in a bad way, but we didn't write that. We wrote it straight, only I had decided, in my coke-enhanced arrogance, that I was an artist. I wrote in long speeches on the nature of life, I tried to structure the whole thing in an experimental manner, I stretched narrative and filled the script with sea-symbolism. The lifeboatman's name was Billy McCabe. The script was called *McCabe's Ocean and the Electrical Face*. I thought I had written a masterpiece. The production company did not agree. They hired a third writer, a friend of mine called Poe Glancy, to rewrite the whole thing as a conventional *Based On A True Story* TV movie. They re-named it *Lifeboat in a Storm*. It was the *TV Quick* pick of the week, and my name was on the credits although little of my work remained. I tried to have my name taken off the credits in a fit of artistic pique. I was an asshole, but the industry was filled with assholes so nobody seemed very much to mind. Maybe I acted more of an asshole in the industry than I otherwise would have done, to *fit in* you see: but I was a good man when I wasn't hanging out with the industry crowd. It sounds up-my-own-ass of me to say so, but that's how I was: in the *real* world I donated nearly a hundred thousand dollars to charity. I worked for a while for a Shelter, manning the phones, until I had to quit because of time pressures. I went to political meetings, and doorstopped for liberal politicians. When Sally Boyden ran as minority candidate for New York mayor I endorsed her, gave her campaign money. When Pablo Elevado attempted to muster support for his bid to become the first Hispanic Democrat presidential candidate, I was a supporter, in a small way. I gave his campaign money too. I met Elevado several times, and for a while I hung out with Han Morales, George Christolides, Jenny Newport, all those people. I couldn't exactly call them friends; but I supported the cause. It was the cause that was important. I still believed the world could be made a better world. You find that hard to credit?

I still believe that. If you don't believe the same, that's your loss.

Did I tell you I was raised a Catholic? My father was a

Polish Jew but he converted after he came to the States and he married a Catholic Pole, so I was taken to mass and confession and such when I was a kid. The only part of it I liked was confession. I liked the way that the priest couldn't tell anybody else what you said to him, so no matter how shocking or powerful your words they could not travel outside the confessional. *How long since your last confession?* Father I killed a man, I killed two men. A silence. That grille, like an apothecary's cabinet without the drawers. *My son, I am saddened to hear you say so. Is this a joke? I must remind you that it is a great sin to mock God's offices. God is not mocked.* Are you gonna absolve me, or what? Chewing gum, kicking at the dark wood of the partition with my toes. Actually I killed more than two men, it was more like six men. I peed on them too, when they were dead, took a dump on them after they died. They're all dead, pop, pop – *my son, how old are you?* I'm fifteen, father. *Fred!* (in a much sterner voice, for this was, after all, my priest and he knew me) *I know you're no more than twelve. I'll not stand for this. Lie to a priest? Who do you think you're fooling? Did you really harm some men? I don't believe you did. You must listen to me when I say that your soul is in very severe danger with this sort of joking. The confessional is no place for joking. I am going to ask you to go away and think seriously about what you've done, I mean your levity and your disrespect for God, and you'll come back tomorrow in a penitent frame of mind to say sorry to God and to me for this wickedness.* It scared me, actually, because his voice was straining with suppressed anger, with actual anger, and it is an upsetting thing to realize that you have angered a priest. But when I was out of the church I felt a glorious sensation of transcendent levity begin to suffuse me, because I knew *he could tell nobody about it.* The secrecy of the confessional protected me. I could have hugged myself in glee; it seemed to my twelve-year-old mind to be the perfect crime. The victim had taken a vow never to give the perpetrator away. But when I got back home from school the next day, Father Terrell was sitting in the kitchen with my mother. They both looked very sternly at me when I came in, and all that buzzing and fearfulness frothed through my young body. It was a thrilling fizz in the solar plexus that I associated, even at that age, with sex. I knew he had told my Ma. I knew he had betrayed the most sacred of his vows in order to discipline a twelve-year-old tearaway who had done nothing more, for Christ's sake, than prank about. This was terrifying in the most profound way. I was shaking – was actually shaking, like a spastic child. This was in part fear of my Ma's wrath, for that could be a terrible thing, but it was also (I don't think I'm being fatuous when I say this) the rending of the veil of the temple, the crumbling away of my trust in the Church. Father Terrell stood when I came in and said, 'Fred, I've explained to your mother that you came to confession yesterday in a wholly inappropriate frame of mind.' I couldn't hold my words in. I positively squealed, 'You can't tell! You're not allowed to tell!'

'I have not told her the precise details,' said the priest in a pained tone, but I knew in my heart that he had broken his vow, and I believe that he knew it too. He wouldn't have made that temporizing statement otherwise. So then there was a lot more talk; my Ma grabbing my elbow and making me sit on my stool by the table and listen to a lecture on proper respect, and the wrong sort of friends, and God seeing everything. By then, of course, it was much too late. An adult might say that the church is not in its priests, but in God. I don't know about that; maybe it's true. But to a kid the church is a mysterious and polytheistic place, the Pope the chief god, bishops and priests lesser deities. Without wanting to sound bombastic, I knew that day what it felt like to be betrayed by one's god.

You might say that a person never quite gets away from it, the Church. A person never quite *wants* to. As an adult I refused to make public demonstrations of religious faith, but the sense of it still haunted my mind. I can be more precise: I hadn't much time for the God of my youth, he seemed to me too patriarchal, too Jewish, too thou-shaltn't. Christ – well, Christ was fine and such, but to my adult sensibilities he seemed too *hippy*; his love thing was too fluid, too free. I knew a guy at college called Henry Haglund, a sweet but sentimental gay man. He was Catholic too, I think, or maybe he was Lutheran, I can't remember. But the point is that he was fixated on Christ, on Christ's love, on (a poster in his room) the well-defined musculature of Christ's abdomen as he strained on the cross – all the love, *strenuous* love and *painful* love, all that, the effort-reward ratio linked like that. That wasn't for me. But the Holy Spirit, though – now there you have it, *there* you have something that still pushed my god-button. Nebulous, in a way, yet also precise: a cloud of unknowing that was also a dove with Persil-white wings and a beak sharp to shear the green branch. Sublime. In some sense I decided that the Sublime would be my god. I even thought that the Holy Spirit would be (this sort of hubris was common enough in the television industry) my Muse – for I was increasingly certain, inside my mind, that I was an *artist.* I would sit at my Mac and close my eyes, hold out my arms, palms flat down, and slow my breathing, trying consciously to open myself, to let the spirit flow into me and through me, a great, glorious streamer; so that I could become – let's say – the comet, creating-creating-creating at the front in an incandescent nub, whilst behind me poured a great trail of light and spiritus sanctus and glory.

Jesus, to think of it. And I really believed it. I believed I was making *Art* as I sat at my keyboard clicking and tapping, and writing dialogue between Paul and Paula, and blocking in long shot, cut to, dolly pan, sketching prissy little stage directions about images and actors' movements. I was writing a screenplay, leaving the banality of TV behind for the hope of Hollywood and Oscars and respect and The Whole Thing. I had fantasies of a $60 million budget. I toyed with casting this or that current star in the key roles. The story (I think I believed this, it's a little hazy in my memory, but I think I believed that) the story was literally being dictated to me directly by the Holy Spirit – by, let's not forget, thirty three point three recurring of the God-head. And that infinite recurrence also, in its way, a sublime and a mystic thing.

This is the story:

The opening scene is set in the Waldorf Astoria, in New York, on 19th November 2001. Enron's bankers are assembled in these opulent surroundings. They are about to be told that to the $13 billion reported debts for the 3rd Quarter of 2001 must be added a previously undisclosed $25 billion of additional debt. The commercial behemoth, America's eighth biggest corporation, is about to topple. It is on the very edge of falling. My three key protagonists are present in this hotel at this time: first, Paul 'T-Bird' Lanborn, an Enron junior manager. Second, his girlfriend Paula Potocki. And third, Marshall Porter, a senior Enron executive. Now, T-Bird, foolishly, has run up gambling debts of over a million dollars. He decides that the way to dispose of these debts is to fold them into Enron's enormous losses, losing them in sums so vast that a few extra millions will not be noticed. 'The perfect robbery,' he says, 'is the robbery where the stolen money is not even noticed, where it is lost in the welter of bankruptcy and disaster.' I made a mental note to revise that word 'welter' in a future draft, it's not really a Paul word ('bunch' would be a Paul word; 'fucking mess' would be Paul). If the mafia, from whom T-Bird had unwisely borrowed the money with which to gamble, don't get it back by the end of the day then they will kill – not T-Bird himself, no no, but his woman, the beautiful Paula. Paula doesn't know this; she believes it is her handsome T-Bird who is at risk from the mob. The situation is desperate. T-Bird decides that Paula will seduce Marshall, the senior exec guy, who is graying-depressed-burntout and whom they reason will be susceptible to Paula's pneumatic charms. She will persuade him, blackmail him if necessary, to pass the required money to a company T-Bird has set up to that end, a purely notional company that will, by a complex legal maneuver, become another Enron satellite holding. Paula is not happy with the notion of bedding the old man, for he is not comely; but she wants to save her lover from what she thinks will be his grisly death, and so she goes along with this plan. The monetary transfer must happen before the bankers are informed of the desperate levels of Enron debt, and all assets are frozen, but it must happen close to the wire or it will be noticed in audit and the embezzlers will go to jail. There you have the ingredients; the deadline (which shrinks before the characters, as the story develops); the love triangle; Paula's half-hearted decision to bed silver-haired Marshall for her boyfriend's sake, little knowing that it is her own life on the line; T-Bird's own agonized guilt at the duplicitous way he is handling Paula (whom he really loves, in his way), his worry that is at the same time feeding his addictive gambling personality. I wrote it all, sex, excitement, social comment, a twist in the end. I thought it genius. It was so *much* more than just a thriller. It was *art*. I wanted to call it not *Gambler's Luck* or *The Seduction Conspiracy* or any Hollywood title like that, but rather *In At The Death of the Whale*, the whale being the corporation at the heart of the thing (one character in the script says 'a whale is a weasel built by committee'). You see, the Ghost had inspired me to produce *art*. I even picked out an epigraph for the movie, to be shown as white characters on a plain blue backdrop before the opening shot. It was from George W Bush's birthday letter to Kenneth Lay, the Enron chairman, in 1997 on the occasion of Lay's fifty-fifth birthday: '55 years old! Wow! That is really old. Thank goodness you have such a young and beautiful wife.' That was a real letter. Bush actually sent that letter.

I had the highest hopes for this project, I really did. But it was not picked up as a movie by any studio, no matter now many coca-fuelled lunches I sat through with contacts and friends (most of the coca, I should say, deposited inside my own nose during those lunches: Hollywood's vibe in those days was health food and restraint, and most producers and movers and shakers that I met with ostentatiously did not indulge). I turned it into a TV serial, four episodes, one day, a sort of mini-*24*. When nobody bought this, I transformed it again into a TV series, stretching the action over several weeks to fill a pilot episode and twenty episodes. But no dice, no dice, nobody was interested.

So I sat down again and rewrote it as a novel, a big 600-page thudder of a book, wedging in lengthy paragraphs of descriptive prose between the pre-existing dialog. I wrote in long bursts, 12-hour sessions, 20-hour sessions, followed by exhaustive collapse asleep in my clothes on top of the covers of my hotel bed. Into the descriptive passages of my novel I swept all the crumbs and litter of the zeitgeist. I devoured TV and magazines and newspapers for gobbets and snippets and flavor and cultural e-numbers to give the whole ragbag *verisimilitude*, for crying out loud – piling details and details onto my characters, an abusive childhood here, a dirt-colored wart on the brow there, *live you fuckers, live*. An article that I chanced to read in *NY Day* resulted in me allocating an obsession with chess to Marshall, a fascination with Bobby Fischer's games and lifestyle, the 1974 match in which Karpov won the right to challenge Fischer as world champion, and took the title by default when Fischer didn't show – checkerboard shirts in Marshall's wardrobe, chess-piece-shaped topiary in his Hamptons place, and a mental tic of translating trading terms into chess notation in his head. I read a book about the Vilna ghetto and the camps in 1943–44 and gave Paula a Lithuanian Jew grandfather, and modern liberal Jew parents, and a yearning in her $200k per annum life to return one day to the old country, to get back before the Fall to the Old World's brick towns and green fields and giant skies. The composition was all random, like this, but I told myself that this was OK because life is random. My coke-fizzing head felt sure that was the case. At the same time, and without finding the contradiction in the least discommoding, I also told myself that *it was all part of a grander plan*, that the Spirit was guiding me, that I was being inspired.

I worked in a whole subplot about 9/11 and then changed it to March 11 Madrid, and then took it out again as too much the obvious gesture. I wrote vastly indulgent passages of descriptive prose and congratulated myself on their accomplishment. Marshall's jowls sagged like an old woman's breasts. Paula had a neatly trimmed mat of pubic hair, like the bristles of a black toothbrush. The snout of a jumbo on the runway looked like a white whale in sunglasses. The bags under Marshall's eyes seemed, to Paul's coked-up sensibilities, to be smiles, almost like mockery. I wrote a scene in a casino to give Paul backstory to highlight his gambling addiction: a croupier pulling cards from a boxed stack like a slatecutter working a slab to prise off wafers. The chips as fossilised money. The chips clinking as they are shunted over the baize like loose teeth. I tried to think myself inside the mind of a gambling addict, I made the mental effort to *be* Paul. The way the click of the ball as it rattled in the roulette was like something falling into place inside his head, how it was the perfectly tooled clockwork sound of *rightness*, the sound that released the catch of tension deep inside him and allowed his muscles to relax even as he strained forward in excitement to see where the ball was going to settle. Red carpets soft as sand underfoot. The air under the electric chandeliers balmy as a summer's night. Croupiers and waitresses in black and white, discretion personified. Every player a lord of the earth, a princess, royalty in their own egos, all of them only ever one deal, one turn away from unimaginable wealth. What did I know? I'd never even been to a casino. I had seen them on the TV.

Nobody bought my novel. It interested no publisher, and no agent was prepared to represent me. I became bitter. Why didn't the cosmos understand my genius? Something was wrong somewhere, and my fundamental self-belief, my coke-arrogance, could not believe the wrongness was in any sense mine.

You see, I felt I had *art* inside me, a beautiful super-annuated fetus, and I felt it urgently, I felt it was spring-loaded for release. I thought I had to *get it out* somehow. I had to put it somewhere, I was itching, cocaine-itching to put it out there, somewhere, I no longer even cared where – like a fifteen year old, desperate to place his dick in something other than his right hand. Got to, got to. But nobody would take it, no cheerleader would indulge me, nobody was interested. I became bitter. The coke didn't help. I probably became a little paranoid. Or more than a little.

But there are other ways of expressing one's creativity. Other modes of art. I found one. The 9/11 terrorists, to return to that wearisome subject, *they* were artists. They got it out there. Nobody ignored *their* genius.

I haven't taken cocaine for years now. Of course, I should say, I'm glad to be clean, I'm much better off without it, much smoother. And I can sleep properly, without waking in a sweat and a jolt. But at the same time I'm not glad. I'm far from glad. I miss it. If I found some I'd take it. If there were some right here, right now, I'd stop writing this and take it in a flash. Life with cocaine as opposed to life without it: soda water compared to regular tapwater. You want tapwater with your bourbon? No, you don't.

So, I can picture the disdain on your face as you read this, hey he thunk of his terrorism as art, hey he had *pretensions* in his bombing and murdering. But that's not it at all. I tell you: the Spirit moved me. Are you going to contradict me? What good will that do? You think the Holy Spirit is mocked? It is not. You can't joke it away. By this stage, however, it was no longer really the Holy Spirit, it wasn't a Catholic thing to my conscious mind any more. It was a Catholic thing to my subconscious, maybe, but I'm not answerable for that. To my conscious mind it was now Hegel's *Geist*, it was the Spirit of History. It was Destiny. What was wrong was the System? Everything was wrong. It had to be pulled down and rebuilt, entire. Freedom was supposed to be our reason for existing. You want to tell me we had freedom in the old USA? You want to tell me we have it now? Oh, yeah, you *want* to tell me that, but you can't, because you *know* it is not true.

I did my job, and it was crazily well paid. Cleaners and nurses and front-line troops earned a few dollars a day, and I earned hundreds of thousands, which I spent at once, saving none of it, blowing it all on blow and hotel bills and extravagance. I wrote a kindergarten show about a kitchen in which puppeteers brought foam-built microwave and coffee-maker and pans to life to talk amongst themselves and have little adventures, called *Kitchen Capers* (title changed to *The Kitchen Krew!* by the studio). But at the same time I started chatting online to liberty-minded people – real liberty that is. I started going to face-to-face meetings. I joined the American Workers' Party. I would have joined before but I had been timid at the prospect of my name coming to the attention of the industry as a Communist, I would have lost work. But I was able to join in secret, to pay the money and go to the meetings and nobody else knew.

The one thing that turned me around more than any other was the declaration of the War on Terror. You remember that? 'Terrorist' became the word to describe any anti-government activist. Don't misunderstand me; I was in New York (in New York state to be exact) on September 11th, and I was as shocked and as appalled as anybody else. But the War on Terror had nothing to do with that. How could it have anything to do with that? It was about *definitions*, about blanking out the page of history and starting again. After 9/11 *any* protestor, any freedom fighter, any contrarian, anybody exercising their rights to free speech and free thought – anybody who opposed the government at all – was scratched out and rewritten as 'terrorist'. If the government had had this idea in the 1960s do you know what they would have done? Martin Luther King would have been a terrorist. Malcolm X certainly would have been a terrorist. The American Revolution was a terrorist act and George Washington was certainly a terrorist. Anti-war protestors were terrorists. Nelson Mandela was a terrorist. John Garnier was a terrorist. Fucking Gandhi was a terrorist. Sesto Bruscantini was a terrorist. It was just, like, ridiculous.

The government egregiously identified itself as anti-terrorist. The only place an anti-governmentalist could go was to become an *anti*-anti-terrorist. To *inhabit*, in other words, terrorism, to reclaim it, to do it better. To force a sense on the people that Freedom must be fought for. Freedom is not something handed to us by our benign superiors; it's something we claim, we seize in blood-stained hands. The AWP understood that. That's how America was made, wasn't it? You want to tell me it wasn't?

Now, I know this: you want names, and details, and conspiracies dissected and displayed to your gaze. I say again: no. Is that on the record?

The AWP used to meet in rooms behind bars, in private houses. It was organized on a cadre basis, so I only knew maybe eight people in all my time hanging out with them. Henry Muller was one; another guy called Stramm, I knew him as Hoper Stramm and sometimes as Doper Stramm, I'm not sure of his first name. It may have been Karl or Carl. You can have those names; I'm assuming that they're both under the snow, those guys. Two people who I know survived the snow who used to come to meetings were the Evanses, Robertson and Anne; I bumped into them in New NY; they were on their way somewhere and stopping in the barracks there for a week. Holland Coates. Benton Taney. Carolyn Usher. A guy called DeBoer from Canada (I saw the name DeBoer in a post-Snow document a while back, so if it's the same guy maybe he survived the Snow too). It was like a family, the AWP, the cadre-sized groupings gave it that sort of scale. Not lecture halls filled with hundreds of Maoists with their fists in the air, but half a dozen people sitting round a kitchen table trying to figure out how to make the world a little better. Trying to figure out how to help people – maybe it does sound just a little pathetic when I put it in those terms, but after all what else were we trying to do but help people? What's so wrong in that?

They liked me because I had lots of money, but not only for that reason. I was excited, and committed, and I was good with words. Words were my skill, and a lot of my contribution. I wrote thousands of words for the party newsletters, and although it was anonymous (the Party spoke through me, I didn't express my own ego) I have to say some of that writing was damn good. I also contributed direct action – it wasn't just words. The party was the only good part of my life for a long time.

I went to meet my wife. At this time she was staying in the apartment I'd bought her (Bridgeport NY) whilst I was staying in a hotel. This was before we divorced. We met in a restaurant called *Tips* which specialized in serving the juicy extremities of food rather than the whole shebang: tender wedges of chicken, asparagus-ends, the tips of carrots and leeks. I sat in the lot inside my car and sniffed up a quantity of powder from off of the back of a paperback novel and into my nose. Then I wiped the book clean and put it in my jacket pocket, because I was still reading. The novel was called *The Eight Folds of Heaven*, but I can't remember who wrote it. I was wearing a black Boss jacket with a *Matrix* T-shirt under it, yellow corduroy pants, sneakers, no socks. Male-pattern baldness was already the most noticeable feature on my skull. My face was prematurely lined, because the coke meant I didn't sleep much, and because it was wearing me out. I can be frank about that. So I sniffed up some more of the stuff preparatory to meeting my wife and got out of the car. It was dark in the parking lot.

When the coke went up into my head this is what I experienced. First, I had a sensation of clenching inside my head, as if my skull were filled not with bone and brain but with pure muscle, and I was flexing that muscle inward all at once. Then there was the tingling, an abrupt warmth that was near-numbness and the urge to sneeze, an urge I resisted because I believed (I'm sure irrationally) that sneezing after snorting wasted some few crumbs of cocaine that had not yet been absorbed into my blood. So I sat there, wide eyes, head slightly back, as a sort-of equilibrium settled in my sinuses and I did not sneeze. But as I sat, there came along with the equilibrium a gathering sense of elation. I could feel confidence gelling inside me, awareness of the million possibilities of life and of my own ability to access them all. A crescendo. Immediately before taking the stuff I had been anxious, fretful: but that all went away. All my anxiety melted, washed out by self-confidence.

I had been worried during my drive to the restaurant, because I had been cheating on my wife, and because I felt that my wife suspected this fact. I had been worried that the meeting was going to be awkward and upsetting. But now, as I looked again at the circumstance, I felt I could cakewalk it, I felt it was going to be easy. Fuck it. She might wail a time, but I'd bring her round, I'd sweet-talk her, promise her, I'd *show* her I loved her, that she was the one who mattered most to me. I'd whirl her away with sheer force of personality. What did a little fucking around matter? Everybody did it. It was all alright.

She was sitting at the table by herself when I came into the restaurant. She looked up at me as I stood over her and said, 'You're high', with a disgusted tone. I said, 'Only at the fact of seeing you again, my love,' speaking a little too rapidly. I was staring a little, looking at every single thing in the restaurant in quick order. Fidgeting a little. I sat down.

For half an hour she said almost nothing. I gabbled my way through the menu, the drinks, the thing I was writing, the Fox guy who maybe would pick it up, the state of the world. She said very little. By the time the food came, and after a peck of wine, I could feel the high slipping away, but that only made me want to cling more desperately to it. I finished half of my food, but I wasn't very hungry. I lit a cigarette, and she scowled at me. 'Non-smoking,' she said, pointing to the little plastic pyramid on the middle of the table upon which was drawn, diagrammatically, a smoking man's profile inside a red circle with a red bar across it, cancelling him out, erasing him. I felt wobbly. The man in the red circle was me. The restaurant staff had put the sign there specifically as a message to me. I was being erased, wiped out of the picture. I extinguished my cigarette by dropping it in my nearly full glass of wine. The restaurant staff and my wife were plotting somehow. I waved down a waiter and insisted, noisily, angrily, that my wine be replaced, that my wine had a cigarette stub in it. My wife said, 'Fred, what's the matter with you?' This was only a manner of speech, she wanted to rebuke me; she didn't want actually to know what the matter was with me. The waiter, sullen, brought me a new glass. I grinned, I decided to brazen it out. I wolfed down a chocolate dessert, a mousse in a scalloped glass bowl. I said, 'Tasty, tasty.' Then I said, 'Chocolatey, chocolatey.' This struck me as funny, and I giggled. But my wife's face was stern, and the hilarity left me. 'I gotta go to the bathroom,' I said, feeling in my inside jacket pocket for my little bag of powder. 'You're going to get high again,' my wife said, dryly, 'and we've only been here an hour.'

'It's the bathroom, honey,' I told her. 'When a man's gotta go, he's gotta go.' I put a John-Wayney inflection on the word *gotta*. Western. Shoot-from-the-hip. I stood up.

'If you go off right now to snort in the men's room,' she said, looking up at me, 'then I'm fucking *out* of here, I'm leaving you forever. Sit down, down.'

'Come on.'

'I'm serious.'

'When I gotta go,' I said, less certainly. 'I gotta go.' The John-Wayney vocal tic didn't seem so funny this time.

'I'm serious, Fred,' she said. 'I'm serious as divorce. I'm leaving you – if you break our meal to take more drugs.'

I sat down. 'You make it sound,' I said, but I couldn't

think how to finish the sentence. I drank some more wine, brought out another cigarette, and then remembered about the man's profile in the red circle with the erasure sign lancing through his cheek. I put the cigarette back in the pack. It occurred to me to say, 'Jesus, tough crowd,' in a low voice, as if that would be funny. My wife did not laugh.

Then what happened was that all the exhilaration, all the self-belief and sense of possibility, flipped right about. If you've taken drugs you'll know what I mean. It happens when you're cocktailed on a number of chemicals, and when you're tired, and when you're in a no-way-out situation of whatever kind. You'll brazen it, brazen it, and then suddenly you'll be crying, begging, apologizing. I didn't cry, at least. At least I did not actually cry. I said, 'Look, Mary, Mary I'm sorry.'

She quizzed me with her eyes. With her eyebrows only, actually.

I slumped. I felt so exhausted I could have slept right there, at the table. At the same time I was twitchy, fidgety. 'Look, I wanted to meet up with you,' I said, 'and I wanted to talk to you. I've got something to tell you. I guess you know about it. Maybe you do. But I love you. Let's put that on the table right now, I love you. OK?'

'You think I'm a fucking idiot,' she said, but in a passionless sort of way.

'It's been a bit crazy with this Fox project, and before that with the, the, other thing, the thing. I've not been a brilliant, you know, husband, I know. But I decided, actually as I drive over, as I *drove* over, I decided to turn over a leaf. You're right about the, stuff, about the gear. I'm going to cut down.' Then, because her face seemed to darken as I said that, I said, hurriedly, 'Cut down as a prelude to quitting, really giving it all up, it's the best way, if you just flat quit then you've more chance of falling back off the cart, but if you pace it, cut down, gradually come down, then you'll *stay* off it.' There was a hiatus as a waiter took our plates, and I looked intensely at the tablecloth. When the waiter was gone, I said, 'And I want to say something else, because, you know, to turn over a leaf I'll need your support more than ever, so I don't want there to be any secrets.'

'Denise told me that she saw you and Caroline go into the viewing room together at the Frieland bash.'

This information took a moment to assemble itself in my brain, my poor battered and leaky brain. 'Uh,' I said. 'Caro, yes. I wanted to talk to you about Caroline.'

'It was Caroline you wanted to talk to me about?'

'Uh, yeah, I wanted to. It was that one time.'

'It wasn't that one time.'

'No, there were other times. But it – look, this is going to sound cliché, inevitably, inevitably, but it was a stupid and a nothing thing. A fling. It was a fling.'

'Have there been others?'

'Look. Can I say that I'm sorry? Can I just say that?'

'Don't get mad at me.'

'I wasn't getting mad.'

'You said can I say sorry in a angry sort of way.'

'I'm sorry,' I said, losing momentum, 'I'm sorry I said sorry wrong, and I'm sorry about, uh, Caro. I stopped seeing her.' But I had seen her that afternoon, and planned on seeing her the following day as well. The day before that I had seen a woman called Anna, from Hong Kong, who was visiting Warner. She had gone with me, I think, in the mistaken belief that I was an important bigshot studio type, and I didn't like to disabuse her of her beliefs. Belief is important, after all, and disillusionment is the cruelest thing. I was also paying two women, on alternate weeks, to come to my hotel room so that I could have sex with them; one called Maria – like my wife, as I told her – and the other called Misty. I had enjoyed congress with Maria three days before. I had told her to lie on her front on the bed and read a copy of *House Beautiful* magazine that I happened to have in my room whilst I watched myself in the wall-to-floor mirror move back and forth on her with my belly against her back. I often instructed Maria to act in some seemingly bored manner when we were intimate: to act like a manne-quin, to watch the TV, to hunch forward and paint her nails whilst I came into her from behind. I thought that was kind of a cool way of doing it. She was a squashed-face, skinny, Hispanic woman, and I bet she's under the snow now, dead and frozen like all the rest of them.

Before the Snow I more or less lived in hotels. I called my hotel room 'my study'. I told people that I could only work in hotel rooms.

I said to my wife, 'I'm sorry, I really am.'

She said: 'Are you saying sorry because you're genuinely penitent, or because you want to get sorry out of the way before going back to it?' She may not have used the priest-phrase *genuinely penitent*, I may be embellishing my memory when I report that, but this was the gist of it.

I was really struck by that, by what my wife said to me. Because that's true, isn't it? That *saying* sorry is only ever a going-through-the-motions, like in the confessional. It's only form. I have said I am sorry, and what else is there to say? There's nothing else to say, sorry doesn't span the space between people. *Being* sorry is a wholly other thing, though. Saying is sinning, going to the confessional, and then sin-ning again the next day. Being sorry is not sinning any more. If you genuinely were sorry, in your inmost being, it would be almost vulgar, almost disgusting, to open yourself and show the world those emotional viscera.

'Things,' I told my wife, 'have just really been getting on top of me lately. Everything's been kind of getting on top of me.'

'The drugs are on top of you,' she said, with scorn. And as far as she was concerned, I knew, I was just dying under a massive drift of the white powder, crushed and killed and buried and dead. But I shook my head, 'It's not that, it's not that.'

'Would you like coffee?' said the waiter, standing a little way off. I nodded, and then I said, 'Yeah, yeah,' and magically – as if by divine inspiration – there was a whole speech in my brain, a fluent, an eloquent and compelling speech. And the gist of the speech was this: that coffee was also a drug. Indeed that caffeine and cocaine were essentially, Platonically, *chemically*, practically the same thing, only one was black and one was white, only one was socially accepted and the other socially stigmatized. And that this sort of chemical-apartheid, this ridiculously arbitrary prejudice against one drug but not the other, was symptomatic of the insaneness of how society worked. Why shouldn't people be allowed to take whatever chemicals they liked, if it didn't harm others? How did the land founded on the notion of freedom get to be so fucking-nanny-like that it denied its citizens the freedom to do what they liked, if it didn't harm others? How did my drinking *this cup of coffee here*, or sniffing this other miniature pyramid of white powder *there*, harm anybody but myself? Who had the right to tell me *not* to do *either* of these things? Because, when it all came down to it, there are only two things, there *is* only black and white, there is only freedom or fascism, and which was it to be? Which side to choose? It was all there, like a speech printed on vellum, and all I had to do was say it, and Mary would understand, and she would give me her blessing, and hug me.

But I didn't say a word of that. The words just did not come out of my mouth. My mouth felt dry, actually.

Mary said: 'We can do this thing through lawyers, or we can just do it. There's a website where we can both log on, and they generate the legal papers, and I can, or you can, file them. It'll be cheaper.'

'Cheaper,' I said.

'Not that money is an issue,' she said, scornfully. 'You got a pile of money, I know.' I thought: how can she be so scornful of money? Isn't money just another symbol of freedom?

'Hey,' I said, and I pressed both my palms flat against my face, my hands blade-to-blade to make a mask, my two little fingers against my nose, my thumbs on the side of my cheekbones.

'Jesus,' I heard her say, 'why *not just stop* the amateur dramatics?'

'Sure,' I said between my hands.

'Or hire lawyers if you want to,' she said, getting up from the table. 'If you want to. I only thought the website and all would be quicker and easier.'

Lawyers: now, lawyers are part of the problem, don't you think? Before the Snow or after. It's not exactly an original position, attacking lawyers; but wouldn't it be better, just better, if the Law were like the instructions to a blender? Instead of like the arcane mysteries of the temple of Bla-Bla that only the initiated high priests understand? Like the warranty on a blender: you claim, you get. Can you imagine how things would be if you had to hire a lawyer to claim when you bought a faulty blender from the store? As it is (as it used to be), you take the thing back and that same afternoon you get a new blender. But under the Law you'd spend thousands of dollars and the best part of a year and then you'd get your blender, or not if the store hired better lawyers. It's so stupid we don't even see how stupid it is anymore. We're in the blizzard and we don't see the blizzard, we think the world is just all white about us.

You're a lawyer, yes?

I had a heart attack. That happened when I was in a steak restaurant with two friends, Mare Obenreizer and Solomon Chifadza. My divorce was behind me. Mare was a writer like me, and Sol worked in business. He was a business trouble-shooter. We were all having a meal together, because we were old friends. Sol was talking, saying about some company or other he'd audited, how he'd gone in and come out a fortnight later. 'I saved them four hundred thousand a year,' he was saying. He repeated the sum as three sentences: 'Four. Hundred. Thousand.' Then he said, 'I told them how to smarten up, slim down. I ran up 20,000 bones on my own.' Then he was telling another story about how he planned to buy up a shipwreck, this grain ship wrecked on the coast of Mexico somewhere, snap it up, going for a song, who else would want to buy a wrecked ship? – spine broken, this ship – and all the grain swollen and spoilt, salt water in all the grain compartments. Snap it up for a song, since the cargo was ruined and the ship could not be made sea-worthy. 'But you know what I'll do?' He waggled his eyebrows. I leant a little towards him, holding my beer bottle so that its red-white label rested against my cheek, because it was a very warm night. 'This is what I'll do,' he said. 'Truck some pigs down there, Texas pigs, and have them fattened on that fucking grain. The boat went down in the estuary for Christ's sake, I'll guess it's not even that salty, the water there. The water in an estuary is not necessarily *all* salt?'

'The water,' said Mare, with a drunk man's seriousness, 'in an estuary is not necessarily all that salty.'

'I'll be prince of pigs,' said Sol. 'Pigs eat whatever.' He said *whatever* like a teenage girl, for laughs. 'They'll eat cigar ends, sawdust, you-say-what. Ship them back up for sausages and pork bellies, and I'll make moo-chow die-near-ow.' Mare laughed at this. He was drunk enough to laugh at anything. I smiled, but it was as much a grimace as anything, because there was a soreness in my ribs and up in my shoulder, over on my left side. It felt like an indigestive pain, a sort of hot, burning pain. Sometimes I get little catches of pain in my chest when I breathe in deeply, which I think (I've asked doctors) has to do with a slight tendency to inflammation of the pleural membranes, inflammation that the residue of my unhealthy lifestyle brings on me from time to time. That pain usually catches in my chest for a breath or two and then goes away. I figured I was experiencing that same thing.

I was wearing a lemon-colored hessian jacket, with a black Dandy Warhols T-shirt under it. I hadn't changed the shirt in a couple of days.

Sol said mucho dinero again in his comedy accent.

Mare said Robert die-near-ow, and laughed; and Sol laughed.

I widened my grimace, because the pain was growing fast. Then my elbow slipped from the table and I slumped. The beer bottle fell from my hand. It tap-tapped on the table and it fell over, vomiting beer and suds from its tiny glass mouth. The pain had suddenly swollen, had become very fierce, like a broken bone. It didn't recede, it was lodged in my torso like rock. It grew harder. I gasped as I slid to the floor. The last thing I remember was Sol's face: the black freckles on his beef-colored skin looking like dark glitter, and his wide face stretched wider with this huge fucking grin as I dropped to the floor. This, let me assure you, is what death feels like. I know what dying feels like. Your blood runs to fire and acid in your chest and shoulders, and you can't stop yourself falling to the floor, and everything is blanked out with the pain. I was down on the floor. I told myself, man you are down *lying* on the *floor* now. Up above I could still hear them laughing deeper, laughing louder, thinking I was only fooling around. A massively dense pressure was crushing my chest and my shoulder from front and back at once, squeezing and squeezing until beads of blood (I am sure) were wrung out of my very bones. It was agonizing.

That was my heart attack. I was conscious all the way in the ambulance, but the pain was so fierce I couldn't speak, I could barely breathe. Sol rode with me. His flat wide face kept looming over me and he kept saying things like 'you hang in there' and 'nearly there now'. Then we were at the hospital, and Mare had taken a taxi and arrived before us. He manifested his concern in a different manner to Sol, by joking with me, and jollying me, by calling me names like 'a hell of a cuss' and 'you old boozer' in an Irish accent, and 'hurry up an' get well, I wanna go back to the bar'. These two approaches, Sol's concern and Mare's joking, represented their diverse personalities.

Surgeons operated.

And the next day, when I was all alone, and the sunlight was so fierce through the window in my room that it made my eyes water, the doctor came by. 'I am not the police,' he told me. I said, OK. 'If you keep taking cocaine,' he said, 'at the rate it was yesterday present in your blood then you can look to have half a dozen heart attacks like this a year until you eventually die. I wouldn't give you even a year until that happens. Until,' he repeated, in case I had misconstrued, 'you die. Yes? It will bury you. Yes? You certainly won't reach forty-five. Understand: I am not even talking about the alcohol and the cigarettes and who-knows-what-else. I am only talking about the cocaine and about the weaknesses of your constitution. Yes?'

I said yes, I was meek, and alarmed at what the doctor said.

After he left I sat in the bed and stared at the folds of white blanket over my feet. I thought of shrouds.

But in a little while my spirit revived. I prepared a speech for the doctor, rehearsing it mentally over and over. I planned to call the nurse and ask her to bring the doctor. Then when he came to see me I would tell him that he was wrong about cocaine. I didn't need to cut it out entirely – reduce it a little maybe, but not total abstinence. I would tell him that in moderation it was merely a useful stimulant, not unlike coffee. I'd tell him that Sigmund Freud took cocaine, and credited it with much of his best work. Moreover, I'd say, doc, I'd say, you have to understand the *environment* in which I work. I work in the movies (this wasn't true, but that's what I was going to tell the doctor). Everybody in the movies takes cocaine (this, again, was only a half-truth, but what the hey). If I abstained people would think I was weird, I would lose work, friends and contacts would avoid me. So you see, doc, it is a *necessity* that I am able to indulge, just a little bit, from time to time. So what I want, doc, what I *need*, is for you to give me some medical leeway – come up with some medication, some treatment – some regime I can adopt – which will enable me still to get high, drink, smoke, screw, work for twenty-hour shifts, and do all the other things I *need* to do. I imagined the doctor replying *but it is*

217

illegal in a timorous voice, and at that point I would add: maybe it is, although you and I – we are rational adults, and we can agree that it should not be illegal in a so-called free country. However, granted that, technically, it is illegal. Here is one of the beauties of our little conversation, doc. Because there is such a thing as doctor-patient confidence, isn't there? If you prescribe me something to deal with the powder then there's no need for the police ever to hear about it. Do you see?'

I never had this conversation with my doctor. Of course my doctor would have told the police. There's no such thing as patient-doctor confidentiality.

It took me months to recuperate from the operation. My chest hurt much of the time, embers from the pain of the attack itself. To be precise, it hurt where they had separated the ribs to get at the throbbing organ, a luggage-seam of stitching and plasticated scar tissue red-pink against my yellower flesh. Eventually this hurt wore away, and I began to feel more like my old self. But there was an important change in the world. My insides had been on view to the world. That was what I kept thinking. I looked at a copy of the consent form I had signed, and I noticed that the hospital retained the right to film operations for training purposes. I couldn't find out, nobody seemed to know, if this had happened with my operation. But I became convinced it had. I became convinced that the world had seen my red and glisteny insides. That's not a comfortable thought, you know.

Then my ex-wife published a book. I read it with bulging eyes. That fucking book. I wondered, in my more paranoid moments, if she had carried a tape machine around with her to record our every conversation, our most private conversations – it was uncanny how she reproduced word-for-word the things I had said. She described our love life. She wrote out our arguments in the form of little playlets in the text, possibly as an oblique satire on what I did for a living: twenty pages of prose, then four pages of 'FRED:' and

'MARY:' and our every twist and wriggle of language recorded there. It devastated me to read it. I was still recovering from heart surgery, for Christ's sake. There's an H G Wells short story in which the world ends and all the people come for judgment; dictators stand proud and defiant ready to hear the list of their terrible crimes from the Recording Angel, only instead of reciting their majestically evil doings the angel relates their petty, venal, everyday failings, and this they cannot bear to hear. This is too humiliating. My ex-wife's book was like that. She called it *Living With an Adulterer*, and she dedicated it, without permission, to Hillary Clinton (you believe that?) and 'To All The Women Who Love Their Men Despite Their Men'. It was published by a women's press, and it did very well. It stayed in the *NY Times* Hot Hundred for five months. It became a morning-TV talking point. It was widely reviewed. In between the little playlets of our spats were sections of gray prose that analyzed the fault of our culture, how men were trained not to care, how they expected their women to make them a Home but how they Abused that Home and still expected it to Be There For Them. There was a chapter on 'So-Called Biological Imperatives' as an acculturated justification men used to allow themselves to have sex with other women. 'If *some* men can resist these So-Called Biological Imperatives,' she wrote, 'then *all* men can. Indeed, if many men simply do not feel these So-Called Biological Imperatives, then we can legitimately ask – Do They Even Exist? If they did, we'd expect *all* men to feel them, just as *all* men can grow beards or pee standing up.' There was a lot of capitalization in the text, which gave the book a oddly Germanic feel. That, and the hectoring tone. There was a photograph of my wife on the back cover in a dark power suit, sitting on a chair with her legs and her arms crossed, looking gloweringly at the camera.

But, Christ, there were conversations here that I had assumed were private, were just between myself and my wife. Our sex life, for Christ's sake? The things I said in anger? That's hardly fair. The time I met her in the restaurant, and I was a little high, and the things we said before she told me she wanted a divorce – it was all there, only I was malodorous and twitchy, constantly looking over my shoulders, and my skin was spotty, and I was rubbing my nose with the back of my hand like a screen-cliché junkie. Our wedding night was there, when I got a little too drunk, and took some pills, and had to throw up in the hotel bathroom for a little while. That was there. Is, I wondered, nothing sacred? I spoke to a lawyer, to see if the book was actionable. She told me that unless I had specified with my wife prior to any conversation with her that the content of said conversation was to be regarded as confidential, then a court would be unlikely to uphold any charges on grounds of breach of confidentiality. I said, heated, pepped up on a little powder, who the fuck makes that sort of stipulation before talking to their spouse? The lawyer shrugged. She was wearing a blue suit, jacket and skirt, not unlike the outfit my wife was wearing in her author photograph.

After that meeting I walked the city for a while in a sort of fugue state, my vision narrowed with hopelessness and anger. I went into a bookshop and stood in front of a display of *Living With an Adulterer*. More in sorrow than rage I took one of the books from the display and started tearing it. The checkout boy came round to remonstrate with me. The manager came too. I was crying. Jesus, that was a low point. I ripped four copies, ripped the covers off. 'It's a betrayal,' I kept saying. 'I'm making a protest,' I said. The bookstore was in a mall, and the mall had a security guy and he came by, told me to stop, sir, desist, sir, and eventually he grabbed me in a neck-lock from behind. 'It's a betrayal,' I told him. 'Sure it is,' he told me. 'You going to calm yourself?' 'I'm calm,' I said. 'I'm calm.' I paid for the four books, and the checkout guy insisted on giving me the books themselves in a plastic bag to carry away with me, even though I didn't want them, what would I do with four ripped-up books? So then I wandered the city for a while carrying those four ripped-up books in a plastic bag, not knowing where I was going, not knowing what to do. Still holding the bag I put my credit card into a public phone and called my ex-wife. I got her answermachine. I blabbed into that, for a long time. 'I'm sorry, I'm so sorry,' I said. 'Fuck it, Mary, I'm so sorry.' It was pathetic. I thought about suicide. I didn't think through the specifics, but only the general idea of it. Then I went into a bar and through to the rest room, and I sat in a cubicle and sniffed up a little pile of cocaine powder. It made my sore heart hurry in my chest, and made my blood pump with a scary vigor. I told myself, 'This is it, this is the death, my system has been overloaded, I'm going to be found dead slumped on the john in some bar somewhere, just as the doctor said.' But I didn't die, obviously, and after a while, and after some more sniffing, I felt a little better. I washed in cold water, and walked out of the bar leaving the bag of torn books in the cubicle.

That was a low point.

The AWP gave me focus, helped me through that time. They were closer than my friends. My friends, not to put too fine a point on it, were fucking useless. Sol came to see me, and he creased his face in a serious mask, and said to me, 'Look, I talked to a friend of mine, a detox guy. I told him about you.'

'You told him about me?' I said, wiping my nose with the palm of my hand. 'Jesus, Sol.'

'I'm worried, man,' he said. 'About you. He's confidential, man, he'll keep it to himself. And, like, it's not that *unusual* in your business is it now? – a habit, a certain *loss* of control. You know?'

'I thought you were *discreet*, man,' I told him, severely. 'I thought you'd respect my confidences.'

'You had a heart attack, you could have died, I talked to my man, he says that detox is a stroll these days, a stroll, compared to what it used to be. It's not cold turkey and sitting in a ring like AA. It's much more modern-day. You want I should set up a session with him?'

'With who?'

'With my friend, man. Get you looked at. You had a heart attack, you could have *died*.'

'I can't believe you went to some stranger and spilled my whole story to him,' I said, growing angry.

'Not some stranger, a friend of mine.'

But the AWP didn't care that I did drugs. That was not the issue for them. Indeed, I had several interesting conversations with my cadre leader on that subject. His name was Mo (for Maurice) Gaché; from Louisiana originally, now resident in New York. A large man, bearded over face and neck like black turf, a ponytail, a meaty nose, the flesh of his face gathered in broad bunches, but tiny little eyes like beads of blue blood squeezed out of that clenched face. During the first quarter of the Year of Our Salvation two-thousand-X I spent a lot of time buzzing between Gaché's house on Third and my latest hotel, the romantically named Cielo di Pisa on Straight. Gunning the engine of my tiny Volvo and zipping through the traffic, parking skew, dashing along the street to Gaché's steps, pushing his bell button as I panted. There was no actual hurry, except that I made myself hurry, I strained to inject urgency into my life to distract myself from the zeroness of it. 'Hi Mo,' I would say, as he opened the door, 'I can't stay, I got the group in forty minutes.' The *group* was a substance-abuse seminar I had agreed to attend three times a week. I had hit another car in a parking lot just as the owner was returning to it. The owner and I had got into an argument over the damage. The police had been called, and I had been arrested. My blood, according to whichever lab the police subcontracted this work to, contained traces of cocaine and amphetamine. I was charged, fined, and ordered to attend the substance abuse meeting thrice a week. The judge had used that exact word: thrice. My attorney had queried it in court: 'Twice a week sir?' Three times, the judge had said, irritably. Three times.

'That fucking group,' Mo said as he let me in.

Mo did not approve of the state poking its nose into what he considered my private business. For him it was symptomatic of everything that was wrong.

I had to wait in the hall whilst he bolted the door. I could not simply stand there quietly. I had to shift the weight inside my body from my left foot to my right – not hopping from foot to foot precisely, but swaying over and then back in staccato little shifts of center-of-gravity; and wiping my nose on the back of my hand, and looking into all the corners and crevices of Mo's hallway, and then thinking that it was kind of gross to wipe my nose on my hand like this, and pulling out one of the silk handkerchiefs I had bought for my constantly streaming nose and blowing phlegm into the fabric. 'I got to use your john before we start,' I told him. 'I'm busting.'

'Sure,' he said.

He knew, of course, but he really didn't care.

Afterwards we sat in Mo's front room. There was a large poster of Trotsky, with a several-lines-long slogan printed over his face, something about sitting in his room and thinking the world was a beautiful place. There were thousands of books on the walls. Mo owned thousands of books. The walls were fish-scaled with their spines. He had net curtains over his windows.

We talked shop – which is to say, terrorism. Do you perk up as I say this? I can picture your reaction precisely. September 11. March 11. But it's ancient history. I don't even know if Mo survived the Snow. I haven't seen him in five years. So we talked about the plans we were making, as a group, for an assault. Three bombs on one day, a Sunday to minimize casualties. A New York newspaper office; a coffee shop; and a blimp exploding over the White House – we were going to hire a blimp in Washington, pack it with explosive, float it over the White House and explode it. The plan wasn't to injure the President, or anybody. It was to make a splash. We were going to paint the words 'True Freedom' on the side of the blimp. When it exploded it would make all the TV networks: images of True Freedom going down in flames over the White House. It would be irresistible visual copy. It would run all over the world. We were doing *something*, at least. We had a statement ready, that I had helped draft. I can't remember all the words of it, not precisely, but it was about freedom. Americans boast that they will live free or die, but they have handed their freedom over to the press, to a tyrannical government, to corporations – to a capitalist world that thinks the freedom to choose latte or espresso is a suitable replacement for the freedom to live, speak and do as you wish. Lots more in that idiom. You get the point. This attack was months in the preparation, but it was never executed.

This is what Mo said, that time, about my drugs. 'You've got some——' he said when I came down from the bathroom, nudging one of his fat fingers at his own hairy upper lip, just below his right nostril, to show me where the traces of powder were on my face. 'Thanks,' I said, feeling embarrassed.

He could tell that I was embarrassed. 'Fuck it,' he said, 'don't feel awkward on my account. Snort all you want. Who's to tell you not to? Government scientists? Who gave *them* – who gave the *police* and the *judiciary* the *right* to *peer* up your ass? You want me to tell you what John Stuart Mill would say about that? About the the gak?'

'You're right,' I said. 'It's my business.'

'It don't signify,' he said.

The TV was on in the corner. Or perhaps this was another time – I think, on reflection, that this was a different time. Evening, not afternoon, and us sitting eating a meal off our laps, and drinking red wine, and watching the TV. It was a reality show. Reality TV was all over the media that season. We'd had *American Idol*, and *The American House*, and *Big Brother*, and *Open Dating*, and this show was called *The Barracks*. It followed twelve recruits in the army, real recruits, only their every hour and every action was captured by hidden cameras and broadcast to the nation.

Usually the case in reality TV was that the public voted off the least-liked members of the cast. On this show that selection was undertaken by the army itself in its usual manner, but the principle was the same. The public chose favorites and tuned in nightly, or tuned into the weekly roundup, to see if this lean, shaven-headed African-American with the handsome face, or this tall and buff and blue-eyed Midwest boy with a winning smile, had survived the training. The public watched that training. The public watched them do everything except piss and shit.

'It's fucking pathological,' said Mo. 'Our obsession with this sort of stuff. It's *symptomatic* of our culture. Something very wrong in our culture, man, that we're so obsessed with this. Prurience, fuck.'

'Yeah,' I said.

'It's like mobile phones,' he said. This was another of his bugbears; the way everybody now was compelled, more or less pressured by our culture, into carrying a mobile phone, Mark of the Beast, so that they could be contacted at any hour of the day or night, no matter where they were. It struck me as a little cranky, this last animus, but for Mo it was all part of the larger picture.

'I guess you could say,' I said, 'that they surrendered their privacy when they joined the army.'

'You ever been in the services?'

This surprised me. I shook my head. 'You?'

'Four years. Man, you accept that the sergeant will force you open like a clam during *parade* and during *exercises* and – yeah. But at *night*, in your bed, with the light's out? – that's your own time.' He gestured at the screen.

The image was from a low-light camera, that greenish Matrix-style color, the gritty, sandy texture of the images, thousands of dots of light and dark coarsely coalescing into the form of one of the soldiers in his bed. A hiss-filled soundtrack from a directional mike, picked up his whispered conversation with the guy in the bed next to him. He was talking about a medical worry he had. It was not clear to

me if he knew the cameras and the microphones were privy
to his comments.

'This is the problem, right here,' said Gaché. 'The state is
working as hard as it can to erode privacy.' I had heard this
speech before, but that didn't bother me. I looked up to
him. It was a good speech, and true. 'Privacy is the enemy,
because the individual cannot be controlled if he has a
fucking little private space of his own. It's George Orwell's
Nineteen Eighty-Four. You ever read Foucault?'

'I never did read Foucault.'

'Bentham – English, from the nineteenth century – he
invented the panopticon, which was a kind of prison, man,
where everybody was on view all the time. Foucault says
that's the model of modern society, only it's now the society
of the Spectacle, we're all on view, not just prisoners – or
we'll all prisoners and it's all the time. There's no privacy, so
nobody can commit a crime. They're shining the light inside
our heads, so we can't think in private any more, thought-
crime is the only crime they're interested in. Ideological
control. What's sick—' and he gestured at the TV again
'—is not that shows like this exist, but that people are so
fucking eager to get on them. Fame is our drug. Fuck, we *all*
want to be famous.'

'Well, famous,' I said. 'But more *rich*. Yeah? And – you
know, respected, and loved, no, adored.'

'Famous,' said Mo, firmly.

'Yeah,' I agreed. 'Famous.'

'Man, we fucking *queue up* to strip and bend over and to
say to the state, go on, take a *good look* up my ass. These
kids—' pointing at the TV '—they already gave up their
body to the state, that's what being a soldier is, but they *got*
to give up their souls too?'

He drained his wine. He got up and waddled through to
the kitchen to put more red in his glass. When he came back
I said:

'I used to work on a reality TV show,'

Gaché grunted. 'That whole industry,' he said, derisively.

'It was called *SponsorCam: Africa*. You remember it?'

Gaché grunted again, meaning either yes he did, or no he didn't.

'We were going to call it *SponsorCam: Sudan*, since the first series was in the Sudan. But the management decided that we needed the word Africa in the title, to try and draw in some African-American demographic. That word's a charm to that demographic. I said, when we do Afghanistan – we planned Afghanistan to be next, only Congress shut us down—'

Another snort of derision from the big man.

'Anyway, *I* said, when we do Afghanistan are we going to call it *SponsorCam: Asia*? Of course not. Anyway,' I said, losing my way a little, and swilling my wine in my glass as if that would sheepdog my thoughts back into their pen. The wine was a Chrysostom, a Cyprus wine. I remember thinking how strange to be drinking wine from Cyprus rather than California or France, but thinking nevertheless how pleasant it tasted; except that my taste was all shot to pieces by the drugs I was taking. It's very hard to sense the nuances of taste when your nose has been sandblasted and bleached on the inside.

We did not make bombs in Mo's basement, like some cack-handed amateurs. The AWP had a fair bit of money, some of that money mine. We made munitions in a property in the middle of Iowa specially bought for that purpose. We bought some of our ordnance openly – God bless America for that – and others through contacts we made at Midwest meetings, or through the internet.

On another occasion – or on the same occasion, I'm not sure – my memory is not as coherent as maybe it should be (I'm minded to blame the drugs, because constant drugs do make the mind sparser and gappier than it otherwise would be) – it may have been that same evening, watching the TV, drinking wine: only I remember another person there, a man called Benton Taney, who was also in the movement. Perhaps he came along later and joined us, or perhaps this whole conversation happened on another occasion. Anyway, Mo turned to me and asked: 'You ever kill anybody before?'

We must have been discussing Direct Action. But it's linked in my mind with my telling Mo about SponsorCam because, when he asked me that question, it was on the tip of my tongue to answer, 'People died on account of me' – that I felt guilt for my involvement in the whole Sponsor-Cam project. I really did. At the time it happened I was so guilty I couldn't sleep. I date my pills from that time. I remember very vividly a character called Tayyib, on that show, who borrowed money from his mother to buy a pistol, went out and shot a market trader with the pistol, took his takings – turned to *grin* at the camera he knew was watching him (the cameras in the market were on poles looking down) – gestured with the still-hot pistol in the direction of home, as if to say I'm going home now, tune in to the camera in my mother's house to watch what I do next – and then went home and paid his mother back the money he had borrowed from her. Paid the money out of the dead man's purse. Of course his ratings went skyward; everybody switched to his mother's camera, and then his own, to see how, or whether, he would explain himself to his mother, to see what he would do next, to see whether, or when, he next killed somebody. Jesus, that *grin*. He didn't tell his mother anything; he paid her the money and took a glass of tea with her, and then went away again. I watched that in my apartment (this was before my staying-in-hotels period), and feeling ill, feeling a horrible sense of, like the Bridge over the River Kwai, *My God What Have I Done?* So what's the thing to do then? To get up the next morning and just go on with your life? Pretend it didn't happen? Deny it had anything to do with you? These did not work for me.

So when Mo said *did you ever kill anyone?* I didn't say any of this to him, because I knew he would mock me. He had a temper on him, that man. He despised me, sometimes, I think. He turned to Benton and said:

'Of course he fucking hasn't. He's a fucking tourist, this one. Watching the revolution from his sofa. Don't worry, *caballero*,' he turned back to me, 'I know what it *takes* to kill a man, and so does Benton here, and we'll do the dirty work.'

'Jesus,' I said, 'Mo.'

'Just – fucking – just—' said Mo, suddenly immensely fierce, those portions of his cheeks visible above his beard blushing poppy-red with his ire, his pip-like eyes straining blue. His anger did sometimes swirl up like that, seemingly from nowhere.

'Hey,' I said, but in a small voice.

'Shut *up*. Jesus you're despicable, you're despicable.'

It occurred to me to say, you take my fucking money though, but of course I didn't say that. I loved him, despite his temper with me. I tell you what: he ridiculed me whenever there was a third party present. One time there was an activist from Detroit called Mary, or Mary-Ann, with us and we were discussing things, and suddenly Mo turned to Mary, or Mary-Ann, and said, 'You know Fred's nick-name in the cadre? Worm-man. He's a shit-eater.' And he laughed, and told a long story about how the police had arrested me for hitting this other person's car, and I had cried like a kid, and tried to confess everything, only I had so much snot in my mouth and my nose from my crying that the police couldn't understand what I was saying. 'Weak link, weak link,' said Mo, laughing again with a thunderous laugh. None of this was true, of course; the police had not arrested me, they'd just questioned me. And I hadn't mentioned anything about the Movement, and I hadn't cried. I don't know where Mo got that story from. *From where he got that story*, I should say.

And on another occasion he punched me. There was a meeting of the cadre, ten of us, in a CD warehouse in an industrial and trading zone on the outskirts of the city, and Mo was late. The rest of us just sat around, sat around, and David (who had the keys to the warehouse) got nervous and nanny-ish when people, bored, started picking at the shrink-wrapping of the slabs of CDs to see what the albums were, 'Don't do that, hey guys, don't do that, my manager'll crucify me,' in a whiny voice. When Mo finally arrived I was keyed up, edgy, and I went over to him and said, 'Where you been, man?' – only that. He swiped at me with his fist, big as a baby's head, and caught me on the side of my temples. I fell straight over, and I heard a pure angel-song ringing noise in my ears, and I saw the perspective of the floor at forty degrees, and people clustering around me. But I was alright again in a quarter of an hour, just a little sore, with a dime-sized bruise on my forehead. Whereas Mo dislocated one of his knuckles with the punch, and his big hand swelled up bigger. We went ahead with the meeting. It was not easy getting all the cadre together at one time, and we decided to go ahead with the meeting rather than reschedule. But Mo sat on a stack of CDs nursing his hurt fist and glowering at me like it was my fault.

Another time, he and I had to drive a van up to Rochester, NY, to pick up something or other. I hired the van under an alias with a false driver's license I'd paid $1100 for, and we drove upstate, and I thought the afternoon was going well: the trees blood-red in their New York fall livery, the sunshine sharp but not too hot. I guess I chattered away somewhat, but Mo joined in as well. I thought we were chatting, chilling, I thought it was going well. Then he said, urgently, 'Pull in, pull in at the rest-stop, at this pit-stop,' and I figured he needed to piss. So we pulled in at this parking lane and he said, 'Get out, get out,' and I climbed out, a little worried. It crossed my mind that he was going to drive away and leave me there, but I told myself, I've got my wallet, I'll walk to the nearest town and hire a car or get a taxi back home. But he didn't abandon me beside the road. He got out too, and then he took off his belt, unthreading it from the loops at the rim of his trousers with exaggerated precision. I said, 'Mo, what are you doing?' Then – do you know what he did? He pushed me down on the ground, held me down with his giant hand on the back of my neck, he pulled down my fucking pants and *whipped* me with the belt. Like he was Dad and I was Junior, like he was disciplining me. It was so humiliating. Cars passed on the road, and we were both right there. They must have seen everything, one grown man whipping another at the side of the road. Nobody stopped, of course. He hit me six times. It hurt. Then he got up, put his belt back, and got back in the passenger side of the van's cockpit. 'Come on,' he said, through the window, as I was picking myself up. 'Come on, let's get going.'

All for the rest of that journey I was trembling. I couldn't even ask him why he'd done what he'd done. But he seemed happier. Chattier.

He acted like that, unpredictable. He was more than a little unhinged – he was touched.

But I loved him. You know why? For two things. For the first, a speech I heard him give to the cadre. He said this: 'You may think of this cadre as family, but it's not family, it's much closer than that. We hold each others' lives in our hands. If you tell anybody outside the family about Pa touching you a bad way or Sister fucking the postman, that's OK, nobody is really hurt, nobody is dead. But you hear things in the cadre, you take them *to the grave with you*. Everybody must understand this. Nothing leaves the cadre. It is sealed, it is a sealed space. This goes beyond the meanings of the word secrecy you have previously come across. This is more than secrecy. Our lives depend on this. If you break this confidence, people die, people die, and – Jesus by Christ – I swear I'll make sure you're one of the people who die, if you break the confidence.'

This was the most beautiful speech I ever heard. Partly it was the 'greater love hath no man' vibe. But, I'll tell you, it was more than that. On another occasion he told a meeting, 'I'd die for you all, you'd all die for me, let's not dwell on that – can't we just take that for granted and move on?' It was the *taking it for granted* that was so moving, as much as

231

the fact of the readiness to sacrifice. But more even than that was the promise of a sanctuary space, a room out of which there would be no leakage. A sealed place, with sealed people, so perfectly insulated from the rest of the word, so friction-free and of itself, that you could spend two hours discussing how to bomb a government building and then zip up your coat and walk on to the sidewalk and marvel that the people you walked through had no idea what you had been talking about, planning, intending to put into action. *That* – that sensation, it was better even than cocaine. To smile at the ordinary people, and to talk to them, and for them not to know what was in your head. It's hard to express. It's a feeling of power, of superiority, but that sounds crude, like I was a bully or that I felt like a bully feels, and that's not it. It's more than that. Above all other things it is a feeling of containment. Can you understand how powerful that feeling can be? Of control, of wholeness, it is what it feels like to be a pure cell, to exist without pollution from outside, without the sense of bleeding one's essence into the gutter, but to *be*, pure as a star. Clean. White. Like the blankness outside. There is such power in blankness. There is power in namelessness. Mo gave me that. It felt that way to me, that he gave me that. Everything else was secondary to that.

I told him stuff, and he kept it to himself. Perhaps that was why he was so blithe about inventing stories about me, like the tale he told that woman about me crying in police custody. This might explain his impulse to fiction.

Here's something I did after the occasion I mentioned earlier, when I had that sort of mini-breakdown – when I walked into that bookshop and started ripping up copies of my ex-wife's book, *Living With an Adulterer*. After that I moved from my old hotel to a new one, because the old room reminded me of that whole shabby episode. I took up a new room in a new hotel, and plugged in my laptop, and set up my printer. This is what I did.

I wrote like a demon. I wrote and wrote, great slabs of

prose like sculptor's marble. I wrote in twenty-hour sessions, wrote until I fell asleep on the floor, or on top of the bed in my clothes, and then I'd get up so eager to write again that I didn't even shower. Inspiration filled my head like great cirrus clouds inside that blue-painted chamber. I ate only room service, I shooed away the cleaners when they came to change the bedding in the morning, I wrote and wrote. The Spirit was in me then, as certainly as my heart or my liver. It streamed into me with all the myriad white particles I breathed in through my nose. White atoms, like the tiny white particles that accumulate to make clouds in the sky. It was the cloud of unknowing. I knew my past, and I wrote it out and made my knowledge unknowledge. I fixed the whole thing in letters, millions of letters. In three weeks I had my completed document, 900KB on my hard drive. This I printed out. I did not revise it, did not correct it in any way, I simply printed it out. It ran to 300 pages, a great brick of paper, that I elastic-banded together and put inside a large envelope. I put the envelope inside my tote bag, a little black vealskin backpack-type thing I used to carry when I was out shopping or whatever. What did I write? What was it about? You might think it was about my ex-wife, but it was hardly at all about that. I wrote about my childhood, my parents, my upbringing, about things that happened. I don't want to say what I wrote. Things that happened, and a few things from later on, but mostly just me, with me as the central character. It was my early life, it was all of it. It was important. I finished it, and printed it out, and sealed it in manila and put the package in my tote bag.

I showered. I stood in the shower for a long time, but I hung my tote bag, with its cargo, on the hook on the back of the bathroom door where I could keep my eye on it. The individual threads of shower water coming down felt like nails at first, very hot and sharp, but after a while I ceased to notice them. It was just the shifting pressure of water on my head and shoulders and back, and the hissing like amplified silence, and the gurgling sounds of the plughole. I soaped myself and rinsed, soaped myself and rinsed, soaped myself and rinsed, all the time looking at the bag hanging on the back of the door.

After that I shaved, dressed, and went back to my computer. I took a sachet of white powder from the drawer of the desk, tipped a little onto the surface of the desk, near the corner. There was a plastic component that I had detached from my laptop, a sort of plastic shoulder just next to the hinge where the screen opened and shut. I had pulled this off, or it had fallen off, I can't remember; but it had two straight plastic edges, each an inch or so long, and I used one of these to marshal the powder into a neater hump. Then I squatted on the floor and positioned my nostril at the side of the desk and sniffed up two nostrilsful.

After my head had settled, and after I had finished twitching and flexing my shoulders and my neck, I felt the joy inside me. My belief was that the joy was always inside me, like my soul, like the Holy Spirit, but it took the cocaine to release it, to give me access to it again.

I turned on my laptop and called up the little icon of my 900KB file. I speared it with the white arrow that moved to my mouse's command. I dragged it over the blue-check wallpaper and put it in the dustbin. My machine spoke to me, saying *Are you sure you want to send 'Memory' to the Recycle Bin?* I clicked yes. Then I opened the Recycle Bin and pulled down a menu to delete it. Another window popped up with a red exclamation mark: *Are you sure you want to delete 'Memory'?* and I clicked yes again with a bubbly sense of elation. It was gone, and gone forever.

Now the only version of the file was a hard copy, in my tote bag. So I sprayed myself with Helios, an eau de cologne I sometimes used, and I walked out of my hotel room for the first time in weeks. I left the hotel and I walked through the streets of the city. I was elated. It is difficult to explain. My whole book was sealed and secret in a satchel slung over my shoulder. Nobody but I knew what was written on those pages. It was the purest form of secret. If somebody – the hotel cleaner, say – went into my room and turned on my laptop and tried to find the file, they would be unsuccessful. It was erased forever. (I later found that there are often ways of retrieving apparently erased files, but I did not know that then. I believed that everything I had written existed only in one hard-copy, portable form). And I was carrying it around with me, like a bomb, watching the passers-by, watching patrol cars cruise past me, watching for something, anything. I achieved a sort of bliss this way, wandering without plan through the city. Once I sat down in a café to have a drink, black coffee, and as I waited for the waiter to bring my drink to my table I became suddenly panicked, I became suddenly convinced that somebody was going to grab my tote-bag and make away with my manuscript. The thought was unbearable to me, that the manuscript would be taken out of my control, that they could take the thing and – I didn't know, but – publish it, put in online, copy it a thousand times and hand it out on the subway. That would have killed me. That would have been more than I could have stood. So I popped up and shuffled round from behind the table, and hurried out before the drink was delivered. I went into a bathroom in a department store, into a cubicle, and sniffed up some more powder, spilling some on the floor. Then I washed my face from the cold tap, hunched over my satchel as I rinsed, clutching it to my belly like a freefalling human clutching his reserve parachute. Then I gobbled some pills that were in my jacket pocket, without knowing what they were. But I was seeking the revelation.

Out on the street again, the gray grids of the city jammed at startling angles to one another, window-grids, street intersections, poles, trash cans. But over it all were great arch-shaped clouds of white. Spiritual white. People blurring past me, and I could feel a pain in my cheeks, in both of my cheeks, and this pain I deduced, after some thought, was because I was grinning so hard, grinning so wide. God was Spirit, in me. He was inspiration and joy and elation, energy, and not love at all. Fancy that – I would never have guessed it without that revelation. I'd been so often told He was love, and I'd believed He was love, but it turns out He's not love at all.

Blocks and towers everywhere all about me, black pyramids on top of gray towers, and in the sky the clouds seemed to mimic the city, cloudscapes firm as icebergs, towering towards heaven, tapering with the abruptness of the perspective. I was standing, pressing my tote-bag into my stomach with both my arms to keep it precious, and people jerked and flowed past me, jerked and flowed, and I was standing next to a Walk-Don't-Walk, leaning against the pole. But I was looking up, and the clouds declared the majesty of unknowing – which is a pompous fucking way of putting it I know, but that's what it was, really what it was. I had tailored myself. I had remade myself into white paper, and I was carrying myself in my own papoose, and the secret was so pure that nobody would ever know it but me. There was a kind of splash of understanding in my mind. You follow: I'm saying here it was as if my mind was a pool, and the clouds were reflected in the surface, and things moved in the underneath, and then I saw, and this is what I saw: the cloud that filled the sky before me, standing on the rooftops of the towers over the road, was a mountain. Then I saw it was the mountain of Purgatory, and the road wound round it from base to summit like the thread of a screw, and this was my path.

It was a vision nobody could see but me.

I'm not sure I've conveyed to you the joy of my tote-bag and my single copy of the manuscript. I could have destroyed it completely, do you see? I owned it, controlled it, nobody but I. Plus, I'll admit, I was exhausted, drained, pepped-up, zinging, my head wasn't quite right.

There's one more thing I have to tell you, and this will interest you because it was a terrorist act. You are interested in that. In the confession of it. Better, it concerns somebody still alive, a military somebody, an (whisper it) *interim presidential* somebody. The climax of my story.

The plan was this: I was to work for the army. It's ironic to think of it now, that this fact saved my life – my association with the army, my fortuitous presence at the barracks at the onset of the snow. And all this was only true because I was there to infiltrate the army, and assassinate Colonel Robinson. He's still alive, as you know, Christ he's the actual embodiment of military-presidential nexus rule, so you know that my attempt was unsuccessful. But it's the intent, the intent, isn't it?

The army advertised, and I applied. They wanted a speech writer, a briefings writer, a civilian to work alongside the military scribblers. Some soldiers worked not on the front line or in catering but for *Stars and Stripes*, or preparing press releases and the like. But the army, in our increasingly media-savvy age, wanted to augment this body of men. They advertised, and Mo brought it to my attention. The cadre discussed it. I would get the job, and then I would have access to the barracks at Stafford County, where the job would be based. This would give the opportunity for a high-profile piece of direct action. I drove up to Stafford County Base and had an interview with two very mild-spoken uniforms, and shook hands with them both. One of them said he remembered *Lifeboat in a Storm*, which I'd put on my CV, that he'd really liked it. It was the TV piece about the lifeboatman who found Jesus. I nodded and smiled and thanked him.

I got that job.

So I started working at Stafford Base. I was not in the army as such, and I did not wear a uniform or do basic training. But I had a lapel badge that got me past the guards on the gate, and – although they swept under my car with metal sticks to check for limpet bombs – they never searched my personal bag. They didn't even look in my trunk. I parked up, I went to an office, and I sat at a word processor and wrote what they asked me to write: press release material, internal material. Sometimes I spent whole days just going over other people's text and prettying it up. It was not exciting. It was not challenging.

But I did not intend to stay there. I had applied for the job under my known name, the name under which I'd written all my TV scripts. But this was not the name on my driver's license, not the birth-certificate name. When I hired vans for the movement I used that other name. I'd even taken out a credit card with that name on the plastic, and a spurious billing address, to cover my tracks. When I had appeared in court on the drugs thing I had given my birth-certificate name, and I'd been tried under my birth-certificate name. When I applied to the military I didn't tell them the name on my birth-certificate was different. It was as if there were two different people. Two secret boxes, each hidden from the other.

And then, after three weeks – so short a time – Mo came up from town and stayed in a motel near the base, and we met up to discuss the plan. We were to hit Colonel Robinson. He was due to give a speech, which I had helped write, to a bunch of journalists and others. He was going to stand at a podium in the auditorium at Stafford, and address a crowd of journalists about the defense of freedom. 'This is the perfect time to hit him. Perfect.'

We were drinking vodka and Kool-Aid. It was snowing outside.

'I've only been in post three weeks,' I said. 'Is it too soon?'

He waved this thought aside. 'Don't be stupid,' he said.

I packed a certain number of grams of plastique into a plastic tube the size of my thumb (a container that had once housed an expensive roll of low-ASA film), a golfball-sized plug like non-sticky Blu-tack. Then I put a wire into the top via a watch battery and a switch. We did this in the bathroom of Mo's hotel room.

The following morning I drove into the camp earlier than usual. It was a cold, bright day. The sun bounced off the snow as off a mirror. The guards smiled at me. They swept under my car with their metal brooms, and waved me on. I parked up and went inside. I made my way to the auditorium.

The spindly paraphernalia of public speaking was stored in a little room appendixed to the main chamber. This I knew. The main auditorium was continually strafed by the lines-of-sight of three surveillance cameras. But the store-room was blind. More, the surveillance cameras in the auditorium itself were not low-light devices. With the lights off I knew – from loitering in the security cockpit by the main entrance to the building pretending to chat to the guards there – that the cameras could see nothing but blocks of shadow layered on blocks of black. I knew in advance what the camera would record: a slant wedge of light as the door was eased open, the silhouette of a man – smooth outline of skull, no face visible – stepping in, the door shutting and the whole screen becoming dark again.

I stood a moment by the door until my eyes adjusted to the dark. Then I stepped nimbly down the central auditor-ium aisle onto the little stage up front, and into the unlocked storeroom at the back. With the storeroom door shut behind me I could turn on the light, and it burst on with a sting to my dark-adjusted eye, the color and almost the flavor of unsweetened grapefruit juice. I fumbled with the microphone, unscrewed, unscrewed, not easily done in silk gloves but I managed it. And then it was open, and I tipped out its hard viscera and replaced them with my own package. I fiddled for a moment with tweezers to extract the wires from the phone's on-off switch mechanism, and to poke my wires, my special wires, into the miniature sockets.

The switch was a tiny cubic nubbin of black plastic on the side of the microphone. It was scored on its topside with three little ridges to aid finger purchase.

I screwed the whole device back together again and re-nested it in its two-fingered perch. Then the light was off, and I was making my way back up the auditorium aisle, and through the main door again.

For twenty minutes I was in another room mingling and drinking coffee with forty people: military, journalists, press officers. I smiled and shook hands, and listened to people saying how much they were looking forward to the colonel's speech. I said, I'm looking forward to it myself – wrote it, after all! They laughed politely.

Here is the point: for a certain space of time, less than an hour certainly, *I knew*, and nobody else did. Not even Mo Gaché, who was sitting in his motel ten miles away waiting for me to report back – even he could not know whether I had successfully planted the device or not. Nobody knew but me. As I laughed and nodded and chatted I felt precisely this elation, that there was a *pure* secret, an unadulterated secret. We filed through to the auditorium, and the ceiling lights were bright overhead, throwing down a brilliantly clear light. I had physically to prevent myself from looking up at the cameras. I knew I could not, that their electric retinas would have captured my face, its expression of triumph, my secret. So I kept my eyes lowered by an act of sheer will. I sat. I looked purposefully at the desk before me (undefiled by graffiti, this being a barracks and not a college lecture hall). I examined the backs of the close-cropped heads of the military people in front of me. I picked up my press-pack in its blue folder, and leafed through it, even though I had written most of it.

Colonel Robinson was on the little stage, chatting with two other brass, and in only minutes he would be dead. The clock's hands semaphored three o'clock. So it was time to begin. I was nodding in response to something the person sitting next to me was saying, but the words were fuzzy and indistinct. I wasn't listening. Instead I was watching as a junior officer fetched a lectern from the store room and placed it midstage. Colonel Robinson's interlocutors were removing themselves to their seats. The Colonel stood at the front, sizing up his audience, his speech folded under his arm. His junior officer had ducked back in the storeroom and re-emerged with the microphone stand, with the microphone itself, and placed this in front of the lectern. This aide squatted, bent knees, straight back, to link the wire from the mike to a wire on the floor, and then he stood straight up again.

He nodded to his superior. Colonel Robinson nodded back and took a step towards the lectern. The junior officer moved to one side, to take a seat in the front row. The moment neared.

But then, as a last gesture, the junior officer stepped back to the lectern to turn on the microphone for the colonel. Of course, in the army, it is out of the question for a senior officer to do something as menial as flicking a small switch for himself. Rank has its privileges, and the first of those is that all such menial chores are handled by juniors. Of course. I should have realized. Or Mo should have realized, because he'd actually been in the fucking army.

My smile was frozen on my face. Everything seemed sticky, everything went slowly. The colonel was six feet from the lectern. His junior was groping on the mike for the switch, took a step closer, brought his face towards the thing to locate the switch. His head drifted slow as a balloon towards the microphone. His thumb caught the nubbin, moved it a millimeter, and it seemed to take a very long time for the switch to cross that tiny distance. I stared. The starburst dazzle of the light caught in my eye, and time stretched.

Time sagged.

Then the gunshot crack brought time back up to speed.

The junior officer was on his back. A ghost of smoke fled the scene towards the ceiling. The murmur of expectant talk had been instantly silenced. Colonel Robinson, standing six yards away, had flinched and frozen, his head withdrawn self-protectively a little way in between his shoulders.

There was silence for the space of four seconds.

Then people started yelling. People stood up. Some hurried to the front. Leather holsters were unbuttoned and pistols were brought out, as if a sniper had been standing at the back of the hall. Even when it became clear that no sniper had felled the lieutenant, the army people kept their pistols in their hands. A gun in the hand makes a certain sort of man feel calmer, like a baby's pacifier.

The explosion had broken the wire-mesh ball from the end of the microphone, and propelled it with force through the cheekbone of Lieutenant Amos – because now, after this event, I was to learn his name, where before he was perfectly anonymous to me, and would have remained in that delicious state of obscurity had I never acted. I got up and rushed to the stage, but a cram of men had assembled around Amos's prone body, and I couldn't get a good look.

I saw, afterwards, via the Argos-eyed medium of TV. I saw photographs, I saw computer-generated diagrams in which Amos's head became a model of spindly neon lines, and the bolus from the end of the microphone a black ball that traveled along a dotted pathway in slow motion, breaking open skin and bone, embedding in the skull, collapsing the orbit of the right eye, snapping the head backwards, bouncing off the corner of the brain pan and traveling down to half-emerge through the roof of his mouth. He was flown that very evening through the falling snow to a military hospital at Godherst. It still wasn't certain he would live. I stood on the concrete outside building 4 (or whichever it was), part of a huddle of a dozen soldiers, bowing as the chopper landed to save our faces from the downdraft, then uncurling ourselves as the stretcher was hurried into the belly of the machine. Snow flurried all around, gray rips and shreds of dusk stirred hugely by the rotor blades. Flakes prickled my face and stung my eyes. Amos was loaded into the machine.

Then the chopper took off, and it quickly shrank to blinking lights in the sky, and its clatter reduced quickly in volume to a murmur. Then it had wholly gone, and there was only the falling snow. A dozen military men, and myself, were standing around in the aftershock of the whole event. Guards had been doubled at the perimeter of the camp. Everybody had been searched. Military police had set up an incident room. My boss, Colonel Bruschetti, clapped my shoulder, told me I'd need to work a few overtime sessions on this one. I said fine, I said OK, anything you need sir. I said, overtime is the least of it. Jesus, I mean (I said) this is terrible, sir, this is terrible.

He nodded. He drew in a deep breath, held it, let it out tragically. 'Terrible,' he said. 'So much evil in the world.'

'Evil,' I said.

'Poor Amos,' he said. 'It wasn't meant for him, I guess it was meant for Robinson.'

'I,' I said, 'guess so.'

He looked up at the night sky, where it seemed that the cold stars had been dislodged in their millions and were fluttering down. Apocalypse as litter. 'This weather,' he said. 'It's unseasonal, this much snow – I've lived here thirteen years, never seen the like.'

'No sir,' I said.

'They got snow in Florida,' he said. 'You heard? In September? In *September*, though?'

'Near October,' I said. 'Sir.'

'But in *Florida*?' he repeated.

He went his way, back to his barracks apartment, and I said, 'See you tomorrow sir,' and I drove out to the motel.

The army snowplows were keeping the roads open, but driving in the dark after the day's excitement was a disconcerting business; the road was flanked by two chalk-colored cliffs of snow that lent a bizarre monotony to the driving experience. The cones of light from my headlights illuminated the same patch of white road, the same flanking white sidewalls, and after a few moments I lost the sense of motion at all. The inch of snow under my tires muffled the noise of the road. I seemed parked in a white box with the lid off, waiting only for the giant hand of God's Spirit to lower a white slab over me and seal me away forever. When I strayed on the silent road, pulling a little to the left, the illusion that it was the wall moving in towards me, rather than I moving towards it, was very hard to shake. I rubbed my face with my palm, trying to wake myself up, but I had fallen into a sort of coma. I was living in a fairytale. The world was freezing around me.

243

Then there was a sign, hurtling forward as if some hurricane force had thrown it straight at me. And this was my turn-off.

Off the main road the army trucks had cleared the way for about half a mile. After that the drifts had been accumulating for a week or more, and I had to pull to a stop. I clambered up and over a two-hundred-yard hump of snow before I got to the motel where Mo was staying. The staff there had tried their best to clear their own front area, but armed only with shovels they hadn't been able to do much. The front door was clear, but the first-floor windows at the back of the motel were snowed in.

I stamped as much snow from my ordinary shoes as I could, wiped it from my shoulders, and ducked into the lobby. The clerk didn't even look up: she was staring at a TV screen. The news was carrying the story. 'Hey!' I said. 'What's that? Is it local?'

'The base,' she said in a dreamy voice, without looking at me. 'Down the road. Terrorists hit it.'

'Man,' I said, rubbing my hands to help my circulation. 'That's severe.'

'Severe,' she echoed in her TV-drugged voice. Her eyes never left the screen.

I went along the corridor and up the stairs to Mo's room. It took several bouts of knocking before he opened the door, and when he did he was holding a gun in his left hand. But he let me in.

'You think that's wise?' I said, nodding at his left hand.

'You could have been police,' he said, gruffly, tossing the gun (actually throwing it) onto the bed.

'And if I *had* been the police, would it have been wise,' I said, 'to have opened the door with a gun in your hand? If they'd have seen that, they'd have, like, pounced. Just act normal, man. Just talk normal to anybody who—'

'You!' he bellowed, suddenly, turning and raising both his hands – the gesture was like that of surrender, but the meaning was exactly the opposite. The meaning was hostility. 'You *don't* tell me what to do – you *fucked it up.* Didn't you? Didn't you? You *hit* the *wrong guy.* The plan wasn't to whack some junior *nobody.*'

'Hey,' I said, backing off a few steps. 'Hey – man—'

He advanced on me. 'One thing you *can't do,*' he said, his voice huge with anger, 'one fucking thing you've *never been able to do* – is talk *street,* don't call me *man,* motherfucker. You're a middle-class fucking college boy, you're a writer, you're a fucking *pussy,* you're a fucking *pansy,* you bald-headed *pussy.* You had a childhood cosseted and pampered – you don't – you don't know – you don't—' His rage spluttered to a temporary halt.

I had backed up against the door. He was standing in front of me, perhaps four feet away, his hands by his face, the palms slightly curled as if he had frozen in the middle of reaching out to wring my neck. His blue-bead eyes were staring.

I swallowed. I could feel my fragile heart thudding.

I looked swiftly about the room, and this is what I saw: the bed was still made, the sheets neat as a rectangle of cardboard, so he had not been asleep. The gun was lying near the pillow, where he had tossed it. The TV, on an articulated arm sticking out of the wall, was showing the news, but the sound was turned down. The bathroom light was on. The mini bar door was wide, and its Lilliputian bottles were scattered, empty, all about the carpet.

I looked straight at Mo. I tried to summon my courage. When he was in one of these rages he could be very hard to handle, but my experience was that the anger often drained away as swiftly as it had come on. I tried to pacify him. I held up my own hands, palms forward, directly in front of my chest. 'Mo,' I said, in a small voice. 'Can we just talk about it?'

His breathing was audible, rough. He was staring un-blinkingly at me. His arms were still up.

'Come on,' I said, wheedling. 'Can I have a drink? Can I just have a drink? Or,' I added, forcing a smile, trying to defuse, 'have you drunk all the drinks?'

This allusion to his drunkenness, though intended comically, tipped him over the edge into rage. I realized as I said it that it was poorly judged. He lurched suddenly towards me, breathing a groan of sheer wrath, his right hand clumped into a fist. My legs jellified, and I just slumped to the floor. I was squealing. I was genuinely, physically terrified of this man. His fist hit the door above me with a splintering thud. It went right through.

An animal panic took me, and I scrabbled like a ferret along the carpet, half rising and half leaping to get up onto the bed and over it to the other side. Mo had turned. 'You fucker,' he said. He didn't shout, he spoke distinctly, clearly. 'You fucker.'

I was gabbling. 'We didn't plan for that eventuality – the junior guy turned on the microphone for Robinson – we should have anticipated that eventuality but we didn't, it's *not my fault*, it's absolutely *not my fault*, that eventuality was not—'

Mo stalked towards me, his huge hands out in front of him like Frankenstein's monster. A splinter of chipboard from the door was stuck in the crevice of two of his fingers.

I leaped up on the bed as he came down the side of it, and jumped down again, keeping the mattress between us. On an impulse I grabbed the gun, and held it in front of me.

'Just be cool, Mo,' I said.

But he was a big man. He reached easily right over the bed and simply plucked the gun from my hand. Then he flipped it around and pointed it at me. I flinched. 'Jesus, Mo, quit this, could you just? Just?' I said, high-pitched. 'Just give me a break? – Can we talk about it? Can we just talk?'

He aimed the gun precisely at my nose, and held it there. I flinched, pulled myself together, tried to look calm, half-flinched again. 'Mo,' I said. 'Mo, Mo.'

'You,' he slurred, loudly. 'You – just stay there.' He slipped the gun into his pocket and stalked straight out of the room.

I let a great tense breath loose itself out of my lungs. With the relaxation came a rush of instant resentment. '*Jesus*, Mo,' I called after him. 'What are you playing at? You coulda given me a heart attack. That's not just a manner of speech with me, you know.'

There was a crash from further along the corridor. I heard plywood splinter. 'Jesus,' I said, more quietly, too quietly for him to hear. 'You'll have security here in a minute.' Although, on the nightshift in a snowed-in motel, I supposed there was little enough to fear from security. I doubted if the cops would even make the effort of calling by, given the drifts outside. This in turn alarmed me further. I had an unsettling vision of Mo sitting on the bed with his feet on my chest, my corpse on the carpet, and nobody even coming to check what the sound of the gunshot was.

Usually, as I said earlier, Mo would be decent with me when it was just the two of us, and would act up, get pissy, get abusive to me when there was a third party as audience. But every now and again he would surprise me.

He emerged at the door to his own room, his arms full of miniature bottles. 'Did you just smash the door down next door?' I asked. 'To get at the minibar?'

'My one's empty,' he mumbled, stepped forward and dropping the dozen or so little bottles onto the mattress.

'What if there'd been somebody in the room?'

He glared at me. 'I been here three days now,' he said. 'I can hear there's nobody next door.'

'But still, hey – I don't want to be all – all criticizing,' I said, still feeling my way for his mood, 'but I suppose I wonder – hell, I wonder whether it wouldn't be an idea to lie a little lower, you know? Not draw attention to ourselves?'

'Fuck you,' he said, dimly. His truncheon fingers were struggling to uncap a tiny bottle of bourbon.

'Hey,' I said. 'What's the matter, man?' I asked.

'I told you,' he said, suddenly fierce, 'not to say—' he took a swig from the little bottle, '—pretending like you're some wiseguy, like you're all street, fuck all that.' He snorted derision. There was an armchair in the corner of the room, positioned for him to watch the TV from, and he slumped into the seat.

I was still standing beside the bed.

'The microphone,' I said. 'It's just one of those things. We neither of us figured that the junior—'

'You don't ever shut up?' cried Mo.

'All I'm trying to say,' I said.

There was silence. Then Mo let out a big sigh.

'I'm surrounded by fucking amateurs,' he wailed. It was almost comical. I felt the urge to laugh. 'I should go it alone – wipe the slate *clean*, leave no *trace*.'

'It's still worth claiming it,' I said. 'It's still a military hit, a legitimate target. We can still claim it, yeah?'

Mo said something to me then. I don't want to report it here. It had to do with something that happened to me when I was a child, a traumatic something: and I had told Mo about it a while back – and wished soon after that I hadn't told him, because he mocked me over it many times, he mocked me in front of other people. He mocked me there, in that motel room, on that night – he rehearsed the thing I had told him, and laughed at me. I can't report what he said without revealing the thing that happened to me when I was a child, and I choose not to tell you that thing – that's my secret. It's buried with the snow. The snow made everything new. The whole world just stopped, and all its secrets are hidden away now where nobody can ever find them.

Let me ask you a question. You're lawyers, right? So: how long, in NUSA, before people start digging up corpse-meat to eat? How longer until that is made *legal*? More than that – how long until it becomes *habitual*, so that we no longer even think twice about it? So that we start to relish it, to think of it as normal? When the regular food-mines run empty – I know, because I chaired a mining committee, that miners come across human bodies all the time, in all

248

manner of sleepy-faced dead positions in the snow, their tissue full of proteins and fats and preserved by the extreme cold. How long until hunger shifts human culture to that food source? There's several years' supply of high-protein food down there, whilst we arrange things up here.

Or has it already happened?

Of course, the government would cover that up, if it's true. You ever see *Soylent Green*?

Let me tell you something else: this I knew from way before. I was always unillusioned about this. You want to know, although you don't ask it, why a nice middle-class Catholic boy like me turned into the enemy of the government and all that, why I followed the path I followed. But I *saw*, early, that this cannibalism was the way the world worked. I saw that when I was very young. So it shouldn't surprise you. The cosmos isn't pain and ugliness and all that adolescent shit, but *of course* it feeds on itself, and *of course* the bigger animals eat the smaller animals and of course the government is the biggest of the animals.

I didn't think you'd understand.

No.

I turned the volume up on the television and sat on the end of the bed drinking raw vodka out of one of the tiny bottles. The news circled back to the microphone bomb every twenty minutes or so, but there wasn't much they could report, and other news crowded it out. Mostly the news was weather. People dying of hypothermia all over, scientists and their theories, global warming. End of the world. With hindsight the weather was truly the big news, but at the time I was impatient, I wanted to see how the media mirror reflected me back to myself. I wanted, you see, to feed on myself. I figured the weather was just a bit of unseasonal snow. I thought there were more important things in the world.

The clouds always used to look so innocent, but they devoured us – didn't they? They opened their mouths and they ate the world. *Fluffy*, my ass.

For quarter of an hour Mo seemed to have fallen asleep. But when I started talking again he woke up. 'I still say we claim it, man,' I argued. 'One soldier's like another, it hardly matters which is which. Let's phone through a claim, before some other organization jumps on our bandwagon. Might as well make the most of it. Mo?'

With his eyes closed, Mo said: 'Wipe the slate clean. Starting again on my own.'

I was looking right at him. His eyes clicked wide open. I almost jumped. It startled me.

He stood up, pushing off from the arm of the chair. Then he took one step forward, so that his considerable bulk was between me and the doorway. The gun came out of his pocket.

'Mo?' I said.

He fired the gun. Jesus, it made one big noise. I thought the walls would split open with the sound of it. I don't know where the bullet went, except that it didn't hit me, but I nearly jumped out of my skin. I screamed. 'Jesus! Mo!'

He moved his hand a fraction, re-aiming, but it was trembling slightly with the drink. He must have been much drunker than I realized. He fired again, and again the bullet went somewhere that wasn't me. I jerked at the sound, I put my hands in front of my face – as if *that* would have been any protection! – I took a step towards him, thinking to run past him out of the door, but I changed my mind, I hovered, and then I just fled. I just fled. I had no courage. I wet myself – only a tiny little, but it was piss and it came out into my trousers, a dime-sized patch of moisture on my pants. I rushed to the window and fumbled stupidly with the catch. I was yelling. The noise was just coming out of my mouth like water from a broken-off pipe. Meaningless noise, vowels only.

There was another gunshot and I fell over, but I hadn't been hit. I don't know why Mo, in that small room, had so much trouble hitting me. Maybe he was simply too drunk. Maybe he wasn't really trying to kill me. But it surely felt as if he was trying to kill me. When I heard that third gunshot my legs just crumpled, and I slumped to the floor. My hand was still on the catch, and I didn't fall all the way. And then, in a sudden rush, the window was open, and I was through, out into the snowflakey darkness.

It was a second-floor room, but the drift was almost that high, so I fell into the brisk softness of the snow, still yelling in fear. I went through the papery surface of the snow and made a man-shaped two-foot shaft before my fall was broken. But I was scrabbling, and clambering out and round, as if the devil himself was behind me. I covered twenty yards, bounding down the chilly flank of the drift towards the main entrance of the motel, and behind me I heard *poc-poc-poc*, soft as a ping-pong ball hitting up-holstery. Gunfire muffled by the snow. Snowflakes regularly spaced throughout a space of, let's say, six hundred cubic meters – extraordinarily effective as a silencer. I thought, from the distant-sounding noises, that my adrenalin had carried me hundreds of feet away from Mo; but I looked over my shoulder and he was barely ten feet behind me. He had jumped out of the window after me, and was standing up to his hips in the drift, pointing and firing with the pistol. The chill of the air slid into my heart then, because I knew he was doing more than just firing drunkenly-randomly, I knew he was actually trying to kill me.

I screamed 'Mo,' and dived, and half-fell, half-slid down to the motel's front door. Feet had cleared the threshold of snow, and my face was close to the lintel. Another *poc*, and brick tile from the doorstep disseminated itself through the air in a foot-wide cloud of tiny pieces. Fragments struck my face. That's how close I was to it.

My first thought had been to get back inside the motel, but it flashed upon me then that Mo would simply follow me, chase me through corridors and rooms until he could finish me off. Better to stay outside, where it was more spacious, where there was more chance of eluding him. I thought of my car. The snow gleamed palely into the distance. But the path I had made coming was still visible – gouges in the snow, here a footstep, another, then a shallow and ragged trench. I hurried, scrabbling rabbit-like with all my limbs.

Once at the top of the drift I made sudden surprising purchase and I was away, heaving my legs to pull them out of the knee-high snow (and this was on a path I had already made), and struggling deeper into shadow and silence. Wading through snow is more like moving through quicksand than it is moving through water, although (ironically) the snow itself *is* water, and *isn't* sand.

Away from the motel everything was covered by a shapeless shadow.

Snow was continually falling through the night. Flakes were all around me, shimmering with their own cold, falling only slowly. My eyes adjusted to the dark. I saw telegraph poles like Arctic trees and, blocky to my left, the indistinct shapes of buildings, snow-cloaked, not lit from within. I did not look behind until I came to the last spur of the road to have been cleared by the army plows, and striding down to my parked car. I had been away, at most, two hours, but the snow had wholly covered the vehicle, reducing its shape to a dolphin profile.

I scraped the door clear with my naked hands, and scooped snow from the windshield too, and got inside panting. The engine took four or five goes to start, and I drove off shudderingly, throwing off great foam-like masses of snow as I went. But I was panicked, still in shock, and my visibility was poor, and the road was markedly worse since I had last driven it. Going downhill as I was I soon lost control of my automobile. I slid over brake-blithe ice into the cliff of white at the side of the road. The impact was hard enough to jar my airbag into deploying.

This crash was too much for my already agitated state of being. I guess I could have emptied the bosom-like pillow of its air, I guess I could have restarted the car, driven off more carefully. But I didn't do that. Instead I tore the door open and tumbled out into the snow, and then the fire-cold of snow against my bare hands galvanized me, the cold-burn up inside my trouser-legs above my socks, and in my face.

I ran.

I slipped and fell several times, but the snow caught me in its soft limbs. Its single, great, soft limb. And I picked myself up, and ran down to the interstate, and then I ran along that. There was no traffic. The street lighting threw elliptical buttresses of light onto the drifts at the side of the road. Patches of light stage-lit the road. I had eight shadows, like swollen spider's legs, following me, stretching out in front of me, leaping up suddenly, swivelling around me as I moved on. The snow was up to my shins, up to my knees, even on this recently cleared stretch of roadway. And the flakes fell inexorably down and down. Packing around us all, packing us tight and safe like expanded polystyrene. All those snow-flakes, all their miniaturized sawtooth profiles.

I stopped running after a while because I was too tired, and my heart was yammering in an alarming way. If I had a heart attack there, I told myself, I would die, I would be dead, nobody would get me to hospital, I'd be a frozen corpse. But as I moved on at walking pace I began to feel very cold, and that scared me more. Snow accumulated in my hair. My hands were dark with the chill. I started shivering uncontrollably. I could try and hold back the tremors, but they came anyway. I tried blowing into my cupped hands but my breath seemed to be coming out of my lungs cold. I couldn't shake the suspicion that I was dead, that Mo had shot me, that I was not walking but haunting. My heart hurt with the physical effort I was making. It was very cold. I was very cold.

I walked and walked. I was tired, freezing. I lost feeling in my feet, in their stupid fucking silk socks and Lazzarone leather shoes. I wept, intermittently. I told myself I was going to get frostbite and lose my toes. I started to halluci-nate a little, so that for instance it seemed to me that the road was slanting upwards with an increasing gradient, although in fact I was crossing a more or less perfectly horizontal terrain. I kept looking over my shoulder, thinking that Mo was there, and even though I could see that he wasn't, even though I could see that I was alone except for the swarm of snowflakes all around, and my elastic swarm of shadows. But I couldn't shake the sense that somebody else was with me. I was trudging now, pulling my leg muscles through the motions of walking with great effort. I said things to my invisible companion. I addressed him as Mo, as my wife, I don't know what I said. I don't know what I did. I don't know how long it took me to get back to the camp. I don't know anything. My mind is a perfect blank.

Eventually I reached the camp.

The guards were surprised to see me, but I told them my car had gone off the road into a drift, that I couldn't get it out, that I'd been walking for hours to get back. They took me through, into the same infirmary where Lieutenant Amos had, earlier, had his wounded head examined. They wrapped me in blankets, gave me hot soup in a styrofoam container. They gave me sanctuary. Isn't it strange that my own people, that Mo, had been so unwelcoming? And that the people I was warring against, the military themselves, were being so good to me? This was an irony I had cause to consider and reconsider over the following months, as the snowfall became intolerable. I was treated for minor frost-bite in my left little toe. I could not leave the base. Then nobody could leave the base. People, mostly soldiers, struggled through the continual blizzard to find sanctuary with us. Copters went out and came back with supplies and fuel, and throughout the whole time of the snow we only lost two of those machines. The base command formed an emergency committee, chaired by Colonel Robinson, the same man that I had failed to kill. The process began by which the base tore itself up, dug itself up to the surface of the snow and re-established itself on mesh and balloon-supported platforms. I don't remember how many times that happened, except that I helped, I did what I could.

Everything else was lost in the welter (that's *my* kind of word, welter) of experiences. It was an exhausting, but also a glorious time. And contact with similar bases resulted, four months later, in the formation of New-New York, the augmentation of several platforms from around the area. And – I don't need to tell you any of this – you were there, or you were in a similar base, somewhere else.

But I'll say this: I meditated a great deal, in those days, on patterns I could see in the swirl all about me. For instance: the pattern made by, on the one hand, my failure to shoot the Colonel, the man who was then elected the first Interim President of our new fucking world order, and on the other, by Mo's failure to shoot me in the motel that time. Another instance: my heart attack and the breakdown of my marriage, they're facets of the same thing, the same over-stimulation, the same heart's-pain. The surgeon's account of my heart attack and my wife's account of our marriage were equally unforgiving, but equally misguided (since, as for the doctor's judgment, aren't I still alive? He's not. And, as for my wife, well, all I'll say is that she was wrong, she was *not right* in her caricature account of our wedded life. We were happy, sometimes. We were in love, some of the time).

Another instance: the pattern made by my early career in reality TV, the camera eye always on its subjects, and God's eye, which is always on us. Like the people in the Sponsor-Cam experiment I guess we act up for God, we try to grab His attention. Jesus, *notice* me! Anything – murder, adultery, heresy, *anything* – is better than being ignored by God. How could anybody bear to be ignored by God? I'll let you into a secret, too: the snowstorm that possessed the world for all those many, many months, it seemed to me that this storm was nothing less than the Spirit itself, its ice-fire kiss as it swallowed our world whole. Of course most people were too sinful to endure that contact. Of course there were only one hundred and forty four thousand who survived – I've seen official figures, but I've never trusted official figures, I'll go with my estimate, it comes from a higher source. I have been most struck by the prophetic element in my vision, the vision I saw that afternoon in old New York City – I was seeing the path that was destined humanity, the arduous but purifying climb up and up the snowy flanks of Purgatory. Isn't that where we are? There's nothing new in a man being inspired to prophesy by the Ghost of God. You shouldn't be surprised that it happened to me. Perhaps I've been more reticent about it than some other prophets, but that's because I understand the essential truth of God *is His secrecy* – why else does he hide from us, why else does he throw the myriad beauties of the world in our eyes except as a distraction, a smokescreen, to deflect our prying? So many people look at the world and can't see God, and they don't seem to understand that it's precisely this hiddenness, it's precisely this secrecy, that is the whole point of God. Imagine if God were visible to all, sitting in a triune throne in the heavens for all to see – how would the world be different?

You can't answer me. It would be different – we'd all be dead of terror, we'd all be dead of shame, we'd all be cowed. But God hides in the snowstorm, and hides in the pillar of cloud, and hides in the cold fire of sunlight, and we can get on with our lives. That's the secret of our existence.

You want me to boil it all down to a motto? You want me to Reader's Digest it? Authority abuses. That's what Authority does, it's in its nature, it can't help it. That's why God, who is wise and compassionate, does not force His authority upon us. You're in the army, I know, you're in the actual army, so I guess you've sold yourself to that system, you accept the abuse, you bow down to the authority. Maybe you tell yourself that you believe in it, that authority can be good. But that doesn't change the fact of it. In your heart you know the fact of it, it does no good, it abuses. So, the only question that remains for us to answer is: what are we to do in the teeth of this abuse? Should we take it? Should we resist?

The second one, of course.

I could simply scrawl that phrase, Authority Abuses, in ten-yard-high graffiti all over the base: that would testify to the truth of it. But people see words without reading them, they read them without understanding them, you have to find another way of expressing their truth, a way that cannot be so easily ignored.

And it seems to me now that the Spirit has indeed shaped my life, written it as a properly schematic, aesthetically harmonious whole. How else to explain so many parallels, such balance? It can't be explained otherwise. Take my movie script, that I turned into a book, that got turned down by all the publishers (who are all fucking *dead* now and under the snow, so who's triumphant in the end?) – I couldn't understand, at the time, why nobody saw its genius. But now, with a longer perspective, I think I do see. I think I see that I was actually, proleptically, writing about the collapse of Corporation USA, whose collapse we are still in the process of witnessing – a few bombs in the greenhouses of New London to help that collapse on its way. But my book, that was truth, and the central character – fucked up, yes, addicted to gambling, not true to his woman, yes – was me, fucked up, yes, taking drugs, screwing around, yes. And the denouement of that script: I'd better tell you, you won't know it otherwise, you certainly won't have seen it on any Big Screen or read it in any airport bookshop. The denouement is that Paul pulls it together, that he saves the girl, that he disposes of the debt, and indeed ends up with millions in unmarked, non-sequential notes – that happy ending is what awaits me. I believe it. It's not arrogance that tells me I'm untouchable. It's not schizophrenia, or ego, or insanity, it's the sheer beautiful harmonious truth of things. There are higher powers that look after me. I'm designed for something much more. You see, it's not enough to care, you have to show you care – it's not enough to hate the government, you must act on that hate. It's not enough to love, you have to tell somebody you love them. Isn't that right? Protest and survive.

Sometimes I look at the world and it looks like a drawing – you know what I mean? I mean a drawing, not a special effect or a hallucination, but like one of those super-intricate line drawings of the sort that an idiot-savant, Rain-Man autistic boy might draw, all miniature detail perfectly rendered and fantastically reduplicated.

Or what? I have to shave with a blade now. I used electric before. For a year I've been shaving with the same blade. The edge is practically crenulated. When I shave now it brings up a dozen red full stops under my chin. You think I'm happy about that? You know how expensive tissue paper is nowadays? Tissue paper, for Christ's sake? I saw a man using his key as a letter-opener once. Not only that, I saw a *soldier* using his *bayonet* as a letter-opener once. What do you reckon that means?

Let me, for a moment, say one more thing, let me say something about alien encounter. Doesn't it seem odd to you that, before the snow, aliens used to be so secretive about their abducting, their spread 'em, poke 'em, fuck-off encounters with humanity? Why so furtive? Why would they need to be so furtive? Aliens are always represented in sf and culture as superior beings, aren't they? With the better tech, the higher foreheads, the less body hair as if body hair is the index of bestiality and those guys, those blue-skinned smooth-skinned space guys are just *that much closer* to pure mentation. You know? So why—?

Those invasive aliens. Those lurkers in the woodshed. They're our superiors, they are above us in the cosmic hierarchy. They are like parents, we are like children. They are like government, we are like the governed. That's the connection that's made, isn't it? The aliens come to Crossroads Missouri or to Blankville Idaho and steal some dozen bus drivers or farm workers or whatever from their beds, and the government covers it up. Nobody knows about these abductions because the government covers it up. In other words, the government is their secrecy. Why? Not to prevent cultural panic, for what could be less surprising or more anticipated than an official declaration of aliens among us? No, no, not for those reasons. The government covers up by reflex, because that's what governments do. Two sides of the same coin. Aliens are government, government is alien. So why do they hide? They hide like God. They vanish like God. For the same reasons.

Here's another question: if we have these devices that Seidensticker invented, why not bring them out in the open? Clear snow away, maybe, with them. Put them in reverse gear, undo the snow, why not?

I saw a tomato the other day, a ripe tomato just sitting there on the side like a bomb, its stalk the sparkle of the fuse burning down. Red is the danger colour, isn't it. There's too little red up here.

That's all I want to say for now.

{MS notes, handwritten on verso of final sheet:
well there's very little here that's germane to the matter in hand – not without interest, though, from a legal point of view. And a political one, of course, with Robinson's recent cancer diagnosis. Jerry, could you cross-check with other documentation about the holes in this account? Specif., his mysterious 'something' that he says happened in his childhood about which he is so reticent, presum. abuse, but forewarned is best about that sort of thing before it comes to trial – too often used as a premise for dimin. respon.

Also, why did his cadre leader try to kill him? Did I miss something? Or did he not say why? Tension in the organiz.? Does this have any bearing on his continuation of terrorist tactics in NUSA? This Gaché guy, are we sure he got swallowed by the snow? Please check. KK.

JL: Not abuse, it turns out – it's a strange tale, actually – check doc 12–999B, you'll need a Senatorial OK for clearance, but given the high profile of this case you'll get it. But I can't see the childhood events jeopardizing trial – assuming, like you say, trial goes ahead in the current changing political situation. Do we wait and see whether you-know-who is elected next IP? Or do the wheels of justice grind on nevertheless? I mean do we act as if Robinson will last forever as IP even though we know he's probably only got weeks? Please to excuse me my naïve questions. JL.

PS: File 08–999 is also relevant, personal statement by you-know-who's wife, but it's under seal, I haven't seen it. Worth a subpoena? They might not give it you, but it could be worth trying anyway. JL.

PPS: Just checked with Harriet at records, she hasn't of course seen the file (08–999) either, but she says it's been through the censor, so it almost certainly won't contain any names. Still worth a subpoena? What do you think? JL.

Text Title: [not specified]
Text Code: 341–999

My name is Tira Bojani Sahai. I have been asked by [*This is a Sensitive Document under the terms of the Act of '22. All proper names have been removed for one of the reasons specified in that Act. Access to this name requires Senate Level Clearance; apply to 7–24358–45432–1*] to write a continuation to previous testimony already submitted to the Senate Committee, which I am prepared to do. Afterwards I have agreed to read through my testimony and sign each page as a guarantee of its accuracy of transcription.

I was married to [*Name deleted: see above*] and resident in Liberty [New London] for three years before the events related in this document. I became involved, sexually with [*Name deleted: see above*], but afterwards I became

estranged from him. I have reason to believe that he subsequently commenced an affair with [*Name deleted: see
above*], the wife of [*Name deleted: see above*]. I was aware,
or I had suspicions, that [*Name deleted: see above*] had
become involved in terrorist activities – this was after I had
ended my affair with him. The political climate was tense,
heated almost to the point of hysteria. People had died in
the various explosions. There was a great deal of animosity.
I met with [*Name deleted: see above*], who begged me to
intercede on his behalf with my husband. He was scared for
his life. My husband left town on unspecified military
activities. I heard that [*Name deleted: see above*] had been
arrested on suspected terrorist charges. Then four soldiers
arrived at the door of my own apartment, and I was placed
under arrest myself.

I was taken in the night by three military police to a
holding station on the outskirts of Liberty, and there I
stayed for an unspecified amount of time. I estimate that I
was there for at least a month.

I was interrogated many times: asked hundreds of questions, most of them variations of the one question: was I
involved in the bombings? No, I said, no. But they reconfig-
ured the question, dressed it in different guises, and asked
and asked and asked. How did I know [*Name deleted*]? I
worked on a committee he chaired. Wasn't it true that I had
had an affair with him? Oh God, how embarrassing, yes that
was true. But it ended a year ago, and I have had no dealings
with him since then. No dealings at all? Almost no dealings.
Do you expect us to believe that? Do you really expect us to
believe that?

I have no expectations at all.

I was, to begin with, in a cell in Liberty, built out of metal,
prefabricated wall. I could see the places where bolts the size
of my big toe clasped the coigns of these walls together. But
the floor had been carpeted, the little bed was well provided
with blankets, and a hot pipe ran along the floor of the

right-hand wall, so I was comfortable enough. Opposite this was a window latticed with the sort of ironwork shop-keepers use to swathe their shop fronts with at night to discourage thieves. Used to use, I should say. The view from this window was not extensive: I could see the corner of the L-shaped block in which I was being kept. I could see a stretch of wall over the way, and poking above it a com-munications pole cobwebbed at its top with a fan-spread of metal wires.

Was I frightened, alarmed for my future? Of course. It was a very frightening time. I think I assumed that execution awaited those convicted of terrorism, although this was never made plain for me. And I assumed that in the super-heated political climate of Liberty at that time I would certainly be found guilty. And yet the monotony of living in a cell, a monotony broken only by the delivery of food, and the arrival of guards to take me for another bout of interrogation, was, in its way, a soothing thing. When a life's routines have been disarranged as comprehensively as mine had been, under arrest, regular routines become the last architecture of sane existence. Had that been taken away (had I been woken in the night, moved continually, never allowed to settle) I would have fared much worse.

Outside my cell I was aware, from time to time, of the rhythms of city life. I heard helicopters pass overhead, and truck engines clearing their throats, and sometimes I heard people's voices. But most of all I heard, as did everybody in Liberty, the continued bombardment. One day I counted four distinct detonations: the pea-whistle of approach, the slam-banging of the explosions themselves. I asked my guards about these, and sometimes received accounts of the ruination of a housing block, or the collapse of a warehouse wall. But sometimes I would receive only sour expressions, and I was reminded that, to these guards, I was myself somehow implicated in the continuing bombardment.

But one thing was obvious even to me, in my seclusion: every explosion, whether near at hand and startling or further away and muffled by distance, was preceded by the whine of an object hurtling through air. These were not, as were the first two bombs, devices placed by hands and left to blow up: these flew in from outside the city.

After several weeks the interrogations stopped. Shortly after that I was transferred to another cell, one I shared with three others. I spent, I think, five days in this cell. It was not a large space, and the four of us were cramped, sleeping in two bunkbeds. I recognised two of my new cellmates in the vague way one recognises everybody in a small town. But I knew the third very well. Her name was [*Name deleted*], and she was the wife of a senior military officer, and she had also, I was sure, had had an affair with [*Name deleted*], and *he* had been the cause of all my troubles. She was very mournful when I came into her cell. She almost fell upon me with joy, just for the pleasure of seeing a familiar face. I was almost so pleased to see her long black hair, her beautiful face, that it came close to modifying my previous animadversion.

For the first days we spent together she clung to me, in the desperation of her fear. It was almost impossible, in the face of her sorrow, *not* to try and console her, although I felt a certain repulsion as well. She presented the aspect of a bottomless hunger for such consolation. Her black hair was almost the emblem of that black-hole urgency, and she gobbled up my company, my words of reassurance, everything about me. The curious thing is that I saw, eventually, beyond this. It turned out that there *was* a ground to her need, there was a fundamental point which, when touched, settled her anxiety: but it took me several weeks to understand it.

'What's going to happen?' she would say.

'I don't know.'

'Don't *you* say that,' she would complain. 'Don't you say that.'

And so the next time she asked, 'Do you think they're going to execute us? Do you think they're going to use torture?' I would say, 'Of course not, of course not,' and she could draw strength from that. My speaking was enough. 'It's going to be OK,' I would say, hugging her, and feeling her heart kicking like a restless thing against my collar bone. 'Everything'll be fine.' Finally I found myself saying, 'You stick with me, I'll make sure it's OK.' And she would purr, like a cat.

It took me several weeks to understand it, but once I did I found comfort in it myself. I could only reach that calm place in myself by passing through her heart. I don't mean to speak in riddles, but you have to understand how completely *physical beauty* draws a veil over a person, even the beauty of one woman in the eyes of another. When you look at a beautiful person you will, almost inevitably, see the beauty, not the person. [*Name deleted*]'s tears of anxiety, her querulous complaints about the food and the cold, her phases of incessant, nagging questions ('what will they do with us? Will they put us on trial? Will we be executed? Will we ever get out of jail?' – to none of which I knew the answer any better than her) – all this seemed only an aspect of a weakness wholly consonant with her physical beauty. It fitted, like light throwing shadow. And over the weeks I realised that this wasn't *her* at all, in any meaningful sense. Underneath the face and the hair and the figure and the carefully modulated voice was something much more interesting, something wilful and real, a selfishness concentrated into something powerful and authentic. I began to see her differently, as if she were steeped in a clear stillness, like the transparent air through which a dawn or a sunset achieves its imponderable depth. More, perhaps more importantly, I could believe that only I could see that about her. To other women she was merely annoying, and to other men merely attractive, but to me she was something more. This was her pole star, and it was about this that I oriented myself. The other dots in her constellation, her

privileged birth, her background of wealth, private education, her pre-Snow litany of ski-trips and Bahamian
summers and tedious but well-monied boyfriends – all that
became perfectly neutral to me.

I know she will read this, which of course influences what
I say here. Perhaps it's enough to say that in two weeks we
became very close. Circumstances had thrown us together. I
don't, really, want to say too much about this; it's none of
your business. I'll say a bit more about it in a little while, but
I don't want to dwell on it. People will read this document,
and perhaps it will cause trouble for me.

Then one morning we were all taken out of the prison
block. We were handcuffed and hustled over the bright
snow to a military aircraft. Several cell-fuls of prisoners
were brought out and prodded into the belly of the plane,
and then the doors were shut and we rattled and dragged
our way along the snow and up into the sky.

'God knows where they're taking us now,' said [*Name
deleted*].

The flight lasted a few hours. Then the plane landed on a
dry-slope grid, which rattled and burred underneath the
wheels. It took a long time, or so it seemed to me, for us
to come to a complete stop. Then we were hustled out by
the guards, eleven of us in droopy-roped handcuffs, standing blinking in the sunshine. The air was sharp in my
throat after the mugginess inside the plane, but at the same
time I could feel the warmth of the sun as a palpable pressure on my skin. I lifted both my hands to push my hood
back.

'Warm sun, cold air,' said [*Name deleted*]. She had
uncovered her own lustrous hair.

'Summer,' I said. 'Snow.'

We were both squinnying into the hard white light, the
bright sky and the brighter land. Wind had scraped gentle
undulations with oddly sharp ridges between them, over all

the snow in front of us, but otherwise the land was as featureless as a blank page all the way to the horizon.

Behind us, eight hundred yards away, was a wired-in enclosure, a hectare in size, with wooden barracks and larger storage sheds. Frost-dulled items of military hardware – sled-tanks, one-man planes, guns – were just visible between the buildings.

'To see a bear,' said [*Name deleted*]. She sighed. 'Even one. Just to see one white bear . . .'

'Polar bears? You're kidding,' I said. 'What's for them to eat?'

'Hn,' she agreed.

We stood for about an hour. There was nowhere to sit. My legs grew tired. 'Should we sit down?' I asked [*Name deleted*]. Such friends had we become. She had become the friend you seize on during your first terrifying day at school, the person to cling to and who clings to you. 'Should we?'

'I don't want to get my clothes wet,' she said.

'Wet? But that snow is powder dry. It's cold, sure, but in fact it's too cold to be wet. It's like deep-frozen pearls.'

She laughed briefly at this, as at a palpable absurdity. But it was nothing but the truth. The snow was so dry it squeaked like polystyrene when we walked upon it. Nevertheless, we neither of us sat down. We'd lived with the snow for years, and still somewhere in our heads we couldn't rid ourselves of the belief that this was ordinary slushy snow. We hadn't, even yet, come to terms with the reality.

Eventually a knot of military men formed at the open gateway to the camp, and started marching towards us. Our guards perked up, and herded us into a line. 'Maybe,' said [*Name deleted*] to me sardonically as we stood side by side, 'they'll explain why they've brought us out here.'

'To have us shot,' said somebody further along; a man.

'No,' said [*Name deleted*], loudly, as if trying to persuade herself. She shook her head, her long black hair a pendulum. 'They could'a shot us in Liberty. They wouldn't waste the gas on flying us out here if all they wanted to do was—'

She stopped, because the military men had arrived and were standing before us.

'Good morning,' said the first of them, calling the words distinctly and clearly in the bright air. He leaned his head forward to give special emphasis to some of his words, which added a jerky earnestness to his speech. 'Welcome to *Camp Yalta*,' he shouted. He grinned and adjusted his sunglasses on the bridge of his nose with one finger. 'Why is this *temporary military structure* called Camp Yalta?' He didn't wait for an answer to his own question. 'It's a little joke that you may come to appreciate in a *little while*. Shortly you will be led to a *secure barracks building* inside the camp, and you will be processed in due course – I should remind you that *you are not prisoners*, and do not have access to the rights of legal representation and so forth. You are *internees* under the provision of the terrorism act.' He looked up and down the line, grinning.

It was then that I recognised him. Something familiar about him had been nagging at me, and that grin brought the memory back. I had met this man before. His name was [*Name deleted*]. I had met him before, during my very earliest days in Liberty. He was the one of my husband's subalterns who had first made representations to me about his commander's desire to marry me – I had called him 'Pander', after the fashion by which we invent daft names for the people around us, for our own personal satisfactions. I had never particularly liked him, and indeed had lost track of what had happened to him, except that he had been promoted and had passed from my husband's staff early on in our marriage. I think he went to New NY for a while.

But here he was, strutting and crowing.

'I'm not going to ask if anybody has *any questions*,' he said, smiling, 'because if I do you will *invent* stupid questions to vex me, and I'm not in the mood. *I have no sympathy for terrorists*.' He beamed enormously at us, as if seeking our approval for this manifestation of virtuous civic zeal. 'But before you take your place in the secure barracks,

268

there is one set of orders I must carry out. These orders come directly from [*Name deleted*].'

I jumped a little to hear my husband's name. I had not been expecting it.

'The general reports that his wife,' Pander was saying, 'has been transported here in this plane. I have orders to *separate her* from the *other prisoners* and have her delivered individually to the advance camp, where [*Name deleted*] is *conducting operations* out on the snow. Would Tira [*Name deleted*] make herself known to me please?'

'That's me,' I called.

Everybody looked at me. I blushed a little, I think. It embarrassed me to be the centre of attention, so unexpectedly. It embarrassed me to realise that [*Name deleted*] had had me in his thoughts, that he still cared enough for me, despite all our troubles as a couple, to want to rescue me from this situation. Most of all it embarrassed me to think that I would soon be freed from this penal gang of internees – I worried what the others would think of me. Of course they would hate me. I would hate any of them who received this sort of special treatment.

Pander had walked over to me and was looking carefully at me. He said: 'I don't think so.'

'I beg your pardon?'

'Lady,' he said. 'I could almost admire your chutzpah. But if we trucked you all the way to [*Name deleted*], and he said *this ain't my wife*, we'd only have to truck you all the way back. You don't want to put us to that bother. You'd wouldn't like us after. We might hold a grudge.'

'But,' I said, 'I am his wife.'

Pander nodded. 'Your name?'

'Tira Sahai,' I said. 'Tira [*Name deleted*]. Tira London.'

He shook his head. 'Tira [*Name deleted*] I just *gave you*. The others, I don't know what they are. I'll tell you, lady, I *know the woman* I'm looking for.'

I was genuinely baffled. 'But I'm the woman,' I said.

He shook his head, once, to cut me off. 'Listen,' he said.

'You didn't hear what I said? I know this woman. I was the man who *introduced* [*Name deleted*] to his wife, I was at the meet, and I spoke to her, helped *set up* the relationship.'

'That's right,' I said. 'I remember you.'

He shook his head again. 'You think my memory is pie-eyed? You think *I don't remember* the woman I introduced to the general? It's only *two years* since.'

'But it's me,' I said.

'Once is chutzpah,' he said, taking one step away from me. 'That's almost likeable, that shows *spirit*. But to *persevere* like this, that's just annoying. That's kind of crazy.'

'I really don't understand what game you're playing at,' I said.

'You *know* me?' he said, suddenly snarling. 'You know *my name*? You met me before?'

And in that instant I couldn't remember his name at all. I could only remember that I had christened him *Pander* in my own head. Obviously I couldn't tell him that. And, looking back on this moment, I don't believe it would have made any difference if I had been able to remember. He would have dismissed the fact – I'd seen him about Liberty, I'd heard of him, one of the guards had told me, there would have been some explanation he would have lighted upon. He had looked at me and decided I was not the woman. It was idiotic. It should have been funny. I'd think of it funny today, if it hadn't had such miserable consequences.

'No,' he snarled at me. 'I thought not. You must be *slow-witted*. When it was me *introduced* the two of them? You think I woulda forgotten that the general married *a white woman*? You think I'd be *fooled into thinking* the general had married a,' there was a catch, a momentary hiccough in the sentence, and he finished, 'black woman? No dice, sister.' He stepped away.

[*Name deleted*] to my left, spoke up. 'But she is, I'll vouch—'

'This!' Pander yelled, suddenly shouting as loud as a

sergeant major. 'This is why *I don't allow* question-and-answer sessions – *you internees*, you're all interested in *wasting our time*. Trying to be tying us in knots! The general's wife is clearly not in this group – I'd recognise her if she was. The fact that *one internee* is prepared to *vouch*,' he almost spat the word, 'for another, that doesn't impress me terribly much.'

I had the sense, almost an instinct, that this was a lifeline, and that I should struggle not to let out of my grasp. I called out. 'I tanned, that's all. I've had two years in the sun – you know what the sun's like up here, even when it's cold. It's tan.'

'Oh, there's *no difference*,' Pander called, with sarcastic inflection, ' 'tween suntan and *black skin*.'

'It's only my face – and hands,' I said, eagerly. 'Look, I'll show you—' scrabbling at my coat, '—my stomach is really pale. I haven't been out sunbathing or anything. Look—'

'Stop that!' Pander yelled. He sounded sincerely outraged. One of his men made as if to step over to me, and I dropped my hands by my side.

'Come on,' I implored. 'Jesus, take another look at me. Take me to my husband, he'll confirm.'

'That's that,' shouted Pander, returning to his men. 'That's enough. I'll tell the general his wife was not aboard the transport. You will all go to your barracks now, and get settled in, and you'll be interrogated in due course.' It was in this manner that my suntan changed the course of my life. I could dwell, even if only for a moment, on the alternative path events could have followed, except for Pander's stupidity, or except for my own stupid tanned skin. I could, perhaps, have flown to the base further out in the snow where my husband was trying his best to conduct negotiations with the outsiders, to prevent their continuing bombardment of Liberty. And, following the successful completion of this, he would, perhaps, have taken me with him back to New NY. I would have been first lady to his Interim President. I would have become well-travelled, influential, a power in the land. Instead of which I've spent most of my life since that day in a small room. Instead of which I've never got beyond Liberty, and probably never will. But I'm getting ahead of myself.

We were marched inside the fenced area and into a baldly furnished wooden and metal room. There were six beds, for the eleven of us.

'We should double up,' said somebody. I didn't know his name.

'We could sleep shifts,' said somebody else.

We sat around on the beds for hours, talking nervously about what was gong to happen. One by one, we were shuffled off by guards, 'to be interviewed' they said. 'To be shot,' said [*Name deleted*] nervously, laughing a little, because nobody seemed to be coming back after they were escorted out of the room.

'We'll be alright,' I said to her. We were sitting on the same bed.

'Shall we share this bed?' she asked.

'Sure,' I said. I put my hand on her forearm, and smiled at her.

Several hours passed before it was my turn to be interrogated. A guard was at the door.

I was led over the yard and into a more substantial-looking building. Down a corridor we paused outside a door, whilst the guard knocked.

Through the door was a room, a table, two chairs. An officer was sitting in one of the chairs. The guard stopped by the door.

I sat myself in the vacant chair, and rested my cuffed wrists on the table. The officer interrogating me was reading a file, wholly absorbed in it. I decided to sit patiently for a while, to play the situation cleverly, but the truth is I have never been a particularly patient person.

'Is there any chance,' I asked, 'that you could take these cuffs off?'

The interrogator stopped reading and looked up at me. He had a fine, rather feminine face; dark brown hair, a long column of nose curling into two scrolled elegances over his nostrils, thin lips, a broad scholar's brow. His brown eyes were serious, and his scooped-out cheeks gave him a monkish cast. But he was wearing the same uniform as Pander, as my husband, as the whole military world, and I immediately mistrusted my instinct to like him.

'Surely,' he said, in a Midwest accent. He gestured to the guard at the door, who flourished a key, and in moments my hands were free.

'Thank you,' I said.

'You know why you're here?' he asked me, putting the folder down but not meeting my gaze.

'I,' I said. 'I don't know. I've been accused of terrorist crimes – but I'm entirely innocent of—'

'We're not interested in that,' he said.

I stared at him. 'Not interested in my innocence?'

'Not interested in those alleged crimes.'

This took the wind from my sails. I sat back. 'Oh,' I said. 'Well, I guess I assumed that was why I was here.'

'Do you know [*Name deleted*]?'

'Yes,' I said. 'I haven't seen him in a long time. I heard he was arrested.' In fact, I had assumed he was dead. 'Is he here?'

'*He* says he had an "affair" with you.' The officer raised his eyebrows to indicate the scare quotes around 'affair'.

'Yes,' I said.

He hummed for a moment at that. 'That's interesting. He's not a very reliable source – not reliable, you see. He claims to have had affairs with several women, some married to high-placed military figures.'

'My husband—' I started to say.

He talked straight over me. He didn't raise his voice, he just talked through my words as if his voice had substance and mine was transparent. 'My superior officer, who knows [*Name deleted*]'s wife personally, has already briefed me that you are not the person you have been claiming to be.'

'This is ridiculous,' I said.

'Frankly, I don't care. It's [*Name deleted*] we're interested in, not you.'

'Him? Why? I'll tell you, you know, he's not the criminal mastermind he sometimes pretends to be.' This, looking back, was a rather spiteful thing to say, but I was startled, unsettled.

'He is,' he replied, 'a greater danger than even he realises.' This quietened me.

'Is he here?' I asked eventually. 'Is he in this camp?'

'He's outside. You can speak to him in a moment.'

'Oh,' I said, surprised.

'Events,' said my interrogator, 'are coming to a head. We are trying to gather all relevant material. It is likely that you will only sit here, and be returned to Liberty in due course, but we can't be sure. You will face charges for,' he gestured with his left hand, 'impersonating a senior officer's wife, I'm sorry,' and he almost smiled, 'of course that's not a specific crime, in actual legal terms, but you take the point – you *will* face the consequences of your deception, however we decide to frame the charge.'

'This is insane,' I said. 'It's like *Alice in Wonderland*. Why not just get hold of the general and ask him to come take a look at me?'

My interrogator looked at me. 'I've been told that you've insisted on a personal meeting with the general before, several times. With a, shall we say, *suspicious* energy. Frankly, Ms – Ms – what shall we call you?'

'Call me [*Name deleted*],' I said, getting angry.

'Well, that's exactly what we can't determine,' he said. 'Whether you're simply delusional – and you wouldn't be the first person to suffer the delusion that you're married to the IP, or in this case the *future* IP. Or whether you have some sinister ulterior motive. Your insistence on meeting the general suggests to me the latter. A possible assassination attempt, perhaps?'

'This is such a crazy thing, it's beyond crazy,' I said. 'If he's here he can just take a look at me, from a distance if you like – he's probably going to bump into me anyway, isn't he, if I stay here for any length of time? It's not a large camp.'

'The general isn't here.'

'He isn't?'

'He's several miles from here.'

'What – out on the ice?'

'He's in the middle of the most delicate negotiations. Negotiations that hold the possibility of – not only peace – not only respite from attack – *but also* the possibility of future survival for the whole human race.' He said this in such a deadpan, sincere way that it did not at all sound overblown.

'Jesus,' I said.

He inclined his head a little. 'Indeed. There's an immense amount at stake, more than you can easily imagine. He can hardly walk away from these negotiations on the whim of any deluded woman who comes in here claiming to be his wife. Can he now?'

'Negotiations with whom?' I asked.

He nodded, slowly, as if I had said something with which he agreed. 'We're not far from an announcement,' he said. 'In the meantime you're free to move about the camp. But not to leave it. It would be extremely foolish of you to leave the camp anyway, since we're sixty miles from Liberty in you-don't-know-which direction. If you wandered away you'd be dead in days, and probably in hours. But, so that there is no misunderstanding, if you move outside the camp boundary the guards have the authority to shoot you.'

'Negotiations?' I said.

'You'd be best advised,' he went on, 'to stay in the barracks to which you've been assigned. That way you'll at least stay warm, and fed. Goodbye.'

The guard came to stand behind my chair. Looking at him, and at my interrogator, I stood up. 'But,' I said, 'I know lots of other senior officers. I know plenty of people on [*Name deleted*]'s staff who could vouch for me – I know [*Name deleted*], isn't he a colonel?'

The next thing I was being shuffled to the door of the small room.

'Wait,' I called. 'You said [*Name deleted*] was here. Can I see him?'

'Ah,' said my interrogator, with dry distaste, 'your "lover". He's here. Outside, to the left. Door at the end of the corridor. That's where I last saw him. But,' he sat up straight, twisted in his seat. 'I'd warn you.'

'Warn me?'

'Only that he is not to be trusted. He is a fantasist. In my judgement you can trust about a third of what he says. About a third is true, a third is altered from some recognisable truth, and a third is pure fantasy. He used to be a writer you know.'

'He told me that.'

The interrogator shrugged. 'He has acquired the habit of fiction, like an addiction. He told us, for instance, that he was abducted by aliens as a child. He was quite . . . graphic in his accounts of it. Unpleasant.' He shook his head.

And, with that, I was shuffled through the door and left to wander down the corridor outside by myself. Minutes earlier I had been cuffed and guarded, now I was free to meander about the compound. I wasn't sure what had happened to make the difference.

And there was a door at the end of the corridor, and I passed through it into the intense bright light of sun-on-snow, and, just as I had been told, [*Name deleted*] was sitting on an empty packing case.

He looked up at me as I stepped out, his face blank.

I looked around, drew in one lungful of cold air, then another. Everything glittered. The sunlight was positively painful. I wished for shades, but I had none.

'I thought you were dead,' I said, taking a seat on a case next to his. He looked exactly as I remembered him: the lined and cracked expanse of baldness, the twitchy movements, the lively eyes. But there was something diffuse, something uncharacteristically loose, about his manner that belonged to a different person. I couldn't quite put my finger on it.

He squinnied at me. 'Nice to see you too. I'm sure.'

'What are you doing here?' I asked. 'What, for that matter, am *I* doing here?'

'Ah,' he said. He shaded his eyes with the flat of his hand. 'Great things are afoot. The greatest in human history. I'm almost embarrassed to say that I'm at the heart of them.'

'You are?'

'You see those clouds?' he said, suddenly pointing at two or three foamy clouds in the zenith. 'Didn't you used to love cloud-watching? We thought clouds had destroyed the world. Hey, didn't we? The snow comes out of the clouds, and the clouds cover the earth, and the *snow* covers the earth and—' He broke off.

'Are you alright?' I asked.

'Sure,' he said. 'Surely. Surely.'

'You seem a little – I don't know. Is something wrong?'

'It's been a lot to take in,' he said. 'I thought it was the same thing, as in, like, the *snow* had come out of the *clouds*. Bu' it turns out it didn't at all. So, it turns out the Snow didn't come outta there at all. Man,' he said, 'that takes us back doesn't it? The Snow, when it started. You remember that first flake of snow? And you thought this is just another snowfall there've been a million like this already – only there haven't. You remember? It wasn't like any previous snowfall. And now, we know that's truer than we thought. That very first snowflake, it's—' he broke off again.

It was as if he were conducting a monologue, and it didn't really matter who was listening. It was if he had barely registered that I was there at all. It was very odd.

'Did you find your Sidewinder memo?' I asked.

'What?'

'You used to tell me that there was a memo by a guy

called Sidewinder, a government scientist, that gave the real reason for the Snow.'

'The Seidensticker memo,' he said.

'Yeah that. Did you ever find it?'

An expression of cunning came into his face, and for the first time in our conversation I had a real sense of the old [*Name deleted*], the conspiracy theorist, the believer, the guy with whom I had had an affair. 'You know what?' he said. 'That was a smokescreen.'

'A smokescreen.'

'Yes,' he said, leaning towards me, and speaking more urgently. 'Wheels within wheels. Misinformation. The government had its official story, and it had its unofficial story. It had the both of them. The government had its official story, that Russians started the snow with their nuclear industry. But who's going to believe that? I mean, really? How could *so much snow* come about that way anyway? . . . It doesn't make any sense when you stop to think of it. Jesus, a *kindergarten* kid could figure out that this wasn't the way the snow came. So they laid a false trail, they invented the Seidensticker memo. You know what? I don't even know if there is a real Seidensticker, I don't even know if he exists! But it's some made-up story in his memo, about scientific advances that turned the oceans to snow – that's not especially believable either, though, is it?'

'I don't know,' I said uncertainly.

'Of course not. But why did the government lay this elaborate false trail? Why forge this memo in the first place, unless the truth – the actual truth – were so incendiary that it had to be covered up at all costs?'

'What truth?'

'The real reason for the snow. What else?' He averted his eyes, and his voice shifted to a mumble. 'And I'm the key to it. They wrote the memo to provide a spurious justification for the Snow for those few people canny enough to see through the "official" story and seek for the truth. But the real truth was behind that memo. And I'm the key to it.'

'I've just been,' I said, gesturing to the door with my head, 'in there, being interrogated by some guy . . .'

'Colonel Fairford.'

'Was that his name? OK, Fairford. He interrogated me. Although to be fair, you couldn't really call that an interrogation. It was really . . . I don't know, *soft*.' [*Name deleted*] chuckled, as if this amused him. 'But,' I added, 'he mentioned you.'

'He did?'

'He said you weren't to be trusted.'

This seemed to amuse [*Name deleted*] further. He grinned. Lines bunched up at the corners of his eyes like millipede legs.

'I told him,' I went on, 'that I knew you, and knew how far you were to be trusted. But he said one thing about you I didn't know.'

'What was that?'

'He told me,' I said, grinning at the stupidity of it, 'that you claim to have been abducted by aliens when you were a kid!'

His reaction surprised me. I was ready to laugh with him at this absurdity, but instead he looked horrified. He leapt up off the case and stalked around in a small circle. 'Jesus!' he howled. 'Jesus Christ! I told him that in confidence, and he's blurting it out to everybody! I told him in the *strictest confidence*. Christ, why does he have to tell the whole world? Is nothing sacred, is nothing secret? Christ alive!'

'Hey,' I said. 'It's OK. It's me. Remember?'

He stopped and looked at me, but nothing in his look made me confident that he really knew who I was. His mind was considerably more unhinged than it had been the last time I had met him.

'You got to promise me,' he said, with desperate earnestness, 'not to repeat that *to anybody*. That's absolutely secret. Nobody must know – Jesus can't I have a *single* secret that's just mine?'

'Alright, alright,' I said, trying to mollify him. 'You can calm down, it's alright. I'm not going to tell anybody.'

'It's a secret!'

'In which case I have to ask, why did you tell it to – him, to – Fairfax in there.'

'Fairford.'

'Yes.'

'Oh, oh, I thought it was relevant,' he replied, throwing his hands up in a melodramatic gesture. 'I was trying to help. I thought it would help. Given the current negotiations.'

'Yes,' I said, getting up off the crate myself to move my limbs and get my blood circulating again. 'Fairford said something about that too. What's happening? What negotiations? With whom?'

'It's really cool, actually,' he said. His whole manner changed again, becoming once more secretive and adolescent. His moods were highly volatile. 'Who'd have known it? We all thought the clouds had eaten the Earth, but in fact it was something completely different – war of the worlds, invasion.' He chuckled, and then, with a teenager's abruptness, he was off, running with an ungainly trot across the open space at the centre of the compound.

That night I lay in the narrow, hard little bed with [*Name deleted*], and she put her arms about me, and I put my arms about her. I told myself it was to stop myself falling out of the bed, which was part of it. But it also pressed her bony body up against mine, it also brought her heat into my skin, under my skin. Her hair, unwashed for months, did not smell bad; on the contrary, it had an attractively organic smell, the real animal McCoy. I pressed my face against it.

It was dark. We cuddled together like schoolgirls.

'Do you know what? I never used to like you,' I whispered, into her ear. 'Isn't that stupid?'

She didn't reply for a moment. Then she said: 'I always liked *you*. I was always – drawn, to you.'

'Oh,' I said. 'I'm sorry, I was an idiot. I,' and I stalled, uncertain how to phrase it without sounding stupid, 'I like you now.'

She laughed, a low fluid sound. 'Ditto,' she said.

We cuddled closer.

We took comfort in one another.

'Your husband, though,' I said. I felt her go tense in my arms. 'Hey,' I said, 'hey. I'm only saying.'

'I'm sorry. Ain't it stupid?' She spoke softly.

'I guess he knows you're here?'

'I had a fling – I guess you could call it a fling. With you-know-who.'

'[Name deleted]?'

'The very same.' She sighed, minutely. 'You and he were an item, too, weren't you?'

I sighed myself. 'I don't know why, now, when I look back, but yeah, but yeah. He's here, you know. He's in the camp. I saw him today, talked a bit with him, and – man – he's gone loopy.'

I could sense her smiling in the dark; some minute shift in her facial muscles. 'Loopy,' she said. 'That's so British. That's such a British way of putting it. Nuts. Loco.'

'I mean it, though,' I said. 'He was always a bit unhinged, but he's got much worse. I don't know what they did to him in interrogation, but his mind is losing it.'

She was quiet for a bit. 'He found out,' she said in a smaller voice.

'[Name deleted]?'

'No, my husband,' she said, with bitterness in her voice. 'You remember he was running for the Senate? He had these major ambitions, these political ambitions. That's what upset him the most, I think, when he found out. Not the personal betrayal, but the damage to his political career.'

'He was angry?'

'Sure enough,' she said. 'He was all *have you any idea of the damage?* and *how could you do this?* and *you've betrayed not just me but Liberty, you've deprived them of a man who would have been a fine Senator.*' She snorted. 'As if. He was *so* pompous.' (The word 'so' came out through her Swanee-whistle accent as a reverse-inflected 'sew'.) 'He strode up and down. Do you know the worst thing he said?'

'What?'

'He said, *if it had to be an affair, couldn't you have picked a less politically damaging man?* Can you believe that? I honest-to-god don't think he minded me having sex with somebody else, I think he could only think about the political fallout. But then they arrested [*Name deleted*], and then they arrested me. I guess [*Name deleted*] gave up all his names straight away.'

'Never a brave or discreet man. Did your husband not get you bailed?'

She snorted again. 'He came to see me, told me it was the best place for me, that he was filing a legal separation. I said, good. I told him: good, I'm glad. I told him, I wish I'd had the courage to tell him what I'd thought of him before. Selfish. Oh, he was disgusting sometimes.' She shuddered in my arms, and I held her more closely. 'Not *like* your husband,' she added, slyly.

'He was out of Liberty when I was arrested,' I said. 'On manoeuvres somewhere, I don't know. When we stepped off the plane – and that guy told me that Crow wanted . . .'

'Crow?'

'That's how I call him, my husband. He looks kind of like a crow, with the big nose. Or I used to think so. But when that guy said Crow wanted me to be separated from the prisoners and brought to him – I couldn't believe it.'

'Wasn't that weird?' she said, her accent bending the diphthong in 'weird' into fluting outlandishness. 'That whole scene?'

'I know,' I said.

'I *know*,' she echoed. 'When he wouldn't believe that you were you? He really couldn't see past your skin. Did he really not recognise you from before?'

'I guess not.'

'That's so racist,' she said.

'It's not unusual,' I said.

'It's outrageous,' she said, her voice growing louder. 'What an asshole. I tried to speak up for you, but he just slapped me down. I remember him from Liberty, and he was always this ass-kissing, toady little guy. When I was still with my husband, he'd a *jumped* if I spoke to him. He'd have been all, hel*lo*, how interesting, my, my.'

'Times change,' I said.

'Hey!' called somebody from a nearby bed. 'Will you girls keep it down? We're trying to get some sleep, for Christ's sake.'

'Sorry,' we said, together.

She was quiet for a long time. 'You wanted to grab that chance,' she said, finally, in a whisper.

'Grab?'

'The chance to get out of this internment camp – if that's what this place is. I don't know. When that guy read out your husband's name. You wanted to grab the chance.'

'I guess so,' I said. 'But it wasn't to be.'

'I can understand that,' she said. 'I can understand you wanting to get away. But I'm glad you didn't go.'

And I held her more tightly, and she held me more tightly. And we fell asleep. I'm not going to put down in writing some of the things we did, because it's none of your business. Besides, the current NUSA climate – or so I understand, from my secluded position – is increasingly puritanical, so it would probably only inflame somebody or other. On the one hand there's a lot of irrelevant physical description, but that's just bodies – under the regime of hunger in which everybody in NUSA lived all bodies were bony, men and women; and there really is surprisingly little difference between male bodies and female bodies under such circumstances. On the other hand, there is stuff like love, tenderness, affection, support, words which the world has tried to discredit by making them sound ridiculous, childish, sentimental. But these are important words. These are the only important words. And it is no dishonour that they are childish; that, as I said, she and I were like nervous schoolgirls on their first day of school, holding hands and helping one another through.

That's all I want to say about that.

We were a week in the camp, each day the same as the next. Internees were permitted to wander about uncuffed, but Pander would sometimes repeat the warning that should we leave the perimeter his men had license to shoot at us.

There were six buildings, five of wood and one of prefab metal walls and roof. There was a vehicle park, in which two snow-tanks, a couple of snow-bikes and some crates were stored. A helicopter was swaddled with a tarpaulin outside the fence, next to the grid airstrip on which our plane had landed. From time to time, on odd days, a plane would fly in with supplies, and depart after an hour. Sometimes it would depart towards the west, and sometimes towards the east.

I spent most of that week with [*Name deleted*]. She and I stuck together, and we slept together. She told me about her life before the Snow, and I told her about mine. She was solicitous on the subject of Minnie.

On the other hand, there was [*Name deleted*], who was usually to be found sitting on crates outside one of the army buildings. He sat there, his head burnt brown by the sun, like an old Buddhist monk. Sometimes he would rock backwards and forwards, talking gently to himself. It was pitiful.

[*Name deleted*] would have nothing to do with him. I couldn't draw her on the subject of her affair with him, either. I think she felt ashamed to have gotten herself caught up in such a situation. I didn't press her.

Nevertheless, I found myself caught up with him, the mad old monk, almost despite myself. I suppose I need to explain how it was that I found myself outside the fence with him, in the dark small hours of the morning, trudging across the ice.

He came up behind me one afternoon when I was standing at the wire, looking over the pure white monotony of the landscape beyond. 'I know the truth of it,' he said.

'Hi, [*Name deleted*],' I said. 'How you doing?'

'The *truth* of the *snow*,' he said urgently, like an old tramp haranguingly panhandling me. He took hold of my elbow. 'C'mon, the *truth* of it, you want to *know* the truth of it?'

'Let go my arm,' I said, but I didn't snap at him. 'Jesus, you *were always* like this, you know. So intense, so obsessed with truth, such a pain in the arse. You always believed the truth was a hidden thing, a secret thing. Did you ever think that maybe the truth isn't like that? You ever think that? Maybe the truth is exactly what you can see, and not hidden at all? Maybe the truth is in plain view.'

He seemed delighted at this. 'At last, you *get it*,' he said. 'At last, somebody gets it. That's it! The truth is all around! Look at all this snow, lying all around. The sheer amount of it, that's the truth!'

'You're crazy,' I said genially. 'That's just, that's nonsense. How is that truth?'

'Look at the snow,' he urged me, 'and tell me where it came from.'

I ignored him, but he repeated the question, and so to humour him, I said: 'It fell from the clouds,' as if to a kid.

'So *much*, though? Could so much fall from the clouds?'

'[*Name deleted*], I don't see what you're getting at. It's all there, so I guess so much could. So much did, after all.'

But he was shaking his head. 'That's what I mean. Use your noggin.' And he wandered off.

Another day I went over to him, and talked to him for half an hour or more. We talked about the camp, about the snow. He said to me, 'They're at a camp, you know. They're negotiating.' I said, 'I heard there were some negotiations goings on, but I don't see with who – unless it's the Australians.' 'No,' said [*Name deleted*]. 'It's *aliens*.' I almost laughed, but stopped myself, remembering how upset he had become on a previous occasion when I laughed at his alien-abduction story. Then he said, 'General [*Name deleted*] is there, he's leading the negotiations.' I said, 'My husband.' He said, 'Who are you again?' with genuine puzzlement in his eyes.

I knew his wits were badly disarranged.

The third occasion was late in one afternoon. I wasn't with [*Name deleted*] because she had gone for an afternoon lie-down, and I was standing alone when he came up to me. 'You want to meet them?' he asked me. 'You want me to take you there?'

'Where's that, [*Name deleted*]?' I asked, indulgent.

'Your husband.'

'So you know who I am today, do you?' I smiled.

'I'm serious,' he said. 'I'm serious. It's a few hours' walk. You can meet them – the aliens, they're ready to meet me. I talk to them.'

'You talk to them?'

'They,' he said, 'talk to me.'

His gaze was hard, determined, convinced. It was almost convincing, the complete conviction with which he carried it off. 'Really?'

'This is the way to do it,' he said. 'We get out before dawn, under the fence. We walk for a couple of hours. Then we're at the out-camp, where your husband is. Don't you want to go meet your husband?'

I thought to myself: it would cut the Gordian knot of the ridiculous official refusal to recognise me. It would be worth it just to see Pander reprimanded for not obeying his superior's orders. I pictured the scene: 'I told you to bring me my wife, here she is, why have you been keeping her with the other internees?' It would be worth it just for that. I didn't believe [*Name deleted*] about the aliens, of course, but I was more prepared to believe that he really knew the way to where my husband was. Perhaps he did know.

'How do you know?' I asked him. 'How do you know where he is?'

'I've been there. I've been involved in the negotiations.'

'You? Negotiating with Australians?'

'No,' he said, petulant. 'No, there's no Australians. But

286

they flew me to the for'ard base a couple times. It's due east of here, maybe four hours' walk. Do you want to go or not?' Why else,' he pressed me, 'why else do you think they brought me here?'

'Why did they bring any of us?'

'Me?' he insisted. 'Why did they bring *me*?'

'Jesus, [*Name deleted*], I don't know.'

'To play a part in the negotiations,' he said simply. 'I'm the key, I'm the chosen one. I'll come get you before dawn.'

His words got under my skin. That night I couldn't sleep properly. Perhaps my sleeplessness, my muddyheadedness, played a part in it. I lay in [*Name deleted*]'s arms, and her breathing was soothing, but I became conscious of aches in my neck and shoulders. I executed complicated, super-slow movements to extricate my arm from behind her back, to unhook my leg from between hers, without waking her up. I tried lying facing away from her, or turning back to her. But no matter what I did I could not sleep. He had got to me, even in his broken-down madness. Eventually, after what seemed an eternity, I got up. I couldn't sleep.

The windows of the block were still black, I got up, put on my boots and coat, and went outside. [*Name deleted*] was sitting just by the door in the darkness.

When I came through he stood up as if he had been expecting me, as if it were the most natural thing in the world. 'Come on,' he said.

'Look,' I said, meaning to add, this is crazy, we can't just stroll out over the snow. But I didn't say that. I just followed him across the compound. He made his way to the fence and went down on all fours. As I approached I could see that he was digging at the snow at the foot of the fence.

'I changed my mind, I don't think we should leave the compound,' I said, as I came over to him. But he ignored me. He was madder than ever. 'They talk to me,' he said as he scrabbled at the snow, 'they talk *through* me – I'm the

287

key. I'm like the universal translator. You ever see *Star Trek*? And *they* – and the *army* – want to use me for their own ends. But I won't be used. I'm too canny for them. I communicate what I want to communicate.' He laughed.

'You're crazy,' I told him, hugging myself for warmth.

He dug with a splintered board from a packing crate, and I stood watching him. You shouldn't, by the way, get the impression that this camp was like a prisoner-of-war place, or any of that movie cliché (assuming you've seen any of those sorts of movie). There were no guard towers, no searchlights, no guards patrolling the border with Alsatians – nothing like that. The guards were probably all asleep. Surely they were. There was nowhere to escape to, that's the point. [*Name deleted*] said he knew where my husband was camped, and he said it was a doable walk over the ice, but I only half believed him. And failing that we were sixty miles from Liberty in god-knows-what direction, and thousands of miles of snow desert at the end of every other compass point. Why would we be so foolish as to break out? Still, Pander's words kept going round in my head, my men have orders to shoot anyone found outside the compound, and I was getting panicky.

'Are you sure,' I said to [*Name deleted*], as he dug, 'that you know what you're doing?'

'Are you sure that you know the *truth*?' he replied. He was hip deep in the hole he had dug.

The snow glittered all around, steely grey-blue under the quarter-moon.

'You know what a psychiatrist would call it,' I told him, hugging myself and wishing for the thousandth time that I had a cigarette. 'He would call it your hypomanic state. It alternates with depressive periods. The colonel said that your grasp on reality was poor, that you were a fantasist,' He wasn't listening to any of this. 'It means you're mad. You're a suitable case for treatment.'

'Here we go,' he gasped, pulling the bottom of the fence

towards him where it had come free of its ground, like a rotten tooth. He ducked down, and wriggled up on the other side. 'Come on! Come on!'

I took one last look at the camp. 'If Pander had only believed me,' I said, wistfully, 'I'd be with my husband right now, and I wouldn't have to do this ridiculous thing.' But I dropped into the hole, pulled the wire over my head and shoulders and clambered up on the outside.

We started away immediately at a trot, heading easterly towards a gleaming bar of paler sky. 'It's nearly dawn,' I said.

He was laughing, softly. It didn't reassure me about his sanity. 'On a flat plane,' he told me, as if reciting a school lesson, 'the horizon is further away than it would be in an undulating landscape. Accordingly we must travel further than we otherwise would to get out of sight of the camp.'

'We're leaving,' I pointed out, 'a pretty obvious trail.' Not only the hole dug under the fence, but scratchy footmarks over the frozen foam of the snow.

'That doesn't matter, that doesn't matter,' [Name deleted] cackled. 'We'll be over the horizon by dawn, and then they'll come – then they'll come – then it won't matter. They talk to me, I understand them. None of the *others* understand them. Maybe this time I'll ask them for sanctuary.'

'Sure,' I said, panting a little to keep up with him. 'They can take us into their spaceship, give us a nice cooked breakfast. They eat breakfast, do they?'

He giggled at this. 'You're funny,' he said. It was like being with a hyperactive and slightly paranoid thirteen-year-old.

The going was good, the snow firm enough under foot with the night's hardened carapace of frost. It would start to soften as the sun rose. During the day open snow became a much more treacherous place, liable to open suddenly beneath the unwary foot, cracking and bubbling slowly, opening cold lips to form crevasses of various sizes. The best time to walk on open snow is at night. But of course you know that already.

We walked well, we covered the ground, with ease. It was hard to tell the time, except that the sky to the east grew paler, more platinum-blue, the light suffusing up through the purple and black of the night sky, rising as slowly as osmosis. The stars changed their hue, thinning and then vanishing in the growing light. There were several silk-effect clouds hanging near the horizon, darker blue against the lighter blue-rinse colour of the sky. By the time these clouds had turned mustard- and orange-coloured with the imminent sun we had walked so far that the camp could no longer be seen behind us. [*Name deleted*] was singing in a warbly tenor:

> Here come the sun, doo-doo-doo
> Here come the sun, doo-doo-doo
> Here come the sun

My leg muscles were starting to complain at the constant trudging, but I also felt a certain elation – to be out of the camp, to have committed myself to some action (even so crazy an action as [*Name deleted*]'s) rather than just to be sitting around passively. And also, I'll confess, I was curious to see what strange little green-men [*Name deleted*] was going to conjure out of the snow. I wanted to see him bring his fantasy to the point of proof. I had no idea. I had absolutely no idea.

The sun put itself a millimetre above ground, like a red-shining periscope checking out the world above, and [*Name deleted*] called out 'Day! Day!'

'Can we stop now?' I asked. 'We're out of sight of the camp.'

'But look around you!' he said, throwing his arms wide and wheeling about. 'Look! Look!'

I looked. The sharp angle of new sunlight threw a giantess's shadow behind me, stretching with ludicrous extension almost (it seemed) to the far horizon. [*Name deleted*]'s shadow was similarly elongated. And the plane of snow that looked, by night or in clear day, smooth as paper, was revealed by the oblique illumination to be fantastically pitted and carved, grotesquely distorted into a million humps and pools. A million little knobs of snow caught pink-and honey-coloured light and appeared to litter the world with semi-precious pebbles. A million jags in the surface stretched shadow in weird, witch-like shapes. Undulations in the snow, like beach sand at low tide, were here emphasised by the light into fantastical horizontal staircases, scattered architectural or giants-causeway features strewn in broken-off array. The purple of the receding night sky westward blended with the pink and orange and blue of the coming daylight. The white snow took all these colours, held them, and assumed jewel-like scintillations and threads of sheer colour as luminescent as an aurora.

'Isn't it beautiful!' hooted [*Name deleted*]. He was dancing from foot to foot, like the old guy in the *Treasure of the Sierra Madre*. That last sentence will only make sense if you've seen that movie.

'Very pretty,' I said. I flopped down to rest my legs, folding them underneath me as I sat on the snow.

The sun had moved above the rim of the world now, a neon-red carbuncle. The clouds near the horizon were shreds of claret. Everything was roseate light, blue immensity, blurring to purple in the west, everything was silence, except for [*Name deleted*] hooting and the scrape of his dancing feet on the snow.

'Look at those colours,' he called. 'Salmon,' he yelled. 'Tomato! Pumpkin! Hay! Eggshell blue! Eggshell blue!'

'You're quite excited,' I observed. 'You want to calm down, maybe?'

He hurried over to me. 'I could forgive them, you know – they made the Earth a beautiful thing. You realise how beautiful when you see it like this. Not mud and pollution and people everywhere breeding like maggots, but everything picked clean and pure, just pure colours and open expanse, and clear light!'

'You mean the snow?' I said.

'It's better this way. It's purer this way. The Earth isn't *infested* with people the way it used to be. That's all I'm saying.'

'That's a pretty Nazi thing to say,' I said.

He sat himself down beside me, his eyes scintillating with reflected glory. 'Say,' he said. 'What did you say your name was?'

My stomach turned over a little. I kept forgetting how insane he really was. 'Tira,' I told him. 'I'm Tira – don't you remember? Jesus, [*Name deleted*], we were lovers for months – don't you remember that? Have you lost that much of your mind?'

'Sure, sure,' he said, waving his mittens in the space between us. 'I just forgot. There's a lot to think about, it crowds out the newer stuff. Listen – Tira, yeah – listen, I'll tell you something. This is secret, right? You mustn't tell anybody. Anybody at all. OK?'

'OK,' I said.

'When I was a kid—' he said, and stopped. He rubbed his beard with his mittens. 'This is the most secret of secrets,' he said. 'You understand?'

'If it's so secret,' I said, 'why are you telling me?'

He ignored this. 'When I was a kid I was,' he paused, dramatically, and then said, 'abducted by aliens. I know! I know!' He spoke as if I had reacted with amazement, when of course I had not. 'It's fantastical – but it happened. They took me from my bed, not once but many times. They took me to a metal room, and . . . did stuff to me, I don't want, I don't want to tell you about that. And I never understood it, I used to try and pretend it wasn't happening. But I don't want to talk about that. They were different-looking from *these* aliens, they had arms and legs.'

He stopped, as if musing. So I prompted: 'These aliens don't have arms or legs?'

'Of course not, of course not. They live in the snow, do you see? This is their medium. Those other ones, I don't – I haven't quite worked out what the relationship is between those other aliens and these new aliens. But, man, they speak to me! That's why the military flew me out here, to parley with them. They asked for me! You believe that? The ETs. They asked for me by name!'

'Hey,' I said. This sounded even more insane to me.

'Or,' he said, in more thoughtful mode. 'Maybe they brought me out because they'd been copying me. Then when I was here they discovered I could talk to them. Maybe they didn't ask for me by name, didn't ask for me by – but that doesn't matter.'

'How do you mean, copying? Copying you?'

'Hey, when I lived in Liberty I was the leader of the freedom fighters. It was a secret. I wouldn't expect you to know about that. It was a secret.'

'What are you talking about?' I said. 'Have you lost your mind completely? Don't you remember all those conversations we had when we were . . .'

He waved his mittens, dismissing me. 'Never mind that, never mind that. You need to understand this about them: they're not what you'd expect.'

'What would I expect?'

'Oh, I couldn't say. But science fiction – you know—'

'Sure,' I said. '[Name deleted], are you going to . . . show me these creatures of yours? Are you, I don't know, doing to call them forth, or something?'

'Not little green men,' said [Name deleted], as if I hadn't spoken. 'Not blobs and tentacles. Science fiction made us believe that invaders would come in saucers, and blast the White House with lasers, and march over our landscape in killing machines, and suchlike shit. But, when you think about it, that's not a very sensible way of proceeding. We wouldn't invade Mars that way, would we? So why should Mars invade us that way?'

'So these aliens are Martians?'

'Martians?' repeated [*Name deleted*], his face clouding. 'What do you mean? Of course not. The point – the point – is, is that if we invaded Mars we'd terraform first. Wouldn't we? We'd need the world to be prepared for our arrival. Seeding the atmosphere, working over the ground. Wouldn't we?'

'So your aliens,' I said. The whole conversation had an unreal quality to it. 'They terraformed Earth? With the snow?'

He put his arms about me, bringing his face close to mine. His eyes were agitated, it was difficult to say whether with joy or fear. 'That first flake, it wasn't like any snow that had fallen before. You remember that first flake? And, and, and,' he added, releasing me, and standing up, 'when you *think* about it – but who actually *thinks* about it? No, people don't think about it, they take it for granted, they live in the world of habit and tomorrow'll-be-like-yesterday, day-after-tomorrow'll-be-like-day-before-yesterday – that's the limit of their thought. But if, if, anybody had sat down to think about it, everything would have been clear.'

'Clear?' I echoed, because it seemed to me far from clear.

'*All this snow?* How could *this enormous amount* of snow come out of our little earthly clouds? No way. It would *have* to come from outside. It's so obvious when you think about it. You know what comets are? Snow. You know how many you'd need to send into the atmosphere? Little ones sure, but enough of them to keep supplying the higher atmosphere with granules of snow, granules of ice. And it snows, and it snows, and after a while the world is no longer inhospitable meadows and inhospitable mountains and inhospitable oceans – after a while it's nothing but snow. If you think about it, it becomes clear.'

'So aliens . . .' I said, but I couldn't think how to finish the sentence.

He sat down on the snow in front of me. The sun was a fist's breadth above the horizon, its fire more orangey than before.

'We used to think that water was an essential, a sine qua

non,' he said, very rapidly. 'But, of course, for a more developed form of life any fluid, any solvent, anything capable of . . . you see, there are many differences between the metabolic logic of them and us, but plenty of the higher functions are comparable. Still, they don't like the sorts of heat we like. It's uncomfortable for them. I'm guessing here, of course, but I reckon it's a logical guess. Given the volatility of ethyl-based circulation at – you'd say, at *room temperature*. We still say room temperature, don't we? Even when our rooms are freezing. By rights, room temperature ought now to mean however-many-degrees below, and—'

He stopped.

The next thing he was talking about was the circulatory system of the aliens. A lot of this passed straight through my brain: it was disjointed, and some of it was stickily technical. But I remember him going on and on about their circulatory system, how it was gravity-driven, not pump-driven, not heart-driven, they must constantly up-end themselves, let their let's-call-it-blood sift down their systems, upend themselves again. There was no way he could know this, of course. With hindsight it looks like the most random speculation, and it bears no relation to the reality.

'This,' I said, for the nth time, 'is crazy.'

'Look around you!' he bellowed, throwing his arms wide. 'This is their doing!'

'They live in the snow?' I said.

'You ever read *Dune*? You ever see the TV version? That's them, those worms. They thread through and through the snow. *That*'s where they live!'

'I never read *Dune*,' I said. 'But wasn't it on telly . . . ?'

I thought of what Colonel Fairford had called him: a fantasist, a born liar, don't trust his words. From thinking it was too weird to be a lie, I started thinking that he'd concocted it all out of some old sf novel he'd read once. '[*Name deleted*],' I said. 'This is incredible. I mean that in the actual sense of the word. I mean literally that it's hard for me to believe it's credible.'

For a long time, perhaps a minute, [*Name deleted*] stood upright on the snow. He seemed to be staring at the western horizon. When he finally spoke it was in a different voice, a calmer and saner-sounding voice. The old [*Name deleted*] seemed, briefly, to have returned.

'I worry,' he said, 'that perhaps they have gotten inside my head. My moods seem to be – since first meeting them—' He trailed off.

I got to my feet, and started over to him. 'Hey,' I said. 'Don't be glum.'

'They bombed the hospital,' he said, bleakly. That stopped me in my tracks. I had an instant, and vivid, memory of picking a severed hand out of the wreckage of the hospital. 'That's not *Dune*,' he said, meditative.

'I guess that does sound more *Independence Day*,' I said. 'That sounds more like *War of the Worlds*. I mean, bombing us. That sounds to me more like the kind of thing an invading alien would do.'

Abruptly, he was hypomanic again. He swirled round, his voice accelerated, acquired a headlong rapidity. 'But that's the really weird thing, it's not like that *at all*. Jesus, I can't tell you how hard it's been trying to talk with them. Trying to talk. They are—' and he spun round and round like a dervish, his arms out, '—they – are capricious,' he said. He stopped, a little unsteady on his feet. 'Capricious,' he said. 'That's the word for them.'

'Capricious,' I said.

'But it's more than that. They are *capricious* in their *capriciousness*. They can't even be consistent in being capricious. Sometimes they *are* rational – serious, logical, predictable. Sometimes they act for reasons that are obviously self-interest. Sometimes they deal in terror, in power – and we surely understand those things. That's how we act. We understand power. But we don't understand power manifested only intermittently. Does that make sense?'

'Not,' I said, 'really.'

He paused, mulled over his own words. Then he opened

his mouth and another gabbling rush came out. 'It's a human constant, power, isn't it though? Some humans have power wrested from them, but we – just – don't – *give it away*. They do. They do. We can't work out why. It's not predictable. They seem enthusiastic. They seem to get carried away by *imitating* things – us, say – and you think, hey, that's all they are! They're interstellar children, they're just really impressionable, they've been captivated by some new fad, and it happens to be us. But if you think that you're just wrong. Or, I heard somebody say, they're guilty for having all but wiped out our life form, and their guilt makes them act strangely. But I don't figure it's guilt. It's not predictable the way guilt is. When the bombs went off in Liberty they just copied the explosions. That's all. They sent projectiles into the city to make more explosions – it's like they thought we were blowing ourselves up *for fun* and they wanted to show us they could be fun too. Sending explosive globes raining down on the city. Why? I don't know. Copying us. Why should they? It's like the British invade India, they steamroller over India, and force every Indian into British schools and the British army and the British way of life. And then, having committed that force majeur, they start themselves spontaneously wearing turbans and saris and drinking tea and riding elephants.' He threw his hands up, shaking his head. 'Is that the way imperialisation happens?'

'I don't know,' I said.

'The military sent dozens of squads to them – armed, of course. Aliens are invading, and now they're bombarding us – are you surprised they want to keep these facts from the people? Think of the panic. Sometimes, though, they seek out the soldiers and they say, "Hey hey, shoot us, there's the fatal spot, beneath the head," in this singsong voice. Impossible to say if they're being happy or sad, delirious or depressed-suicidal. Sometimes they act that way en masse. Sometimes it's one or two. But, again – sometimes they respond as if to a threat. I mean, the way *we* respond to a threat.'

He shook his head.

'They hunt,' he said. 'They show astonishing co-ordination over large groups. They show self-protecting, rational, animal behaviour. They hunt like sharks. The men stationed out on the ice call them Great Whites. You know?'

'Sharks,' I said. 'I don't like the sound of that. Have we been invaded by alien sharks? And they speak English, do they?' That sounded to me more like a sf-TV alien, stepping out of the saucer and just happening to speak perfect English.

[Name deleted]'s eyes were suddenly very wide, as if he had been goosed. 'Man!' he exclaimed, as if it had struck him for the first time. 'It's exciting, though! I mean, the end of the world, and *now* we meet the aliens. And – they learned our language really quickly. Idiosyncratically, sure, it's not Harvard English, but nevertheless. Nevertheless. We assumed that they must be like us in some deep way, to have picked up our language so quickly. But it's not so, it's not so at all. They don't seem to have a language of their own at all. We can't learn their language, find out what their core concepts are, all that – because they have none. Great white aliens.'

I felt a tremor in the snow.

'It's like,' said [Name deleted], 'they conquered the world, and now they're at a loss what to do with it.'

'Jesus, [Name deleted],' I said, starting as another tremor in the snow vibrated the soles of my feet. 'What's that?'

He seemed much calmer now. 'Here they come,' he said.

What happened next is hard for me to remember with any precision – which is more than a little ironic, since I'm sure that for most people reading this document it is only this part that you're actually interested in.

This is what I remember. A plate-shaped cloud seemed to have slid along the sky and into the zenith. The sun was yellow, as tall above the horizon as I was. The richer colours had drained out of the sky, but the east was still pink and the west was still gentian blue. The snow trembled, and trembled, and [*Name deleted*] dropped to his knees like a religious ecstatic.

The ice rippled and sagged a little to my right.

'There's a chopper,' I called.

A helicopter was visible in the sky away to the west, its cockpit glinting like landing lights, gold and white.

I felt something wriggling inside my head, like maggots. Under the bone of my skull. My own thoughts, like solid things in my brain-matter, thought and memories, flickers of epileptic light at the edges of my vision. I think it was the stress at that moment. Who knows what terrible carnivorous creatures were moving through the snow under my very feet, sifting the snow like earthworms through earth. [*Name deleted*] was making a high-pitched ululating noise. The chopper's distorted throb was reaching me through the air – the police, the army, coming after us for fleeing the camp, and Pander's words kept coming back to me: 'My men have orders to shoot anyone found outside the fence.' It was all happening at once.

A circle of snow six yards in diameter cracked, sank, broke into boulders of white, and then fell suddenly away. I was a couple of yards from the lip of this hole. I saw something, corpse-white, flecked with flat patches of cream-coloured squares that could have been intermittent scales, move in the hole, curl around it like a cat settling to sleep in its bed. I stepped back, I felt this overwhelming revulsion. It was as if a plague pit had opened up.

'They don't have a ship!' squealed [*Name deleted*], as if in ecstasy. Perhaps the realisation had just come to him. 'They don't travel through space *that way* – gleaming control panels and flashing lights and – *ugh*—' All the breath left him and he flopped forward.

'[*Name deleted*],' I called. But the noise of the chopper was much louder now, and I could barely even hear my own voice.

He was getting slowly to his feet, saying something that I couldn't hear over the noise of the rotor blades above me. I saw movement again in the hole.

Then bullets started pounding into the ground. The helicopter's side-mounted gatlings were thrumming and spinning, and sparks and puffs of detonation were splashing all around the hole and inside it too, throwing up white dust, chalk-like fragments of snow, and such an enormous noise that it overwrote even the crash of the rotors.

I threw my arms about my head in terror and danced away from the hole, away from the tempest of bullets. The snow was turned, in short order, into a kind of fog, as if powder-fine snow were falling again. Everything went misty, I could see nothing. I was screaming something. I don't know what I was screaming.

The noise of the gatlings stopped, and the powder swiftly arranged itself in flowing lines and curls under the force of the rotor blades. In moments the air was clear again.

Something broke from the snow. It popped up as neatly as a flying-fish through the surface of the ocean, a brown-edged trail of smoke through the sky arcing swiftly up and coming down. It missed the airborne 'copter by feet and hit the snow a few hundred yards further away with a grand, fiery explosion. An oval of fire swelled quickly, turned brown and grey with smoke and sent out skeetering tentacles of smoke. In moments it was over, except for a rising plume of black and a crater, except that the shockwave pushed out, an invisible hand, and shoved me over onto my back.

I lay there, my ears ringing, and heard a second projectile descending, and heard a second explosion. The chopper's noise was receding, as if its pilot had decided to fly away from this attack. The throb of the motors became quieter and quieter and then I couldn't hear them at all. The tinnitus in my head faded.

I picked myself up from the snow. Particles of snow were all over me, as if I had been dusted with sugar. All over my arms and hands, my legs and body, my face and head.

The white light reflected from the snow all around me made it hard to see the craters left by the explosions. Even the hole that had appeared right next to me seemed to have gone. Perhaps its walls had collapsed and snow had filled the hole. I couldn't see [*Name deleted*] anywhere. In fact I couldn't see very much at all. The white of the snow was brighter than usual, too bright, lit not by the sun but by some inner element that pushed a sharp and a washing-over whiteness everywhere. I shielded my eyes with my mittened paw, but it did no good.

The sky was bleached, blank as bone. The snow was shining on the sky, instead of the other way around. I thought to myself, what's happening here? I thought to myself, have I got snow blindness?

I thought I heard [*Name deleted*] talking. He sounded close, no more than six feet away from me. He was saying, 'They're not all the same, any more than we're all the same.' I turned, turned, but I couldn't see him anywhere. The voice had the ghostly burr of hallucination. 'They don't present a unified front,' he was saying. 'They can be hostile to us and friendly to us at the same time. Don't we act the same way?'

I felt afraid. I felt very alone, on this shining white plane. I couldn't for the life of me work out where [*Name deleted*]'s voice was coming from. I was no longer even sure where I was.

'Where are you?' I called.

'What we have to do,' he was saying, his voice smaller and less distinct as if he were retreating from me as he spoke, 'is understand the imperial mindset. Now that's not a straightforward thing.'

There was nothing. There was a silence so perfect it felt artificial; not the sound of wind in my ears, not the thread of my own pulse in my inner ear, nothing at all.

'Hello?' I called, and the word crashed like an explosion. My own utterance made me flinch, it was so loud.

My spoken word did not echo.

I turned slowly through three hundred and sixty degrees, and on all sides I was faced with the mathematically flat plane, the sharp whiteness, the bleached sky. I dropped to the floor and slipped my hand out of my mitten, and the snow was cool to the touch but not icy, a granular whiteness like cold sand. It was as if my fingers' nerves had been dulled somehow, and could no longer register the sharpness of their sensations. I couldn't understand what had happened. It occurred to me that I had been killed, or fatally wounded, during the helicopter attack, or during the explosions afterwards, and that I was now lying on the actual snow as on a deathbed. Perhaps I was experiencing death. Perhaps this is what death feels like. This blank white plane, this could be the afterlife – a life in the wastes of the snow, an afterlife there too. I tried to make sense of it, and in a strange way it did make sense. Warrior religions like the Vikings' promised a warrior's afterlife of feasting and slaying. Hunter religions like Native American faiths promised an afterlife in eternal hunting grounds. Shepherd religions like Christianity promise a shepherd's heaven of safe green fields and mild weather. What if our afterlife is wholly determined by our life? What if people who live amongst the snow spend eternity in the snow after they die? The thought was nearly unbearable to me: to think that death would provide no escape from this monotony.

'No,' I yelled, and the word hurt my ears, and made my head throb, it was so loud. And yet, once again, there was no echo; the word vanished as soon as it was spoken.

Then I had the sensation of insects crawling inside my head, a gritty, itchy sensation right in the middle of my head. Pulling off my mittens I tried to screw my little fingers into both my ears to reach the itch. 'Ah!' I hummed. 'Ah!' I was humming to try and reach the itch with sound waves, to take the edge off it. My own humming sounded vast, headachey, but the sound stopped as soon as I stopped.

The bright snow was parting in front of me. A gap opened up in the crust, and snow tumbled inwards from its lips. The gap widened, and the snow shifted around it. Something bone-white moved in the space. It reared slowly up.

It occurred to me then that perhaps the reason I couldn't see [Name deleted] was that he had been buried. Perhaps the snow had collapsed upon him and carried him down into the hole that had been created earlier. I thought to myself, distantly, that I should be trying to dig him out. But at the same time I was hypnotised by the giant worm that was rising up in front of me. I was face to face with the alien.

Then, with a rushing insight, I understood who this being was. Not an alien, of course, but rather my daughter. She had taken a strange form, that can't be denied. She was wormy, dragon-sized, with a grey-white forward portion, and then feathers, or not feathers because each frond twitched and wriggled with life; cream-coloured scales, or fins, or something; but a mouth with a purple-brown pulsing action somewhere behind the fourfold crinkle of its lips; and behind the complicated business of the midsection was a great swelling, elephantine and indistinct, mostly still buried in the snow. In the snow. But she – it – would shift, and pull herself-itself round, and I would get the sense of something more complicated, segment upon segment and each different from the other.

'You're big,' I said. 'You've grown so big.'

The words were normal-sized. They didn't boom or hurt my ears. They were conversation words, not solitude words, and much more comfortable to my ears.

Minnie swirled slowly, and the snowtop ice growled and cracked, and her sheer size broke atoms of snow from the surface and sent them scurrying into the wind. *This season I am big*, she conceded. Her skin pulsed and vibrated, turning purple-black as it did so. Perhaps that was how the sound was produced. I could have laughed, or cried, or repeated her manner of speech. This season? As if it were a fashion show.

'I missed you,' I said. 'I'm sorry you went away.'

This season I am big, said the creature again, and then I couldn't see it as Minnie any more, but as a great ugly worm, long as a skyscraper laid flat. It was almost as if this monster had devoured Minnie's body, had nosed under the snow, through the buried streets, into the crushed rooms until it had found Minnie's body, and swallowed it python-like.

I shouted. 'I'll kill you,' I said. 'You are so ugly,' I said.

To kill strike below the shoulder, said the creature, arcing the second, icicle-feathered-segment of its monstrous body out of the snow to present itself to my aim. The calmness, the blandness even, with which it faced its own death struck me forcefully. I sat on the ground. The stiff ice crackled under my snow-clothes. I wanted to cry, to weep and howl, but tears didn't come. Sometimes they don't. There are times when you want to cry, as a demonstration of the turmoil inside you, and the tears simply don't come through. The monster withdrew itself into the snow before me, until only its grey forward segment, with its sore-looking multi-lip mouth, was visible. *To kill strike below the shoulder,* said the creature.

'Dragon,' I said. I drew a deep breath. 'Where did you learn English?'

This season I am big, said the dragon.

'I don't understand what you mean.'

The dragon seemed to murmur to itself, to twist in the ice a little, as if it were considering my questions.

'What I mean to say,' I said, with a new lucidity, 'is that – maybe you don't grow the way organisms from this world grow – to start small and to grow larger and larger. Maybe it's not like that for you. Maybe you fluctuate in size.'

The study has been longfold, said the dragon.

I pondered this. 'What do you mean? I don't understand the word.'

The period of study has taken long, said the dragon.

'Study? What?'

The period of study has taken long, said the dragon. *At the beginning we spoke fax.*

And I had the understanding that the creatures had stud-ied us through electronic communication, and that for some reason fax-messages had sounded to them more like intelligent interaction than human speech. I don't know how I knew this. I could present you with some theories as to how; maybe I imagined the whole thing. Maybe the creature said *facts*, not *fax*, and the vivid mental picture distracted me from the truth of it. I don't know. I don't know.

Taken long-ish talking has has at and, said the dragon.

I got to my feet again. 'What drew you to me? Can you read my mind? Is that it?' I was quite excited. 'Are you only speaking in my mind? Maybe the words I hear are just sounding inside my brain. You can sense my pain, my loss, and that's what's drawn you to me – my daughter, my beautiful, dead daughter. You know about that, don't you. You know about that.'

This season I am big, said the dragon.

'OK, OK,' I said. 'I'm going too fast for you. It's OK. I can slow it down. We can slow it down. Let's talk, slow as you like.' I was consumed by intellectual curiosity. I was talking with a creature from another star.

It was necessary tenfold to break through the crust that forms on the surface of any *object superheated supercooled*, said the dragon, with a weird emphasis. *This season I am big*, it added.

Again I experienced a clear mental picture. I can't be certain, to be honest with you, that this was the result of some alien telepathic suggestion. Maybe my brain was merely playing tricks with me. I have a vivid imagination. Perhaps I imagined the whole thing, influenced by [*Name deleted*]'s gabbling about science fiction and *Dune* and so on. Maybe that was all. But I *saw* a meteor landing in soft snow, and then I saw the hard surface forming on the snow, and then meteors crashing down with tremendous acceleration to punch through the crust and reach the soft snow underneath. I saw all that, and with a salmon-like leap my heart reached a new level of understanding. That these creatures not only lived in the snow, they were the *authors* of the snow.

As if following my thoughts, the beast curled its horse-head-sized snout, with its strange maw, sweeping it left and right past my face. There was a grassy, alcoholic smell.

'It's your element, isn't it?' I said.

It was necessary sixfold to break through the crust that forms on the surface of any object superheated supercooled, said the dragon. *It was necessary twofold to break through the crust that forms on the surface of,* said the dragon.

It withdrew abruptly into the snow, drawing back like a tortoise pulling its head back into his shell. There was an earthquake-like rumble, and the crust bulged away to my right. The grey snout of the creature emerged, and fragments of ice adhered to it like the skin of sugar on a crème brulée. *Taken longfold talking has has at and,* said the dragon.

I saw everything. I saw the alien world, snow-covered, creatures swimming through the snow like fish swim in our oceans, but superintelligent creatures, creatures with inquisitive minds, mapping the cosmos, planning their next move. I saw the terraforming of Earth from their point of view, co-ordinating a thousand sub-cometary lumps in oblique trajectories to graze our atmosphere. I saw them falling to Earth themselves inside boulder-sized ice blocks, nascent forms, no larger than a thumb – or – no – larger than a pollen grain. I don't know. I can't say whether this was telepathic suggestion by the creatures, or something else. Maybe it was just my imagination.

And I blinked,

blinked, and I was alone, and

blinked, and I was in the chopper, and a man in uniform was leaning across me, in front of me, yelling right in my face. He was hanging on a strap with his left hand, and waving in my face with his right. I was sitting there, seeing this man, and behind him the inner wall of the chopper. Everything seemed to have changed very abruptly from bright whiteness to close, dark, noisy. I could see a small window in the wall, through which everything was blank and white. The engine was very loud.

The man was shouting, 'Count for me, backwards,' and I took my gaze from the white window, and the metal fittings of the 'copter's hold, and tried to focus on him, upon this man. It was enormously hard to concentrate. His face seemed to decompose and recompose in front of me – there was his nose, his chin, his left eye, his forehead, his ears, his right eye, but they didn't seem to cohere in a single image. 'Can you do that for me?' he yelled.

'What?' I said.

'Good!' he said, looking pleased, his eyebrows shooting up. 'OK, good, stay with me now, stay with me. Can you *count*, can you *count backwards* from ten, for me please?'

'Count?'

I could see, then, what was wrong with his face. He had no mouth. But I thought to myself, if he has no mouth, how is he asking me to count?

'Backwards,' he said again.

And then, with a conceptual coming-together in my head, I understood what the problem was. I could see that he was wearing a plastic mask over his mouth. That what I had taken for his chin was actually this mask.

'Why are—?' I asked.

He nodded, vigorously, and raised his voice again, as if the noise of the chopper were making it impossible for us to communicate.

'Can you please count backwards . . . ?'

'Ten,' I said, looking around the space. Two soldiers, also in masks, were sitting on a low metal bar on the far side of the compartment. Some boxes and cases were on the floor to the right of me. 'Nine,' I said. 'Nine ten, eight nine ten.'

'Backwards,' the man yelled again.

'Ten eight nine,' I said. 'Ten nine eight. Why are you wearing a mask?'

'What?'

'Why are you guys all wearing masks?'

He nodded, 'Very good, very good,' he said. 'This is very good. Can you go *back* all the way from *ten* to *one* for me?'

We landed back at the internment camp, and I was hurried from the 'copter into a metal prefab, where another group of masked men, this time in doctors' clothes, were waiting for me. They had a heater going in a booth, and asked me to strip, which I did without shame or embarrassment. They examined my skin, but paid particular attention to my nose and my mouth. They peered in my mouth with black plastic-snouted instruments.

They gave me a mask of my own, linked via a black rubber tube to an atomiser of some kind. When I breathed in this device scattered a warm mist of, it felt like, water into my lungs. I coughed, but they insisted I keep going. 'What is it?' I asked, coughing and coughing. 'Is it water?'

'No,' they said. 'A very different chemical.'

I dressed in new clothes: thermal undergarments, woollen top, hiker's trousers, socks, gloves, hat. I sat on a chair in a room by myself for a length of time: minutes, perhaps, half an hour perhaps.

Doctors came and went.

Two men came in, one of them a doctor the other with a camcorder. It was rare to see such technology in our post-Snow world. They pulled up chairs and sat opposite me. They were both wearing surgical masks.

'What did you see?' they asked me.

'Where?'

'Out on the snow. With [Name deleted].'

'How about him?' I inquired, my memory prompted. I had fled the compound with him. We had walked through the pre-dawn, and into the rising sun. We had seen the snow transformed into a landscape of jewels and lights, we had seen the white become multicoloured. But in all my journey back in the helicopter I had forgotten entirely about him. 'Is he OK? Is he alright?'

But they didn't want to talk about him. 'What did you see?' they asked.

'I saw my daughter.'

They didn't seem to think this was outlandish. 'Your daughter?'

'She's dead,' I said, with the gritty prickle of tears behind my eyes. 'She's dead and under the snow, and she's been dead for years. But she was there. I don't know how, I don't know how exactly. I saw a monster. I saw this giant worm, this dragon, but it was also Minnie, somehow.'

'I see,' said the doctor.

The man taping it on the camcorder didn't say anything.

'Minnie,' I said, because I felt I needed to explain it to them, 'was my daughter.'

'I see,' said the doctor.

I heard myself. 'It sounds crazy, doesn't it! It sounds mad.'

'Not at all,' said the doctor. 'A few more questions. Did you used to smoke?'

I wasn't expecting that question. 'Did I smoke?'

'That's right.'

'Yeah, I used to. You can't get the fags nowadays.'

'The—?'

'Cigarettes. I haven't smoked one in years. But I used to, yes.'

'We can see it in your lungs. Your lungs should,' he said, simpering a little as he said this, 'be a healthy pink colour, but yours are black. Black!' he said.

'OK,' I said, feeling annoyed. 'There's no need to lecture me. I've quit, yeah?'

'Not at all,' said the doctor. 'It's almost funny. These black lungs have almost certainly saved your life.'

'What do you mean?' I asked. 'What do you mean, it's almost funny?'

'I'll tell you, I trained as a doctor,' said the doctor, folding his arms and becoming quite chatty. 'I don't mind telling you – the army paid me through medical school, and I worked as an army surgeon. But most of my work was prevention, touring barracks, talking to the men about sexual health, about keeping strong. I used to lecture them on not smoking. They all smoked, of course, soldiers, mostly, they all smoke. But I'd stand there and say,' and he furrowed his brow in parody of his old lecturing style, '*hey guys, don't smoke, it gives you cancer, it impairs your physical fitness*, and so on. I'd have been the first to lecture you on the health hazards. But now the boot is on the other foot, if you see what I mean. Your smoking altered your lungs, and they don't like that. They like an unpolluted lung. That's the irony, you see. If you'd have followed my advice years ago and quit smoking, then you'd probably be—' He stopped.

'Be what?' I pressed. 'Dead?'

'In a much worse state,' he concluded, looking serious.

'What about [*Name deleted*]? I was out on the snow with him. Where is he now?'

'He has been significantly impaired,' said the doctor.

This unpleasant phrase chimed inside my head. I imagined monstrosities, deformities.

'I don't understand,' I said. 'He used to smoke too – as if that makes any difference to anything.'

'We know,' said the doctor. 'Which is why he's lasted as long as he has. But he also used cocaine, and wore away much of the mucus membrane inside his nose. That gave them an access to the base of the brain pan – we're not exactly sure how it worked.'

'Explain to me,' I said. 'I'm confused.'

'I'm sorry,' he said, getting to his feet. 'I don't have clearance to talk to you about this.'

'You've just *been* talking to me about it!'

'I'm sorry. I'll check in on you tomorrow.'

I spent the night in that room. A soldier in a mask brought in a truckle bed. There were no blankets or pillows, but I was very tired and I slept easily. It was never cold inside that room. I woke in the dark, with no idea what time it was. I woke in the middle of a dream in which Minnie and I were boating together in the middle of a blue lake (although we had never been boating together, she and I, in real life), and she said to me, 'You know what this blue stuff is in the lake, Mum?' and I said, 'Sure, sweetie, it's water,' and she said, 'No, it's a very different chemical. We're crossing the lake of acid.' And in my dream I knew she was right, even though the blue fluid looked so peaceful and limpid. It wasn't hissing or steaming the way you might think acid would. So I pulled the oars out of the water and they were two corroded lumps on poles, like two boiled sweets that had been sucked for too long.

On the far side of the lake was an enormous mountain.

Minnie was standing up and pointing, indicating across the lake at the mountain, spectacularly broad and high with a road running around it at an angle that was virtually horizontal, coiling around the flanks of the mountain like the thread of a screw, and myriad tiny little figures were on the road, walking upwards. And I said, 'Isn't the air clear, we can see every tiny little detail on that mountain road,' (and I was very struck in the dream that I could indeed see these tiny details, even down to the fact that the men marching up were wearing collarless shirts and workman's pants). But when I looked again I could see that Minnie was not pointing at the mountain, but in a different direction. She said, 'There's the criminal.' I didn't want to follow the line of her pointing arm, I didn't want to see the criminal. I had the feeling that he was lying in the middle of the blue lake of acid, a basker, and I didn't want to see it. Perhaps his body was half-eaten away. 'I want to go back,' I said. And Minnie had become [Name deleted], and I knew that he was the criminal, and he was right in the boat with me. I was afraid. I said, again, 'I want to go home.' And [Name deleted] replied, 'Back to that place of sawdust and chopped ice?', speaking with immense disdain, as if I were the most foolish and despicable person in the world to want to return to such a place.

I woke.

They wouldn't let me out of that room. A soldier in a mask brought me food, and when I needed the toilet I used a chamber pot (real old style), which he took away and brought back clean. Not a pleasant job for him, I suppose. It only occurred to me on the second day that they might be conducting tests upon my stool, upon my water.

I spoke to the doctor when he next came to visit me. 'I understand that I'm considered to be a contamination risk of some kind,' I said. 'I only wish I knew what the contamination was supposed to be.'

'I'm not at liberty to say,' he said, smiling, as if this were in itself amusing.

'Where's [*Name deleted*]?' I asked. 'Did you leave him out on the snow?'

'He's in a room not far from here.'

'Is he also in isolation?'

'Naturally.'

'I want to see somebody.'

'You want?'

'I want to see [*Name deleted*].'

'I don't know who that is.'

'She's a woman, in this camp. She's one of the internees brought here. I want to speak to her. I want you to bring her here.'

'I'm sorry to say,' he said, shaking his head a little, 'I can't promise anything.'

I got up and walked towards the doctor. I had the half-formed idea to rip off his mask, to infect him with whatever was in me (whatever the breath of the snow-worm-alien-thing had given me), so that he would understand the frustration of quarantine. So he would have to endure it too.

As if he read my mind he was up and out of the room in a moment.

I reached the door just in time to hear the bolt sliding through to lock it. 'Hey!' I yelled, banging on it. 'Can I at least have something to read? Can I at least have some *reading matter*?'

I banged for five minutes, or ten, I can't be sure. Eventually I gave up. I made myself comfortable and lay on my bed for a long time, running things through my mind. Eventually I fell asleep. It felt as if I had reached the end of something, but I hadn't reached the end. There was one more act to play out.

My room had no windows, so it was impossible for me to know what time it was. But I was asleep, and the room-light was off, so it felt like the middle of the night, when the door started shouting, bang-bang-bang. 'Hold on,' I called, druggily, still half asleep, thinking I was back in my house in Liberty and somebody was at the door. Somebody was smashing at the door, making it bounce in its frame. 'Hey!' I called, coming more awake. 'Hey!'

I sat up, and heard the bolt being withdrawn. The door swung open, and a shadowed figure stepped in, and said, 'So where are the lights?' and I recognised the voice of my former lover, of my companion on the snow on the occasion of my meeting with the aliens: [Name deleted].

He said, 'So where are the lights?'

'On the wall, by the door,' I said, swinging my legs over the edge of the bed.

And the lights came on. And my eyes winced with the brightness. There he was, [Name deleted], his creased, intense face looking nervously all about the room. He was the first person I had seen in days not wearing a mask.

'What's the password?' he asked. He sounded insistent. 'What's the password?'

'Password shit,' I said, rubbing my face.

He had shut the door behind him and was crossing the room to me. 'C'mon, Tira, password, password.' He sat down next to me. He was grinning.

'Oh God,' I said. '[Name deleted], I was asleep, you know?'

'I'll give you a clue,' he was saying, 'but I can only tell you once. You gotta remember it, OK?'

'You know, I'm not in the mood—'

'Remember I told you I was abducted, when I was a kid?

313

That I was an abductee? Remember that? Well, hold that thought, keep it to yourself but hold that thought. The password is "live free or die".'

'Four words,' I said.

'Sure. Live free or die. Enemies of freedom: surveillance, army, government. Face them, even at the risk of death.'

'What are you doing here, [*Name deleted*]?'

'What am I *doing* here? Let's get *out*, hey, Tira? They're holding us as prisoners. I'm come to rescue you. Like Luke Skywalker in the movie, and you're the princess.'

'I'm no princess,' I said, distractedly, because I had just then noticed what he was carrying in his right hand. 'What's that? No, I know what it is, where did you get it?'

He looked down at the gun, held it up to display it. 'This? I found it.'

'Should you – hey, should you be carrying that around?'

'It was a guard's. He was supposed to supervise my inhalations. They got you inhaling?'

'Yeah,' I said, nervously.

'You know what we're inhaling?'

'No.'

He grinned. 'That bother you? Don't you think you should know? Isn't that the point of freedom, to be in charge of your own body?'

'How,' I said, trying to stay calm and keep my voice low, 'how did you get the guard's gun?'

'He didn't believe I was abducted.'

'Didn't?'

'No,' [*Name deleted*] said, sombrely, shaking his head as carefully as a child. 'He mocked it. I couldn't persuade him, of the truth of it. I guess I won't even try any more.'

Everything was very quiet. The door was not quite shut.

'Why not?' I asked.

'They think the visitors, the aliens, have infected us. Think of that! How likely do you reckon it is? They evolved on a completely different world, their cellular structure, their *everything* is completely different to ours. There's just no way our two metabolisms could interact. They won't listen! I can *speak* to them, they *speak* to me, I know. They don't even see them as *worms* – Christ, they've no idea. Some form of fluid aggregation – fuck that. They think they're like an ants' nest. An ant!' he said.

'[*Name deleted*]—'

'Can you believe it? A cloud of *dust*. Intelligent dust! Does that sound *likely* to you? They let billions suffocate under the snow, but some, some conscious decision on their part kept us two alive. Why? Because they have a plan. A plan, and I'm at the centre of it. I tried to explain that to the guard, but he didn't want to listen. Didn't want to hear. It was in his interest to hear, I'd say, to hear that I'm *the one*.'

'Hey,' I said. 'Wait a minute. What about the guard?'

'Came in with this breathing thing, with the long rubber hose. God knows where they dug that up from. Fifty years old. The rubber hose broke.'

'Broke?'

'He's dead, the guard. The hose broke.'

I could feel my heart hurry alarmingly. 'Dead?' I repeated, huskily.

'You wouldn't believe the difficulty I had,' he said. 'I took the hose and managed to get it around his neck, but rubber stretches, you know? I pulled and pulled, and I'm not as strong as I used to be. So I hung on it with all my strength, and my heart started complaining – I don't have a very healthy heart. I had a heart attack you know, before the Snow. I had surgery.'

I said nothing.

He was quiet. After a while, he concluded: 'Anyway, the hose broke, and he fell to the floor. He was pretty grey by then. A kind of dark grey, not blue. I was expecting him to go blue. But his eyes were red – not just red-rimmed, but the whites of his eyes completely red on both sides. It was pretty gross.'

'Are you sure,' I asked, 'that he's dead?'

[*Name deleted*] shrugged. He looked at the gun in his

hand. 'Not breathing,' he said. 'I sat and watched him for a while. Then I took his sidearm. His holster was still buttoned up. He didn't think to unbutton it, take out the weapon and ward me off. He kept scrabbling at his throat, but the hose had stretched and stretched till it was thin as wire, and it had dug right into the flesh of his throat, you couldn't reach it to pull it out. I mean,' he added, more slowly, 'if he'd thought clearer he could have got his gun out, and then he'd still be alive. But he didn't think clearly, so he's dead – it's kind of his fault really. You got to always,' he tapped his forehead with his left forefinger, 'keep one step ahead, mentally.'

I felt nauseous. 'Jesus,' I said.

'He was only a guard,' said [*Name deleted*].

'You're a psycho,' I said, without heat.

'I couldn't *define* that word if you *asked* me,' he said quickly. 'Psycho, what does that even mean? That's just – that's just—' He stopped. He was looking at the gun in his hand. 'That's just a meaningless word,' he concluded, before continuing without pause, 'and I never, I *never* saw the supposed comparison between a gun and a dick, you know? They're not *at all* alike, really, when you think of it. For one thing, a gun has no balls, and it doesn't spray, no *fluid* comes out of it. And you can only use it for one thing. You can only use a gun for one thing, you know, whereas with a dick – you can fuck with it, piss with it, pull on it when you're feeling lonely.' He chuckled.

After a pause he said in a lower tone, 'Six billion dead under our feet and you're going to blame me for one more?'

'Jesus,' I said.

'Alright,' he said, with a sigh. 'I'm sorry, I apologise. Alright? Shall we go?'

'I'm not going anywhere with you,' I said.

'C'mon!' he cried, smiling. 'Don't be pissy.'

'You,' I said, meaning to say, *you revolt me*, but my eye fell on the gun in his hand again, so I repeated, 'I'm not going anywhere with you.'

316

'You're coming,' he said, not smiling.

'Or what?' I said, firing up a little. 'You going to kill me too?'

'I guess,' he said, deadpan, and stood up. The pistol was aimed at my face. A gut-level fear thrummed in my belly, a death-fear, and my heart just galloped. My hands were trembling. I stood up too. 'OK, OK,' I said. 'I'll come, but I'm—'

'You're what?'

'I'm coming, OK. Don't be crazy, alright?'

'We need to speak to them again,' he said, still pointing the gun at my face. 'That means going out on the snow. You got anything warmer to wear? Where's your coat?'

I needed, desperately, to urinate. Everything in the room seemed sharper, more vivid, and every object and space had oriented itself around the gun, its human c-shaped scaffold, its single clear eye looking straight at me. It was the still point. The need to pee passed away, but my hands were still trembling. 'They took my coat,' I said. 'I don't have a coat.' I thought, ridiculously, maybe he'll leave me here when he realises I don't have a coat. It's stupid, I know, but although I believed he was capable of shooting me dead I didn't believe he was capable of herding me out onto the snow in my night-wear.

I was wrong. 'Never mind,' he said. 'They'll keep us warm.'

I had on bedsocks, leggings, a long-sleeved top. At home I sometimes slept in a nightcap, but the army doctors hadn't provided me with one of those. It was in this costume that I stepped out into the corridor, prodded by [Name deleted]'s free hand into an ungainly trot. At the end of the corridor we passed through a door into a sort of hall. Electric lights dangled on cords like shining hanged men. The windows set in the left-hand wall were black, so it was indeed the middle of the night.

A dozen beds were arranged along each wall, so the hallway was a sort of hospital ward. But all the beds were empty, their sheets folded neat as cardboard, their pillows undented. 'Go through,' urged [*Name deleted*] behind me. 'Go through.'

'Where are we going?'

'Outside,' he said.

And we hurried through into a corridor, and into another room, this one apparently the lobby. A private was sitting with his boots on the table in front of him, reading a library book. His gun was leant against the wall behind him, like a broomstick. There was a desk light by his propped-up left boot, and another light over the outside door. [*Name deleted*] actually squealed, with delight or panic, when he saw the private. 'Don't move, don't move!' he yelled, hurrying over to him, the gun in his right arm, and his right arm locked straight out, pointing straight ahead.

'[*Name deleted*],' I said. 'You're scaring me.'

The man said nothing. He looked like he thought maybe he was dreaming. Then he whipped his feet off the table, covered his mouth with his hand and half-fell backwards off his chair onto the floor. 'You stay there!' [*Name deleted*] sang. 'You stay down there! Come on, Tira.' And he grabbed my arm and pulled me through the main entrance and outside.

It was dark outside. The ground glimmered underneath a frost-coloured moon. I immediately began to feel the pain of the chill through my bedsocks, and the air nipped at my neck and face. But I felt an outrush of warmth from my chest which I knew was sheer relief. 'Jesus, [*Name deleted*],' I exhaled. 'I really thought you were going to kill that guy.'

'Take a few down,' he said, but he was facing away from me as he spoke and his words weren't distinct. Maybe he said, 'Take a few of them down.' He pulled me across the frozen yard, where moonlight underwrote every sparkling lump of snow with a crescent of shadow. Boots and tyres had churned the snow up in the day, and the night had settled it in its weird choppy little shapes. I looked up and for a moment [*Name deleted*] had vanished. '[*Name deleted*],' I warbled into the night. '[*Name deleted*]?' A prisoner, now abandoned, I felt not freedom but terror. I peered amongst the chill block shadows of trucks parked close to one another twenty yards from me.

A door squealed, and I looked round to see [*Name deleted*] emerging from a dark little hut. He was carrying keys, which he tinkled in his hand like a little bell. 'Truck,' he said. 'That one, I think.'

Opening the door I clambered up the little ladder and got myself inside the cab of the truck. The seats were sharply cold to the touch, and the chill seemed to have intensified the odour of the space: the smells of metal and creaky plastic and motor oil, to which was added a vaguely mentholated and frowsy essence. 'Wrong one,' said [*Name deleted*], having tried rattlingly to fit the key into the ignition. 'Next one.'

'[*Name deleted*],' I said. 'Where are we going?'

'Come on,' he said.

He climbed down from his side of the truck and I, less eagerly, got out of my side. It occurred to me to run back across the pocketed white of the yard, to try and get help. But then, I thought to myself, what? Wouldn't [*Name deleted*] just shoot me in the back as I ran? Then I thought, to rationalise my decision further, escape to what, anyway? Locked back in a room with no company?

'This one,' he called, and waited for me to come over to the cab of a second truck. 'I think this one matches the tab on the keyring.' He pulled open the passenger door. 'Up you go,' he said.

I think I was still half asleep. It didn't, quite, seem real, despite the glaze of frost on the inside of the truck. He tried the ignition and the engine farted noisily, barked, barked and died. 'It's the cold,' he said. 'The fuel gets a bit frozen. They put an additive in the diesel, you know.'

'You don't say,' I said. '[*Name deleted*], where are we going in this truck? Is it back to Liberty?' But my last word was drowned by the phlegmy rattle of the engine starting. I thought to myself: surely the guy at the front table, the one [*Name deleted*] threatened with his gun – surely he will have gone to get help now. Surely soldiers will rank and block our exit? Surely [*Name deleted*] is about to be recaptured.

But no.

He put the truck in gear and we lurched off. I could hear the crunch of the tires over the snow, and the clatter of the engine cylinders, and then we accelerated rapidly, driving straight for a stretch of fencing. We went straight through with a fantastic crash. That must wake the whole camp, I thought. But the next thing was that we were on the open snow, driving at full throttle, and by the dashboard lights I could see [*Name deleted*]'s face grinning, underlit in green like a Halloween mask.

We drove for hours. I don't know how long exactly. [*Name deleted*] put the headlights on almost as an afterthought after we had been driving for half an hour or so. 'Where are we going?' I asked him. 'Do you even know which direction you're driving?'

I was very aware that he still had the pistol.

You may find this hard to believe, given that I had been kidnapped at gunpoint and was certainly in danger for my life, but what I did next was fall asleep. The driving was monotonous, it was dark, and I was very tired. The stresses had overcome me, I suppose. The blow-heater on the dash was warming me cosily. I fell into a doze slumped in my seat.

I woke abruptly when the whole truck shook and bounced. I yelled out, and tumbled forward, knocking my chest against the dashboard in front of me and banging my forehead against the windscreen. That hurt.

I blinked, sat up. Light was coming in through the windows.

The whole cabin had tilted forward thirty degrees from the horizontal. I looked over to [*Name deleted*]. He was cradling his face in his hands. A wriggle of blood came through his fingers and dripped onto the floor. 'You OK?' I asked.

'My nose,' he replied, with a flattened intonation that was almost comical.

'Jesus,' I said, my heart starting, belatedly, to hammer. 'Did we crash? Did you crash the truck? You idiot.'

'We must,' he said, still cradling his nose, 'have hit a pothole in the snow. Thin crust, small crevasse, I don't know.' He fumbled with the catch of his door, and more or less tumbled out into the dawn light. I stayed where I was. The air coming through the open door was very chilly. I could see [*Name deleted*] fussing about the buried snout of the truck, examining the wheels, rubbing his nose into the crook of his arm. Eventually he got back into the cab and, with some difficulty, pulled the door shut.

'So?' I asked.

'Oh we're stuck,' he said, glumly. 'It don't signify.'

'Where are we?'

He didn't say anything.

'What, hey – [*Name deleted*] – what are we going to do?'

'We're going to wait here. They'll come.'

He tried the engine several times, but it just refused to start. Without the engine, the hot-air blower wouldn't work. It got cold in the cab very quickly.

There wasn't anything else to do. We sat in silence for a long time.

'You ever think about the Spirit?' he asked, after a long time.

All around us was blind, blank, whiteness. It was very cold. The horizon looked only a few hundred yards away; the world could have been a film set, white in every direction under a moon-coloured sky. It shrunk perception. 'Spirit?' I said. I was giving my hands an alternate squeeze and a chafe, but even my breath felt cool. My muscles trembled intermittently, like rabbits about to have their necks wrung. 'Spirit?' I said.

'The Holy Spirit,' he said. 'You won't believe it, maybe, but my whole life has been guided by the Holy Spirit. Kind of like a cloud, floating overhead. My own personal cloud.'

His voice sounded a little less deranged than it had. I hazarded: 'You're religious? Jesus, you're a Christian? I had no idea.'

'No,' he said sharply, 'not like that, not conventional religion. Not sheep and children and all that. But the Spirit, yeah? Inspiration. Respiration, inspiration. It kept you alive, in that building, under the snow. I remember you told me about that. It was them, can't you see? They gave you the air to *respire*, diffused the air out of the snow for to inspire you. Inspiration. The Holy Ghost. When I heard that phrase when I was a kid, I thought of a ghost, like Casper the ghost or something – you know. A sheet floating spectrally in the air, with holes for eyes and mouth, like that was the holy part, and Casper was the ghost part.' He laughed at himself. 'You know what it was like, in church when you were a kid and they'd say holy ghost?'

'I wasn't raised,' I said, somewhat primly, 'in a Christian environment.'

But he wasn't paying attention to what I said. 'The Holy *Spirit*, that's a better phrase. The Spirit. What does it look like? It's particles in air. That's what it looks like. Everything is particles in air, light is particles in air, matter is, spirit is the same thing. The universe is an endless snowfall of atoms. You know who said that? Heraclitus said that. He was an ancient Greek philosopher. They knew a thing or two. Those Greek philosophers. They knew a thing or two, that this is the way the world is, this is simply the way it is. Atoms falling through infinity like an endless, bottomless, fucking *topless* snowfall. That is what is.' His teeth caught, clattered, on the last word. He said: 'Man, it's cold, it's really cold. I got to stretch my legs, I have to stretch my legs to get warm.'

He pulled open the truck door and hopped out. I leaned over and pulled the door shut. I sat back in my seat and tried to wrap myself around myself to keep warm. [*Name deleted*] was yelling at me through the windscreen, 'Come out, hey, Tira, it's warmer in the sunshine.'

I watched him for a while, and eventually – more from boredom than anything else – I clambered out to join him.

There was a minim of heat from the sun, but I still felt wretched with cold. I folded my arms, hands under armpits, and shuffled sluggishly round in a circle. [*Name deleted*] was flinging himself about with crazy energy, throwing his body into a starburst posture and then pulling his limbs in again. 'This is the way to do it!' he said. 'This is the way to do it!'

'What are we *doing* here?' I asked.

He was trying to run on the spot, but the snow under him had been softened by his bouncing and his foot went through the crust. It looked as though he had gone down on one knee. 'They'll come,' he said.

'And then what?' I asked.

'They'll come,' he said, a third time. He was grinning. I don't know if I'd ever seen him so happy.

'It's a kind of infection, you know?' I said, shuffling round to try and keep myself warm. 'They're not worms, or anything like that. I think they're more like bacteria.'

His smile vanished. He struggled up. 'That's a lie. They tell you that? That's a lie.'

'They get inside us, in our brains,' I said. 'They're like intelligent dust. Like bacteria. It's an infection.'

'Don't goad me,' he said, crossly. Then, suddenly, he bellowed. It was like a heifer. 'Oh!' he cried. 'Oh!' He fell backwards and sank a few inches, his arms moving, like a kid making a snow angel. I tutted. He was such a child, really: such a show-off. A spoilt child.

'OK, [*Name deleted*],' I said, becoming more bad-tempered. '*You're* the centre of attention. Everybody look at *you.*'

'God!' he called out, lying on his back. He sounded wheezy. 'I've torn something.'

I assumed he meant a ligament. 'Should have warmed up

before your exercises,' I said, sarcastically. 'Or perhaps those jumpy-things were supposed to be your warm-ups? In which case you should have taken them easier.'

'I can see clover,' he said.

This brought me up short. It seemed like a fantastically strange thing to say, in the circumstances, even for a lunatic like [*Name deleted*]. 'What do you mean?' I asked, starting over to him. 'Did I hear you right?'

'God, God, God,' he said again, more faintly.

'[*Name deleted*]?' I asked. I began to think this was more than horseplay, that something was wrong. 'Are you OK?' I crunched over to him. My feet went into the snow to the ankles. He was lying on his back. His face was concrete-coloured. It looked awful. It was terrifying to see it: grey, scrunched up in pain. 'Christ,' I said, bending down over him. 'What is it?'

His pain rictus was exactly like a grin. He'd drawn his arms up tight at his chest. It occurred to me that he had had a heart attack. 'Jesus,' I said. 'Is it your heart?'

He drew a painful breath, and spoke rapidly and wheezily on the exhalation until his lungs were empty: 'It's a she, Tira, spectre made up of particles of snow where—' He gasped.

I felt a fear freeze solid inside me. 'Don't die, [*Name deleted*],' I said. I had a vision of myself marooned on the snow, miles from anywhere. I had no idea which direction the camp was. I could certainly not extricate the truck from its snow-crater. There was no food. I thought to myself: he dies, what do I do? 'Jesus, are you hurting?'

His face told me he was hurting.

'I have to hurry you to hospital,' I said. But it was an empty thing to say. 'Shall we try and get you in the cab? It'd be warmer in the cab.'

'Cold,' he gasped, as if in confirmation.

But there was no way I could lift him. I pulled at his shoulders in a desultory fashion, couldn't move him, and let him sag back into his indentation in the snow, and he puffed out a cloud of warm breath in the cold air. He exhaled, but he didn't inhale. I think it was then he died. I couldn't see any chest movements. Perhaps he just passed out, and was breathing too shallowly for me to see, but it amounted to the same thing. I put my hand on his face, and it was cold as any snow. I had a distressing flashback: I saw myself in a building trapped under the snow with the man called Jeffreys who's dead now. He broke his leg badly in a fall and died. I remembered [Name deleted] telling me that he'd had a heart attack, in the pre-Snow. And now he'd had one again. '[Name deleted],' I called. '[Name deleted].' I chafed his face. I lifted his arms and pulled them around in the vague hope that it might move blood through his body. I thought of doing chest compressions, I wasn't quite sure how to do them, but I'd seen them on TV, so it was surely possible. But then I thought, wasn't a heart attack a sort of rip or tear in the heart itself? Wouldn't pounding his chest make it worse?

I did nothing. I went and sat in the cab for a long time, and thought about nothing, about nothing at all, about nothing.

That was how [Name deleted] died.

Now, it seems, he's a hero, and we're not to say bad things about him. But I'll say this, I know for certain that his heroism was a wholly involuntary thing. Can a person act heroically after their death? No: a person cannot act at all after their death. But, they say that we need heroes in the new world.

Now I discover that there are under-snow lakes, great oval stretches of water surrounded on all sides by snow. I'm a little hazy on these. As I understand it, these lakes may be the result of volcanic activity at the earth's buried crust. The snow played havoc with tectonics, cooling and fracturing tectonic plates and producing a great deal of vulcanism, which in turn heated scattered pockets of water within the ice. But I was talking to somebody the other day, and they said that the lakes are heated by nuclear power stations, broken and malfunctioning under the snow, so they are one of the functions of human activity. This person said that the water was radioactive, and the fish we grow there and harvest are radioactive too. But better radioactive food, than no food, I suppose.

Then there's the plant growth. I don't know anything about the plant growth, except what every schoolchild knows: that some of the funguses are crystalline, drawing up minerals dissolved in the snow into coral-like patterns, helped by fertilisation from all manner of human waste; but that some of them (I don't know how) are organic, and can be prepared as food. Pretty tasteless food, but better than starving. I suppose. As to whether we owe these new growths to the Others, I have no opinion one way or another. I think, on reflection, I'd prefer to think not. If they destroyed our world, giving us back some mosses is pretty poor recompense. Besides, as I understand it, the Others don't think in terms of cause-effect, of injury-recompense, or anything like that. So if they kept me and Jeffreys alive, under the snow, in that building, diffusing in oxygen and taking away our carbon dioxide – as, perhaps, they did – then it was not because they had a plan. What plan? It was an arbitrary thing. To allow us to live, and billions to die? That doesn't suggest a plan. All I know is that the oxygen came from somewhere, after our pot plants had died. That's all I know.

The day wore on. I was achy in my stomach with hunger, and I drank very little, because it hurt my gums and teeth to suck on the snow. I knew I ought to ingest as much snow as I could for the water, but I was so cold and shivery and I could simply not bring myself to stuff snow in my face.

I got out from time to time to have a look at [Name deleted], in the snow. But he was cold as the world now, and motionless, and I knew he was dead. I tried to formulate a plan, but didn't get very far. Mostly I sat in the cab of the truck and wrapped myself about myself to try and keep warm. But what was the point? You can't answer me that question. What was the point? Death everywhere.

Finally the light started to thicken and the sky darken. I felt a terror come with the darkness, to think I was going to sit in the cab in my nightwear. I told myself I was going to die. So I galvanised myself by force of will. I stepped out into the dusk, and went over to [Name deleted]'s body. I wanted to get the clothes off the corpse, to wrap myself in them. It was not easy work. The sky darkened and darkened over me, as if the coming of night were an impending thunderstorm. The quality of the light became eerie, as it sometimes does at dusk. My fingers were numb with the cold and wouldn't work properly. It took me long minutes to undo each jacket button, and when I had them all undone it was very hard to pull his arms free, to turn his dead weight over and wrench the jacket off. I almost stopped there, I was so tired; but I needed all the clothes, so I turned the body again and picked, picked at the shirt buttons, and then turned him again to pull the shirt off, and then yanked and jarred the vest off. I pulled the pants down. The legs were stiff, frozen straight, whether with rigor mortis or just sheer cold I couldn't tell. It was hard to manoeuvre the pants down the legs, but finally I did it. I had an armful of freezing clothes, saturated with snow. I was shivering so hard I could barely hold them.

I left [Name deleted] lying face down in the snow, naked except for his underpants and his socks. His flesh had a blue-veiny whiteness that reminded me of Stilton.

I think I was hungry to the point of insanity. I had flashes of apprehension that the snow was all sugar, that the ice-crust on top was meringue, that [Name deleted]'s clothes were huge slabs of cold cooked pasta in my arms, that his flesh was soft cheese. My mouth watered. 'Jesus,' I muttered to myself, through banging teeth.

I stood up to return to the cab. But the dusk appeared to have reversed itself all around me. There was a brightness all across the sky. I turned, and turned, and light swelled enormously, terrifyingly, from all the snow, like a colossal world-breaking and silent explosion all around me. The light shone upon the fabric of sky lightening it. Everything became extraordinarily white. Silent white and neon white.

'It's happening again,' I said, turning. But the truck had gone, and [*Name deleted*]'s body had gone, and I dropped the cold clothes from my cold arms.

I expected to see another of the worm-dragons rise up from the ice, but it didn't happen. There was a long stretch of time, perfectly silent and perfectly white.

The light pulsed brighter until it bulged inwards into my line of sight, squeezing all detail into a wash of whiteness. Then it pulled back again, the pulses reduced, and in the middle of my vision was a figure walking towards me, tall, skinny and dark.

Closer. Legs working over the ice, carefully. Arms hanging limp.

Almost reached me.

There was a high pitched hum, like a whistle, and it ceased almost as soon as it had begun. A flicker of more intense brightness ran round the horizon. But I was still there, standing on the bright snow, under a bleached-out sky, with this strange figure walking out of the distance and straight up to me.

When she got close enough, I could see that it was myself. I said: 'Hello there.' What else do you say to yourself?

'Hello,' I replied.

We were standing, face to face.

I said to me: 'If I stand here long enough, you'll pass on by.' I didn't understand what I meant. Then I said, 'How high you've climbed!' I said this with a sort of laugh, a little snickering sound, as if it were a joke. I didn't understand that either.

But I was really there.

'I didn't climb,' I said to me. 'I was carried up.'

'Are you talking about just you,' I said, 'or all of *you*?'

'What do you mean?'

I laughed again, but it wasn't unkind.

My dark face contrasted neatly with the brightness behind and all around. I could look intently at my own shining black hair, my solid nose, my straight brow. I could stare into my own brown eyes, and as I did they were staring into mine. I have not been very much given to staring into mirrors, not since my teenage years, so it was almost a surprise to see just how round and bright my eyes are, to see how Pochahontas-like my face was.

I said to me, 'Such a lot of *water*!'

'It's not the water,' I said, hugging myself in my chill, 'it's the *temperature* of the water. If it were fluid—' I was going to add that if the snow all turned to water we'd all drown; but, for some reason, I didn't say that. Standing out on the snow, conversing with myself, as if it were the most natural thing in the world!

I seemed unimpressed. 'Everything's a fluid at a high enough temperature,' I said.

'I learnt that at school,' I said, disdainful. I peered again at this avatar of myself. 'How come?' I asked, trying to find a way of phrasing the question. 'When I saw you before—'

I inclined my head. 'Before?'

'You were a giant – worm, a sort of dragon. But that's not your form?'

I shrugged. This made me angry.

'No games,' I warned. 'Can't you be straight with me? Can't even *you* be straight with me?'

'I see a lot of *water*,' I said, clearly enunciating each word, and turning my head. 'And some trace *elements*: everywhere. And what do you see?'

'When I encountered you before I was with . . . him,' and I pointed down at the snow, where (I couldn't see, but I knew that) [*Name deleted*] was lying. 'And I think his perceptions influenced mine, but all I want, but all I want to know is, was it a real thing, or only a hallucination? Did his thoughts take concrete form, or did I just dream it?'

329

But in reply this version of myself only repeated; 'I see a lot of *water*.' She smiled, and for a moment – it sounds like vanity to say it – I was struck by just how pretty I was. 'All I'm asking,' I said, 'was, are you manifesting, or is it in my head?'

'Your head,' I said, with a curious little gesture of the left hand, 'is – what? Mostly water, and some trace elements.' I opened my eyes very wide, and suddenly I didn't look so pretty any more. 'Are you *content*?' I asked. 'For how long do you intend to remain content?'

It was such a strange thing to say. I couldn't think of an answer.

That was all that exchanged between us.

The light burned with its perfectly cold flame, all around.

I felt something rise in my head, as if a torus of magnetic charge had passed entirely around it – the magician's hoop passed about the body of the assistant. Things flickered, momently, into photo-negative, such that the snow subliminally became a waste of carbon dust, the sky a canvas of dark grey, and my own face a skeleton flash of whiteness in the middle. Then everything was white again.

And then I was being strapped into a stretcher. Masked men were fussing over my head, fitting me with a helmet, tucking a scarf around my exposed neck. The stretcher was connected to the side of a helicopter. The helicopter schwump-schwumped into flight, and carried me up. I was looking up where the black blades of the machine blurred pale grey in their rotation, and a massive oval veil laid over the blue and the clouds above.

Then I was back at the base. Or I was back in Liberty, I wasn't sure. I felt weak, thin, my head hurt. I would sit up in my bed, in my room, and look about. I called out for Minnie. I believed for a moment that I had fallen asleep in the bedroom of Sam's house in Collier's Wood on a hot summer's afternoon, and I thought I could hear Minnie

330

downstairs. 'Minnie!' I called, feebly. 'Love, what are you doing down there?' But that world was now smothered and cold.

I slept a great deal. I was in a much worse state than before. I lost some of my fingernails. But it wasn't the cold, I think: it was my second dose of *them*. Doctors in full head masks came and went around me, testing me. I had to use the vaporiser, inhaling astringent chemicals of some description or another. Sometimes the chemicals would change, as if the doctors were experimenting with various substances to try and shift the infection, or plaque, or whatever, from my lungs and sinuses. 'It's a different kind,' they'd say, mystified by their own ignorance. I slept, ate, slept, slept. I read. I slept and woke choking, crying out. Each day was like every other day.

One day I napped and woke to find Crow sitting on a chair. 'Hello Tira,' he said.
'Oh,' I said.
It took me an inordinately long time to pull myself into a sitting position. Crow didn't come over to lend me a hand. He was wearing a mask that covered his lower face. My mouth was dry, and I drank some cold, cold water from a misty-glassed cup.
'You been watching me sleep?' I asked.
He nodded. 'You're still beautiful, Tira,' he said, mournfully. 'I've missed you.'
I nodded, as if this were my due. '[*Name deleted*] is dead,' I said. 'I guess he had a heart attack.'
'We know. We found his body on the snow. You were wearing his clothes when we picked you up.'
'Was I? I don't remember putting them on.'
'You met them, didn't you?'
I let my vision defocus. Crow went furry at his edges, the room plumped and blurred. 'I guess,' I said. I could feel the water I had just drunk, like cold mercury in my stomach.

'I'm so sorry, Tira,' said Crow. His voice sounded, I realised with a start, close to tears. 'I'm so sorry.'

'Sorry?'

'It was all a stupid mix-up. I wanted you at my side.'

This made no sense to me. 'At your side?'

'Robinson is stepping down. His health is not good. I'm going forward as the next IP.' He shook his head, as if this were a sorrowful thing.

'But that's great,' I chided. 'Isn't it?'

'Yes,' he said, simply. 'But I was hoping to persuade you – I mean, I know we've had our differences. But we're still man and wife. So I was hoping to persuade you to be First Lady. I was hoping to persuade you to stand by my side. It's important for a man with those sorts of responsibilities to have a helpmeet.' Using that cod-Biblical word summed up so much about Crow. He shook his head again.

'And clearly that's impossible now,' I said.

'I'm so sorry. It's all a stupid misunderstanding. I sent a message to [Name deleted] to meet the plane you were on, and bring you to me. But he says he didn't recognise you when you got off the plane. I guess you've changed. We all have – you're thinner than you used to be.'

'Thinner,' I said, sourly, feeling bile rise, which in turn started to make me feel fully awake for the first time. 'And a different colour.'

Crow shrugged noncommittally. 'Anyway, it's a powerful shame he missed you. If you'd have been with me, you would never have been exposed to the Others' contamination. We could have gone back to Liberty, and then to New NY.'

'You're going to New NY?'

He nodded. 'And I wanted you to come. I wanted it very much. But I guess it can't be helped now. When he missed you at the camp—'

'He didn't *miss* me,' I said, heated. 'I pointed myself out to him.'

'To who?'

332

'To your subaltern, to what's-his-name, [*Name deleted*].'

'It's a shame,' said Crow again, shaking his head. 'A mistake.'

'He fucked up,' I said.

'I guess he did,' said Crow. I might add, with the benefit of my hindsight, that Pander still ended up as Chief of Military Staff under Crow's presidency. So Crow was clearly not that convinced of his incompetence. But I'm getting ahead of myself.

After that initial meeting, Crow came to see me fairly often in the hospital. It was clearly the case that my fleeting encounters with the Others had infected me with something, but the doctors weren't sure with what, or to what end, or with what degree of infectiousness, so I was quarantined. It was deadly, it was dull.

When Crow visited, he usually did not come alone. Perhaps he didn't trust himself to stay emotionally level-headed in a room with me alone. Usually he brought a junior officer along with him.

The two of them would sit on chairs on the far side of the room, wearing their masks, and talk about the Others. Sometimes they got so engrossed in these conversations that it was as if I weren't there.

'You see we assumed,' said Crow, 'that aliens would be *corporeal*, much as we are, maybe with a different arrangement of limbs or sense-organs. But they're not like that at all. We assumed that if they could travel through space, they'd at least be civilised – like us. But they're not like us. They're not civilised. We assumed they'd live in cities, and travel in machines, and have families, or I-don't-know-what. They don't drive cars. They don't live in cities.'

'Oh, I'd say they *do*,' said the junior officer, whose name I didn't know, but who seemed to be on informally chummy terms with my husband. 'I think so, at any rate.'

'Cities,' said Crow, dismissively. 'Where? You check the satellite photos, there just aren't cities, it's white *everywhere*.'

That was the first I knew for sure that the snow was general over the whole globe. I'd still been clinging to the idea that somewhere, some mythical Australia of the mind, was free of snow. It was a shock to realise that this wasn't true. But Crow and the other military guy were still talking about cities.

'That's what I'm saying, General,' the other guy said. 'You think an alien city will be towers and apartment blocks and roads. But why should it be? You've seen the geotherm and sonar studies of the under-snow. The snow is not compacted the way it ought to, it hasn't compacted down regularly. There are areas of greater-than-expected density, and areas of less-than-expected density. Maybe that's what their cities look like.'

'Maybe,' said Crow, dubiously.

'Three-dimensional cities,' said the other guy. 'Cities for cellular beings who live in the snow.'

'Cellular beings?' repeated Crow, as if trying the phrase out in his mouth to see how it sounded.

'Why not? That have bodies, but without *organs*, you know? The balance between individual cells and the whole is – different than the way it is with us.'

'Maybe,' repeated Crow. 'But the point is, they established a connection with us. They copied us, some, but they fought us.' He shook his head. 'We couldn't understand them. It's hard to fight an enemy you don't understand,' Personally I think this was Crow's way of saying *it's impossible to fight an enemy you don't understand*, but that he was constitutionally incapable of uttering the phrase 'it's impossible to fight'. It's not in his nature to say that.

'They copied us, but erratically. They swamped us, and I figure they *must* have known—'

Crow interjected, 'That's not proven.'

'—*must* have known what they were doing, that they were killing billions of sentient creatures. You don't conquer a world in a fit of absence of mind.' He chuckled at this, as if it were a great witticism, and was moved to repeat it. 'You just plain *don't* conquer a world in a fit of absence of mind. So they knew, and then afterwards they felt guilty. Like the British in India in the nineteenth century . . .'

'It's not like that,' said Crow. 'I'm almost certain it's not like that. They don't have the same relationship to motive, to notions of responsibility, guilt, shame, that we do. They're . . .' He searched for the word.

'Capricious,' I said.

He smiled. 'Exactly,' he said.

'So, [*Name deleted*], when he and I were on the snow—' I started, but Crow leant eagerly forward.

'That's precisely it,' he said. 'That's exactly the thing. It's about [*Name deleted*].'

'What about him?'

'I tell you what. He's a hero of the new world.'

At this I almost laughed aloud. 'A month ago you guys were interrogating him as a terrorist. Last week he strangled one of your men. He'd lost his head, he was a *psycho*, he threatened me at gunpoint and dragged me in my night-clothes onto the snow. This is heroic?'

'He died,' said the other guy, laconically. As if that was all that was required to be a hero.

'What he means,' said Crow impatiently, 'is that this is how he must be represented to the people. The people need heroes at a time like this.'

I didn't follow. 'The people?'

'This is important,' said Crow. 'He died, and with him died the belligerence of the Others. It's as simple as that.'

'As simple as . . .'

'They won't attack any more. They've communicated with us. Electronically.'

'Which,' the other guy added, 'just *really* suggests civilisa-tion to me. So – what are we saying – that they can, like, *manipulate* the different electrical valences of water at different low temperatures to confect whole neural nets from nothing, to process billions of bytes? So they can fashion weapons and fire them out of the snow at us? These are both civilised.'

'Well they didn't *say* it was a misunderstanding,' said Crow. 'Not as such. But I guess we can take it as read. They didn't gather, they just didn't understand—'

'This is merely speculation,' interjected the other guy on a warning note.

'—didn't *understand* that we're a race of individuals. I guess they're not, in the same way. Or maybe they are. But the point is, they established communications with [*Name deleted*]. To be strictly accurate, they first tried to establish a connection with two of our guys, two soldiers in the field, but they, both those men died.'

'Don't tell me,' I said. 'Those guys weren't smokers.'

Crow ignored me. 'But [*Name deleted*] didn't die, that's the point, and they set up some sort of two-cans-on-a-wire with him. Or a one-way thing. But anyway, anyway, the point is that they took his aggression, his anger and urgency for war, to *be everybody*. That's how I see it. This, they thought, was *everybody*.'

'We *think*,' warned the other guy, shaking his head, as if warning me off from jumping to conclusions. 'We don't know.'

'Then he died, and they saw what a death was, from the inside if you like. They got to roam around inside a dead man's head. It may be that they don't have death, or if they do they don't recognise it, or don't acknowledge it, or something like that. I think they found [*Name deleted*] dead, and since they assumed he was everybody, or everybody was him, it was a shock to find him a corpse. Maybe that woke them up.'

'They killed those other two guys as well,' said the other guy. 'Before.'

'But *they* were on active duty, so we whisked them outta there pretty quickly. So I guess they didn't get to see first hand what the death thing is like. But with [*Name deleted*], they'd established pathways in his head, they'd laid down this plaque in his brain, and so they could plug into his consciousness, go *in* there, wander about.'

336

'Hypothetical,' said the other guy, unimpressed.

'I don't know,' said Crow. 'Something's certainly changed their view. If he'd'a stayed alive, then maybe they'd still think of us in terms of fighting and hatred. But now they're communicating through equipment, and we're making progress with them.'

'Plaque,' said the other guy, wonderingly.

'Plaque, that's it,' said Crow. 'There's a little bit in your lungs now, Tira, I guess. It's, they tell me, like a site of TB, grown about with living tissue to contain it. Or something like that.'

'I don't understand,' I said.

'I reckon they killed him,' said the other guy, 'to see what would happen.'

'We don't know they did that,' said Crow, hurriedly. 'We've no evidence they did that.'

'We've no evidence either way.'

'Now I guess it *is* possible,' said Crow, 'that they read about [*Name deleted*]'s heart condition in his brain. If that's how their connection works. Or maybe – maybe [*Name deleted*] just had a heart attack, just like that. He was prone, it could have been fortuitous.'

'Fortuitous,' I said.

'Anyway, they're copying us, they're peaceful now.'

'But they bombed the city,' I said.

'Oh that was before,' said Crow, dismissively.

'Let me explain the sequence of events,' said the other guy, pompously. 'When we realised their presence we went onto the snow to combat with them. A couple of our soldiers got contaminated, and died, but they weren't ever properly used as contacts. They were soldiers and at war, and the Others seem to have taken *that* as representative. Besides which, establishing the connection proved fatal: too much of the Others' material was absorbed too quickly by these two soldiers' healthy lungs, and they died of a form of toxic shock. They kept attacking us. When they saw explosions in the city, they bombed the city. They tend to be opycats like that. This was all before [*Name deleted*] had any contact with them.'

'So when did he have contact with them?'

'He was a suspect, and was brought out to the camp for interrogation. But he broke free and ran out on the ice, and that's where they contacted him. After that, he was a transmitter-receiver. That's how he styled himself, anyhow. We flew him out to the advance point to try and use him to communicate with them, but it seems clear that our transmitter-receiver was flawed. He was full of hate.'

'He's a hero of the New World now,' said Crow. 'We better get used to thinking of him as a hero.'

'Because he had a heart attack he's the hero?' I asked, incredulous.

'A death that, whilst in contact with them, has changed their behaviour. It has ended the war. When we break it to the people, I mean the stuff about aliens and the snow, we'll pitch his act as a heroic self-sacrifice. His one death means that the whole of the new world of humanity will survive. You know what? The Others are growing plants for us.'

'Plants?'

'A number of different kinds, actually,' said the other guy. But he was more interested in his own theories about the aliens. 'Do you know what I think? I think they've arranged the snow in differing zones of pressure, because that's what a city is to them.'

'Bacteria building cities,' said Crow, scoffingly.

'So, why not? And you can't hardly call them *bacteria* anyway, that's not accurate.'

'Those maps from geotherm, they don't show any *symmetry*, any balance in the areas of hyper- or hypocompression in the snow.'

'Maybe it's symmetry to them,' persisted the other guy. 'Anyway, the point is this. We kept sinking shafts down through the snow, snow-mines, food-mines. What if our mining disturbed them? What if we were pushing mine-

shafts right through their cities, their equivalents to tov
halls and shopping malls and stuff? What then?'

'It's pretty far-fetched,' said Crow.

'But then maybe they were defending themselves, and it
just happened to coincide with the terrorist bombs. Maybe
they were defending themselves against *our* attack. Don't
you reckon?'

Crow shrugged.

'So now everything's dandy?' I said, incredulous. 'All because [*Name deleted*] had a heart attack?' I couldn't believe
this.

'Not just because of that,' Crow conceded. 'But people
need heroes.'

'And what about me?' I asked. I meant *aren't I a hero too?*
But Crow looked sombre.

'You'll have to stay in quarantine for some time. It might
be possible to fly you back to Liberty, where your quarantine will be more comfortable. But it could be, I can't lie to
you, Tira, it could be years.'

'We don't know how many years,' said the other guy.

'I'm afraid we don't know,' confirmed Crow.

'Could be never,' said the other guy. He shrugged.

I felt disgust. It seemed to me that I had spent all my life
sitting in the corner of a room whilst two old men chatted
amiably with one another, ignoring me. As if I were a little
girl. 'Fuck you,' I said. 'Fuck you both.'

Crow looked very startled at this profanity of mine, his
eyes like polo mints in his long, pendulous face. The other
guy seemed amused.

'Don't be like that, Tira,' said Crow, petulant.

I leant forward, and they both flinched, which gave me a
small pleasure – to think that my contagiousness could be
intimidating. 'You're going to peddle [*Name deleted*] to the
people as a hero. A lie, a lie.'

'People need heroes,' said Crow, again, fingering his mask
nervously.

'What about the Sidewinder memo?'

They looked baffled.

'[*Name deleted*] told me about it,' I snapped. 'The Sydenham, the Sicklehammer, I don't know the name.'

'Seidensticker,' hazarded the other guy.

'That's the one. You leaked that, so that people would blame this guy for the snow. You were covering up the existence of aliens, weren't you? You can't help yourself, can't stop yourself lying to the people. That's like a reflex for you.'

The two men spoke at once. 'You can't underestimate the culture shock inherent in alien encounter . . .' said the other guy. 'Seidensticker's a real guy, the stuff in that memo is true, he's just . . .' said Crow.

They stopped, looked at each other.

'Seidensticker's a real guy,' said Crow, carefully. 'The stuff in that memo is all true. He's just wrong about being responsible for the snow – but he genuinely thought he was. We never leaked the memo, not on purpose. You're unfair to us Tira.' He paused, hummed and hoomed. Then he said, 'Government's gotta govern. It wouldn't be much of a government otherwise. Would it, now.'

'Have you actually *seen* that memo?' said the other guy.

'You lie to the people,' I said. 'I'm so sick of sitting quietly here whilst old men yak away and yak away. You lie all the time. It's instinctive. You just don't know anything else. [*Name deleted*] was right – that memo, passing [*Name deleted*] off as a hero of the people, leaking that, drip-feeding that.' But the fire had gone out of me. I slumped back. '[*Name deleted*] was right about you, right about you all along.'

'I think you're being unfair, Tira,' said Crow again, in a hurt tone. 'Seidensticker developed these electromagnetic sheaths, much more friable than he realized, but—'

'Sir,' said the other guy, more sharply. 'Does she have clearance for this?'

I no longer cared. I felt hugely tired, that's all. I wanted to sleep again. I lay down, and turned my back to the two of them.

I heard them get up and leave, and when the door clicked shut I shuffled myself onto my back. Almost at once the door opened again. Crow re-entered, this time solus.

'Tira?' he asked.

'What is it?'

He sat in the same chair he had occupied before. Then he stood up, pulled the chair a little closer to my bed, put it down and sat again. He was silent for a while.

'What is it?' I asked again, turning my horizontal head to look at him.

'I wanted to talk,' he said. 'I wanted to talk with you, alone.'

'So,' I said. 'Talk.'

But he was silent for another stretch of time.

With a gasp of irritation, I pulled myself upright and swung my legs over the edge of the bed. 'You don't seem to be doing much talking,' I said.

'I don't know how to do it,' he replied, simply. I detected sadness in his voice, and almost despite myself I was conscious of a degree of pity.

'Just come straight out with it,' I suggested.

He shook his head, but then said, 'I love you,' in a strained voice. My stomach clenched, like on a roller-coaster ride at the lip of the highest peak. I felt very uncomfortable. I could see that Crow was crying. Actual tears, warm as his body, dripping over his hunger-sculpted cheekbones and falling through the air. Actual tears. I had never before seen him cry. It was as shocking a thing as I could imagine. 'I love you,' he said, 'I love you, I love you so much, I love you, ah!' This last word was a sharply indrawn breath, a sob, and then he put his hands to his face. [*Name deleted*] had used to do that from time to time with me, but with him it was always just play-acting, amateur dramatics, one of his many *look-at-me!* strategies. But with Crow it was different. It was really quite upsetting. For all my problems with Crow over the years I had always thought of him as

341

ong. I had never seen him cry. This, however, seemed like breakage.

'OK,' I said. I didn't know what to say. I hazarded, 'Hey,' and then, 'don't cry,' but it sounded false, so I shut up.

'Jesus,' said Crow, the most extreme expletive I ever heard him use. 'I'm sorry, Tira, I'm sorry.'

'It's alright,' I said.

'It's all so – messed up,' he said, wiping his eyes with the blades of his hands. 'Oh Jesus, what's *wrong* with me?'

'It's alright,' I said, again.

He sniffed. 'But of course it's not,' he said. 'Not alright.' There was a large inward breath, and a shuddery exhalation. 'I'm making a fool of myself.'

'It's OK,' I said.

He shook his head. 'I know it's foolish, I can't help it. But I ask myself over and over, How did it go wrong? I always ask myself, what did I do wrong? I guess it's sentimental of me, but I always figured – you know,' he was shuffling in his chair, uncomfortable with this sort of emotional talk, 'I always figured, love would be enough. But however much I loved you, you just didn't,' and his voice wobbled. He coughed. 'You just didn't,' he concluded, more sternly, 'love me. So I guess, maybe it wouldn't ever work out.'

'Well,' I said. 'It wasn't quite like *that*, was it?'

He looked straight at me with rheumy, baffled eyes. 'How do you mean?'

'Well,' I said, starting feeling uncomfortable. 'You know what it was that put the – distance between us. We both know what it was.'

'What?'

'Come on, don't play games.'

'Tira,' he said, leaning towards me a little, 'no, seriously. What?'

'Well if you want me to be brutal, it was when you found out I was – you know what.'

'What?'

A spurt of remembered anger carried me over the hump

342

of embarrassment. 'You do *remember* the conversation we had about me being Indian, don't you? You do – you must. Don't pretend you don't remember that, don't rewrite history. You thought I was a white girl, and when you found out otherwise you couldn't hack it.'

Crow just looked confused. 'I couldn't – do what?'

'Couldn't hack it, couldn't – cope with it, couldn't deal with it.'

'I don't know what you're talking about,' he said.

This fired me up. 'Don't play these games. I was there. Don't you remember, you thought I was called London, but I told you that was only the city where I came from? Don't you remember that?'

He nodded very slowly, and then fiddled with his mask as if it were irritating the skin around his mouth. 'I do remember that. That was funny! I thought maybe you were related to Jack London, the writer! What a doofus I was!'

'I'm glad,' I said, furious, 'that the memory amuses you, arsehole.'

'That had nothing to do with – us becoming – estranged,' he said, haltingly. 'Is that why you think we grew apart? That's crazy. That had nothing to do with it.'

'OK,' I said, in disgust and fury. 'If you want to rewrite history – no, I can't believe you could just—'

'Hey!' he said, his voice loud and hard for this first time in the conversation. 'Give me *some* credit, for crying out – what? What are you saying? You're saying,' as if the idea was dawning on him for the first time, 'that I turned against you because of your skin colour? How could you *think* that? How could you think that matters to me at all?'

'How could I think? When I *told* you,' I said, jabbing with my finger to emphasize my points, 'that I was Indian, you got all upset.'

He looked baffled. 'Upset? No, no. I guess it took a moment to adjust to it. I'd thought you were Irish, so I guess it was a shock to find out you were Indian. But it was just an adjustment thing. It only took a moment. Hey, *you'd* be the same if the positions were reversed.'

'Adjustment?' I said fiercely. 'You insisted on separate ucking beds.'

'Don't swear, Tira,' he said. His brows had contracted, and now he looked angry.

'I'll swear if I want,' I said. But I didn't swear again.

'The separate beds thing—' he started to say.

'You're going to tell me that wasn't your idea. You're going to tell me it had nothing to do with finding out I was Indian.'

'It *was* my idea, the separate beds thing,' he said. There was a fury of his own in his words now, a compression of his lips and a controlled emphasis of diction. 'It had nothing to do with you being – coloured. I can't *believe* you'd throw that accusation at me! We're still married. Did I ask for a divorce? Did I refuse to have anything to do with you? Sure,' searching his mental Rolodex, 'sure you'd sometimes call me a racist, but you called me lots of things when you were angry, including a homosexual. That was just how you were when you were angry, all passion – that was one of the things that drew me to you. You didn't really think I was a homosexual, and you didn't really think I was a racist. How can you *think* that? That's so insulting.' And the anger in his words mutated sloppily into self-pity again. 'How could you? I love you! I've always loved you!'

'Jesus, just *spare* me the rhetoric,' I said, slumping back. 'You're living a life of pure self-delusion. It'll serve you well as a politician. Jesus, I don't believe this.'

'Believe it or not,' he said. 'I love you, despite everything. We're *married*.'

'So why did you insist on separate beds?'

'Do you really need to ask?'

'It seems,' I said, sarcastic, 'that I do. Yes, apparently I do need to ask.'

'I can't believe,' he said, 'that you need to ask.'

'If it's not your revulsion at—' I started to say.

'You were,' he cried, 'committing adultery with another man!' There was a pause. 'That was the reason,' he added, in

344

a lower voice. 'Jesus, Tira, I'm only human. I try to forg⸻
to turn the other cheek, as Christ commands us, but ther⸻
only so much I can do. There was only so much I coul⸻
bear.'

'That,' I said, slowly, 'was afterwards—'

But Crow was in the middle of a spiel now. 'I loved you, and I still love you. But did you ever think of *me*? We were married, and I tried to do well by you, to do the right things by you as a husband should. But when we were – intimate, in the marital bed, it was *always me*. Wasn't it? It was always me that – initiated it. Just once, just one time, I'd have liked it to have been you, you coming on to me. If you want me to put it in those terms, those vulgar terms. But it never was, was it? Was it, though?'

'I thought,' I mumbled, 'that was how you liked it.'

'Of course not. Of course I wanted to feel that you wanted to do – that as much as I did. I wanted it to be a mutual thing, a loving thing. So I stopped making my advances to you, and waited to see how long it would be before you—' He was having real difficulty with finding the form of expression for this. 'How long before you initiated intimacy with me. It was a long wait, though, Tira, wasn't it?'

'This was all after you'd exploded at me for being Indian,' I said.

'I did not *explode*,' he said, firmly. 'It makes no difference to me, your skin colour. It made no difference back then, and it doesn't now.'

'Well,' I said, casting my mind back. 'Maybe not exploded. But you were upset, I remember that. And I remember you insisting we have separate beds not long after that.'

'I wanted separate beds after you started your affair with – Oh, Jesus, you know who. Are you surprised I wanted separate beds when I found out about that?'

'It was the other way about,' I said. 'I started seeing [*Name deleted*] *after* you insisted on separate beds.'

'Your memory is wrong,' he said, simple as that. 'And the

confidence with which he spoke unsettled my
thoughts. Was I wrong? Had I misremembered the sequence
of events? Because it is easy to do that, isn't it: to think A
happened before B when in fact it happened after.

The last thing Crow said to me was: 'It can't be, it breaks
my heart. If only you'd come to me when you first arrived! If
only you'd never been contaminated by the Others! Then we
could rebuild. But not now – it breaks my heart, it breaks my
heart, because I love you.' And he started bawling again,
starting crying so the tears dribbled, giving his hollowed
cheeks a melted wax look. Then he screeched, 'We could
have been happy, you could have come to Newny with me as
my wife, my consort, my partner – but you decided you
needed this other man. Jesus! It *broke* my dignity, it broke my
self-respect, Jesus it broke my heart.' He stopped, he seemed
to get a grip on himself. 'It's too late now, anyway. If you'd
have come straight to me, we could have patched things over.
But it's out of my hands now. You've been, I'm sorry,
infected. I'd better say goodbye, I'd better.'

Then he left the room.

This evening, after writing that last passage, as I put the light
out in my little room, I heard somebody singing in the street
outside. My little window, with the graph-paper grid of wire
lines running through the glass, allows sight out over a
stretch of road, a little yard opposite. Tonight was a full
moon, shining on the snow, and the voice I heard was either
a woman's or perhaps a high-pitched man's, maybe a boy.
The army is full of boys. He was standing at the corner of
the street, and because there was only moonlight and starlight outside I couldn't quite see him. This is what he sang:

> Queen and huntress, chaste and fair,
> Seated in a silver chair:
> Hesperus entreat your light
> Goddess excellently bright
> You who make a day of night

I think I've put the words down right. I thought they lovely, so I scribbled them down there and then. It sou like a hymn, but it is obviously addressed to the moon.

That same moon, up there: I can see her as I write.

The prevailing winds across the frozen Atlantic are west to east.

Crow went to New NY, and has been IP for four years now, and I am still here. I am still officially quarantined, but I am not confined to this room. I can wander the streets of Liberty, although I must not leave the city. The activity of the Others was close to this city, apparently confined to over-UK and not in the over-US (as we must not now call it). The Senate seems to think that the whole of Liberty has been compromised in some way. So I can go about the city. I can be with the woman I call, when others are around, my friend. There is a new puritanism in the new new-world that frowns at certain sorts of relationship. I mentioned her before. We don't live together. She was divorced by her husband, and has a room in a women's block, and she works in a stationery supplier that supplies the military, working with stock and catalogue. I call her my girlfriend, which is a nicely ambiguous phrase. We spend time to-gether, from time to time.

Crow, as I still think of him, is due for re-election soon. He is standing, but there are strong candidates standing against him. I have not seen him in four years, and not spoken to or heard from him personally in three.

And I think back. It still baffles me, the order of events. I have put them down here as I remember them, and I do so in the hope that he will read them. I don't presume to think that I can change his interim-presidential mind, and the more I think about it the less certain I become of the actual order of events. Perhaps it is as I remember it, perhaps Crow is right. I know he is a busy man now, an important man, the leader of this small remnant of humanity. But perhaps he has time to read the occasional document, this one of the many that detail sightings of or encounters with the Others.

...e been quiet for fourteen months now. Away to the ... .he plain of snow is interrupted by the curious plumage ... a crop-field. It makes very beautiful patterns in the ...orning light. Some people, superstitious, refuse to eat ...ood grown for them by the Others, but I have tasted it, and it is good.

In New NY, or near by, a large under-snow lake was discovered. I have heard that it was formed by the uncontrolled nuclear reactor under the snow at Seven Mile Island: I don't know if that's correct. There are the worries about radioactivity, but food is better than no food. Seven breeds of fish live down there: fed by human waste. They do very well. Sometimes they're loaded into open-topped pallets and shipped over the snow-Atlantic. The ambient chill keeps them fresh, although the breeze of their passage can dry them a little – still tasty, though. These barges are computer-guided, and powered by sails, and they glide over the snow without human pilotage. When we've unloaded them we can simply send them on their way, further down to the east, and over a matter of weeks they'll be blown all around the world and back to the over-US. Liberty will, they say, start a lake of its own soon. The greenhouses are doing better, although I'm too cash-poor to taste their food.

I can see the moon as I write. She is barren, of course. The moon landings were before my time, but I've seen the pictures: dry as cement-dust, a world of ashes and corroded breeze-blocks under a sky black as stormcloud and night and death. But that's not how she appears as I look up at her now. She looks white as diamond, she looks pure as the song said, chaste and fair. It seems to me, as I look up, that everything that has happened to this world, this earth, these events to which I was witness – that these events belongs to the same sphere. It seems to me that the old dust-and-ashes moon belongs to the dead time; that now, in our new world, not barren but chaste, not heartless but cruelly fair – that in this new world, the moon is a snow-covered landscape as well. She is our Holy Spirit, presiding over the cour humanity now. I can almost believe that it was from shedding a portion of her cold down upon us, that the snc came in the first place. To take a notional vantage point ou in vacuum, the earth and the moon look now like sister worlds, white-and-white, cold-and-cold, pure-and-pure. We're living in a new phase now, because the page is blank. Paper is blank, slab-like, it's an expensive resource, but at least it's blank.

Appendix

DOCUMENTS ASSEMBLED

The Senate and the People of NUSA have ruled not to make public the foregoing documents. Special advisers have determined that:

(a) with regard to [*Name available to clearing level 7*]; as a former President, and considering his allotted status as Hero of the New World, this standing would be compromised, and the health of the NUSA body-politic damaged, by certain unsubstantiated allegations made in these documents, specifically that he was [i] racist, [ii] cuckolded, [iii] complicit with the alleged invasion force of Others to any degree. None of these claims have any basis in truth.

(b) with regard to [*Name available to clearing level 7*], his own confession may or may not be a forgery. As a recorded Hero of the New World his standing would be compromised, and the health of the NUSA body-politic damaged, by certain details contained in these documents. Reported via public news manifests: '[*Name available to clearing level 7*] gave his life to save the Republic. His sacrifice brought about an end of the war between humanity and the Others. He deserves the title Hero of the New World.'

(c) with regard to a number of other officers in the NUSA military, several of whom now hold senior office in the government: no benefit to the nation can be demonstrated from having those parts of these documents that relate to their earlier lives made public.

By Interim Presidential Order.

A STATEMENT FROM [NAME AVAILABLE TO CLEARE
LEVEL 7]

'The new category of Hero of the New World has ar
immensely positive impact upon public morale. In the
rebuilding of the lives of the human race, it is vital to have
heroes to whom everybody may look up. In future years
schoolchildren will study their life stories as wholesome and
socially cohesive myths. It would damage the precarious
sense of commonality in the NUSA for derogatory and
largely untrue allegations about any Hero of the New
World to come to light. Documents containing such allegations must be censored in various senses. We move on to a
new age!'

This interdiction shall hold for a period of not exceeding
50 years, subject to reappraisal by the Senate.

Theories of the origin and purpose of the Others: put to motion this day, 4–1–10 in Senate.

[i] That they are alien forms of life from another solar
system, having altered this world to make it more habitable
to their physiologies. 18 ayes.

[ii] That they are alien forms of life from within our own
solar system. 1 aye (later struck).

[iii] That they are manifestations of the same catastrophic
circumstances that caused the snow, viz. upheaval in natural
order, mutation of the space-time continuum, created
according to some natural (not supernatural) law. 4 ayes.

[iv] That they are secular apparitions of spiritual conflict,
viz. divine or diabolic intervention, just as the snow is God's
plan for this globe, and the survivors the elect, one day soon
to multiply to the number 144,000 and ushering in the last
days. 17 ayes.

[v] That they are humans, or post-humans, having travelled
through time, this present global catastrophe similarly

voked by time disturbances of some undetermined nature. 2 ayes.

vi] That they do not, in objective terms, exist, being manifestations of certain telekinetic abilities latent in humanity now brought to the surface by extraordinary events, and that all achievements attributed to the Others can in fact be attributed to the individual telepathic and communal telepathic abilities of the new humans, homo superior. 1 aye.

[vii] That they are merely mass hallucinations, and all the apparent circumstances explained as their action may be explained in other, non supernatural ways. 1 aye.

Coda
Tira Bojani Sahai

[1] It's strange to look over all this documentation after so many years. Some of the stuff here I'd forgotten, and some – as with Fred's confession, which I read for the first time two days ago – I'd never known. But other parts of the story are vividly in my mind, and have been there all this time.

It's strange, quite apart from anything else, to see how heavily censored all these papers were – that's so redolent of its era. That more than anything else. That paranoid governmental control. A brow furrowed like low-tide sand. But now it is full twenty years later, and each year has felt full. I feel like an old woman, although I'm still only in my fifties. But things have changed. Some things have stayed the same. Some things have changed.

For example, it seems nowadays foolish and over-sensitive to blank out all those names. Anybody in Nusa, for instance, would be able to deduce my former husband's name, since he, evidently, was the IP who followed Robinson. It's a matter of historical record. Even I appear in the footnotes of the official histories. Other names are also only lightly obscured by the censor's pedantry.

If, as seems likely, this new 'publisher' will print out copies of these collected documents ('for their historical interest' as he puts it) then it is surely stupid to retain these marks of censorship. They date from a less secure time. Here, then, are the names obliterated in the original documents:

George Corvino
Fred Gimble
Edie Bisson

Thomas Pound
Teri Grenert
Frank Robert Gillprazer

Of course, it may be the case, perhaps, that these names are less illuminating. It may be that it is not the names that are important.

[2] We know a great deal more about the Others than we once did, although there remains much we don't know. It is full fifteen years since it was determined that the ordnance they fired down upon Liberty – all the shells and bullets they spat up at army personnel and helicopters and so on – was actually our own; all dredged from the ground-level under-snow. They put out their alien feelers (whatever shape they took) and wormed their way wherever the snow was laid down, into barracks and military storehouses, and retrieved our own ammunition. This they were able to pass up into the upper reaches of the snow and propel upwards.

Liberty was the only city they bombarded: there were no attacks of any kind on the other cities. And it does seem to be the case that they fired at Liberty in a sort of homage. They saw us blowing up our own buildings, and they, sort of, joined in. They saw our troops running around on the ice firing off their weapons at every tremor in the snow and every unexpected thing, and they fired back. With hindsight it becomes almost touching, like a toddler copying the things they see an adult do. It would be banal to say 'they did not understand', but I sometimes think, in terms not wholly removed from that mode of thought, that it may have been their mode of understanding which was simply not the same as ours.

So in Newla, where the city council built the seven towers (the largest architectural undertaking yet of the post-Snow world), the Others seemed to have copied human actions, pulling up minerals from a wide area of under-snow, seeping them upwards (or lifting them, or insinuating them, or

354

however it is they transfer material through the medit
and constructing their own weird and rather beautiful co
structions a few kilometres from the city. I have only see
pictures, but they look like great rust-brown sausages,
blimp-sized termite nests, some thin and towering, some
oval and squat. And most importantly, when Newden set
aside acres of snow, with painfully dug up ground soil and a
solar-powered heating system to stop the earth from freezing, to grow maize and wheat, the Others copied. Their
peculiar snow-crops, constructed (according to the best
scientific intelligence) of displaced minerals and snatches of
salvaged organic material – salvaged we don't know how –
are now grown widely around every city. Some strains are
inedible, but some are nutritious, and two decades of
human tinkering with the plants, cross-breeding and so on,
have produced several quite tasty versions.

And when New NY farmed fish in their under-snow
lagoons, the Others provided their own swimming creatures. The last document by me, 341–999, mentions the
beginnings of human fish farming. Survivors had carried
up live fish eggs with them, and there were several attempts
to create ponds for them to swim in. The first successful
ponds were under-snow, in heated pockets of water made
by, to begin with, heat pollution from the surface of the
Earth; and latterly, closer to the top of the snow, in solar-
powered sinks. We have bred and harvested our fish successfully for many years now. The Others copied us, as they
did in so many things; in Liberty by creating their own fish-
stocked under-snow lagoons. But in New NY they created a
huge under-snow body of liquid water and filled it with
strange creatures, things bred out of the frozen DNA of
dead animals they found underneath the snow, gill-lunged
cows with udder-sized swim bladders but without eyes,
kicking with flap-hoofed hind legs through the black water,
devouring tiny shrimp-like insects that in turn fed on
organic matter dredged from the ground and circulated
through the ecosystem. Dog-headed octopus creatures with

r-like growths upon drifting tail-analogue tentacles. adless birds that flap their way through the under water ith diaphanous adapted wings, and who feed by winnowing water into their neck-maw. Humanity came upon this bizarre resource by chance; it existed for several years before we became aware of it. Some say they made it for us, some say they made it for their own purposes, it's impossible to know. But the meat is edible, which is the most important thing. To begin with some people were squeamish about eating such monstrosity, but nowadays we are more practical. It is amazing the things to which people can become habituated.

Now, whether the creature that I saw on the ice, that first time, was one of these experiments – or whether it was indeed a manifestation of the Others, an avatar – or whatever the hell it was – I can't say. Nobody can say.

[3] Publishing is the vogue this season. It reminds the older citizens of pre-Snow times, and it is, I suppose, a diverting novelty for the young. The young outnumber the old. Books are much cheaper than they used to be.

Yesterday I read a new science fiction novel, a sure sign that things are increasingly returning to some sort of pre-Snow normality. It's the seventh new title published this year. There's much more paper now than before. Fancy that!

Science fiction is the literature of choice, of course, for Nusans. It has become the new realism, with historical fiction (as all books about the pre-Snow years must necessarily be called) looked down upon as a lamentable escapism. We try to come to terms with what has happened to the world. There was enough food to eat last year. There has been enough food to eat this year. Next year, we'll see.

The novel, by Donna Avellanos, was a speculative fiction about the Others. It incorporated a great deal about what we now know about them. I mention it because Donna interviewed me before writing the book, and accordingly it's

a novel that incorporates my personal theories a
the Others. People do seek me out sometimes, to ask
about Fred, or about my own adventures. It's those theori
that I want to set down here, in this coda, so that shoulc
somebody in the future pick up and read this mess of
documentation, they would also read my personal beliefs. I
am not a scientist. I have lived almost all my life in Liberty.
Edie and I are still friends, and see one another. With
hindsight it suited neither of us very well to be lovers. We
blew hot and cold with one another for many years, spending intense periods of time together, then arguing explo-
sively over trivialities and breaking up. But always getting
together again. After my husband officially divorced me –
this, as perhaps you'll remember, was after his term as IP – I
found myself working in Liberty stores or bars once again,
which was a strangely debasing echo of my pre-Snow life.
But a person has to work somewhere.

Donna, the writer I mentioned in the previous paragraph,
spent three days with me, asking me questions about my
encounter with the Others. For a while (after the period
recorded in the official documents) there were many such
encounters; but nobody has spoken to an avatar of the
Others in nearly two decades. So people such as myself
(and remember: I met them not once but twice) have
acquired a new celebrity. Mostly I talk about the first
encounter, with Fred on the snow, when for whatever
reason, presumably because Fred's imagination had over-
written the situation, I saw Them as giant snow-worms.
People like to hear about that because it is the more
dramatic and entertaining of my meetings. But it's the
second encounter, when I met a version of myself, that
interested Donna.

When I met Them this second time, they said to me: 'I see
a lot of water, and some trace elements everywhere'. They
told me that my own body was mostly water, with some
trace elements. I think they were deliberately drawing parallels. I think that, for two decades, we've been confused in

.hinking. We think of the snow as the medium in which Others live, whether they live there in cities or in the ..ld, whether they are multicellular beings in the shape of sharks or dragons or termites or whether they are uni-cellular hive-minds, or more like dust, or pollen, or nano-technological creatures of some kind. There have been advocates of all these theories. But I believe (and I am not alone) that we cannot separate out medium from life form. I believe they are the snow. I think the body of snow, which is, as they said, mostly water with trace minerals, is their body. As that officer of my husband's whose name I can't remember now puts it in the document, they are bodies but without organs. They organise on a different level to us. Snow crystals are matrices of water. We have evolved elaborate carbon-based structures, hard skeletons and soft sacs, to contain our vital water; but these aliens, I believe, have evolved a different way. *Their* structure is provided by the forms water adopts when it freezes; they store their chemicals, their electrolytes, their long-chain molecules in their water, rather than (as with us) the other way around (storing their water inside their tissues). This means that they are not limited to specific corporeal forms, but can shift whatever it is they require across the larger scale, moving material in whatever shape is necessary for action, or thought, or reproduction. That's what I think.

Donna agreed with me, and wrote her novel based on this premise. But the book adds some intriguing speculation that is all her own. She thinks that the Others landed on our world, like it was Plymouth Rock, landing on the Native Americans, from another star system – who knows how long they had travelled through the vast chill of deep space, etcetera etcetera. She also doesn't think that they infected us, as most people assume. She thinks (there's no evidence for this, but it makes for a good story) that *we* infected *them*; she thinks we have passed over to them the virus of intelligent consciousness. I'll quote: 'what use would intelli-gence be to these creatures, cruising for millennia through vacuum-dark? It would be a hindrance, a recipe for madness not survival. But now they demonstrate a hectic, undisciplined intelligence. As they copied us in various, seemingly random ways, perhaps they copied us in terms of consciousness too. Perhaps they have been awoken by our own capacity for thought. They got inside our heads, one by one, and they took away our habits and strategies of intelligent thought.'

According to something I heard on the radio a few months ago, only seventeen humans in the whole of the world were ever diagnosed with the infectious plaque in their lungs and/or brains placed there by the Others. I am one of those seventeen. Four of the others died. But the rest of us continue our existences none the worse for our encounters. I think the plaque was one strategy they used, a rare one, and I think it was superseded by more complex and subtle ones. I don't think they were really trying to establish communication, as my first husband thought. I think they were sipping our consciousness to see whether they liked the flavour. I doesn't seem likely to me that they had *no* consciousness at all themselves, as some people insist, for that would leave them nothing more than bugs or plankton, and they are so clearly more than bugs or plankton. But I suppose their consciousness was alien, and not like ours. But I think they liked the form of intelligence they found on our world so much they copied it. I think they sampled it, and sent the virus all around their snow-body until they became agitated and alive with plans – to bomb, to grow imitation plants, to create and populate under-snow seas and so on.

Or perhaps we should think of it this way: maybe this is their life cycle. They pass through space as snowballs, as mindless as embryos. But when they strike a suitable world they fill it, and take from it what they can. Perhaps they are designed to feed on whatever consciousness they find there, just as a caterpillar feeds on whatever leaves are to hand, to build its own mind. Or minds. Perhaps this is why they are helping us to stay alive, providing us with bizarre but edible foods. They want more of our thoughts. That's a less comfortable thought: that we are nothing more to them than a kind of harvest.

Except that – we're still alive. Our numbers increase. There's plenty of food. Anything is possible. We must be hopeful. We have every reason to be hopeful.

[4] There is one more thing I want to say. This new cycle of life. They passed up carbon in various chemical forms, and it is bound into the stalks and fruiting-shells of the plants. Eventually these crops will become self-sustaining, once enough dead matter has accumulated to form a substratum of soil, the manure that all plant life needs. They recycle organic material more directly by feeding it directly into their under-snow lagoons. Since these pools are cut off from the sunlight this will continue to be necessary: if the Others stop supplying the matter for the insect-shrimps and all the rest of the creatures to eat, then humanity will have to supply the gap. In all this they are only doing what food-miners used to do, reusing the buried resources of the world. This pleases me, very deeply. I know that my daughter is one of those resources. It no longer makes me cry to think of it. More than this, it gladdens me to see a child eating a roasted fruit-shell, to think that all those people have not been lost, that they serve a purpose. Eleven years ago I had another daughter, and nine years ago a son. They gladden me too, and for similar reasons. I have come to hate *waste* above all, and in my happier moments I sometimes come to the conclusion that nothing is wasted. Everything endures, though sometimes changed. We're near the summit of the mountain, I feel, and soon we'll be able to leave purgatory behind. I'm convinced of that.

Of course I can't pretend to be a prophet. The prophets belong to a different age. I think that's all I want to say right now. Thank you.